Maggie Alderson is the author of ten novels and four collections of her columns from *Good Weekend* magazine. Her children's book *Evangeline, the Wish Keeper's Helper* was shortlisted for the Prime Minister's Literary Award. Before becoming a full-time author she worked as a journalist and columnist in the UK and Australia, editing several magazines, including *Mode* and British *ELLE*. She writes a Substack called Style Notes and is on Instagram at @maggialderson. She is married and has one daughter.

Would You Rather

Would You Rather

MAGGIE ALDERSON

HarperCollins*Publishers*

HarperCollins*Publishers*
Australia • Brazil • Canada • France • Germany • Holland • India
Italy • Japan • Mexico • New Zealand • Poland • Spain • Sweden
Switzerland • United Kingdom • United States of America

HarperCollins acknowledges the Traditional Custodians
of the lands upon which we live and work, and pays respect
to Elders past and present.

First published on Gadigal Country in Australia in 2024
by HarperCollins*Publishers* Australia Pty Limited
ABN 36 009 913 517
harpercollins.com.au

A catalogue record for this book is available from the National Library of Australia

ISBN 978 1 4607 5206 7 (paperback)
ISBN 978 1 4607 0690 9 (ebook)
ISBN 978 1 4607 3197 0 (audiobook)

Cover design and illustration by Louisa Maggio, HarperCollins Design Studio
Author photograph by Adrian Peacock
Typeset in Bembo Std and Gotham Light by Kirby Jones
Printed and bound in Australia by McPherson's Printing Group

MIX
Paper | Supporting
responsible forestry
FSC
www.fsc.org   FSC® C001695

For Anna Valdinger

2004

Sophie was woken by the bed shaking as two small, very excited, boys jumped on to it with their large Christmas stockings.

'Mummy, Mummy, Mummy,' said Beau, putting his face right up against hers and moving his head from side to side. 'Look, I'm a reindeer, an actual one.'

Sophie had just taken in that her older son – he had recently turned six – was wearing the flashing reindeer antlers his father had put in both the boys' stockings, before he jumped off the bed again and started trotting around the room as though pulling a sleigh, singing the 'Batman smells' version of 'Jingle Bells'.

At the same time, Jack, four, came up the bed and put his arms around her, pressing his warm little cheek against hers.

'Happy Christmas, my mummy,' he said.

'Merry Christmas, Crackerjack,' said Sophie, hugging him back and kissing the top of his dear little head.

It was only then she realised that her husband, Matt, wasn't in the bed beside her. She glanced at the clock and saw it was

5.50am, which was a bit early for a bike ride, even for him. Perhaps he'd heard the boys stirring and had gone down to make her some coffee.

'Where's Daddy?' said Beau, leaping back onto the bed. 'I want to show him my presents. He's going to be really jealous because I've got a Tintin t-shirt and I've got a Snowy too.' He delved into his stocking and brought out a little plastic model of a white terrier, which he bounced around the bed, barking loudly. Sophie was starting to hope the coffee wouldn't be much longer.

'Have either of you got any books in your stockings?' she asked, knowing exactly what was in them.

'Meeeee!' cried both boys and she tucked them in under the covers with her, one on each side, to eat chocolate Santas – she'd worry later about the catastrophic effect of that much sugar before breakfast – while she read them their new stories.

After she'd done both books and Matt still hadn't appeared with life-giving caffeine, she decided to go down and make her own.

When she got to the bottom of the stairs, the boys rushing down with her, dragging their stockings, she saw Matt's beloved bicycle was in its place up on the hallway wall, so he definitely hadn't gone out for a ride on the empty Christmas morning London roads.

Where could he be?

The boys made it into the kitchen before she did and their shrieks made her rush to follow them. Then she stopped dead in the doorway, trying to take in what she was looking at.

Every bit of bare wall had been painted with scenes of a snowy landscape: a frosted pine forest with reindeer, elves and a snowman, with the back of Santa's sledge on the far wall, as though he was just flying out. The white paint had some kind of glitter in it and sparkled as you moved through the room. There were also drifts of fake snow on the floor, which the boys were now throwing into the air with great excitement.

'Whoa!' said Sophie, seeing it raining down on bowls of dates and fruit. 'Don't mess the snow, or you'll spoil it and Santa will be upset.'

So this was why Matt wasn't in bed. He'd been doing this, probably all night. She walked through to the study, off the side of the kitchen, and sure enough, there he was, passed out on the sofa with a blanket over him.

She smiled down at her husband's sleeping form. So handsome, even out sparko, his thick black hair falling over his face, a shadow of stubble on his cheeks. There was a smudge of white glittery paint there too, which was somehow very sexy. He still had that effect on her.

She should have known it would be something like this; one of his spontaneous projects. It wasn't the first time she'd found the kitchen completely repainted without any consultation with her and, as she was a professional food stylist, it could be irritating when she had a big work project on. But, she told herself, that was a small inconvenience for the magic of living with a highly regarded artist who could create something so special for the boys.

She did hope the sleep deprivation wouldn't make him useless for the rest of the day, though. Three of his four brothers were coming for Christmas lunch with their families. There would be eleven very excited and sugared-up boys in the house – and their equally excitable fathers. She would need his help.

But any hope of Matt being able to catch up on his lost sleep was shattered as Beau and Jack found him.

'Daddy!' said Beau, shaking him awake, his reindeer antlers threatening to take out one of Matt's eyes. 'Wake up! You'll never guess what's happened. Santa's been in the kitchen.'

Matt blinked a few times then his face broke into a broad smile as he grabbed both boys and hugged them tight.

'Are you telling me we've had an intruder?' he said, sitting up and rubbing his head, making the hair stand on end. 'In the kitchen? I hope they haven't stolen the Christmas pudding. This could be a disaster.'

Sophie put her hand over her mouth to hide her smile as the boys' eyes widened at the thought.

'They might have got the crackers,' said Beau. 'We'd better go and check. Come on, Daddy, quick.'

Matt allowed the boys to pull him up and drag him through to the kitchen, where he did a good job of expressing astonishment at the scene. Sophie joined him and he put an arm around her, pulling her close, kissing her firmly on the lips.

'Do you like it?' he whispered, a slightly vulnerable expression on his face.

She threw both arms around him, squeezing tight and rubbing her nose against his, hoping she might be able to arrange for them to have a shower together while the boys ate breakfast in front of the telly.

'It's a Christmas miracle, you genius of a man,' she said. 'But you'd better wash that sparkly paint off your face before Beau and Jack notice. It's a bit of a giveaway.'

CHAPTER 1

2024

Sophie saw her the moment she lifted her eyes from the pages of the eulogy to look at the congregation.

Standing at the back of the packed venue, looking straight at her, was a woman about twenty years or so younger than her, not particularly striking, yet Sophie knew exactly who she was. Juliet.

Or Gillette, as Sophie thought of her. She'd certainly cut her like a razor. Slashed everything Sophie had thought she'd known about her life into ribbons.

Or was it Matt who'd done that?

She blinked and looked down again, relieved that people would think she was overcome with devastation at the prospect of reading her husband's eulogy, not that she was in shock, having just looked right into the eyes of his mistress.

And was she imagining that this woman looked – oddly – a little bit like her? A younger, slimmer version. Much slimmer.

Standing up taller and pulling her stomach in, Sophie made herself start reading. After a few stumbles on the first paragraph, she found her voice and the eulogy seemed to go down well. The assembly of family, friends and colleagues laughed where she'd hoped they would and she could feel the frisson of sadness wash through them when she mentioned the plans she and Matt had made for a new, post-children life, away from South London down on the coast, in Hastings.

She couldn't stop her eyes flicking over to Gillette as she read that bit. How would she react to hearing Sophie's heartbreak about the sudden end to the plans that she had in fact already wrecked? Or Matt had. They had, together.

Sophie felt a flash of pure rage and found she was staring at Gillette, who fortunately had her head down. Then Sophie noticed she was wearing a leather jacket – an old biker-style one, that looked horribly like the one Matt used to have. And then she saw there was a Union Jack applique up by the shoulder, on the left side. It *was* Matt's jacket. She hadn't seen it for years – and now she knew why.

Her fury spiked again and she forced herself to snatch her eyes away. Seeing her sons, Beau and Jack, glance at each other nervously, clearly concerned she was about to lose it, she focussed her attention firmly back on the eulogy.

She was very glad when it was done and she could leave the lectern to squeeze onto the front pew again, between her boys. Beau put an arm round her and Jack took her left hand in his and held it tightly, as the first bars of 'Hallelujah' – the Jeff Buckley version, Matt's favourite – started to play.

Lodged in tightly between them, not boys any more but big, grown-up men, and feeling hands on both her shoulders – from Matt's four brothers, who were sitting in the row behind –

she felt propped up by love. They were such a tight clan, those Crommelin men.

With that support, she hoped that, for a while, she could just exist and experience the rest of the service and not angst about when – or whether at all, ever – to tell them the truth about their beloved father and brother. Just for those few minutes, she wanted to remember the Matt she had known and loved so passionately for over thirty years. She needed to grieve him, not think about how he'd told her he was leaving her for his mistress and wasn't coming with her to Hastings.

So she was glad of the distraction when Beau stood up to read a poem he'd chosen, wearing one of his father's suits, a charity-shop double-breasted pinstripe, flashing the bright paisley lining at the crowd as he stepped up to the lectern, prompting a laugh of poignant recognition.

Sophie glanced at Jack and he smiled gently at her, tears in his eyes, still holding her hand. She smiled back, weakly, trying to tune her brain into Beau's spirited reading of part of Allen Ginsberg's 'Howl', as, despite all her efforts to block it out, the sequence of events on that awful day nearly two weeks earlier replayed in her head, as it had ever since.

She'd been standing in the kitchen on January fifth, trying to get back into work after the break, kneading dough for a Turkish bread recipe from a cookbook she was styling, when Matt had come in.

Leaning on a chair at the other side of the table, he'd told her – completely calmly – that he wasn't moving to Hastings with her after all, but was going to stay in London to start a new life 'with Juliet'.

No further explanation, just the name, as though his words were all perfectly normal.

He'd made that appalling announcement and then – refusing to answer any questions, saying he was going to give her some time to take it in before they talked about 'the details' – he'd set off on his bike, leaving her standing in the doorway, blood-drained and weak-kneed in uncomprehending shock, with flour all over her hands.

Still in that state a couple of hours later – minus the flour, dough abandoned – too stunned even to cry, she was sending him increasingly hysterical messages, demanding he come back and explain himself, when there was a knock on the door.

Sophie opened it to find two policewomen standing there. They asked politely if they could come in and then, sitting with her at the kitchen table, told her Matt was dead.

He'd been knocked off his bike on the Old Kent Road by a lorry driver who was turning right and texting at the same time. Matt had died immediately, they said. Nothing could have been done.

'The stupid vain idiot never would wear a helmet,' Sophie had said, 'in case it spoiled his fucking hair.'

Then the tears had finally sprung forth as she wondered if he'd seen her text calling him a 'spineless bastard' before he died.

She was glad to be distracted from those thoughts when Matt's four brothers got up together to present a simultaneously heartbreaking and hilarious tribute to him with a slideshow of family photos and video clips. They referred to him as 'Matt the Twat' and 'Twat Matt' all the way through it, which made Sophie, Beau and Jack laugh slightly hysterically. It so captured the Crommelin family dynamic, a constant tug of war between undying love and brutal competitiveness.

The tribute helped Sophie hold it together for the rest of the service, and as it came to an end, she glanced behind her to see rows and rows of people crying as Pink Floyd's 'Brain Damage' played, picked by Beau and Jack. Their father would have roared with laughter at their choice of the track, considering the nature of his death, and despite everything, Sophie was glad the whole event had been so perfect for him.

The spineless bastard.

Half an hour later, she was standing in the ghastly function room upstairs at Matt's favourite local boozer, the Red Lion. With its low, knotty-pine ceiling and carpet that was sticky under foot, the pub had pretty much nothing going for it in terms of décor, original features, food, welcome or quality of drinks. Which was exactly why Matt had loved it. He'd said it was 'authentic'.

'It's what he would have wanted,' said Beau, offering his mother a tin foil tray of nasty-looking sausage rolls.

'Make sure the white wine's a bit warm, to go with them,' said Sophie.

'I was tempted to get plastic cups,' said Beau. 'Just to create that genuine private-view atmosphere.'

She smiled at him, happy to have a moment of respite. Her face was beginning to ache from holding it together as she talked to a seemingly endless train of old friends, extended family, Matt's colleagues, art critics, artists, gallery owners and students old and current. All offering the most heartfelt and sincere condolences to the woman they saw as his loving wife and support, his best friend and true love. The tragic widow.

If only they bloody knew.

Seeking a moment alone, she went to the loo, coming out of the cubicle to find Bella, the wife of Matt's oldest brother, standing at the mirror doing her lipstick.

'Darling,' Bella said, spinning round and clasping Sophie's hands. 'If you can't stand it another minute, just tell me and Thomas will have our driver whisk you away. You don't have to endure another moment in this dreadful place. We can pop you into Claridge's and you can just snuggle up and have room service and a massage and anything you want.'

Sophie smiled at her. She loved Bella. They'd been comrades for years in their roles as 'Crommelin WAGs', as the wives and girlfriends of the five brothers called themselves. She was genuinely well meaning but did always find a way to remind everyone just how rich she and Thomas were.

'You know he has an account there,' Bella continued. 'So there's always a room for Thomas, a suite actually, complimentary fizz, you know …' She wrinkled her nose conspiratorially and Sophie almost had to stifle a giggle. How Matt would have loved this.

'You're very kind, Bella,' she said. 'And although it's tough, I do want to see everyone here. I'll be at home with the boys later and I want to spend as much time as I can with Jack before he goes back to Brisbane.'

'Of course,' said Bella, smiling at her with what Sophie could see was sincere understanding. 'You need your boys more than anything right now, but do remember you can come down to us in the country any weekend you want. We're so close to Babington House, as you know, so we can have a lovely spa day there. Thomas has an account.'

Sophie gave her a big hug, genuinely grateful for the good intentions – and the laugh, which had given her a boost to go back and face the room full of lovely people who genuinely cared about her. And who she couldn't be honest with ever again.

She took a detour round the far side of the room to avoid one of the other Crommelin WAGs, who she could see was trying to catch her attention. Not because she didn't love Freya – she and her husband, Sebastian, and their kids were the part of the family Sophie and Matt were closest to – she just wasn't feeling up to that sister-in-law's ultra-keen perception. Freya was a columnist on one of the big broadsheet newspapers and Sophie was sure she would immediately know something was up with her, even beyond the unique stress of this occasion.

Five minutes later, talking to some of Matt's devoted students, one of whom was openly sobbing, Sophie thought she was doing pretty well despite it all when she spotted Gillette standing against the wall, near the door, on her own.

Gillette had come to the wake.

What the hell?

Turning up uninvited at the funeral was bad enough, but to tag along to this most personal of gatherings – and still wearing his leather jacket – defied belief.

But at least it seemed she didn't seem to know anybody.

Sophie had no idea how Matt had met his new 'friend', or anything else about her, but she'd assumed there had to be a crossover somewhere in their acquaintance. It was one of the many things that appalled her – wondering who of their friends had known about Matt's new liaison before she did.

Looking at her, standing there like she had a right to be at Matt's wake, lit a hot anger inside Sophie. She wasn't going to take it. She was going to go over there and demand Gillette leave immediately, but then she realised that even if people weren't openly looking at her, she was inevitably the centre of attention. Everyone would see her do it and want to know why.

With a famously verbose art critic approaching, no doubt to asphyxiate her with white-wine breath and a spray of sausage roll crumbs, Sophie smiled and held a finger up to him to indicate she would be back and reached over to tug the arm of her best friend, Reyansh. He was at Sophie's side in an instant.

'What's up, babe?' he asked in a low voice, taking hold of both her hands and looking at her with tender concern. 'You look like you've seen a ghost – oops, sorry. Not the best expression on this occasion.'

He grinned and Sophie smiled back, shaking her head indulgently before pulling him close.

'Don't look now,' she whispered, 'but there is a woman at your five o'clock, standing by the wall, near the door ...'

Rey stepped back and elaborately took off his jacket, incorporating a glance over his right shoulder as a natural part of the manoeuvre. 'That one in a cheap leather jacket who looks like a less refined version of you?' he said, turning back.

Sophie winced. So she hadn't imagined that. How pathetic men were.

'I think the words you are actually looking for is younger and less fat, but yes, that one,' she said. 'Can you do me a favour?'

Rey nodded, his eyes open wide.

'Can you casually head over there and start chatting to her? Find out her name – and if it's Juliet, will you politely ask her to leave? Use force if you have to.'

'Consider it done, ma'am,' he said. 'But can I make a formal request that you tell me why one day?'

'Of course,' said Sophie, automatically crossing her fingers behind her back. She had no intention of telling him, or anyone else. Ever. What good could it possibly do?

Beau was standing outside the pub pulling on a roll-up he'd cadged off one of his cousins. He didn't smoke, but he'd needed a reason to sneak off and be alone for a few minutes. Making conversation with lovely people who got tears in their eyes or actually broke down while talking to him about his father felt like the most exhausting thing he'd ever done. He'd rather run an ultra-marathon with his annoyingly sporty brother than ever do this again.

And there was also a tiny part of him that was expecting his dad to walk in and reveal that the whole thing had been one of his art projects. That he'd been filming it all with hidden cameras to make one of his famous video installations: 'My Death' by Matthew Crommelin.

After all, he'd videoed their granny's last illness and actual death and turned it into an artwork. This would be a great companion piece.

Trying to blow smoke rings and watching his pathetic attempts condense in the frosty air, Beau heard the side door of the pub open and shut and then two people talking quietly. One of them was Rey. He could pick that voice out anywhere, even though his mum's best friend seemed to be reining in his usual megaphone volume. Why was he doing that?

Beau edged towards the corner of the building to listen. Maybe Rey was in on it with his dad and they were planning the reveal, but as he got closer he could hear that the other voice was female.

'It's nothing personal,' said Rey. 'But considering the nature of the occasion, if, as you tell me, you don't actually know anyone here, it's probably best if you slip away. It's a bit, you know, intrusive.'

'I didn't mean to cause trouble by coming today,' said the woman, speaking quietly but urgently, a catch in her voice as though she was trying not to cry. 'I do see now it was a very bad idea, but I only found out this morning that Matt had died and I wasn't thinking straight. You see, I was hoping I could speak to Sophie. To tell her it's not what it seems. Please tell her that. I'm so sorry for her loss and it's not what it seems.'

Beau dropped the cigarette, instinctively backing up against the wall, aware he was eavesdropping on a conversation the people having it clearly wanted to keep private. This woman, whoever she was, sounded genuinely distressed – and what had she just said? 'It's not what it seems'?

What wasn't? And if she didn't know anyone at this wake, why was she mentioning his parents' names?

He started to put his head round the corner gingerly, to see if he could sneak a look at her, when a figure came round it at speed, sweeping past him.

Beau ducked down, pretending to tie a shoelace – although he was actually wearing his father's red lizard-skin cowboy boots – and looked up as the person passed to see the back of a woman with mid-length, dark blonde hair wearing what was clearly his father's old leather jacket. What the fuck?

It had the Clash logo painted on the back, he'd know it anywhere – and he'd been wondering where it was, surprised not to find it when he'd gone through his dad's clothes at his mother's request.

He stayed crouched down in case Rey followed, his mind starting to race. Who the hell was this woman wearing his father's jacket? Why had Rey just asked her to leave the wake? And what had she meant by wanting to tell Sophie it wasn't what it seemed?

As he turned it all over in his head, another thing came into his mind. Something his father had said to him the last time they'd had a drink together in this very pub. When he'd said, out of nowhere, 'I've met someone.' But before Beau could ask him what he meant, one of Matt's loud friends had turned up and the conversation had ended. And he'd never had another chance to talk to him about it, because that was the last time Beau had ever seen his father.

Was this woman somehow connected with that? Was that how she had his father's jacket?

Standing up, Beau peeped round the corner to make sure Rey had gone back inside then squared his shoulders, ready to face the wake again.

For the time being, he just had to keep it together, to support his mother and his entire extended family. His Uncle Seb was a total mess. But one day he was going to have to bloody well find out who that woman was. However unpleasant it might turn out to be.

Juliet threw the leather jacket onto the back seat of her car. Hard. Really, she'd like to jump up and down on it and chuck it into the nearest dustbin, but she knew she couldn't. It wasn't hers to throw away.

What had she been thinking, wearing that stupid thing? She'd only put it on because it seemed weird to be carrying a jacket at a funeral. At least it was black.

But really, she hadn't been thinking at all, because if she had, she never would have gone to that service, let alone the bloody wake. Now she was furious with herself and the situation, she could feel an anxiety attack building up. A sob escaped, but bracing herself against the car door, breathing slow and deep, she made herself calm down. She had to get back to the office, be normal. She had work to do, an important Zoom meeting. A lot of people depended on her. She didn't have the luxury of a personal life crisis.

When her breathing was even again, she slid into the smooth cream leather driver's seat and checked her face in the mirror. There was a bit of mascara seepage, so she grabbed a wet wipe from the stash she kept in the glove box and fixed it up. With some eyedrops from the bottle she always had in her handbag and a fresh slick of lippie, she felt restored. Enough, at least.

She sat, looking out at the bleak pub car park, still able to hear the noise from the party, if you could call it that. She was glad that nice man had asked her to come outside. What had he said his name was? Ray?

'I can see you don't know anyone here, Juliet,' he'd said, after she'd introduced herself in return. Just her first name. 'And you look a bit peaky. Shall we go outside and get some fresh air? I could do with some myself.'

Standing on the street, in the frosty January air, he'd offered her some sugar-free gum, stuffing four pieces into his own mouth.

'Not very exciting,' he'd said. 'But since I gave up the death sticks I do miss the comradery of popping outside for a ciggie, so now I share this stuff with people instead. It's quite revolting really, so at least it ticks that box.'

They'd stood there for a moment chewing, Juliet feeling increasingly nervous about what she should say when he inevitably asked her how she knew Matt.

'Isn't this the worst pub ever?' Rey had said. 'Typical of Matt to make this his local, with all the cool bars there are in this area now. He loved how basic it is. Always particular, always contrary, our Matt. Maybe he brought you here ...'

He'd turned and looked at her steadily. Her mouth had gone dry. Rey reached out and touched her shoulder.

'I'm pretty sure he didn't, actually,' he said, not unkindly. 'Look, it's nothing personal, Juliet, but considering the nature of the occasion, as you don't know anyone, it's probably best if you slip away. It's a bit, you know, intrusive.'

Then she'd babbled all that stupid stuff about wanting to tell Sophie it wasn't what it seemed. Oh, why had she done that? She had no idea who Ray was nor how he was connected to the family and the worst thing would be for him to say something to Sophie without the full explanation.

But, on the other hand, he was the only person she'd had any contact with. She should have got his bloody number, she thought, as she started the car.

How the hell was she going to get Matt's jacket back to the family now?

2019

Juliet was standing in the gallery of Phillips auctioneers at the north end of Berkeley Square, staring at a painting she was thinking of buying. She bought her art from auction houses because she found the galleries that showed the kind of contemporary work she liked a bit intimidating. And she'd had a bad experience with one of the gallerists.

What a pest he'd been, pursuing her relentlessly for her business once he'd found out who she was – and then more personally. Yuck.

'Do you like this picture?' said a man's voice suddenly, near her.

She glanced to her left to see who was there, assuming the remark had been addressed to someone else, but there was just her and a man, a bit older than her, quite tall, black hair.

She didn't answer. She knew all the opening gambits and she really couldn't be bothered. This was her happy time, indulging in her private pleasure of looking at works of art and sometimes buying them. She wasn't there to make friends. Or get picked up.

So she ignored him and carried on staring at the painting, although her happy contemplation was now infected with a prickle of irritation that this man hadn't got the message and moved on.

'I thought I liked it,' he said, looking at the artwork, not at her. 'I really respond to the colours, they are jewel-like and satisfying and the paint surface has an appealing silky texture, but the more I look, the more I see how derivative it is of Rothko. I didn't see it at first, because the strips of colour are narrow and his are wide, but the way the paint fades out at the edges is just too similar.'

It was almost as though the painting changed in front of Juliet's eyes as he spoke. What had seemed rich and alluring – and just right for her inner hallway – did somehow now look like a bad version of Rothko. It was like wrapping paper: visually appealing but no real depth.

Without thinking, she turned to look at the man again. At the same moment, he glanced over at her, smiled broadly and walked off.

Heading deliberately in the opposite direction – which meant going back past paintings she'd already looked at, another irritation – Juliet continued her tour of the preview, but she couldn't quite lose herself in it as she normally did. She kept wondering what that man might say about each painting she was looking at. But she pressed on. This auction of late twentieth-century British works was one she had been particularly looking forward to.

Eventually, she came to a work that engaged her properly. She already had a small piece by the same artist that she loved and didn't know she'd also done large pieces like this. Like the painting Juliet owned, it was abstract, but with discernible objects in it, which was what she liked so much. It was as though there was a story in there, if you could only figure it out.

She glanced at the catalogue she was holding and found the entry for it. The estimate was right in the sweet spot for her, the mid-five figures. She turned down the corner of the page and carried on looking at the painting.

She didn't know how long she'd been standing there when she became aware of someone next to her. It was the same guy. The black hair, messy curls. He was smiling at the canvas, nodding slowly.

'Beautiful,' he said. 'Just beautiful.'

'Do you think so?' she asked, in spite of herself. It broke all her rules about not engaging with men like this, but after what he'd said about the last picture, she genuinely wanted to know what he thought of this one. Annoying though that was.

'Yes. Do you like it?'

'I do. Very much. I already own a small picture by this artist and I'm thinking to bid on this one.'

She saw one of his eyebrows go up just enough to make her curse herself. Why had she said that?

'I don't think you'll regret it,' he said. 'I own a few of her paintings myself.'

And smiling again, he'd tipped an imaginary hat and walked off.

CHAPTER 2

Sophie got on the Hastings train at London Bridge station, the fifth carriage, as agreed, and there was Rey, waving his arms at her.

'Cooee, darling,' he called out. 'Over here. You can sit facing, I'll be back to the engine. I'll only be a little bit sick.'

She slid into the seat opposite as Rey took two pre-mixed cans of pina colada out of his bag and put them down in front of her, followed by two packets of crisps. He tore one open and stuffed a few into his mouth.

'It's nine forty-five on a Wednesday morning,' said Sophie, as he popped the tag on one of the cans and took an enthusiastic swig, 'and you're drinking tinned cocktails and inhaling crisps. No wonder you're going to be sick.'

'We're going to the seaside. We've got to get in the mood, girl.'

He opened the other can and pushed it across the table towards her. Sophie took a tentative sip and tried not to grimace. It was so sweet. She'd just pretend to drink it, he'd never know.

'Cheers!' she said, taking a fake gulp.

'Up yours. Here's to a day out, a new life and a fabulous new house.' He turned and rootled around in the Goyard tote bag on the seat next to him and slapped an interiors magazine on the table. 'There are some nice ideas in here,' he said, his mouth full of crisps. 'It's a kitchen special.'

Rey was mad about interiors. To look at him, with his rainbow-coloured scarf and the high-crowned apple green Vivienne Westwood hat he'd taken off and put on the table, you'd think he was a fashion stylist or creative of some kind. He was actually a fully qualified accountant who made a very good living flipping property, never going a single penny over budget on the remodelling.

He flicked through the pages of the magazine until he found what he was looking for, then turned it to show Sophie, pointing to a double-page spread of a kitchen.

'Look at this one. No handles, cork floors … Forget those Pinterest boards I sent you, I'm getting a whole new vision for your kitchen.'

'Rey,' said Sophie, reaching out and putting her hand over his, squeezing it lightly. 'I don't know if I'm going to move into that house now. I might just put it straight back on the market and find something else. That's why I'm going today, to have another look and decide.'

He took a long pull on his pina colada. Sophie could almost see the words *Money? Problems with probate? Tricky will? No will?* tracking across his forehead, like a Reuters screen.

'It's not because I can't afford it,' she said and paused to take a breath. Then she took a big pull on the can of sugary cocktail. It was foul, but she needed it. She opened the bag of crisps Rey had put in front of her and put a few in her mouth to take the taste away. 'It's a lovely house, Rey, but I don't think I could bear to live in it, because I chose it with Matt and I would be constantly reminded that he wasn't there ...' She paused. *Because I would be permanently angry. Red-mist furious.*

Was now the time to tell him everything about Matt's betrayal? How he'd told her he wasn't moving to Hastings with her the day after they'd exchanged contracts on the sale of their family home and the purchase of the Hastings one, so she would have to move, whether she wanted to or not. Surely, if there was anyone she could share the hideous truth with, it was Rey?

But, no, she couldn't, because once she'd told one person, the toxic genie would be out of the bottle.

That was something Matt used to say: 'If you want to keep a secret, don't tell anybody.' And, as it turned out, he'd known a lot more about keeping secrets than she'd realised.

Rey said nothing, just carried on eating his crisps.

'I think it would just make me too sad,' Sophie said, slipping back into the lie. 'Living in the house we'd chosen together for the exciting new stage of life we were going to share there.' She took another sip of the hideous drink to stop herself laying it on any thicker. She'd gone a bit flowery there. 'Before he got flattened,' she added.

She tilted the drink can again and was surprised to find she was draining it. She did wonder how she could talk about Matt's death in such a brutal way, but somehow a crude cartoon version of it was easier to sit with than a sensitive pencil sketch.

She tipped the can right up to see if there was a drop left, glad of the buzz of the cheap cocktail. It was so exhausting, keeping up the front of being the grieving widow. Sometimes she longed to let the wronged wife out.

'So if you decide not to move into that house,' said Rey, 'are you going to look for another one in Hastings? I just need to know whether to keep my professional property sonar on or not.'

'I'm going to have a look, see what else is there. Our house in London is sold, there's no going back on that, so I have to find somewhere else to live. There could be something amazing down there.'

'Well, let's go through these house mags then. To get in the mood.'

He started opening them at pages already marked with sticky notes and Sophie pretended to be taking an interest, but it felt like a massive effort. She already had a kitchen she loved, which she was being forced to move out of. The thought of designing a new one had zero appeal and brought up all the same old questions about the house sale. Had the whole moving to Hastings project – Matt's idea – just been an elaborate plan to get her to sell the family home and leave London so he could fund his new life with Gillette? She'd never know.

Rey seemed to pick up on her lack of enthusiasm. 'That's enough of that for now,' he said, closing the magazines. He put his hand in his bag and plonked two more cans on the table. 'Mojitos. They have healing powers.'

Sophie couldn't help smiling as she reached for one. She snapped it open and took a big gulp. Revolting. She took another. 'Have you got any more crisps?'

Rey smiled and reached into his bag again, pulling out two packets of Hula Hoops. 'I always have these with me,' he said. 'In case I'm ever starving.'

'Unlikely,' said Sophie and they burst out laughing. Rey's love of food was one of the many things that had bound them together as friends.

They munched and sipped and looked out of the window at the countryside, which was getting lovely now.

'Tell me something, Soph,' said Rey. 'I'm sorry to bring up Matt's funeral, but that woman you asked me to eject from the wake, what was the story there? You promised you'd tell me.'

Sophie was glad she had her head back, taking a long draw on the mojito, so he couldn't see the expression of horror that must have jumped onto her face. She swallowed and attempted to gather herself.

'Oh,' she said. 'That ...'

'Yes,' said Rey, looking at her steadily. A bit too steadily.

'She had a thing about Matt,' said Sophie quickly. 'Like a groupie-type situation. A bit of a stalker.'

'How did you work out it was her?'

Sophie's brain raced. 'Because she didn't seem to know anyone at the funeral or the wake. And Matt had told me about her, including the name.'

The best cover-ups were always closest to the truth.

'Okay,' said Rey. 'That makes sense then.'

'What does?' said Sophie, alarmed.

'She was actually very decent about leaving, but she did say something that was a bit weird. I had decided not to mention it, because you've got enough on, but now you've told me she was an actual stalker, perhaps you should know.'

Sophie felt sick. She was stuffing Hula Hoops in like an automaton. 'Tell me,' she said, crumbs flying out of her mouth.

'Juliet said she hadn't meant to cause any trouble by coming to the funeral, but she had hoped to get a chance to talk to you—'

Sophie snorted with derision.

'She said she wanted to tell you,' he continued, 'that it wasn't what it seemed. That's it, she said, "It's not what it seems", and then she left. She did seem genuinely distressed.'

'Oh, poor her.'

'So you haven't heard anything else from her?'

She shook her head. 'No. I think she's crawled back under her rock. Found someone else to glom onto.' She raised her can to him and took a sip, glancing out of the window, giving herself a moment to take in what Rey had just told her. *It's not what it seems*. What wasn't? What did that mean? Was it her imagination that Matt had said he was leaving her for someone called Juliet, which happened to be the name of this mystery woman at the funeral?

'Are you okay?' asked Rey.

'I'm fine. It's just remembering that day brings it all back, you know?'

He reached over, squeezing her hand. 'So let's not talk about any of that anymore, let's enjoy our day by the seaside and waste some estate agents' time and then eat chips.'

'Works for me,' said Sophie.

Down on the coast, it was a surprisingly sunny day for early February and, well rugged-up against the cold, Sophie was glad to be outside, walking uphill from the sea front.

She and Rey strolled in silence, arm in arm, and Sophie wondered if it was residual grumpiness from the cocktails on the train that had made every house and flat they'd looked at that morning seem so wrong, but she didn't think that was it. Some of them she didn't even remember booking appointments for. The estate agents must have thrown extras in.

'Well, I couldn't live in any of those,' she said. 'So do you agree I should just abandon the Hastings move idea? Buy another house in London? Stay where I know everything and where my friends are. You, the people I work with, Beau ...'

'And where would that house be? Next to the house you've just sold? And where would you put your test kitchen, since you've given notice on the fabulous studio you've rented for twenty years?'

Sophie slumped at the thought. Losing that space was one of the things that really bugged her.

'And,' he continued, putting a hand on her arm and closing his eyes, 'stop and smell the air here. It feels like silk on my ravaged London lungs. Like Veuve Clicquot after drain water.'

Sophie did as he said, closing her eyes and taking a long, slow breath. He was right. She opened her eyes again and looked back over her shoulder at the sea, wintery sunshine sparkling on the waves. 'It's the third sunniest town in the UK too,' she said.

Matt had done comprehensive research into many such metrics, possibly because he really was planning to move there – or maybe as part of an elaborate smokescreen.

'What's not to love about that?' said Rey. 'And I honestly think it would be great for you to have a new adventure in a new town. I know you have all your pals in London, but everything there is so tied up with Matt. It will all be fresh here – a new life you will create for yourself, on your own terms, no memories to trip you up.'

'Maybe you're right,' she said, remembering her first visit to Liberty's after Matt had died. It had never occurred to her that it would be upsetting to go there – their favourite shop –

without him, but it had hit her like a face-on collision. She'd run back out onto the street, sobbing.

As they came up the rise of West Hill Road, St Leonards, Sophie could spot the house ahead of them by the colour of the front door. Baby lilac. She remembered it because Matt had vowed to be waiting with a pot of black gloss paint for the moment the sale was completed. He had hated pastel colours with a vengeance. One of his many little quirks.

The estate agent was waiting outside for them and Sophie felt strangely nervous as he opened the door.

'No harm in having another look,' she said to Rey, mostly to reassure herself.

She stood in the large hall and looked round, taking it all in again – the generous proportions, doors opening off into rooms she knew were equally spacious. She waited for a tidal wave of devastating Matt associations to hit her, but it didn't come. But then, when she thought about it, she'd only viewed this house with him once. The other times, when they'd been deciding whether they were going to make an offer on it, she'd come down without him, first with Rey and then with Beau. Matt had never had time for another visit.

A whole scenario of how he would have used those days in London with her safely out of the way in Hastings flashed across her mind, in technicolour.

Grieving widow, she reminded herself. *Gridow*.

'Oh, I forgot about all this amazing space,' Rey was saying. 'You could have the biggest Christmas tree. Come on, let's look at the kitchen. Now I'm here again, I'm thinking natural textures set against cooler tones ...'

He headed on through that door, but Sophie turned left into the room that was officially the dining room, which she had planned to use a studio. It had a second door at the far end that lead directly into the kitchen and two large windows with lots of northern light. Looking at it again, she could clearly picture a raised podium in the middle with a plate of food on it, a camera angled down on a tripod, ready to shoot, and open shelves on all the walls to house her props within easy reach.

Before she even stepped through the far door into the kitchen, where Rey had his tape measure out, Sophie knew she was going to move in.

'Cork floors,' Rey was saying. 'Like I said, for your poor old-lady-standing-up-cooking feet and OSB board for the cupboards. It will glow.'

'Pink,' she said, firmly. 'I'm going to have a pink kitchen. Pastel pink.'

The colour Matt most detested.

Rey's eyebrows were nearly reaching his hairline as Sophie turned to the estate agent.

'Thanks for letting me see the house again,' she said. 'I've been having buyer wobbles, but seeing it again, I'm ready to complete as quickly as possible.'

'Great,' he said. 'I'll ring the office and find out where things are up to with the vendor's solicitors.'

'Yay,' said Rey, shaking his arms over his head in triumph. 'I'm so happy. I didn't want to bully you, but I did think you were totally insane to think of letting this house go. The sea views alone.'

'Let's go and look at them,' said Sophie.

They went round the whole house, Sophie's excitement increasing with every room.

'So which bedroom are you going to have?' she asked Rey as they walked back down the stairs.

'Oh, I won't need a room here. I will come and see you, don't worry, I just have other plans for where I'm going to stay.'

Sophie stared at him. She couldn't imagine what he meant. Did he know other people in Hastings? One of the whole points of buying such a big place was to have room for friends – and he was her best friend.

He started laughing. 'Remember that beautiful flat on the seafront we saw this morning? The one you didn't know we were going to see? I bought it.'

'I did wonder why I was looking at a two-bedder with no garden.'

'I spotted it on Rightmove and slipped it into our plans. And I did the deal while you were in the loo at the café, because I wanted to surprise you. I've wanted a place out of town for a while – and I'll be just down the cliff from you.'

Sophie flung her arms around him. 'This is the best news. I won't be all alone here.'

'You certainly won't.'

'And we'll get so fit going up and down that steep path between our places,' said Sophie, feeling almost light-hearted.

'Perhaps we should get a funicular railway installed. Like the two in the Old Town, going up the cliff from my street to yours.'

'Or a very long rope ladder.'

'We can abseil down—'

'Or, if you've been mixing the cocktails,' said Sophie, 'possibly actually fly.'

2009

Sophie and Matt were in Liberty. It was his favourite shop and, as always, he insisted on getting the old wooden lift up to the top floor and then coming down by the stairs, taking in every single square metre on the way.

'Look,' he said, in the tableware department on the third floor, 'they've got dinner plates in the style of blue plaques. How brilliant. "Agatha Christie lived here". Sigmund Freud, Jimi Hendrix. How great would a whole wall of those look? And you could have fictional characters ... "The Jabberwocky lived here", "Eeyore lived here". That would be cool.'

Sophie smiled at him. He always noticed things she'd missed.

'I could paint it,' said Matt, his face lit up with an expression she knew so well. Beau looked the same on entering a sweet shop. Possibility.

'I know you could,' said Sophie, laughing. 'That's what I'm worried about.'

'Sophie Crommelin, food stylist, amazing mother and very sexy lady lived here ...' He pulled her to him and nuzzled her neck.

Sophie closed her eyes. He could still make her feel giddy, even after having two kids together.

'Right,' he said. 'Mustn't let myself get hot and bothered. We are here on a mission to buy you a dress, an interesting dress.'

Sophie's spirits dropped a little. 'Can I have some say in it?' Matt had very particular ideas about what he thought she should wear and they didn't always quite align with hers.

'Of course,' said Matt. 'Let's see what they've got. I just want you to look as beautiful as you are. To strut your stuff a bit. He's bringing his new trophy girlfriend and I want to show him that two can play that game.'

They were having dinner that night with a prominent gallerist from New York, who was possibly interested in representing Matt there. It was a big deal. He had a gallery in LA too.

'Okay,' she said. 'I'll be your human Barbie doll. For one night only. But I haven't exactly got a Barbie figure these days.'

'There's nothing wrong with your figure,' said Matt, reaching down to squeeze her buttock. 'You can show these New Yorkers what a real woman looks like. All his girlfriends look like chicken carcasses.'

Sophie didn't relish the idea of being on show, but decided if it would help to clinch the gallery deal by making Matt feel just a bit more confident, she'd play along. He never interfered in what she wore day to day and she hadn't really changed the way she dressed since they'd met. The jeans and tops had changed shape – and gone up a couple of sizes – but it was pretty much the same gear. That was her style and he said he liked it, so she could indulge him in this occasional dress-up game.

They arrived in the women's designer clothes area and Sophie was immediately drawn to a dress in full tiers of different printed silks. It was beautiful, but the price tag made her flinch – nearly £2000.

'Are you sure we shouldn't go down to the more accessible fashion floor?' she said to Matt, who was looking through the rails with a concentrated expression she knew well. The building could fall down around him when he was in that zone and he wouldn't notice.

'No,' he said firmly. 'You're having the best. You've got to spend it to make it. I want to show this guy we mean business. This is good ...' He pulled out a silk slip dress in a beautiful shade of café au lait.

'That's a really beautiful ... petticoat,' she said. 'It's a nightdress. I couldn't wear it in public.'

'Try it on,' said Matt. 'Just see.'

Sophie went into the changing room to put the dress on and had to admit it was lovely. The bias cut made it cling to her body, but in a flattering way. She was a lot more curvy since she'd had the boys, but in this dress, her body did seem to go in and out in the right places.

Matt stuck his head round the curtain of the changing room and whistled. 'Yes,' he said, nodding. 'That one. It looks amazing on you – and I've chosen the shoes too. You can see them when we get home.'

As Sophie had suspected, when they got back in the early afternoon and she took the shoes out of the box, they were skimpy sandals with very high heels. She put them on with the dress and attempted to walk round the bedroom.

'You really want me to go out like this?' she asked him, nearly falling over as she caught one of the heels on the rug.

'Oh, definitely,' said Matt, coming over and wrapping his arms around her. He took hold of the dress at the hem and pulled it slowly up her body, cupping her buttocks in his hands.

'Shouldn't we hang the dress up?' she said, as he started to slowly walk her towards the bed.

'No,' said Matt. 'It will look better a bit lived in – and keep the shoes on too,' he added, gently pushing her down.

Afterwards, when she was lying in his arms in a state of deep contentment, Matt ran his hand over her hair and smiled at her.

'The way you're feeling now,' he said, 'remember it when you walk into the restaurant tonight.'

And then he made love to her again.

CHAPTER 3

Juliet woke up as a small but forceful missile landed on her bed.

'Mummy!' the missile said, nimbly inserting herself under the covers and snuggling up. 'You're nice.'

Juliet put her arms round her darling girl and kissed the top of her head, with its tangle of dark curls. 'You're nice too, my little dumpling,' she said, and as she spoke, a powerful wave of nausea rolled over her. She turned her head and dry-retched over the side of the bed.

'What are you doing?' said Cassady, sitting up and leaning over to see if there was anything interesting to look at.

'Oh, I think I've got a bit of an upset tummy. I'll be fine when I've had some breakfast.'

But even the thought of food brought the nausea back and she curled up on her side to ride it out, one arm holding onto her daughter.

She hadn't even bothered to do a pregnancy test. She'd known she was knocked up the moment she realised her period was late. Her breasts were tender and bigger, she had a constant strange feeling of being at sea – and now, the morning sickness. All just like the first time.

She glanced at her watch. 7.25, Monday morning. Normally she would be up and dressed, spending precious time with her daughter, before leaving for the gym and then work. The nanny would arrive any minute.

Forcing herself to get out of bed, she handed Cassady a tablet tuned to a children's TV app and went to shower and dress.

Then, remembering that a bath helped relieve the nausea, she weighed up the benefit against the extra time and ran a shallow one. Rubbing body wash over herself, she stopped when she got to her belly, looking down at it, the reality that a new life was growing in there properly sinking in.

She was thrilled because she dearly wanted Cassady to have a sibling, but now it was all so much more complicated. She closed her eyes and squeezed them tightly, desperate to stop the tears she could feel forming. She couldn't cope with turning up at the studio with a puffy face on top of everything else.

And what was she crying for? She forced herself to switch her brain back into strict efficient functioning mode. She'd been doing that most of her life, shutting away the difficult things she didn't want to distract her, and it had become such a natural setting for her she liked to think of it as her superpower.

It had certainly contributed to her business success, being able to push all the other intrusive and inconvenient things away.

You must really want to be born, she thought, gently stroking the skin over where the tiny cluster of cells inside her was multiplying into a human being. And just as with darling Cassady, it had taken just one impetuous fuck to make it happen – with this one on Christmas Day, of all days.

Although of course it was exactly because it had been that particular day that she'd had a moment of weakness and allowed him to come over.

Juliet put her mental brakes on, hard. No. She was not going there. Not then, not ever. That box was closed. Fastened with chains and padlocks and stored in a forgotten warehouse. Which might have burned down.

She put her palms over her eyes so she could marshal her thoughts into their permitted arrangements when there was a gentle tap on the door. It was the nanny, Ligaya, just letting her know she was there.

Juliet snapped to, forcing herself up and out of the bath. She had a jewellery empire to run.

CHAPTER 4

Beau woke up, blinking, wondering where he was, which wasn't an unfamiliar sensation for him. He actually loved it. Made him feel alive.

He turned to look at the woman he'd just spent the night with. Flora. Great girl. Really good fun and very beautiful. He loved her tumbling strawberry blonde curls, although he didn't have a particular type or a preference in hair colour, or any other attributes. What he loved was variety and Flora was a rare bird.

He put his arms behind his head and ran over the events of the previous evening with a great sense of satisfaction. He'd bumped into her in one of his favourite bars, which he'd popped into after finishing his restaurant shift. They'd had a few drinks and laughs, some dancing and then a spectacularly good time back at her place.

Flora really was great. Good to talk to as well as the other stuff. She was a legal translator, working in human rights law. So she had a serious brain as well as a great body. How many times had they hooked up now? With some regret, he calculated that this made it four. Two over his limit. This had to be the last time.

Looking at her pretty freckled face, her lips slightly parted in sleep, he felt familiar stirrings, which made him carefully lift his legs out from under the duvet and stand up. Giving in to what biology was currently suggesting would make things tricky.

He grabbed the bits of his clothing that littered the bedroom floor and tiptoed out to the sitting room where the rest was strewn about. After getting dressed, he looked down at his hands and the profusion of chunky rings on his fingers.

After some consideration, he removed the two that were on his right pinky, selecting one, then he fished in his jacket pocket for a small length of ribbon that he tied round the ring. Printed on it was the word 'Mojobo', followed by his Instagram tag.

He crept back into the bedroom and looked down at Flora, feeling an unfamiliar pang. She really was good fun and so smart. And if he was honest with himself, he did really have a bit of a thing for long curly hair …

He weighed the ring in his hand before placing it gently on the pillow next to her head, then turned and walked out as quickly and quietly as he could.

As he strode down the street, the trees thick with leaves, things flowering in front gardens, bright morning sunshine making even this grimy part of East London look pretty, Beau hoped Flora would like his way of saying goodbye and thank you.

But then he hesitated, half turning, wondering if he should go back and wake her up with a cup of tea and a chat instead.

A few friends had teased him recently that he was becoming an urban myth – the Hackney Ring Man – and a couple of women he had met out and about had spotted his rings and asked if he was the man who left one as a calling card.

One of them had said: 'Are you that ring wanker?'

Both times he had confirmed that, yes, he was the man who left a ring – and told them that he did it out of respect and that he'd never ghost a woman. He left it as a gift, with his ribbon on it so they could contact him via Instagram if they wanted to, and he could explain how much he'd enjoyed spending time with them but that he wasn't in a position to commit to anything more formal.

The woman who'd called him a wanker had then suggested, rather tartly, that another way of doing that would be to wait for the woman to wake up and tell her to her face. Then she'd walked off, throwing, 'Arsehole', over her shoulder. The other woman had just rolled her eyes and turned away from him.

Was he a wanker arsehole? He thought the ring thing was romantic and respectful. People his age met and got it on every night of the week, never to see each other again, so wasn't it good to make it a more memorable experience in some way? He started walking again. It would have been nice to have a cup of tea with Flora, but it would be just a bit too cosy and he didn't want to give her the idea he was up for anything more committed. There was no way he was taking that on right now. Not with all the other stuff he had to deal with.

Feeling his mood lowering at the thought of it all, Beau upped his pace, pushing his thick black hair off his forehead and putting a deliberate spring in his step, which came naturally in his father's cowboy boots.

Seeing a woman blatantly checking him out from the bus stop opposite, he smiled at her and kept walking. It happened all the time. He didn't go looking for it. Women hit on him every day and, in the right circs, he was happy to respond. Good times for all. He just didn't want to have a relationship.

He was only twenty-five, making jewellery was his focus, he worked long hours waitering in a trendy restaurant to survive and he didn't want any other commitments. It wasn't exactly unusual for a guy his age and he thought his ring routine was nicer than just legging it, which he knew a lot of his friends did – men and women.

He came to a bus stop on a route that would take him to his flat but decided to walk straight to his studio instead, which was in a building next to Regent's Canal. He never rushed to take a shower after an encounter like the one the night before. He wanted Flora's scent on his body for as long as possible, it would help him work. He was at his most creative with a bit of a hangover and the hum of a hot night still lingering in his loins. He hammered those feelings and scents into the metal of his rings, every one of them a unique piece.

No wonder so many of his clients were in the music business – or aspired to be. One of his first customers had told him his rings had 'mojo' and that had inspired the brand name, Mojobo.

He ran up the concrete stairs to his studio, taking them two at a time. Sam wasn't in, which he was glad about, because as much as Beau liked him, he was rather too keen on a chat. A long chat, which often segued straight into a long lunch. With beer. Beau had some interesting ideas floating around in his head and didn't want any distractions. Something that looked floral and deeply sexual at the same time … He wanted to get going on it.

He pulled the last ring he'd been working on out of the old tea tin where he stored his works in progress, popped it over the metal rod used to hold rings while he worked on them and blasted it with his hand torch. That design hadn't been going anywhere and he always found a bit of destruction at the start of a project fired up his creative juices. And the more 'rules' he broke while he was making something, the better the final result seemed to be.

He did always wear his safety goggles, though, and with those on, and his big headphones on over the top, he felt like some kind of mad professor. He put his Rolling Stones playlist on shuffle, always good to get things flowing.

But as the unmistakable first notes of 'Gimme Shelter' played out, Beau was hit by a memory so powerful it was like being physically punched in the gut: the last kitchen disco he'd had with his parents, which had happened spontaneously one random night when he'd put that particular track on.

He could so clearly remember Matt's overjoyed reaction.

'Oh, my perfect child,' he'd said, hugging Beau as they all got into the groove, Sophie waving her wooden spoon in the air as she danced. 'Never have I had greater confirmation that we've done a good job bringing you up than your choice of this track.'

Beau realised he was sitting in his studio frozen, holding the ring rod in the air with one hand, the torch in the other. It was lucky it wasn't turned on. He might have set fire to his bloody hair.

Slumping, he let his forehead rest on the workbench as he sobbed, before sitting up and wiping his eyes on his sleeves. It was five months and twenty-two days since his father had died and the grief still often ambushed him like this. And whenever he had one of these shocks it would set his brain off on the same track, like a video in one of his father's installations on constant repeat. Him and Matt in the Red Lion. The last drink they'd had there, when he'd said that weird thing.

'The thing is, Beausie,' he'd said, 'I'm not going be around so much in the future.' For a moment Beau had thought he was going to tell him he had an incurable disease or something, but then he'd said those words Beau so desperately wished he could forget: 'I've met someone.'

Then that same mental loop brought him back to the conversation he'd overheard at the wake between Rey and that woman in his father's leather jacket. Was she the 'someone'? Although he dreaded it with all his being, Beau knew he was going to have to find out. He'd been avoiding it all this time, using his grief as an excuse, but that weird thing his dad had said wasn't going to go away just because he wanted it to.

He had to protect his mother.

2006

Sophie was sitting on a picnic rug with three other Crommelin WAGS, watching their respective husbands and sons play in their annual family rounders match. This hard-fought contest happened every year as one of the highlights of the group holiday, when the whole clan gathered in a large rented house in Devon. Both events were mandatory, although second-to-youngest brother Oliver and his wife, Liz, had got out of it some years before by moving to Singapore.

'Well played!' yelled Bella, wife of Thomas, when her fifteen-year-old son Hugo hit a long ball.

It sailed over the head of one of the younger cousins, who had been put way out as a distant fielder and now went to look for it with little method or enthusiasm.

'Well done, Leaf,' called out his mother, the wife of the youngest Crommelin, Conrad. 'Very graceful.'

Sophie mentally rolled her eyes. Freya did it in real time.

Leaf's mother, Willow, had tried to get the rounders match scrapped, because, she said, she and Conrad 'didn't believe in competitive sport', but it had turned out that her husband's Crommelin genes trumped her beliefs. He couldn't resist an opportunity to triumph over his big brothers now that his younger age was an advantage rather than the handicap it had been through his childhood.

But none of them could stay infuriated with her for long. She was pregnant with her fourth baby, which was a big deal for all of them.

'So, Willow,' said Freya, 'are you going to put us all out of our misery and find out the sex of this baby you're carrying? Sebastian and I are longing to go to the mini-Glastonbury that Bella and Thomas have promised to throw if it's a girl. I'm sure Thomas will be able to get Taylor Swift to headline, with the Rolling Stones and probably Elvis ... They're all on his payroll, aren't they, Bella?'

Sophie couldn't help feeling a bit sorry for Bella, who was never quite sure whether Freya was complimenting or openly deriding her – and it was a fine balance, fuelled by an equal mix of affectionate teasing and retaliation for the constant boasting.

'Well, he did meet Chris Martin at an event recently,' said Bella, 'so perhaps he could get Coldplay, but anyway, we'll have the great DJs and party bands who do all our big dos, so come on, Willow, do tell us. It would be so wonderful for us all to have a little girl in the family.'

So far, their branch of Crommelins was on their third boys-only generation. Matt's father had been one of seven brothers, his generation were five, and to date they had all had sons, so there were now twelve boy cousins, eleven of them old enough to play in this game, although two were let off by living on the other side of the world.

Sophie turned her attention back to the game, to see that after two more young ones had been summarily bowled out, Beau, who had just turned eight, was up for batting against the fifteen-year-old. It was an unfortunate pairing. Hugo was a bit of a bully, making no allowances for younger boys up against bowling skills honed on the cricket pitches of his elite school.

'Come on, Hugo,' Bella called out, to Sophie's irritation. The older boy hardly needed encouragement when facing a child nearly half his age who, Sophie knew, hated this rounders match more than anything else in his life.

Jack loved games, but Beau really didn't. He wasn't very co-ordinated and – probably more importantly – he just didn't care. He hadn't inherited the Crommelin win-or-die spirit, but had no choice but to go through this each year.

Sophie wanted to run over and bat for him, but she could see by the expression on her son's face that he was determined to do his best. Jack had already scored some rounders and Beau didn't want to be the one to let his dad down.

'Loser,' said Hugo, when Beau failed to make any contact with the first throw, but it was a Crommelin rule that batters under the age of ten got the best of three balls.

Hugo bowled again, a terrifying spin that Beau jumped out of the way of.

'What a wimp!' said Hugo.

The little shit. Sophie had to restrain herself. She glanced over at Bella to see if she'd noticed that her teenage son was terrorising a much younger boy, but her sister-in-law was beaming with delight, no doubt congratulating herself that the school fees were worth every penny.

Thomas had a little more compassion.

'No fast bowling, Hugo,' he shouted across the field. 'This is a friendly match, not Eton/Harrow. Save your best spins for that. Just make sure you're in the First bloody Eleven next year.'

He'd got a little boast in, Sophie noted, but she was touched he'd intervened.

Beau's face was tight with concentration as Hugo prepared to send out the third and final bowl and Sophie was delighted – and somewhat amazed – to see the bat connect perfectly with the ball, which flew high into the air and sailed across the field.

The problem was that no one was more surprised than Beau, who just stood there watching it soar away.

'Run, you little hero,' yelled Sebastian, captain of Beau's team, and in his confusion, Beau started running the wrong way round the posts as the rest of his team screamed at him and the other side roared with laughter. Hugo was actually clutching his sides.

Ha bloody ha, thought Sophie.

Then out of nowhere came Matt, scooping his son up under one arm like a stolen piglet and running round the posts, not once but twice, before one of his nephews on the opposing team fielded the ball back to a now furious Hugo at the stumps.

'That's bloody cheating,' he was saying. 'That's not a rounder! Your team should lose points for that, it's pathetic. Beau can't even run. It's a miracle he ever hit it. He's pathetic.'

Thomas approached his oldest son with a stern expression on his face. 'That was a champion bit of sportsmanship from the Blue Team,' he said. 'A great hit by Beau and true teamwork so, as the head of the family, I declare them the winners, on creativity as well as points. And you, my boy, need to learn to think more laterally. You won't get anywhere in life thinking in a box. It's not the Crommelin way.'

That was the ultimate reproof and, looking suitably admonished, Hugo went over to sit with his mother, who immediately raided the picnic basket for him.

Beau came rushing over to Sophie.

'Did you see, Mummy?' he said. 'I whacked it.'

'You certainly did,' said Sophie, hugging him. 'And you scored two rounders.'

'With Dad's help,' said Beau, looking a bit uncertain.

'You did it the Crommelin way,' said Sophie. 'You heard what Uncle Thomas said.'

Beau looked happy again and scampered off to join his cousins. Sophie stood up and went over to Matt, who was emptying a bottle of water down his throat. She put her arms round him from behind and laid her cheek on his back. His t-shirt was quite wet with sweat. She liked it.

He turned round and hugged her back, lifting her chin up and kissing her on the lips.

'You,' said Sophie, looking up at him, so handsome with his cheeks all pink from running, 'are the best dad in the world.'

CHAPTER 5

Sophie was having a party. Well, it was more like she'd had a party thrust upon her.

'Having fun?' Thomas asked as he filled her glass with sparkling wine.

'Yes, great,' said Sophie, hoping it sounded more genuine than it felt.

He and Sebastian had come down to help her unpack the stuff from the old house, which had been in storage for a few months while the renovation work was being done on the new one. And Jack had come over from Australia to muck in too. Now it was pretty much sorted, they'd decided she needed to have a housewarming party before they all went home. She hadn't had a say in it.

Normal Crommelin behaviour.

But it was good to have a test run of the adjusted layout of the house, she told herself, observing the flow of people from the kitchen to the dining area in the new extension, on to the sitting room and then back round through the hall to the kitchen.

The circular plan worked really well for entertaining, just as Rey had said it would. It was just hard dealing with having so many people in it. Especially as she didn't know any of them. Somehow, Thomas and Sebastian had managed to find a surprising number of people to invite in a town where neither of them had ever been before. Jack told her they'd put something on Facebook to make the connections. Sophie had come off social media since Matt had died – it made her feel too exposed – and the very thought of what they might have posted made her shudder. 'Tragic dead artist's wife seeks like-minded Hastings folk for fun and friendship.' Ugh.

She wished Rey was there.

'How do you like this fizz?' asked Thomas, holding up his glass to look at the wine against the light.

'It's very nice,' she said. 'What is it?'

'Local gear. An old mate of mine moved down here a few years ago and he makes it. He's got a whole vineyard thing going. Repurposed the family property. He donated a couple of cases for the party, which was decent of him. He's supposed to be coming tonight, so I'll introduce you. Nice chap. We were young guns together at Warburg's. Now, who else haven't you met?'

'I've just got to go and ask Jack something,' said Sophie, needing a moment's respite from pretending to be delighted to meet new people. She'd just got into the sitting room when someone grasped her arm.

'Hi, Sophie,' said a woman who looked vaguely familiar, but nothing more than that. She had long grey hair, with a centre parting.

'Hi,' replied Sophie as brightly as she could muster, having no idea who this person was.

'I'm Lorraine,' the woman said, smiling with her eyes tightly crinkled up and her head on one side. 'My husband,

Terry, used to work with Matt at Goldsmiths? We had lunch one time, when you two came down here house hunting? I'm so sorry about Matt.'

Maaaaatt.

Sophie forced herself to smile. It took a big effort. This Lorraine was speaking in a particular patronising tone of voice that some people seemed to feel compelled to use when mentioning Matt. She was sure she meant well, but it still made Sophie's skin crawl.

'You're very kind,' she managed to get out, remembering the lunch now. Lorraine did something with felt, which she'd talked about a lot, referring to it every time as 'my work'. Matt had been funny about it afterwards, calling everything he touched 'my work' in a sappy voice. He hadn't liked the husband much either, who was clearly resentful of Matt's success.

'You must come for supper,' Lorraine was saying, still with that half-cocked smile on her face and the Sunday-school tone. 'I'll message you on Insta? We have a great girls' night once a month. You'll love it.'

A girls' night? Was that how it was going to be now? Not invited with the men anymore? Was that still a thing? Fear of the predatory widow? Great. More crap to deal with. She was a pridow as well as a gridow.

'Is your lovely husband here?' Sophie asked, smiling back at Lorraine with her own head on one side. 'I'd love to say hi to him.' *Terrrrrrrrrrrry.*

It had the desired effect. Lorraine's patronising smile dropped. 'Yes,' she said, tightly. 'I think Terry might be in the kitchen ...'

'I'll go and see. I need to check on the food anyway. I've got something super in my oven.' She couldn't help smiling to herself as she turned away.

She walked right into Sebastian. He smiled back at her.

'Good to see you cracking a grin, Soph,' he said, putting an arm round her and giving her a hug. 'Are you enjoying the party?'

Sophie paused before replying. She liked all Matt's brothers but had always got on best with Sebastian, perhaps because he was the most like Matt. The other one who'd gone to art college.

'I don't quite know, Seb,' she said.

He looked at her, his intelligent eyes full of caring concern, but the Crommelin mischief still there too. His colouring was lighter than Matt's, his hair dark brown rather than black, but he had the same firm jaw line and full lips. The genes Beau had inherited. Jack looked more like her.

'I'm so grateful to you and Thomas for everything you've done, but I just don't really know what I'm feeling most of the time these days. Comfortably numb, I suppose.'

Sebastian nodded. 'That makes sense. And I'm glad you trust me enough to be honest with me about it. I did wonder whether this was a bit "too soon".'

He said it in the particular way that had been an ongoing joke between him and Matt and it made Sophie smile to hear it again. Sebastian had exactly the light touch people like Lorraine didn't have.

'But you know how Thomas likes to push everything forward,' he continued. 'Fall in, men, quick march … and I've found over the years it's easiest just to go along with it. Matt was the only one who ever stood up to him.'

Sophie gave him a little hug. He'd looked so bleak as he said it. He'd lost a brother, she reminded herself, his best friend, really. It wasn't all about her, and although Sebastian and Matt had been a bit competitive, as the two 'arty' ones in the family, they had also been particularly close.

'How's Freya?'

'Oh, you know,' he said, 'telling everyone what to think as usual. Especially me.'

'Well, she is paid to have opinions.'

'True – and doesn't she know it.'

'I love Freya,' said Sophie. 'She's hilarious.'

'She does coat her missiles with mirth,' said Sebastian. 'Otherwise she'd be unbearable. And you know she loves you too, Soph. Please don't become a stranger now you're down here. You know you can ring me any time you need to talk to someone, and if you ever want a shot of London energy, come up and stay with us. We'd both love that.'

'Thanks, Seb,' said Sophie. 'I will, but now I've got to go and check on the food.'

She kissed him on the cheek and headed out to the hall, starting to feel desperate to have a moment on her own. She glanced at the stairs, wondering if anyone would notice if she went up to her room for a bit and lay down on the bed, but as she hesitated, someone knocked on the front door.

Screaming internally, Sophie opened it to find a man about her age, perhaps a little older, with grey hair and appealingly crinkly eyes. He was smiling and holding a large box.

'Hi,' said Sophie, plastering on a welcoming expression, 'come in.' *Come in to my house, total stranger, and join all the other people I don't know.*

'Hello. Are you Sophie?'

She nodded.

'I'm Charlie Renton,' he said, waving his fingers as well as he could while holding the heavy-looking carton. 'I would shake your hand, but mine are a bit full.'

'Gosh,' said Sophie, noticing that the brand name on the box was the same as the delicious sparkling wine Thomas had organised, although the box was an oddly flat shape for wine. 'Is this more of that wonderful bubbly? Was it you who gave us that?'

Charlie nodded. 'But this is a different version. In tins. Where shall I put it?'

'That's so kind of you,' said Sophie. 'And how clever to can it. Can I give you hand?'

'Just show me where you want it,' said Charlie. 'I'll follow you.'

She led the way through to the kitchen and helped him put the wine down next to some garden tubs full of ice that Thomas had arranged next to the central island, where he'd set up the bar. Charlie crammed as many cans as he could in among the ice and, as he stood up, Sophie noticed he was wearing faded pink corduroy trousers held up by pink braces. On his feet were pink wellington boots.

She couldn't help smiling.

'Sorry about my, er, look,' he said. 'Work gear. I didn't have time to change. One of my people injured themselves and I've been at A&E for four hours. His wife turned up eventually, so I was able to get over here.'

'Gosh,' said Sophie. 'Thanks so much for coming after that – and you do fit in rather well in my pink kitchen in those trousers. It's almost camouflage. Would you like a glass of your lovely fizz, or do you go straight from the tin?'

'The tins are great. I'd love to know what you think of them, but if there's a bottle open, I'll have a glass. If it's not a pain for you.'

'I'll get you one.'

He deserved one of her nice champagne flutes, she thought, not the cheap party glasses, and headed over to the far side of the room to find one. As she opened the cupboard door, she heard Thomas's unmistakable voice.

'Charlie boy! Good man! You finally made it. Are you living on country time now?'

Then there was the unmistakable sound of Thomas's usual back slapping and Sophie heard Charlie say, 'Good man ...' and she glanced round to see him slapping Thomas back.

Just another of Thomas's apparently endless network of City boys, despite the endearing trousers. They were like stags, or hares, those men, with their weird courtship rituals. She could just imagine Matt rolling his eyes at Sebastian at this point and then the two of them would have disappeared off together somewhere, leaving Thomas with his hearty friend. The Arties and the Hearties had been another of Matt and Sebastian's ongoing jokes.

A wave of intense sadness washed over her as she remembered how they used to make each other laugh about it. The sudden sense of loss was so overwhelming she had to hold onto the countertop with her spare hand to steady herself. In that moment, she would have given absolutely anything to have Matt walk through the door. Even the Matt who had made that awful announcement to her. She just wanted him back, whatever he'd done. She wanted his arms around her. The void was unbearable.

She hadn't realised she was standing stock still, staring into space with an empty champagne flute in her hand, until Charlie appeared at her side.

'Is that for me?' he said, quietly.

'Oh, yes,' said Sophie. 'Sorry, I was distracted.'

He reached for the glass and put his other hand gently on her shoulder, looking into her eyes. 'I'm so sorry about your husband,' he said, in a gentle but normal voice, no pious simpering. 'Thomas told me what happened to Matt. Just awful. Tom was so proud of his brilliant artist brother. Such a terrible shock for you all, especially you and your sons. Absolute shit.'

Sophie gazed back at him, a bit stunned, and found she was smiling, although she could also feel tears forming in her eyes.

'Thanks, Charlie,' she said. 'That's exactly what it is. Utter crap.'

He patted her shoulder – was that the version of the man-to-man back slapping that their mob used for women? – and looked as though he was about to say something else, but before he could speak, Thomas joined them, his overbearing presence like a planet eclipsing the sun.

'Ah, good man, you've met the sis-in-law,' he said, clapping Charlie's back some more.

They must be quite bruised by the end of a day of it, Sophie thought.

'Sophie, this is Charles Renton, the bloke I was telling you about. Wine. We call him Charlie.'

'Yes,' said Sophie. 'We've met, and Charlie has very kindly

brought another case of his lovely fizz – in tins, which is exciting.'

'Fair play,' said Thomas, rubbing his hands together. 'Well, best we finish it, eh? You can always bunk down here, Charlie boy, so you don't have to stay off the booze and drive back to the farm down tiny lanes in the pitch black. I know how lethal they are from Somerset. That's we why keep a full-time driver down there now ...'

Here we go, thought Sophie, wondering how long this boast-a-thon would last and feeling extremely irritated that Thomas had just invited a total stranger to stay the night in her house. Even though he did seem nice, it was too much. The thought of more back slapping at breakfast was too much.

So she was glad to hear Jack calling her from the direction of the dining room.

'My son wants me,' she said, turning back to Charlie. 'Once again, thank you so much for all the wine.'

'You're very welcome,' he said. 'Perhaps you'd like to come and see where I make it sometime.'

'I'd love to.'

'Thomas has my number.'

'Ah, yes, I'll ping it over to you,' said Thomas. 'If I can figure out how to do it on my new Apple watch. It's the latest one, great bit of kit, I just had it sent over from the States.'

Sophie saw him lift his left wrist to demonstrate and grabbed her opportunity to leg it over to Jack.

'Hey, Mumpty,' he said, putting his arm round her and kissing the side of her head. 'I thought you might like a break from the Hearties.'

Sophie smiled, happy that he remembered the joke too.

'Uncle Seb and I have got a bit of an Arties' colony going in here and we thought you should join us. It's really fun. Your neighbours are epic.'

Sophie still flinched a bit whenever she went into the dining room because it was furnished with the big table from the old house with the mash-up of old chairs that Matt had customised. Including the one with Mickey Mouse ears that he had always sat on. He'd carved and painted the ears himself and screwed them on to the back of an old school chair. Everybody loved it – especially the boys – but Sophie could hardly bear to look at it. He'd been leaning on it when he'd made his announcement.

She was relieved to see Sebastian was sitting on it, which softened the impact, in between two older women, who were her neighbours.

'This is where the real party is,' said Sebastian. 'I'm getting all the red-hot Hastings goss from Agata and Olive here. You've really lucked out with your neighbours.'

'Haven't I?' she said, sitting down. 'You two were so great when all the building work was going on. I don't know how I'll ever be able to thank you.' She raised her glass to each woman in turn.

'You're more than welcome, sweetheart,' said the younger of the two women. She looked like she was in her early seventies and was wearing old denim dungarees with a stripey Breton shirt, a red bandana knotted at her neck. 'We're stoked to have you here, aren't we, Ags? Three good women in a row, now.'

'And the people before …' said the older woman, bringing her hands up in the air by her head. She had a strong accent, something middle European. 'They were so boring. How do you say it, Olive? Like shitty bat?'

As they laughed, Sebastian put his arm round the old lady's birdlike shoulders and gave her a gentle squeeze, grinning as he caught Sophie's eye. Sophie knew exactly what he was telling her. He loved the characterful old girl in her Napoleonic-shaped orange hat and bold graphic sweater – and Matt would have too.

Sophie smiled back. That was the first thing she'd thought when she'd met Agata, who always seemed to wear a striking hat of some kind. Matt would immediately have asked if he could draw her.

'Agata's got something to tell you,' said Sebastian. 'Go on, tell Sophie about the cake.' He held up a plate with a slice of the poppy seed cake Sophie had made for the party from a recipe Agata had given her, written out in shaky handwriting.

'Did I make it wrong?' asked Sophie. 'Is it horrid?'

'No, darling,' said Agata. 'It is beautiful, but I have a confession to make.'

'OK …' said Sophie, puzzled.

'You know how I told you it was my aunt's recipe from Czechoslovakia, before the war … I'm afraid it was not. I copied it out of *Good Housekeeping* last week, but I thought you would like the story – and I knew I would like the cake, so …'

Sophie looked at her blankly, taking it in, then burst out laughing, throwing her head back and really letting go.

The rest of the group joined in and when they all calmed down again, Sophie realised she'd just had one of those rare, precious moments when she'd forgotten about Matt and all the complications of being the gridow/wronged wife hybrid and had just been herself again, if only for that tiny instant.

Buoyed up, she allowed herself to hope that living in this house, with these two doughty women on either side, might be just what she needed to get through it.

CHAPTER 6

Beau was standing just inside his father's studio, holding tight to the door handle to keep himself upright.

Grief had just done that sucker-punch thing to him again. As much as the impact of seeing everything inside, just as his dad had left it, there was the unmistakable smell: a combination of oil paint and turps and paper and spray glue, with a hint of coffee and even the powerfully spicy aftershave Matt had worn. Or was he imagining that?

As he looked around the space, he could see why his mother wanted to put off packing it up. She'd been uncharacteristically short with him when he'd suggested they should get on with it. There was just so much of it. Plus she'd said Matt's gallerist and Goldsmiths wanted to curate it all. But he thought the overwhelming sense of Matt's presence must be part of it too. It would be too much for her.

His poor mum. It was horrible seeing her so stressed. She was normally the rock of the family, calm and organised, keeping everything going, but Beau could see how she was struggling. He did his best, and Rey was a great friend, but there was only so much they could do. At least Jack had come home for a couple of weeks to help her unpack in the new house.

Two of his uncles were there too, which was great. He fished his phone out of his pocket and scrolled through to find some pics Jack had sent him of them all eating fish and chips and drinking wine on the beach in the early evening. There she was, sitting between Thomas and Sebastian, each of them with a protective arm around her, looking caring. She was smiling, but he could still see it in her eyes. That haunted look.

He couldn't bear it. And that was exactly why he was in his father's studio, to have a look around in case there was anything lurking there that could hurt her even more.

Beau sighed deeply and walked into the middle of the space, taking it all in. He hadn't actually been there very often. Although Matt always had multiple projects on the go that everyone had to know about, he'd been very private about this work space. He'd never had assistants and didn't really like anyone going there, except for the models he sometimes used.

Beau's eye fell on the chaise longue on the far side of the room, stuffing coming out of the seat, random paint splodges on the velvet. It had always been there, but now it took on a new and unwelcome significance. Was that why Matt had always been so cagey about his precious studio? He'd made claims for it as a holy shrine of creativity, a fragile ecosystem conducive to his work – but was it really his secret knocking shop?

Beau shuddered at the thought, because it reminded him what he was there for. To snoop. He didn't have anything to go on apart from what his father had told him that last time at the Red Lion, the woman at the wake wearing Matt's jacket – and the weird thing she'd said to Rey. But as much as Beau kept telling himself he was probably imagining the whole thing, he couldn't unhear those words: 'I've met someone.' That had been presented as a fact.

So he needed to find out what it was all about.

After tilting his neck from side to side a couple of times to ease the tension, he went over to the desk area, which was scattered with pieces of paper. There was a coffee cup on it, dregs still inside it. Beau closed his eyes and touched it lightly with his fingers, looking for connection. There was nothing. He felt stupid for even hoping and that gave him a push to keep going.

He sifted through the papers, finding pages torn from magazines, a council tax bill and a bank statement, which he didn't look at. He might be secretly poking around in his late father's stuff, in a space he wasn't supposed to be in, but he wasn't that low.

The desk was made out of an old door resting on two metal filing cabinets. Beau pulled open a drawer and was surprised to find it carefully organised with labelled folders arranged alphabetically: *America*; *Angels*; *Artists*; *Brass Bands*; *Bullets*; *Cakes*; *Corduroy*; *Dogs*. He pulled out the *Dogs* folder and it was full of torn-out pages from magazines with photographs of dogs on them. *Eagles, Eggs, Eccentrics* were the same deal.

So Matt had built up his own visual reference library, with physical pictures, not the Google searches Beau used when he wanted some inspiration. When they did clear the space out, he would ask his mum if he could keep this archive. It was the best of his dad, this kind of thing.

He tried L for *Lover*, M for *Mistress* and W for *Woman*, but there was nothing. He opened the other three drawers and it was all the same: carefully filed pictures. What an obsessive man his father had been.

With that area exhausted of possibilities, Beau looked round the space and headed over to the shelves that lined the far wall. There were lots of art books and magazines and the kind of random objects Matt liked to have around. A troll doll with bright green hair. A real Campbell's tomato soup tin, like the one immortalised by Andy Warhol. An amateur-looking ship in an old milk bottle, the masts made from cocktail sticks. A pottery pig that Beau had made at junior school.

He flicked through the canvases stacked against the walls, so many of them, at different stages, all interesting, but nothing that helped his search. Would these all go to some kind of hideous auction now?

He was beginning to think he couldn't stand to be in there much longer and it was probably all a big waste of time anyway, when he noticed that the bottom shelves of the bookcases were stacked with black hardback sketchbooks of various sizes. There were loads of them, which wasn't surprising, because Matt always had one on him.

Pulling out a few and flicking through the pages, Beau could see there wasn't any system of use with the sketchbooks. All the drawings were dated and they could skip years from page to page within one book. It seemed like his father must have just picked up whichever one took his fancy on a particular day.

Another classic Matt-ism, thought Beau. What a great way to torture anyone who might want to do a study of his work, which they probably would.

He pulled out one of the smaller books, turning the pages and stopping suddenly when he saw a sketch that was clearly of him. Blowing out birthday candles on a cake. Six of them.

My Beau, my own boy was written next to it in Matt's unmistakable spiky handwriting.

Beau slumped onto the floor. He remembered the party and the cake, a pirate ship, which Sophie had made, of course. He had no memory of Matt sketching; he'd been too excited about having his friends there, the games, the presents, the food. And all the time his father had been drawing him, with love.

He let the book drop. What was he doing poking around in his father's private stuff? Matt might be dead and gone, but he still had to allow him some respect. Yes, he'd said something very disturbing when they'd last spent time together, but was that justification for Beau to go ferreting around like some kind of amateur detective?

Any hanky-panky Matt might have been up to had been abruptly interrupted by his death, so why go looking for it? Sophie had suffered a terrible loss – but been spared another. He should just leave it all well alone.

Beau stood up. It was time to go. This had been a mistake.

But when he picked up the sketchbook again to put it back on the shelf, it fell open on the last page. There was a beautiful pen-and-ink drawing of a naked woman who seemed to be asleep. She was pregnant.

His first thought was it must be his mother, but it came after drawings of him and Jack, so it wasn't her pregnant with them – and the face just wasn't Sophie's. Matt had drawn her so many times, it had almost become a signature the way he perfectly captured her face in just a few lines.

Although this was very loosely sketched, it was clearly a different woman. She was pregnant and naked, lying among tangled sheets. It didn't look like a drawing of an artist's model – there was a deep intimacy in the composition.

There were words on the sketch too. *My girl cooking.*

It didn't make any sense at first, but then Beau suddenly felt slightly sick. Was this so-called 'girl', in the context, 'cooking' a baby?

Did he have a half-brother or -sister somewhere?

CHAPTER 7

Juliet was in her office, talking to her PR, Rachel Rathbone, on the phone. Or rather, Juliet was listening while Rachel talked. She wasn't happy.

'You have to embrace being wanted for yourself, not just for your product,' she was saying. 'All my other clients are screaming for the opportunities I bring you, that you keep turning down. It's driving me nuts. What you have to understand, Juliet, is that you are as desirable a package as your product. You've created this business all on your own, from nothing. A whole new sector of fine jewellery, sold in the best stores in the world, with a shop on Walton Street. You're still young-ish, ha ha, you're beautiful, independent, very successful – and a single mother. Like your wonderful work, you are a sparkling gem, and it's time you used that.'

Juliet sighed. She'd heard it all before. Pretty much every time they spoke, because Rachel was always wanting her to do interviews for glossy magazines that were based around her. Juliet totally understood that was the norm, but she just didn't want to do it.

'I don't want to be one of those women who flog their brand through their personal life,' she said.

'Well, in that case,' said Rachel, 'I suggest you change your product from being fine jewellery, to making rivets or guttering. It's a luxury brand, and like all of them, as well as the object itself, we're selling the idea of a fabulous lifestyle: wafting around Positano in a Pucci kaftan and a Giuliette pendant, arriving at the Serpentine summer party looking amazing in a Valentino dress with a Giuliette–Valentino collaboration bracelet on your wrist. Both of which, I may remind you, you did last summer. You have a successful business, you look great – and you're a mum. You are living the dream your product projects, so you're the best person to sell it. The end.'

Rachel waited a beat before adding her punch line: 'And if you don't do this interview, I will resign from handling your business. I've got you the cover of the *Sunday Times Style* section, basically the Holy Grail for a brand like yours, and they want a portrait of you to go with the article, so if you say no, you are disrespecting what I do and I will wave you goodbye. And you know me well enough to know I mean it.'

Juliet did. It was what she loved about Rachel. They were very alike.

'Can it just be a head shot?' she asked.

'Why?' said Rachel, a suspicious edge in her voice.

'I'm six months pregnant.'

Rachel hooted. 'Oh, that's going to be heaven for the journalist. The perfect excuse to ask about the mystery father of your mystery children. Is it the same father?'

'No comment,' said Juliet.

'Well, I'm telling you now,' said Rachel. 'That approach won't work in an interview for the *Sunday Times*. Not even for the fluffy fashion section. They're all rottweilers in there, even the ones in designer shoes, and your mystery act is only going to make them more determined to find out the truth, because refusing to talk about it just makes it seem like the father's identity must be some massive big deal – George Clooney, Prince William, Boris Johnson. Get my drift? So I think we need to decide how you're going to answer that question. I'll coach you. Question one: Who is the father of your children?'

For a moment, Juliet was too appalled to answer. Just saying she wouldn't talk about it had always seemed the most honest way to approach it.

'Sperm donor,' she said before she'd even thought it through properly. 'It was a sperm donor. Both of them from the same one, so they are full siblings. I've always wanted to have children, but I'm so committed to my business, I don't have time for a relationship, so it seemed the most efficient way to do it.'

Almost true, she told herself.

'Great,' said Rachel. 'Very modern, they'll love that at the paper. In fact, that's a story I could place everywhere. I can see the headline now: "No father by choice – is this the true modern family?" Shall I make some calls?'

'No,' said Juliet, firmly. 'I'll say it for this interview – and any others in the future that will really help promote my brand, but I'm not going to be the poster girl for sperm donor babies, okay?'

'Well, that's all fine, but just make sure you stay as successful and hot as you are now. Because the moment your brand loses its lustre, you might be glad of any hook you can grab to get yourself some publicity – and, as you know, I'm the girl to get it for you.'

'My jewellery will get the publicity for me.'

'You're right, to an extent. Your jewellery is that fabulous or I wouldn't have taken your account on. I only work with brands when I keenly want the friends and family discount for myself, but just don't forget that you are a very important part of the package too.'

'Fine,' said Juliet, 'but can you still ask about just doing a head shot?'

'No!' said Rachel and slammed down the phone.

2019

Juliet was at an auction at Sotheby's. The lot she was planning to bid on was quite far back in the catalogue, but she liked to sit through the earlier pieces to get a feel for the atmosphere of a sale, how heated the room was. Her years of buying precious gems on the global market had honed her skills for any kind of trading. If she felt a sale room was overexcited, which sometimes happened if there was one special lot in it, or people bidding who didn't have much experience, or just too many people there, she would leave, no matter how much she loved a painting.

That was why she always went to the auctions and didn't bid online or over the phone. She also enjoyed the sense of occasion and would often bump into clients there, so it was a good place to wear her newest pieces. She'd made sales from that which had paid for whatever she'd bought in the auction room.

Figuring it would be at least another twenty minutes until her lot came up, she decided to go and get a coffee to sharpen her mind for the fight. As she walked out into the lobby, she saw him – the man from the Phillips' showroom. He noticed her at the same time and raised his hand in greeting.

Before she'd had time to move away, he was next to her.

'Hello,' he said. 'We meet again. Fellow auction house haunters. Are you buying tonight?'

'Possibly,' said Juliet, thinking it was none of his bloody business and planning to keep on walking, but then he spoke again.

'Did you buy the Lizzie Cromer we looked at that time?' he said.

She nodded, immediately regretting it, and then when he looked down, leafing through the catalogue he was holding, she thought – with relief – that the exchange was over and took a step towards the coffee bar.

'Hang on,' he said, holding the catalogue open and pointing at one of the pictures. 'Is this what you've got your eye on this evening?'

Juliet stared. It was exactly the piece she was interested in. Caught off guard, she said, 'How did you know?'

'Because it's the only thing I'd buy tonight,' he said, smiling in a way that put her at ease, although all her warning bells were ringing simultaneously. Had he stalked her in some way? Or seen her looking at the lots for this show, by chance? He'd said he was an 'auction house haunter', so it was possible he'd been there at the same time. She'd been in more than once to look at this sale, which increased the odds of that, and she had stood in front of that particular painting for a long time.

'Are you buying?' she said, to throw his attention off her and give her more time to suss him out.

'No,' he said. 'I just like watching the circus and being around the pictures. I'm getting a coffee, do you want one?'

And against all her better judgement, she said yes.

CHAPTER 8

Sophie was lying in her bed, looking at the sun streaming in around the edges of the curtains, trying to find the energy to get up and open them. She knew she'd feel better when she saw that amazing sea view, but the thought of doing anything other than lying completely flat seemed impossibly hard. Even turning her head to look at the window had been a big effort.

She sighed deeply. She'd been quite relieved when Thomas and Sebastian had left the day after the party. They'd been amazing help with the unpacking, and the party had been good fun in the end, but having them there had put her on edge. As much as she tried to push it aside, their presence was a constant reminder of Matt's betrayal, because of her permanent terror of blurting something out.

She felt like the woman with two brains.

Sophie squeezed her eyes shut to try to make it all go away. Then she just lay looking up at the ceiling, listening to the silence. Saturday morning and the house was dead. It was so quiet she could hear the blood in her ears.

From the moment the house had become hers it had been hectic with activity and full of people. Rey had stayed the first few nights and then popped up and down from London, overseeing the builders – his regular team – who had stayed with her to get it all done as quickly as possible. They had been good company and constantly hungry, which she'd loved, so she'd been kept busy cooking endless fry-ups and great batches of bacon sandwiches. It had been like having teenage boys again. Then the unpacking and the party …

She'd had some lovely time after that, just her and Jack, but he'd gone back to Brisbane the day before and now she was alone. This was what every morning would be like now, in this stupidly big house. Howlingly empty.

Sophie felt something like panic start to rise up inside her. She wasn't strong enough to survive this level of change on her own.

Leaving London, setting up somewhere completely new, getting used to a strange house, doing it alone – all on top of losing Matt to a horrible death, while simultaneously losing him to another woman. It was too much.

Juliet. Gillette. The name came into her head as it constantly did, like some kind of grotesque earworm. Was the woman at the funeral definitely that person? The one Matt was leaving her for? The same name and a random person she'd never seen before coming to the funeral – and wearing Matt's old biker jacket. It couldn't be a coincidence.

But now Matt was dead, did it matter?

Sophie kept coming back to the idea that other people in her situation would be fixated on tracking this Juliet down and confronting her. But what good would it do to know more? Surely it would make things worse.

No. Sophie was going to put all her energy into making her new life.

She was hoping that, if she just let it slide, that appalling last conversation with Matt – a freakish one-off event in over thirty happy years together – would somehow fade away over time and she could just be Sophie the Grieving Widow. Sophie the Betrayed Wife could disappear forever.

Which made her decide it was now finally time to do something she'd been putting off. Sitting up, she opened her bedside drawer and took out a phone. Matt's phone. She hadn't been able to bring herself to look at it since he'd died, too afraid of what she might find there, but now she had a reason to do so.

If she could erase all mentions of the foul Juliet on his phone, it would feel like she was really wiped from her life. She plugged the phone in and tapped Matt's birthday into the code. The phone immediately opened and she held her finger over the contacts icon, but just couldn't get herself to tap it.

What was she going to do before she erased it all? Read their emails? See pictures of them together? She couldn't face it.

For a moment she lay back against the pillow, looking up at the ceiling, and then she sat up again and opened the text thread between herself and Matt. Without reading them closely, she found her way back to the first hysterical message she'd sent him on that dreadful day and deleted them all right to the last one – where she'd called him a spineless bastard. Then she turned the phone off again and threw it down to the end of the bed. She'd put it somewhere obscure and let the idea of it fade away.

She'd already done that with his laptop, which was in some random box in the attic, where she hoped it would never be found again. Beau had asked her about it and she'd told him she feared the desirable Macbook had been nicked in the move.

Feeling better for making a decision, she picked up her own phone and saw she had several messages. There was one from Jack in Brisbane saying he missed her. Darling boy. One from Beau with a video of baby pandas on a slide. Also darling boy. And one from Sebastian, with one of his brilliant little drawings, depicting Sophie sitting between Olive and Agata. *The Three Graces of West Hill Road*, he'd written. Sophie smiled.

The next was from her agent, apologising for texting on a Saturday, and asking Sophie if she was feeling ready to discuss a possible work project.

Sophie replied, *YES, PLEASE!* Now she really did have a reason to get out of bed and get going.

Work was exactly what she needed. Not moving house work, renovation work, smiling at strangers work, keeping up a front for the family work and certainly not grubbing around in Matt's sordid business work – real, absorbing work. Making beautiful food and styling photographs of it that would make other people want to cook it and eat it. *Her* work.

She hadn't realised until she read that text how much she'd missed it. The prospect of getting stuck in again made her almost spring out of bed and over to the window, where she threw the curtains open.

The view was even more uplifting than she'd expected, the sea filling the horizon, properly blue in the full summer sun, seagulls wheeling around.

She was still gazing at it when her phone pinged again with a message from an unknown number.

Hi Sophie, it said. *Charlie Renton here. Fizz Charlie. Got your number from Thomas. Thanks so much for the party. It was great to meet you. Come out and see the grapes and if there's anything local*

you need a hand with – decent dentist, shoe menders, butcher etc – give
me a bell x

Sophie smiled and created a contact for him: 'Charlie Fizz'. She was sure Thomas had put him up to the giving-a-hand offer, but she didn't mind. It was good to know there was someone in the area she could ask for help and he seemed like a nice bloke.

Buoyed up by the improvement in her morning, Sophie got dressed, made coffee and called her agent, who told her the project was a debut cookbook from a young woman who had a popular Instagram recipe feed.

Sophie opened Instagram on her laptop. Tamar Brown was a sweet name and she was a very pretty young woman too, Sophie saw, scrolling down the posts, with long dark curly hair and beautiful green eyes.

So the persona was great, always a good start – but the food pictures brought Sophie up sharp. They were really well done, with appealing dishes, many of them sprinkled with sparkling pomegranate seeds, displayed in lovely weathered-looking pottery bowls. Just the sort of things Sophie snapped up when she travelled.

The photographs were also well taken. Sophie could see thought had gone into them, and the accompanying recipes were great too. Simply and well explained, with properly balanced ingredients, and intros that made you curious to try them. Sophie could clearly imagine what they would taste like as she read them. She could practically smell them.

She scrolled back to read the profile.

London based, food mad, sharing the joy from my Georgian
heritage. Sasiamnovnoa tkveni gatsnoba.

Sophie copied the unfamiliar language over into Google. The phrase meant 'nice to meet you' in Georgian. Cute. She texted her agent to say she was interested in doing the book and when her agent replied with Tamar Brown's number, Sophie messaged her to set up a meeting.

Then she went through to her prop room/photographic studio, feeling ready to tackle sorting it out now she had a reason to do it.

She paused in the doorway, taking the room in. There were numerous stacks of jumbled plates, bowls and dishes, plus platters, cutlery, jugs and glassware in a big muddle on the floor and surfaces. It was quite overwhelming, but with the prospect of an exciting project to work on, she had a deadline to get the organising done.

Putting on a playlist called Up Cheering that Beau had made for her, she started with the plates, using the raised photographic table in the centre of the room to sort them into groups by style – white, blue and white, vintage floral, ethnic, art pottery, mid-century, contemporary and so on. Then she stood back and assessed the shelving she had meticulously designed to store everything according to how often she used them, with the most frequent at direct hand level.

She filled the first three layers of shelves, then realised she would need her step ladder to reach the next one. Fetching it from the garden shed, she put it next to the shelves and picked up a pile of plates. But when she turned back to the ladder, she realised she couldn't step up onto it while holding the stack of china. She tried going up the ladder and then bending down to pick up the plates, but they were too far down.

Sophie stood stock still on the third rung of the ladder, frozen, letting the reality sink in. This job was crucial if she was going to get back to work, but she couldn't finish it on her own.

Then it all rushed in. How Matt should have been there helping her ...

But no. Even if he hadn't died, he wouldn't have been there anyway, he would have been off somewhere with his horrid little tart.

Once again, being reminded of it was almost like a physical assault. If she was still in London, there were numerous people who would have been delighted to pop over to come to the aid of the widowed – or the abandoned – Sophie. One or the other.

Instead, she was widowed Sophie *and* abandoned Sophie, marooned in this strange house in this weird little town where she hardly knew anyone and where she couldn't even sort out her plates.

All the upbeat energy drained out of her and she carefully got herself down the ladder and onto solid ground. She could feel tears building up – and something more like panic.

But, she told herself, she couldn't give in to it. This was her new reality and she had to cope. Freaking out was not an option. She needed to get back to work and to do that, she had to set up her prop room.

Bracing herself against the table, trying to think of nice things like fluffy kittens and freshly risen sponge cakes, Sophie battled to get her feelings back under control. Then her phone rang and she rushed to answer it. Whoever it was, it would be a distraction.

She squinted down at the screen. Rey! Brilliant.

'Hello, hunty,' he said, chuckling.

Sophie could hear loud music in the background. It wasn't even three in the afternoon and it sounded like he was having a party.

'Just calling in to say hi to my best gal. How are you doing?'

'I'm good, thank you, Reysie baby,' she said. 'I'm just sorting out my prop room—'

'Open another one,' he was saying before she'd finished speaking, in a voice that Sophie could tell was directed at someone else. 'The Veuve. Sorry, darling,' he said, coming back to her. 'Tippy has come down and, as you know, he always brings the party with him. Oooh, I love this track ...'

Sophie felt a twinge of resentment. She would have so loved to ask Rey to come and help her with the plates, but she hadn't even known he was down that weekend and there was no chance of it happening with Tippy on the scene.

Even as she thought it, she rebuked herself. Rey had done so much for her already.

'Anyway,' he continued, 'just checking in to see if you want to come out with us tonight. We're going to that fabulous pub, the Fountain. It's a drag night and Tippy wants to check out the competition. She might do a show for them. We're in negotiations.'

Sophie knew Tippy well. Tippy Molong, a drag queen of great repute in London circles. Rey called him 'she' in the drag context, but he was happy with whatever pronoun anyone wanted to throw at him – that's what he'd told Sophie one night, while dressed in a full-length gold sequin gown and a huge bouffant red wig, with his scruffy black beard.

'So,' continued Rey, 'do you fancy having a little party time? I'm working on having my first St Leonards hell hangover.'

Sophie paused. Was that what she needed? A complete distraction from all this? Alcoholic oblivion, even? Or would she put a dampener on their fun? She didn't want to become the sad friend who people had to include out of guilt.

No, she had to work out how to do this. How to live this weird new solo life that had been thrust upon her.

'That's so lovely of you to think of me, Reysie pops,' she said. 'But I've got to get on with what I'm doing, so I won't come *out* out, but I am going to pop down for a quick swim in a minute, so I'll swing by yours to say hi to Tippy, if that fits in.'

And then, she told herself, if she felt like it, she could still run away from reality with Rey and Tippy and their always generous stock of booze. Keeping her options open seemed like the only way to cope with these strange days.

'Can you pass me that stack with the gold rims, please?' Sophie asked from the top of the stepladder.

'Righty ho,' said Charlie, passing the pile of plates up. 'Not much to go now. It's looking great.'

'Thanks to you. I hope you didn't mind me taking you up on your offer of assistance so soon.'

She'd had the idea to ask Charlie if he could help with the plates while she was having her swim.

'I'm delighted to be useful,' he said. 'And Saturday is always a good day, because I usually come in to St Leonards to have breakfast and mooch about, to be among humanity a bit. So I was already in the 'hood when I got your text.'

'I'm not normally so pushy,' said Sophie, taking the pile of plates from him. 'But I'm getting back to work soon. It's my first project for months and the first time I've worked in this kitchen and studio, so it's quite a big deal for me.'

'I can understand that. Thomas has told me about your work with the cookbooks. He's very proud of you.'

'Really?' she said, turning to look at him in amazement. 'I didn't think he even knows what I do.'

He laughed. 'Well, he does stop boasting about himself long enough sometimes to take in what other people get up to,' he said. 'Underneath all that nonsense, I've always thought old Tommy boy is a little bit insecure. When we worked together as youngsters, I used to hear a lot about how he came from a creative family, but he'd chosen to channel his creativity into making money.'

Sophie paused to take that in, then glanced at Charlie. He looked different to how she remembered him from the party. Perhaps it was because he wasn't wearing the pink cord trousers and matching wellies. He was in jeans and an ironed shirt, a nice belt. She noted the H buckle, rather sophisticated for St Leonards, where it was all vintage workwear and authentic heritage brands. He was quite unusual, not having a beard. Or thumb rings.

'Well, I never knew that about Thomas,' she said. 'So you've known him a long time, then?'

'We were terrified little City of London baby beans together, starting out, pretending to be tough, and we've always stayed in touch, had each other's backs – not just to stick a knife in. Thomas was always one of the good guys. So many of them are absolutely vile.'

'Is that why you gave it up to make wine?'

She saw his face fall a little before he recovered himself.

'Yeah,' he said, a little too brightly. 'That was mostly it. I'd had enough of the nonsense, plus the family land was sitting there doing nothing much after my folks shuffled off and it seemed like the time to leave London. As you have.'

Sophie made herself nod and smile at that, wondering if a shadow had just crossed her own face.

'It's quite a collection you've got here,' said Charlie, looking round.

Was he changing the subject? And if he was, was it for his sake or hers? Either way, she was relieved.

She followed his gaze, taking in the transformed space, the shelves now full of plates, bowls and serving dishes of all different kinds in neat groups. A set of copper pans hung from hooks, and there were areas for jugs, vases, gravy boats and her collection of pressed glass, with cake stands, dessert bowls and even banana-split plates, baskets with cutlery and table linen. There were vintage tea sets, a whole shelf of assorted teapots and a deep stack of old wooden chopping boards propped against the wall.

'Kind of a life's work,' she said, feeling a deep sense of satisfaction, something she realised had been entirely absent since she'd left London. None of the work on the house had made her feel like this. 'Even when I was a teenager I couldn't go past a white dairy jug in a charity shop – and of course, in those days, there was so much great stuff out there. It's getting harder to find good things all the time.'

'Well, you've moved to the right place for that.'

'Yes, the junk shops were one of the attractions for moving here,' said Sophie, laughing and simultaneously pushing away a memory of Matt's delight in finding a yard in the Old Town crammed high with crap – or treasure, depending how you looked at it. He'd bought a vintage Canadian snowshoe; just the one, which had amused him.

'I think it's just these interesting rhomboids to go now,' said Charlie, holding up a pile of particularly ugly dinner plates.

'Yes, those really are hideous,' said Sophie, shaking her head.

'You might still come across food plated like this in some of the older restaurants down here. They are reluctant to let all the details of nouvelle cuisine go.'

'I'll stick to the hipster joints then,' said Sophie. 'I hate square plates with a passion and these are even worse – I think they make all food look wrong, but every now and again a client wants them, so I have to have some, but they are going all the way up here, on the very top shelf, in the hope I won't ever need them again.'

She was still at the top of the ladder when there was a loud knock on the front door.

'I'll go,' said Charlie. 'You need to arrange the rhomboids.'

Sophie wondered who on earth it could be, until she heard a familiar voice wishing a cheery 'G'day' to Charlie.

'Wow,' said Olive, walking into the studio, 'this looks beaut.'

'Thank you,' said Sophie, coming down the ladder. 'I'm starting work soon, so I had to get it done and Charlie very kindly came to help because realised I couldn't do it on my own ...' Her voice caught, dammit.

Olive came over and put her arm round her. 'Ah,' she said. 'You'll be right, darls. Just one of those hidden rocks on the widow's walk that come out of nowhere and trip you up. They're fuckers. But always remember you've got me next door any time you need help. Don't even knock, just walk in.'

'It can be tough getting used to living on your own,' said Charlie. 'It still punches me in the guts sometimes. So, as Olive says, just ring me if you need help with anything – anything at all.'

'Thank you,' said Sophie, smiling at them both, knowing they meant it.

'You've got some nice pots here,' said Olive, turning over a small bowl with splashes of lighter glaze against shades of brown. 'Where did you get these? They're natural glazes, like I use. I'm a ceramicist, can't remember if I ever told you that.'

'No. I didn't know. How wonderful. My mum made them in the 1970s. Went to evening classes.'

'You can't beat the touch of the human hand,' said Olive.

'The best use of a hand regarding the plates up there,' said Charlie, pointing to the rhomboids on the top shelf, 'would be to hold a hammer to smash them.'

They laughed and Sophie felt completely relieved from her mini wobble.

'Thanks to you, Charlie, I think we've done it in here,' she said. 'Would you both like a cup of tea? I've got cake … Or a drink? It's nearly six, if that's your yard arm, and I'll be starting supper soon, so why don't you both stay and eat with me?'

Please, she thought, not feeling ready for her first solo dinner in the house yet.

'I've got a better idea,' said Olive. 'Why don't you come round to mine? That's what I popped over to say.'

'I'd love to,' said Sophie. 'Are you sure?'

'Stop being so fucking English,' said Olive. 'Come at seven and bring some grog. And don't be late, that's another English thing that gives me the shits. Seven. And you're welcome too, of course, Charlie.'

'Oh, that's very kind, Olive,' he said. 'I would have loved that, but I've got something on.' He glanced at his watch. 'I better trot off actually.'

Sophie showed the two of them out, giving Charlie a sincere hug of thanks and telling Olive she'd see her later.

As she walked back into the studio and moved the jugs of cutlery a bit to the left and then back again, she realised she was humming the theme tune from *Neighbours*.

CHAPTER 9

Sophie approached Olive's door on the dot of 7pm and, acting on her earlier instructions, opened it and walked in.

'Hi!' she called out. 'It's Sophie.'

It was odd being in a house that was an exact mirror image of her own: the same but completely different. The hallway walls were covered, floor to ceiling, with paintings, just like at their old house. Sophie's walls were still mostly bare, apart from a few family photos.

'In the back, darls,' Olive called.

Sophie found her standing at a range and Agata sitting at an old farmhouse-style table.

'Grab yourself a glass,' said Olive, jerking her head in the direction of a pine dresser, which was crammed with stuff.

On her way to get it, Sophie passed Agata. 'How lovely to see you,' said Sophie, kissing her soft cheek. 'I didn't know you were coming.'

'Oh, me and Olive,' she said, 'we always have dinner on Saturday, if we have nothing else on. Which is every Saturday.'

She was wearing a yellow hat, which reminded Sophie she'd never seen her without one. And she'd never seen Olive in anything except those dungarees. She wondered what her uniform would become over the years.

'And usually here,' Agata continued, 'because I can't cook.' She threw her arms up in the air as she said it, as if making a great announcement, the light flashing off her bracelets.

'She's not kidding about the cooking,' said Olive. 'Agata's food could poison a dog, but sometimes she gets in a big old tin of caviar and I make the blinis and we have them at her house.'

'With iced vodka,' said Agata. 'You'll see ...'

'That sounds wonderful,' said Sophie, sitting next to her at the table.

Olive came over with a bottle of wine and filled Sophie's glass, then picked up her own, holding it high in the air. 'I propose a toast,' she said. 'To the West Hill Widows.'

'The West Hill Widows!' said Sophie and Agata and they all clinked glasses.

'We're both so glad you bought next door,' said Olive, after plonking a large earthenware pot in the centre of the table and filling three bowls. 'Obviously because you're nice, but we were worried it could be another care home. Nothing against them, people have to live somewhere, but there's already one down this road and two in the next street. It's getting a bit institutionalised.'

'All those old people,' said Agata. 'Nightmare!'

Sophie laughed and then took a mouthful of the stew on her plate. 'This is delicious. Is it Elizabeth David?'

'Spot on,' said Olive. 'Well, it started with her, when I first made it a hundred years ago. I kind of do my own thing now.'

'It's mutton, isn't it?'

'Hogget,' said Olive. 'Salt-marsh hogget, at least a year old. More flavour – and I don't like eating the really little ones.'

'You can get that down here?'

'Absolutely. I know the farmer. I also know a great butcher. I'll take you. And if you're buying fish, there's only one place to go – Rock-A-Nore Fisheries, bloke called Sonny.'

As Olive refilled her wine glass Sophie realise how quickly she'd emptied it. She was having a bit of a party night after all. Good.

'So tell us your story, Soph,' said Olive. 'I know you're a widow – and I'm genuinely sorry for your loss – but that's all I know. When did he cark it?'

For a moment Sophie was too surprised to answer, but then she smiled. Olive's blunt approach was such a blessed relief after all the simpering stuff.

'January,' she said. 'January fifth.'

'Shit!' said Olive. 'That's only six months. You're barely hatched. Are you telling me you've sold your house and moved down here since he popped off? How did you manage that?'

'We'd already sold our London house before he died. We'd exchanged contracts the day before the accident, actually, so it could all go through quickly.'

'And you've done all those renovations as well,' said Agata. 'Which is also very stressful. This is why I haven't done any since the early seventies.'

'I've never done any,' said Olive. 'But seriously, Sophie, if you put all those things into one of those stress measure things, you'd be off the scale. If you were a US marine, you wouldn't be allowed shore leave.'

Sophie looked down, her eyes pricking with tears. Hearing it put like that brought everything home. She'd just got on with it all. She hadn't felt she had any choice about it. And Olive and Agata didn't even know the whole of it. No one did.

She looked up and saw the two of them watching her with great compassion. Agata was smiling gently. Olive had tears in her eyes.

'Ah, babes,' she said, getting up from her chair and folding Sophie into a big warm hug.

To her horror, Sophie found she was weeping onto Olive's Breton-striped shoulder.

'Let it out,' she said, patting Sophie's back gently. 'No one ever got better holding tears in, they turn rancid inside you. Let it go. You've been through a lot. A hell of a lot. But you will survive it – you just have to look at us two to know that. It's a shitshow to get there, but you'll do it. You've got us, you've got your beautiful sons and you just need to be kind to yourself. You'll be right.'

She gave Sophie a squeeze and then sat down again.

Sophie wiped away the tears with her napkin and blinked up at her neighbours. 'Thank you,' she said, 'it's so great to be with people who know what it's like. Who've actually been through this. It's made people so weird with me.'

'What happened?' asked Agata. 'It's painful, but it's good to tell it. My husband dropped dead in our back garden from a heart attack, digging his precious roses. I found him when he didn't come in for his cocktail. That's my story.'

'Mine drank himself to death, the stupid sod,' said Olive. 'Well, it was liver cancer that took him off, but drink did the damage.'

They were so straightforward about it, Sophie felt able to just launch in herself. Normally she dreaded telling people what had happened; she couldn't bear seeing the horror on their faces.

'Mine was on a very busy road on his bicycle and he got run over by a texting truck driver. He was killed instantly. He wasn't wearing a helmet, because he was a vain idiot and didn't want to spoil his hair.'

She was slightly taken aback by the venom she heard in the last words as she said them. She saw Olive's expression change.

'Did you like him?' she asked, in her usual blunt tone.

Sophie paused and sighed, loudly. 'I thought I did,' she said, which was as near to the truth as she could get. 'We were married thirty years, very happily, he was an amazing man, a wonderful father, but in the end, I don't know … It could have been avoided, all this change and trauma. If he'd just worn a helmet.'

If he hadn't betrayed me.

'It is normal to hate someone you love for dying,' said Agata. 'I hate my husband for what he did to me. Why didn't he die at work? Why did I have to find him in our lovely garden? I don't go out in it now. I thought about moving, but thank God I didn't, because the next year, this one moved in.' She patted Olive's hand affectionately. 'I know he didn't do it on purpose,' she continued. 'But I'm still angry he died before me. I loved him dearly, we had a great marriage – as good as someone as damaged as me could expect to have – but he was not supposed to die before me and leave me. I've been left too much, so for that, I hate him. It's not rational, but it's the truth.'

Sophie turned to Olive. 'Do you hate your husband for dying?'

'I hated him before he died,' Olive said. 'It's no fun living with an alcoholic. But I loved him too. He was the best before the booze got him and even when he was fully into that he was still great before he got ugly drunk. He was the love of my life, but in the end I was glad when he died because I couldn't bear to see him, the state he was in at the end.'

Sophie rested her chin on her hand and tried to take it all in. Agata loved her husband but hated him for dying before her. Olive loved hers but was glad he had died.

She had loved hers, but hated him for what he'd done before he died. And was there a tiny little part of her that was glad he'd died rather than go off with another woman?

Once again, she wondered how she would ever be able to come to terms with all the different sides of it. It was too much. But here were these women, who seemed content in themselves, at peace with life, and they'd both had complicated bereavements too.

It was a lot to take in, but it gave her hope.

CHAPTER 10

Juliet was standing outside Rachel's house, her right forefinger poised over the doorbell. She didn't have to press it. There was still time to run.

She was furious with herself for agreeing to bring Cassady to the fourth birthday party of Rachel's son, but when Rachel wanted you to do something, it was hard to say no. That was why she was so good at her job.

Just when Juliet had decided she was going to flee, the door opened and a man was standing there, wearing a pointy polka-dot party hat.

Cassady immediately started laughing. 'You look funny,' she said, pointing at the hat.

'Not as funny as you,' the man said, pulling a goofy face.

'It's rude to point, Cassady,' said Juliet.

'Ah,' he said, switching his gaze to her, smiling broadly and putting out his hand to shake hers. 'If this is Cassady, you must be Juliet. I'm Simon, Rachel's husband. I'm delighted to meet you, Rachel has told me so much about you. Come in.'

Before Juliet could think of any way to back out of it, Cassady had raced down the hall, heading for the sound of children's voices at the back of the house. Juliet had no choice but to follow her.

'Juliet!' she heard someone say and saw Rachel coming towards her, beaming. She threw her arms round Juliet and hugged her.

'I'm so happy you made it,' she said. 'I thought you might bail. I know how antisocial you are and I'm determined to make you mingle more – like your daughter there. Isn't she a great little mixer?'

Juliet couldn't help a mother's proud smile springing to her face in response, even though she knew exactly what Rachel was up to. *Be more Cassady.*

'Now,' said Rachel, leading her by the arm, 'I would offer you some bubbly, but you're not allowed, so how about some elderflower? It's a bit fizzy, so you can pretend …'

Then somehow, as Rachel kept talking and leading her into the room, Juliet found she was standing next to a couple of women about her age, who both looked vaguely familiar.

'Right,' said Rachel. 'I'll just get you the elderflower, Juliet, and you can chat to Nicole and Dottie, who you probably already know. Nicole has recently taken over at *Glossy*, and Dottie, of course, is at *Her* … This is Juliet Mylan of wonderful Giuliette jewellery, which I know you both adore. You had that lovely still life in last month, thank you, Nic.'

And so, Juliet realised, she was talking to two magazine editors.

'Oh, yes,' she said. 'Thank you so much for that picture, Nicole, it was amazing, a whole page. We were thrilled.'

'You're very welcome,' said Nicole, smiling coolly. 'It was a stunning piece. Did you see it, Dottie? A brooch like an amazing eye, with a piece of green aventurine quartz for the iris and a diamond tear hanging in the corner, quivering as though it is just about to fall … I gave it a whole page. Of course, it's wonderful having the editorial space to let something special breathe like that.'

'Yes, I did see that,' said Dottie, with a strained smile. 'It was amazing. We wanted to use that brooch too, but you'd got in first and insisted on an exclusive.'

She turned to Juliet. 'That's the problem with being a weekly. The monthlies beat us to things because they have to shoot everything months ahead, but then we are able to respond to things as they happen, so we are always more current and, of course, we have so many more readers, going out with the biggest-selling Sunday newspaper in the country and then, of course, there are our online readers, reaching nearly two hundred million people, globally.'

Juliet saw Dottie's eyes flick over to Nicole's face to see if her dart had hit the target. The sour expression told Juliet it had.

'Well, we have a lot of new designs coming out,' she said, thinking she better keep talking to stop things escalating. 'I've done a version of the eye as a ring and a pendant, in different colours. Perhaps you'd like to come to the studio to see them … we could have lunch.'

'That would be great,' said Dottie.

'And you, as well, of course,' said Juliet quickly, turning to Nicole. 'Together, or, er, separately …'

How did Rachel handle this? This wasn't a work thing, it was a family birthday party, so it seemed she was personal friends with both these women who clearly hated each other's guts.

She was relieved when Nicole was distracted by something in the kitchen.

'Quiller!' she called out, rushing off. 'Stop that immediately!'

Juliet turned to see her take hold of a small boy who was sitting under the kitchen table, happily unwrapping the presents.

Dottie laughed. 'That'll teach her to send him to forest school,' she said. 'And call him a stupid name, poor kid.'

Juliet couldn't help smiling at her.

'So you're going again,' said Dottie, pointing at Juliet's now very obvious bump.

'Yes,' said Juliet. 'How many children do you have?' Anything to get the focus off her.

'Three. I'm insane – and not at all good at remembering to take the pill. Was yours a mistake?'

Juliet was silenced by the brazenly intrusive question. 'Definitely not a mistake,' she said, after a beat. 'I wanted Cassady to have a sibling.'

I must have wanted that deep down, she told herself, *or I wouldn't have had contraception-free sex with a man I had sworn I would never see again.*

'Is this one going to have a father?' asked Dottie. 'There's no dad around at the moment, is there? That's what I've heard.'

'Well,' said Juliet, consciously composing herself, 'there is a father biologically …'

Dottie laughed and Juliet felt more confident. It was an opportunity to practice for the *Style* section interview.

'But not after that part of it,' Juliet continued, 'which is by sperm donor.' She better get used to saying that – but she was surprised when it brought up a vivid image of Matt's face. His lovely smile. She felt bad, dismissing him in that way. He'd given her the most important thing in her life – Cassady – and now another priceless gift was on the way too.

She realised Dottie was looking at her expectantly and snapped herself back to attention. 'After that, I actively chose to raise my children as a single mother. It's what I want. I'm so busy with the business, I don't want a relationship, but I've always wanted a family. I think we're so lucky these days that we have options. Don't you?'

Dottie nodded, looking thoughtful. 'So you consciously never coupled with their father ... interesting.'

She had a look on her face that Juliet recognised from conversations with Rachel. Dottie had spotted a good angle.

'Who is the father of your children?' added Juliet, deciding to direct her intrusive questions back at her.

'Touché,' said Dottie. 'Three different ones and it does make life complicated, especially as I'm still living with the second father and he doesn't know the youngest isn't his, but you just have to get on with it, don't you?'

Juliet nodded. That sounded like a scenario almost as complicated as hers. She liked Dottie's honesty.

'As long as the kids are happy, I don't think any of that matters, do you?' said Juliet.

'No,' said Dottie, grinning. 'Secret mummy magic, all of it.'

Juliet smiled back.

'I would love to come for that lunch,' said Dottie. 'If you're still offering it. But not with vinegar tits, if that's okay? Just us two.'

Juliet couldn't help laughing. 'I'll message you on Insta,' she said.

'I think we should do a profile of you in the mag,' said Dottie. 'About how you balance your working life with your children and your decision to go it alone. What you just said about being lucky to have the option to do that.'

'That would be great,' said Juliet. 'As long as it's mainly about the business—'

'No,' said Dottie, 'it would mainly be about glamorous you and your novel parenting setup. Rachel's told me about your reluctance to promote your own profile, but you are what's interesting to our two million women readers. They will also read about your jewellery in the course of the article, and see the fab pictures, but it's your lifestyle that will make them aspire to buy at least a scented candle from the fragrance range you are inevitably going to do ...'

'It's a deal,' said Juliet, laughing. 'And you know, that's really not a bad idea – a fragrance range.' She realised she was looking forward to having lunch with Dottie.

CHAPTER 11

Sophie was sitting at a big table with two of Matt's brothers and their wives. They were at Sebastian and Freya's house in Highgate, North London.

'Are you okay?' asked Freya, sitting down beside her after clearing the plates from the table. 'It's not weird being here?'

'It's lovely being here,' said Sophie. 'I've got so many happy memories of being at this house with you and Seb and Matt and all our kids, and of course it's always a joy to see you and the others.'

Freya gave Sophie a little hug. 'It's so good to see you, Soph,' she said. 'We do miss you terribly, now you're all the way down there in Hastings. I know we lived at opposite ends of London, but just knowing you were in the same city made a difference somehow.'

'Well, it's great to be back for a couple of days,' said Sophie. 'Especially in a radically different part of town. I'm definitely not ready to go back to Peckham any time soon – or possibly ever. But it's great to be here.'

'Well, one of the reasons Seb and I have asked you here tonight is to tell you that we want you to think of this as your official London home. With the boys gone, we're rattling around and it would be lovely to have regular visits from you.'

'That's so kind.'

'I can imagine that living all the way down there now, practically in Calais, you must be desperate for some stimulating London life,' said Freya, with the cool, appraising look in her eyes that always made Sophie feel like an insect with a sharp pin poised over it.

'I actually love it,' she said. 'I'm surprised how much. The house is great and it's really wonderful opening my curtains every morning to a dazzling sea view.'

'You've only been there a few months, that's hardly going to sustain your interest after the initial novelty wears off, is it? A bit of filthy water tricked into looking blue by an accident of the light is hardly the National Gallery or the Groucho Club.'

Sophie knew Freya well enough to understand that she wasn't being deliberately unpleasant. Her amusingly barbed way of expressing her thoughts was what had made her such a successful columnist, and over the years, it had become her dominant mode.

'Well, it's enough for now,' said Sophie, glad to see Sebastian coming back into the large eat-in kitchen and sitting room, brandishing a bottle of wine.

'This is the one, Thommo,' he was saying, twisting off the metal cap with a flourish. 'Marvellous stuff. Eight ninety-nine from Aldi.'

'You are joking, I hope,' said Thomas. 'It can't possibly be any good at that price. All the newspaper wine hacks who promote this kind of muck are on the take from the supermarkets. You can't get a decent red under forty quid and it has to be French, with a bloody cork.'

'This was recommended by the wine writer in the *Clarion*,' said Freya. 'And I can promise you that nobody who works there takes cash for comment – including me and Seb.'

'Quite right,' said Sebastian, filling everyone's glasses. 'They give it great reviews because it's brilliant value for the price. If they said crap stuff was good, the readers would suss them out and revolt.'

'I know this wine,' said Sophie, recognising the label. Rey had bought loads of it after reading a write-up in a Sunday supplement. 'It's terrific stuff.'

Thomas picked up his glass gingerly and took a sniff. Sophie saw his eyebrows go up before he sipped. 'Bloody hell,' he said, 'it's actually rather good.'

'I told you,' said Sebastian. 'Anyway, you don't have to buy it – you can go the full Berry Bros and shell out for cases of sixty-pound clarets, so leave this for the rest of us, but stop being such a stupid snob about it.'

'Is it really from Argentina?' said Thomas, looking genuinely perplexed.

'Yes!' said Sophie and Sebastian together.

'That's where all the best Malbecs come from,' said Sophie. 'There's good wine from China now too.'

'And what about that mate of yours who supplied the fizz for Sophie's party?' said Sebastian. 'He's making that in Sussex and it was bloody good.'

'Ah, yes,' said Thomas, swirling the wine around in the glass and holding it up to the light before taking another considered sip followed by a lot of mouth swilling. 'But, of course, the terroir in that part of Sussex is famously on the same geological strip as Reims, so the soil is perfect for bubbly and these days the climate is actually better in Sussex.'

Sophie caught Sebastian's eye and he pulled a funny face, pursing up his lips and screwing up his nose as though he was tasting something nasty.

'And yes. Charlie,' said Thomas. 'Good man. Have you seen him, Soph?'

'Yes,' she said. 'He kindly came over to help me with something in the house. He's very nice.'

'Good. Have him for dinner. He needs a bit of decent company, it's lonely for him out on that farm with just grape pickers for company. You could cheer each other up.'

'Are you trying to set up our recently widowed sister-in-law, Thomas Crommelin, you massive sleaze?' said Sebastian, picking up the metal bottle top and throwing it at him.

'What?' said Thomas, catching the missile in mid-air with his right hand and tossing it back with deadly aim. Sebastian ducked. 'Of course I'm bloody not. It's just Charlie's a good man—'

'So you keep saying,' said Freya.

'He really is lovely,' said Bella. 'And he's been through a lot, poor darling. I think he'd be a great friend for you to have down there, Sophie, he knows everyone in the area. You'd meet some super people.'

Sophie could imagine the kind of people Bella meant. Not the sort who always wore dungarees, or pretended recipes were from their aunt, or even created works of art from felt. Although at least Charlie's cords and wellies had been pink, which did show a more independent mind than Bella and

Thomas's usual friends, who all seemed to wear the same clothes, drive the same cars and send their children to the same schools.

'I've already invited him for dinner,' she said. 'It's the least I can do after all his kindness and I do want to see his setup.'

'See!' said Sebastian. 'I told you there was more to it than a handy local contact. See his setup, indeed.'

Her in-laws all laughed uproariously and Sophie found she was grinning. It felt so good to be with the people who were the nearest thing to siblings she'd ever had. She was still aware of monitoring what she said, but perhaps she was getting used to that.

Bella caught her eye and smiled with such genuine caring affection, Sophie was really touched. It was all the years of shared experience laid down between them, she thought. Like layers of sedimentary rock.

After they finished eating, they headed over to two large sofas to have coffee. Then Freya took Bella upstairs to show her a dress she'd bought for a big party. Sophie had already seen it, so she stayed put, chatting companionably with Sebastian and Thomas, until Thomas headed off to the loo.

Sebastian moved sofas to be next to Sophie, taking one of her hands in his and lifting it to his lips, before putting it down again on her lap. 'How are you really?'

'Up and down,' said Sophie. 'In and out, round and round ...' She shrugged. 'Sometimes, I wake up and the sun's streaming through the curtains and I get up and look out at the sea and feel quite excited about life. But at other times, I can barely lift my head from the pillow.'

'It must be so much to process.'

You can't imagine how much, thought Sophie, but she only smiled sadly at him, appreciating his sincere concern and knowing he was suffering too.

'But how are you about it all?' she asked him. 'I do know it's not just me who's grieving. You lost your brother.'

'And my best friend,' he said. 'To be entirely honest, Soph, I'm pretty much destroyed. I feel bad saying that to you, because, of course, your grief trumps mine—'

'Nonsense!' she said, sitting up straight. 'There's no ranking. We're all in this together and I don't want you – or Thomas or the others – ever to think you have to put my feelings before your own. We've all lost Matt and we're all going to have that huge void in our lives forever now.'

Sebastian sighed deeply and Sophie saw a tear roll down his cheek. She reached over and wiped it away; then, when the rolling tears turned into something more like sobs, she put her arms round him as he cried, wetting the shoulder of her dress.

'I'm sorry—' he started to say.

'Shhh,' said Sophie, stroking his hair and looking over his head to see Freya walking down the steps into the living area.

She looked surprised and Sophie pulled a distressed rictus face at her to try to convey what was going on. Freya nodded, closing her eyes to show she understood. Then she turned and ushered Bella and Thomas, who were coming down behind her, back along the corridor towards the main sitting room.

Sophie kept stroking Sebastian's head until he stopped crying and pulled back.

'I'm sorry, Sophie,' he said. 'I keep it in all the time and it just came out then.'

'Good,' she said, taking his hands in hers and squeezing them. 'You have to let it out sometimes and I'm the best person to do it with.'

'I've probably got snot all over my face,' he said with a wry smile, more like his usual self.

'You haven't, but here's a tissue,' said Sophie, reaching into her bag. 'Talk about him. Tell me what you miss about him. It will help me.'

'He was my bastard. We were always trying to outdo each other and making a lot of stupid fuss about it in public. Nobody ever competed with me more, but no one ever supported me more either. He was a big-deal international artist, but he never made me feel like some sad little cartoonist – he made me feel he was even a bit proud of me.'

'A bit? He boasted about you to everybody. You remember how the walls of our downstairs loo were covered in your framed drawings? He would take people in there to show them: "My brother did these." And I'm going to put them all up again at the new house, by the way. I'm proud of you too.'

Sebastian smiled. 'Thanks,' he said. 'Did he really boast about me?'

'Yes! He would show total strangers in cafés your front-page cartoon and say, "That's my brother. Seb, the famous cartoonist, is my big brother." And he'd tell people in the art world that you are actually a much more important artist than him, because all your work is time-tied and will become historic, whereas his will become completely irrelevant in just a few years.'

'Wow,' said Sebastian. 'Thanks for telling me that. Of course, it's typical of Matt that he had to get killed for me to find out that he actually respected my work. Face to face, we constantly told each other we were shit. What's wrong with us?'

'You're just Crommelins,' said Sophie.

Sebastian laughed and gave her a hug. 'I don't think anyone has ever got us like you do,' he said. 'Freya puts up with it – it's all copy to her – Bella lives in a world of her own, based entirely around family and keeping other women away from Tom, and the other two WAGs moved their Crommelins away to avoid us.'

'Yeah, Singapore is pretty extreme,' said Sophie, 'although somehow Conrad and Willow manage to make Somerset seem even further.'

'It's so good to see you,' said Sebastian. 'Don't be a stranger. You know you can stay here any time, don't you?'

She nodded. 'Freya said that to me earlier. It's very kind of you both.'

'It's not kind. We want to see you as much as we can. In fact ...'

He got up and Sophie watched him go over to the kitchen island. He had a different build from Matt, taller and slimmer, but there was something about his walk that was so like Matt's, it gave her a sharp pang to see it.

'Here,' he said coming back and pressing something into her hand. 'The keys to your London home. We mean it. Come any time.'

CHAPTER 12

Beau was sitting in the Red Lion, cursing his decision to make it the venue for a meeting he was having serious regrets about setting up at all.

He was having a drink with Joe, the technician from Goldsmiths who had been a great mate of his father's, to see if he could eke any information out of him about what Matt might have been up to. *Ugh*, thought Beau, feeling slightly sick, although that might have been because of the swirly patterned carpet his feet were sticking to. He must have been out of his mind to suggest this place, but it had seemed the right way in with Joe, to say he wanted to have a drink in his dad's local with one of his pub buddies.

It was all slightly desperate, because Beau knew Joe and his father would never have shared anything personal, but as they said in cop shows, any kind of lead might help.

Of course, Rey was the obvious person to ask. He was the one who'd been talking to that woman at the wake. He might know her name. But Beau didn't see how he could bring the matter up with his mother's best friend without triggering a conversation that he didn't trust himself to have. Or how he could be sure Rey wouldn't pass it on to Sophie. He had to keep it all close, Beau told himself again; it was the only way he could handle it.

He took a long draw on the lager, then drained the glass, opening his mouth in a grimace at the horrible metallic aftertaste. No, Joe was the only person he could think of and Beau was up at the bar ordering another pint of poison when he strolled in.

'Hello, Beau, you soft little twat,' said Joe in his raw South London accent, gripping Beau in a hug he thought might crack his ribs.

Beau had to smile at the burly man with his lined face and big grin with quite a few teeth missing.

'Good call to come here,' said Joe. 'Take up your dad's place in the Lion, claim his table.'

Beau glanced over to the spot where Matt had always sat. The perfect place to see – and be seen by – everyone who came in. It was empty.

'That's your table now, my boy,' said Joe, clasping Beau's biceps so hard he thought his arms might be permanently withered. 'That's how we do it round here.'

'Great,' said Beau, trying to sound enthusiastic. A lifetime season ticket to the Red Lion hadn't ever been an ambition, but he led the way over to the table and they sat down.

'So, how are you doing, my diamond?'

'Oh, you know,' said Beau. 'Quite shit really, but you just have to keep going, don't you?'

'Ain't that the truth?' said Joe, necking half his pint in one go. 'And what about your dear ma? How she's getting on? I'm going to go down and see her soon, hang your dad's paintings for her. I have suggested a few days for it, but she says she's too busy working, which is good, right?'

'Yes,' said Beau. 'Mum's got a new project on, which is the best thing for her, but it would be amazing to get Dad's work up. The new house is weird without it.'

They chatted a bit more and Joe got another round in. Beau took advantage of him greeting a pal to pour most of his lager into a half-dead houseplant next to the table.

'Tell me,' he said when Joe returned, 'was there anything in particular my dad was working on that you knew of? His gallerist wants to do a full inventory ...' He trailed off. He really hadn't thought this through.

Joe laughed. 'Well, you know your dad, he was working on a million things, as usual. There was a lot of stuff in his studio at the college and the minute I heard the terrible news, I boxed it all up and put it in a safe place. Coded labels, so only I know what's what. Didn't want any greedy little hands poking around in there. So you don't have to worry about any of that.'

'Thanks, Joe. That was really thoughtful. Were there any particular themes you were aware of in that work? We've been through the stuff in his other studio and it feels like there's not much new there, so we thought his most recent output must be at the college. There's going to be a big retrospective and the gallerist doesn't want to miss out on fresh, unseen stuff that could be in it.'

That bit was true. Jack had told him the gallerist had been hassling their mum about it when they were doing the unpacking. Uncle Seb had got on the phone in the end and told him to back off.

Joe looked thoughtful, poking his tongue into the gaps where the missing teeth had been. 'Well, he hadn't been doing so much of the video stuff lately. He'd gone back to a lot of drawing and he was always collecting stuff, as you know, so there's plenty of random crap in those boxes. But there was one new thing he was getting stuck on – you know how he'd start going on and on about something?'

'Oh, yes. What was it this time?'

'Auctions. The posh ones. Sotheby's, Phillips, those geezers … He was always going off there and then he'd come in the next day and do loads of drawings and sketches around that. As far as I could tell, he was planning to work up some installations on that theme. If you look through the stuff I've got boxed up, you should be able to see where he was going with it.'

'Oh, that is interesting. I know some of his stuff has been sold in those auctions for a lot more than he ever got paid for it, so maybe it's something around that.'

'Well, let me know when you want to look in them boxes.'

'Thanks,' said Beau. 'I will.'

And he knew he'd have to. Even though he dreaded it, with all his heart.

CHAPTER 13

Sophie had been up since 6am, getting everything ready for Tamar Brown's first visit. She was feeling far more nervous than she normally did when starting a new book project. But this was a big deal: her first work since Matt had died, the first in the new house, the new kitchen and the new studio. Plus it was Tamar's first book, so she wanted to smooth the way for her too.

She whisked through the ground floor rooms one more time, twitching flowers and plumping cushions, feeling strangely self-conscious about a new work collaborator coming to the house. That was the big difference between here and her old studio, she reflected. That had been separate from her home, a purely working space where she'd done so many projects it had built up a wonderful creative hum over the years.

The new house seemed sterile and contrived by comparison and she had her first pang of doubt about the pink kitchen. Had she wasted a lot of money teaching her dead husband a lesson?

For a moment she stood frozen, feeling completely lost, but then told herself to buck up and get on with it. She put on another of Beau's playlists – this one was called Get Stuff

Done – tied on her striped apron and started making a walnut and honey brittle from a recipe on Tamar's Instagram feed.

She met Tamar at the station and then helped her carry one of those jumbo plaid bags you buy in markets into the house. Sophie hoped it contained lots of the lovely bowls that were in Tamar's pictures.

'Sorry about the bag,' said Tamar as they hauled it in. 'I'm going to stay down in Hastings for a bit, with a friend.'

'No problem,' said Sophie. 'Come through. Leave it anywhere.'

'Something smells good,' Tamar said as they went into the kitchen, and when she saw the cookies cooling on the wire, her face lit up. 'You made the gozinaki! That's so lovely, thank you.'

'It's a great recipe,' said Sophie. 'All the ones I've tried from your Instagram are. You're a great cook, Tamar, I'm really excited to be doing this book with you. Now, what would you like to drink with your sweet? Coffee, tea, herbal …?'

'Actually, I've brought something for you that would go really nicely with them.'

Tamar went back out to the hall, rummaged in the bag and came back with a small packet, which she put on the kitchen island. 'It's Georgian white tea,' she said. 'Georgia used to be a big tea-producing nation, but after the fall of the Soviet Union, it all got abandoned. Now they're building it up again. It tastes best out of glass.'

'Gosh, I didn't know that,' said Sophie, already feeling warm towards this young woman. 'I've got some tea glasses – is it better brewed in glass as well?'

Tamar nodded and Sophie went to the studio to get her glass teapot.

'Come and have a look in here,' she said, popping her head back into the kitchen. It's my new studio and prop room.'

'Wow,' said Tamar, looking round at the shelves with wide eyes. 'This is amazing. What incredible things you have. Are we going to shoot the pictures in here?'

Sophie could see she was checking out the light from the two large windows. 'If you'd like to. It will be my first project here and I'm so glad it's your book. I think we can do something really great. We can discuss photographers with the publisher once we've got to know each other.'

Back in the kitchen, they sat on the stools at the island, sipping the refreshing tea and eating the brittle.

'This is great,' said Sophie. 'Walnuts and honey both feature a lot in Georgian food, don't they?'

'Yes,' said Tamar. 'Although these are mostly a New Year thing.'

'Oops, I should have read the small print. I'm so interested to find out more about all the traditions from you. What is your Georgian heritage? That's a very British surname you have – and with your lovely first name, I wondered if you're from Devon. Are you named after the river?'

To her surprise, Tamar's face fell. 'Tamar is a traditional Georgian name,' she said, recovering herself. 'My mother was Georgian. My father was British, hence good old Brown.'

Her mother 'was', her father 'was', noted Sophie. Had she lost both of them when still so young? Despite feeling a rush of empathy, Sophie decided it wasn't the time to pursue it. A working relationship in its early stages was a delicate thing.

Tamar picked up another piece of the nutty treat and examined it closely. 'It was my grandmother who taught me to make this food,' she said, after taking a bite and another sip of tea. 'My recipes are all from her.'

A slew of questions immediately jumped into Sophie's mind as she pictured this grandmother, a lovely old lady, possibly with long grey plaits, wearing an embroidered peasant blouse. *Is she still alive? Does she live in the UK? And can we do a wonderful black and white portrait of the two of you together?*

But Tamar was looking at Sophie and smiling in a way that seemed to imply that – with all due politeness – the subject was closed.

'Right,' said Sophie, brightly. 'The first thing we need to do is see what sort of look and feel we each envisage the book having, to make sure we are on the same page – forgive the pun.' She led the way over to the bookshelves that covered the whole wall between the studio and the kitchen. 'As you can see, I've got quite a collection of food books.'

'You're not kidding,' said Tamar, standing next to her and studying the spines.

'It's a personal obsession – and a professional requirement. I need to see what's coming out, so I don't do anything similar. I buy anything which looks interesting, publishers send them to me and friends are always buying me vintage ones they find in charity shops.'

She passed Tamar a 1960s American book that was full of garish, slightly out-of-focus photographs of weird salads made with jelly. Matt had found it in a thrift store in LA.

Tamar laughed. 'So you have the what not to do, as well as the good stuff,' she said, turning it round to show a picture to Sophie. 'Maybe we should use Tupperware in our shoot.'

They laughed.

'So,' said Sophie, 'have a look and pull out whatever books appeal – and some you hate – and I'll do the same and we can go through them and see what we both think will work for your book.'

'My book!' said Tamar, her face lighting up. 'I still can't really believe it. A dream come true, all thanks to Instagram.'

'All thanks to your beautiful pictures and great recipes,' said Sophie, resisting an urge to give this endearing young woman a hug.

After some time happily browsing the shelves side by side, they carried the piles of books they'd selected to the dining table so they could spread them out with key pages open. Sophie had put a shawl over the Mickey Mouse chair and found it much easier to be in the room without that deafening reminder. Looking at the table piled with books, she felt good.

Trying to bring things into focus, she had gathered books specifically about food from different regions, which meant they were within the same genre as Tamar's book. She'd pulled out Thai food, Irish food, Andalucian food, Tuscan food, Indian food, Vietnamese street food and many more. Some of them great, some not. She wanted to show how varied and beautiful they could be, but was surprised to see a little frown appear between Tamar's eyebrows as she looked at them.

'Everything okay?' asked Sophie.

'Yes, fine,' said Tamar, picking up a book about Icelandic food and leafing through it in a desultory way. 'Gosh, I don't think I could eat a puffin.' Then she picked up the one about Andalucian food and sighed audibly.

'But I'm getting a slightly bored vibe,' said Sophie, laughing.

'I'm sorry,' said Tamar. 'These books are all very beautiful and I do understand that they're about food from specific places, as my recipes are, but I have to be honest and tell you I'm hoping we can find a slightly different way into it for my book. I don't want it to be like a travel guide to Georgia – like this kind of thing ...' She held up the Andalucian book to show a double-page picture of pigs grazing acorns in a wood, tended by a man in a traditional-looking hat, then turned a few pages to show shots of market stalls and old women with wrinkled faces carrying baskets of produce.

'I suppose that is a bit of a cliché,' said Sophie, who had already started researching similar shots of Georgian scenes on picture-library websites. 'And I must admit, I had rather assumed that would be our way in – especially as it's a less well-known country. Everybody has seen a million photos of Provençal markets and Greek fishermen, but Georgia is still exotic to us.'

Tamar looked thoughtful, flicking through a book about Southern Indian food.

'The thing is,' she said quietly, looking up at Sophie, 'Georgia is exotic for me too. I've never been there, so I don't have any personal reference for the country – it's just the food I know and love so much. I've kept the essence of the recipes on my feed as my bebia – my grandmother – showed me how to make them, but I've finessed them very much from my viewpoint as a British cook.'

Sophie took it in. There were some vegan recipes on the Instagram thread, which had surprised her in a cuisine from the region. Now she understood they were Tamar's own inventions.

'That's exactly why the recipes are so good,' said Sophie, nodding slowly. 'You have taken the best of traditional Georgian food that works for the modern palate, rather than trying to be painfully authentic.'

'Exactly!' said Tamar, looking delighted that Sophie understood her. 'I'm not an ethnic cook.'

'I love the sound of this. We can do something really fresh and new.'

'I'm so glad you get it. I've said all this to the publisher repeatedly, but she keeps going back to "your lovely book about Georgian food". I always say, "my book of recipes inspired by Georgian food" and it's like she can't hear me.'

Sophie smiled. She knew the publisher in question and Tamar had done a very good impression of her rather strident tone.

'Well, I get it,' she said, 'and I'm revved up to make it leap as fresh off the page as it does when you talk about it and, of course, one of the things we have to think about is how we will present the food. Do you want to put it in a contemporary context, or do you want to use the lovely vessels you use in your Insta pictures? I think they give just the right amount of Georgian visual flavour to your pictures, without labouring it, because they work in a contemporary aesthetic too, perfect for your second-generation idea … Did you bring some down with you?'

Tamar's face creased into a stricken expression. 'I don't have them anymore,' she said quietly.

Sophie could immediately see there was some deep hurt involved. Carrying so much around herself made her acutely aware of it in others.

'Gosh, look at the time,' she said, glancing at her phone. 'You must be starving. I thought we'd go out and grab a bite. Do you feel like fish?'

'Always,' said Tamar. 'Especially when I'm by the sea.'

'Great,' said Sophie. 'And down here, you are usually looking at the very bit of sea where the fish you're eating has come from.'

Sophie led the way down the zig-zag path from her clifftop street to the seafront level. It was a lovely summer day, with bright sunshine and a gentle breeze. They crossed the road to walk along by the beach and Tamar stopped, turning towards the water, spreading her arms out, her face up to the sun.

'Aaah!' she said, then turned back to Sophie with a big smile on her face. 'This is what I need. Lovely sea air and a break from East London's clamour.'

After a pleasant stroll, they walked down steps leading to the lower promenade, where there was a collection of colourful shacks with the words 'Goat Ledge' spelled out along the top.

'Do they specialise in goat?' asked Tamar.

'That's just the historic name for this spot, apparently,' said Sophie. 'It's all local fish, freshly cooked. I come here a lot.' *To avoid having lunch alone in my sickly pink kitchen.*

They ordered food – smiling as they realised they'd chosen the same things – and then found an empty table next to the railing that ran along the side of the pebbly beach. Although it was a weekday, the concrete promenade was busy with people of all ages, strolling along, chatting and laughing, walking dogs, pushing babies, stopping to greet friends.

Sophie sank back in her seat and felt her whole body relax as she surrendered to feeling the sun and the breeze on her skin and watching the colourful passing show with the sound of the waves on the shingle in the background.

But as she relished the moment of peace, she noticed Tamar was busy on her phone, fingers flicking and scrolling, tapping out messages, then going back to the flicking and scrolling. Once she lifted it to her ear, only to bring it down again with a twitch of irritation and go back to the tapping. Her eyes were darting around quite frenetically as she stared at the screen, a frown deepening on her brow.

Just as Sophie began to wonder whether she should say anything, Tamar seemed to realise what she was doing and put her phone down smartly on the table.

'I'm so sorry,' she said, 'that was very rude of me.' She sat up straight as she said it, in a way that Sophie found endearing. She'd probably done the same thing herself many times over the past few months without realising it.

'Is everything alright?' she asked in a tone she hoped sounded genuine rather than intrusive.

'Yes … no,' said Tamar, still sounding a bit flustered. 'Just a stupid thing. Sorry. What were we talking about?'

Sophie was trying to remember when she heard someone say her name. She looked up to see Charlie walking towards them.

'Hi, Sophie,' he was saying, then he turned towards Tamar, holding out his hand. 'Charles Renton.'

'Tamar Brown,' she said, shaking it.

'Hi, Charlie,' said Sophie, surprised to see him. 'Tamar and I are doing a book together. She's come down from London so we can talk about it.' She looked back at Tamar. 'Charlie makes wonderful sparkling wine, just inland from here. Sit down, Charlie, join us for lunch.'

'I'd love to,' he said, glancing at his watch, 'but I'm having a meeting with Mark, who has the wine shop in Norman Road. I do quite a bit of business with him. But let's catch up soon, I really want you to come and see how we make the pop. Mind you, I'll probably see you again before we get around to arranging anything.'

'Really?' said Sophie, wondering what he meant. Was there a social thing coming up that she'd forgotten about?

'Small-town life, Sophie,' he replied. 'You can bump into ten people you know just going to buy a loaf of bread. It can get quite exhausting. Sometimes I drive all the way to the Waitrose in Tenterden just to have a break from the Hastings and St Leonards impromptu social rush.' He laughed and Sophie smiled at him, taking it in. She had bumped into Lorraine, that ghastly felting woman, a couple of times, just out and about. She'd felt a bit stalked, but this explained it.

'Well,' she said, 'let's not rely on that. I want to thank you properly for your help setting up my props. I'll invite you for dinner.'

'I'll look forward to it,' he said, and as he turned to say goodbye to Tamar, Sophie looked over at her too. She was on her phone again, tapping even more furiously and starting to look very stressed.

'I'll be off then,' he said, raising his eyebrows at Sophie in a way that conveyed he could see she had something to sort out with Tamar and was going to leave her to it.

Sophie nodded in acknowledgement and, after he left, turned to Tamar, putting her hand gently on her arm. 'Are you sure, you're okay?'

Tamar's head shot up and she looked almost surprised to see Sophie. She groaned. 'I'm so sorry,' she said. 'You must think I'm a nut job, but I have got a bit of a situation on. I don't want to bother you with it, because I'm down here to work.'

'While we're working together, Tamar,' said Sophie, 'we're a team. Tell me what's worrying you.'

Tamar looked back at her and then started talking very fast. 'It's the friend I'm supposed to be staying with down here, she's not replying to any of my messages. I've tried her on Facebook, Instagram, TikTok and she hasn't replied on any of them. I don't understand it. She said I could stay …'

'Have you tried calling her?' asked Sophie quietly, trying to calm her down.

'I don't have her number,' said Tamar. 'She's someone I met on Instagram and we've always chatted on there. When we made this date for me to come down I messaged her to ask if I could stay and she said yes, that would be great, and now I can't make contact with her."

'Do you know where she lives? I could take you there after this. Maybe she's had her phone stolen.' She knew it sounded farfetched as she said it.

Tamar closed her eyes. 'I don't know the address,' she said and dropped her head into her hands, her elbows on the table.

Sophie kept quiet, but then she saw a tear slide off Tamar's cheek and drop onto her lap, closely followed by another one. It seemed a dramatic reaction to the situation, it was only ninety minutes on the train back to London, after all. There had to be more to it.

She stood up and went round the table, sitting down next to Tamar and putting her arm across her shoulder.

'Hey, Tamar,' she said, softly. 'Tell me what's up. I know it can be hard to form the words in these situations, but you will feel better when you tell me, I promise you.'

Tamar sat up and wiped her eyes with each hand. 'The problem is, now I don't have anywhere to stay down here tonight and I don't have anywhere in London either. I'm homeless. I don't have anywhere to live or anyone I can stay with.'

'Well, you do now,' said Sophie, without hesitating. 'You can stay with me tonight and the night after that and so on, whatever you need, until you get things sorted. I'm living in a stupidly big house on my own and I would be delighted to have you.'

Tamar gazed at her, blinking, as if she couldn't quite believe what she'd heard. 'Are you sure? You've only just met me. It would be amazing if I could stay tonight, thank you, but I can go in the morning—'

Sophie raised one finger and smiled. 'It would be lovely for me if you stayed. I lost my husband just this January. My sons are grown up and gone – one of them's in Australia – and I'm living on my own for the first time in my life, in a town where I hardly know anyone. You would be doing me a favour.'

'I'm so sorry about your husband.'

Sophie noted that was her first reaction – to sympathise with her. She was a nice girl.

'You're much too young to be a widow,' Tamar continued, 'and it must be so hard to be going through that in a new place.'

'Thank you for understanding. It has been really tough, but it seemed easier to come down here and have a completely fresh start than trying to get over him where we'd spent our life together.'

'I can see that,' said Tamar. 'But it would be tough wherever you are.'

She knows, thought Sophie.

'So are you going to stay?'

'I would love to,' said Tamar. 'It's so kind of you, but it won't be for long, because I will be getting the advance on the book soon and then I'll be able to set myself up, but it would be amazing if I could stay tonight.'

'See how it goes,' said Sophie. 'With you on site, we can really get cracking on the book.' She smiled fondly at the young woman, happy to see that her face had brightened again, and was then pleased to hear the number being called for their order.

CHAPTER 14

Beau was in his studio, gazing down through his loupe at the ring he was working on and wondering if the suggestion of a vulva he was incorporating into the design was a little too unsubtle. It wasn't an idea he'd worked with before, but that part of human anatomy was rather at the forefront of his consciousness that morning and the shape had just kind of crept into the ring.

He looked at it again and smiled, feeling a familiar twinge, remembering the night before. That had been fun. As had the night before and the one before that. All very different, all great. He was three rings down as a result, so he needed to crack on with rebuilding his stock. Since the disturbing visit to his father's studio, he'd been rather active in the ring-leaving area. He needed the distraction.

He sighed, frowning, as it all came rushing back again. What he knew – and what he didn't know, which was somehow worse. The drink with Joe hadn't turned up anything new, except that he'd have to go and look at the stuff stored at Goldsmiths. Great. Not.

He etched the labia into the ring in more detail, pausing to recall specifics of the previous few nights, which gave him that stirring feeling again.

He smiled to himself and turned up the music when he realised which track had just come on: Marvin Gaye, 'Sexual Healing'. Good times.

He was singing along when he heard the front door of the studio open into the area where Sam worked.

'Hey, Samski,' he called out. 'How's it hanging? Come and tell me the news.'

He glanced up, smiling, looking forward to catching up with his chum, but it wasn't Sam – it was Flora.

'Flora!' he said, dropping his tools and getting to his feet, realising how glad he was to see her. She'd never come to the studio before. 'What a lovely surprise, come in, sit down. Would you like some tea?'

'No, I would not like any tea,' said Flora. She did not look happy. In fact, she looked absolutely furious.

Beau walked towards her. 'Are you okay?' he asked, putting out his arms in case she needed comforting. She really did look distressed.

'Don't you dare touch me,' she hissed at him. 'You've touched me quite enough and God knows how many other women you've used and then insulted with one of your vile rings.'

She threw something and it hit Beau hard on his eyebrow.

'Ow,' he said, putting his hand up. It came away with blood on it. He glanced over to where he'd heard something fall on the floor and saw one of his rings lying under a chair. Was it the one he'd left on her pillow? He couldn't remember. There had been so many recently.

Oh.

'Good,' she said, 'I hope it hurt. I hope it hurt as much as I did when I found that disgusting thing on my pillow, as some kind of vile payment. Who do you think you are, prowling round East London, doing that to women? Treating us like whores. I found out by chance that you've also done it to one of my friends and now we've found six more of your victims and we're pissed off. We've started a Facebook group to see if we can find others.'

Beau was speechless. Victims? No one had been forced to take him home. The rings were a tribute, not an insult.

'I didn't mean it like that,' he said. 'As some kind of payment. That's the last thing I meant. I want to show women how much I respect them—'

Flora snorted. 'Oh,' she said, 'are you a feminist? Did your mummy bring you up to respect women? What you are is a rancid seventies throwback … a pathetic, self-obsessed, woman-desecrating cock jockey. You're *disgusting*. Someone told me they saw you last night in a bar in Shoreditch, on the prowl for your next little snack. Because that's how you treat women, Mr Mojobo, like the greasy leftovers from a chicken shop dinner, last night's pizza crusts and fag ends.'

Beau stared at her, feeling something horribly like tears forming in his eyes. He really hadn't meant it like that. He had been brought up to respect women. He thought he did.

'Well, pound shop Casanova,' said Flora, 'your little game is up. As we speak, these are being put up all over East London.'

She reached into her bag and unrolled a large piece of paper. It was a poster with a photograph of Beau's face on it – taken from his Instagram feed, he noted – with several of his rings displayed along the bottom and emblazoned with the words:

UNWANTED
Women, beware this creep, currently on the booty prowl in Hackney and Bethnal Green, posing as a nice guy. He's not. Look out for the rings.

'We're putting them up over all Shoreditch, Bethnal Green, London Fields and Clapton. It's the twenty-first century, Mojobo, and there's no place for men like you in it.'

'I don't understand,' he said, genuinely bewildered. He knew lots of guys who just left in the night without a word, or gave women fake numbers, or blocked them as soon as they tried to call. He'd even known men who took pictures of women while they were sleeping, naked, and shared them with their friends.

Compared to people like that, he thought he'd been doing something right. That was his intention: a way to end mutually enjoyed casual encounters sweetly.

'Please explain to me—' he started to say, but Flora was already stalking out of the studio.

He slumped into his seat, feeling sick when he caught sight of the ring he'd been working on – and the music ... He turned it off. Was he some kind of sex-addicted, #metoo monster, like she said?

But he'd never forced himself on anyone or put any kind of pressure on them to do things they weren't comfortable with. He always let the woman take the lead. Even in the pick-up, he wasn't the aggressor. If he stood in a bar on his own long enough, someone always hit on him. It didn't usually take long.

He'd wanted to let the women be in charge, to make it a positive experience for both of them, but now it seemed he had been horribly wrong about the whole thing.

Beau picked up his blowtorch and scorched the top of the ring so the vulva shape melted away. He'd have to lay off all that for a while.

He was still sitting there, feeling stunned, blankly staring down at the metal, when his phone pinged. It was a message from a friend with a photograph of one of Flora's posters.

I've just seen this in Homerton, it said. *You've really pissed someone off, Mr Pantsman.*

Beau put his hands over his face as Sam walked in, holding one of the posters.

'Look what I found on our door,' he said, 'and they're all along the street too … What's going on, Beau boy? Are you some kind of costume jewellery Jack the Ripper?'

Beau spent the rest of the day tearing down all the posters he could find, while receiving non-stop forwards and messages from friends – so-called friends – who'd seen them and thought it was hilarious. There were also some from women friends who didn't think it was so funny. And a couple from platonic girlfriends who were supportive. Just two of those.

Then, in what seemed like no time, the poster was all over Instagram and Twitter and it was when somebody called him from the *Evening Standard*, wanting to interview him for a piece about Hackney's notorious ring-leaving lothario, that he decided a trip down to Hastings was needed.

Possibly a long one.

CHAPTER 15

Sophie was woken up by a most delicious smell, like baking bread. Had she left something in the oven? Then she remembered that Tamar had stayed over. She must be up and cooking. How wonderful.

Glancing at her phone, she was amazed to see it was already after 9am and she hadn't woken up once in the night, which was rare for her now. She dressed quickly, embarrassed to be in bed so late, and rushed downstairs to see Tamar taking a tray out of the oven.

'Good morning,' she said. 'Something smells amazing.'

'Morning,' said Tamar. 'I hope you don't mind me cooking in your kitchen. I just wanted to make you some breakfast.'

'I couldn't be more delighted. What is it?' She leaned down to get a closer sniff of the lozenge-shaped breads Tamar was putting on the cooling rack. The baked dough was golden and each one had an egg in the centre.

'These are adjarian khachapuri,' said Tamar. 'A very traditional Georgian thing. It's a cheese bread made with bicarb, not yeast. It's the best breakfast.'

'I think I've seen something like this on your thread.'

'Yes, I do a few versions, but this is the classic, like my bebia used to make me. I haven't actually put these on Insta. They're too personal.'

'Well, I'm all the more honoured that you've cooked them for me then. Would you like some Georgian tea with them?'

Tamar grinned. 'I'd love a cortado, actually,' she said.

When Sophie came over with the coffees, Tamar pushed a small package over to her, wrapped in a plastic carrier bag.

'Shall I open it?' she asked and Tamar nodded.

Unwrapping the layers, she found a small, dumpy earthenware pot with a handle and a lid. 'Oh!' she said. 'One of the lovely pots.'

She glanced at Tamar, remembering what she'd said about not having them any more. Turning it over in her hands, she saw it was clearly handmade, glazed with a lovely lustre to it that looked as though it had come from years of use.

'The only one I have now,' said Tamar.

'That's such a shame. They look so great in your pictures.'

Tamar nodded sadly. 'My bebia had loads of them, but when my auntie cleared out her flat last month, she threw them all out.'

Sophie looked at her, in disbelief. 'She threw them away?'

Tamar nodded. 'She threw everything away except the TV and my laptop, which she kept. She got rid of all my other stuff too, except for what I have in that bag up there.'

Sophie just stared at her, letting it sink in. No wonder she had seemed so fragile.

'Is that why you're homeless?' she asked, quietly.

Tamar nodded.

'So you lived with your grandmother ...' said Sophie, sensing that Tamar might want to talk about it now.

'I can tell you the whole thing, if you like, but from what you've told me about what you've been through recently, probably the last thing you need is to hear my sob story.'

'Not at all,' said Sophie. 'I want to know.'

'Okay, here goes,' said Tamar, draining her coffee. 'The dwelling that has just been emptied of everything, including me, is a council flat in Bethnal Green. Nothing special, but nice enough, two bedrooms. I moved there with my mum and my nan when I was two. When I was fifteen, my mum died of breast cancer.'

'I'm so sorry. It's terrible losing your mum at any age, but at such a vulnerable time for a girl … That must have been awful.'

'It was, but I still had my nan and I was living where I'd always been and I felt secure, because my uncle – my mum's brother, who was quite a successful businessman – bought the flat from the council, so we would have somewhere secure to live. He didn't charge us any rent. He was lovely.'

Sophie caught the 'was' again and saw a sadness pass over Tamar's face.

'When I was twenty and at art college, my bebia died.' She paused. 'Are you sure you want to hear all this? It's really not a bundle of laughs.'

'Keep going,' said Sophie.

'Okay,' said Tamar. 'Anyway, that was horrible, but my nan was in her eighties so it wasn't so surprising and I still had my uncle and the flat to live in, plus by then Bethnal Green had become a really cool place.

'So, I was living at the flat with a friend who paid me some rent, doing my course, putting my recipes on Insta, taking my photos – I was studying photography at college – using my grandma's pots for the pictures and I built a following. It was all great. Then, just as I was starting to get interest from publishers, my uncle died. He had a heart attack and that was it. He didn't look after himself and he paid the price for it. Sadly, so did I.'

Sophie worked it out. Since the age of fifteen, Tamar had lost her mother, her grandmother and her uncle, and her father didn't seem to be on the scene at all. Gosh. 'That's a lot,' she said.

'It gets worse,' said Tamar, smiling wryly. 'So my uncle died and he didn't leave a will, so everything went to his wife, my so-called auntie. A flat in Bethnal Green, even an ex-council one, is worth a nice fat wad of money now, and she threw me out so she can sell it. Of course, I didn't have a lease … And despite all my begging, she wouldn't let me keep any of my grandmother's things. Said it was all hers now, which legally it is. She sent bully boys round while I was packing, so I had to stuff whatever I could grab into that bag up there and I've been sleeping on friends' sofas and trying to make my food in their kitchens ever since. Three months.'

'How could she be so mean?'

'She never liked any of my uncle's "foreign" relatives, as she thought of us. My uncle was good-looking and had money, so that gave him some kind of non-foreigner pass with her, or something. But there is another reason why she particularly hates me.'

Sophie looked at her quizzically.

'My skin is a bit dark for her taste,' said Tamar. 'My dad's parents were from Jamaica. He was born in London, he's as British as you and me, but my auntie doesn't like black people.'

'You are kidding me.'

'I'm not. She's a full-blown bigot. My uncle realised pretty quickly she was horrible, but they had kids and he wouldn't divorce her. He just saw us on his own, kept us separate. I know he always meant to make a will to leave the flat to me, but he never got round to it, and then he died.' She looked down and let out a wobbly sigh.

Sophie paused for a moment, taking it all in, but couldn't think what to say. It was a timely reminder that she wasn't the only one having a hard time.

'Do you fancy a swim?' she said at last.

CHAPTER 16

Cassady was having a playdate with Dottie's youngest daughter, Cricket, at their house in Queen's Park. Juliet was feeling a bit anxious because the moment they'd arrived, the girls had disappeared upstairs and they hadn't seen them since.

She was trying not to think about it, sitting at the table in Dottie's chaotic kitchen, listening to her tell a story about how she'd practically had to steal a car to rescue a fashion shoot that had gone horribly wrong in Mexico. But with one ear permanently cocked for cries of distress from her daughter, Juliet wasn't taking much of it in.

It took a moment for her to realise that Dottie had stopped talking and was looking steadily at her, one eyebrow raised, her arms folded.

'You didn't hear any of that, did you?'

'Sorry,' said Juliet. 'I don't meant to be rude, but I can't help it, I'm anxious about Cassady. They've been so quiet.'

Dottie laughed. 'Great! That's the Holy bloody Grail of parenting. More than three minutes when one of them isn't snivelling, whingeing or giving you a migraine. What's wrong with you?'

'Neurotic single mother?'

'I don't get it, though,' said Dottie. 'How can someone be like Robocop with her business and then a total sap bag with her family?'

Juliet looked away. She liked Dottie and knew she needed to hang out with other mothers to see how they handled stuff, and it was important for Cassady to have friends, but she didn't want to get into any big discussions about anything around family. Minefields in every direction.

'Let's go up and see what they're doing,' said Dottie, standing up. 'I don't want you to fret. You work so bloody hard, you deserve a bit of downtime on a Saturday.'

Juliet followed her upstairs. Two little voices were coming from the master bedroom at the front, not Cricket's room, where they were supposed to be.

'Okay,' said Dottie, 'perhaps we did need to do this.'

She opened the bedroom door and she and Juliet looked in to find the girls sitting on the bed surrounded by sex toys of all kinds and sizes. Each one was holding a whizzing vibrator, giggling and poking each other with it.

Dottie immediately closed the door again and leaned against it, her eyes closed. 'Oh my God,' she said. 'I'm so sorry. We're doing a tried-and-tested feature and we've all taken a load of those things home to, er, test. I thought I'd hidden them well.'

After the initial horror of seeing her precious little tot holding some kind of sculptural pleasure machine – although at least not the large pink phallus Cricket had been wielding – Juliet had to laugh.

'Shall we go and distract them?' she said.

Dottie nodded, her eyes wide. 'You take them downstairs and I'll do a better job of hiding the gear.'

They settled the girls in front of *Mulan* with ice cream – not too much and lots of fruit, at Juliet's instigation – and went back to their seats at the kitchen table.

'So are you always this uptight on playdates?' asked Dottie, happily chewing on a Hob Nob.

'No,' said Juliet.

'Just with me then? I know my house is a junk heap, but I'm not a bad mother really. I've got my oldest one to age ten without any serious injuries. I imagine a lot of your friends have proper security at home. Too much at risk with the Birkin Bag Room and all that. That nursery Cassady goes to has fees higher than Eton and is harder to get into. I read a piece in the *Mail* about it. So do your other friends have multiple nannies and armed guards around the kids at all times when you go to their mansions on playdates?'

'I don't know,' said Juliet. 'This is the first one we've ever been on.'

Dottie's mouth hung open.

'No one from that nursery has ever invited her,' continued Juliet. 'I don't think any of them are normal enough for something like this and if I'm completely honest, I don't really have any friends. I have colleagues at my studio, but they are all my employees, so that's a barrier. So, I work, I hang out with Cassady, I go to the gym and I love looking at paintings. I used go to a lot of auctions to view and buy them, but now I prefer to stay at home with my daughter.' And not rake up too many confusing memories.

'That's not right, Juliet. You've got to have mates. Haven't you got pals from art college, or wherever you went? School? Siblings? Cousins?'

Juliet shook her head, smiling sadly. 'I don't have any extended family and I didn't do the college thing. I hated school and went straight to work as soon as I could. It's always been my focus.'

Survival. Security. Mum.

'Well, that stops today,' said Dottie. 'You've got a friend now. Me. And Rachel – she's a friend.'

'We work together,' said Juliet. *I pay her.*

'But it's all blurred with her. She's friends with all her clients – and with all her press contacts, like me and all the influencers. It's why she's so good at what she does, but we genuinely like each other too. We go on holiday with Rachel and Simon. You and Cass should come next time, we have such a laugh. Meanwhile, we'll have a dinner, the three of us, and Rachel and I will show you how it's done. You can't survive as a mum without friends, Juliet. You'll go nuts.'

Juliet looked at her, tears momentarily smarting in her eyes. She knew only too well that was true. She'd seen it happen, firsthand. When a woman didn't have friends. Or when any friends she did have were systematically blocked out of her life.

'So,' said Dottie, clapping her hands and jumping up from her seat again and heading over to the fridge. 'It's a shame we can't seal this deal with a bottle of wine, but I can have some and I'll make you a nice mocktail – and please don't feel you have to rush off at some official playdate end time. Hang out. Stay for dinner. The girls will love it. I'll text Rachel and see if she wants to pop over. She's only two streets away. What do you say?'

'I say that would be fantastic,' said Juliet. 'And you're right about that nursery Cassady goes to, it's a very stupid place, with very stupid people. I put her in there because I thought it was the best one, but also because I thought the other parents would be good contacts for the business, which they have been.'

She looked down at the rings on her hands. She'd sold them like penny candy at nursery events, but wasn't it far more important that Cassady had nice friends? Friends who were the children of normal people, not from that strange world where the kids had their own drivers and regularly flew alone on private planes but had never been to a park or a supermarket.

'What nursery does Cricket go to?' she asked.

2019

Juliet was having a drink with Matt.

After bumping into him at the Sotheby's auction, she'd agreed – against all her instincts and rules – to meet him at Christie's the following week to look at the lots coming up in their next contemporary art sale. Once again, she'd found his insights on the works fascinating. They were still talking avidly as they left the building. Matt indicated his bicycle, chained to a railing outside. 'I'll walk you to the Tube,' he said.

Juliet agreed, not wanting to tell him she had a driver waiting, and there was something so interesting about this man, endearingly wheeling a bicycle beside her, that she didn't feel ready to end the conversation yet.

So, when they got to St James Street and he'd suggested popping over to Dukes Bar, it seemed like a fun idea.

And there she was, sipping one of their legendary martinis. Another thing she never did, because she had to be up early every morning for her trainer and then on top form for work.

'Cheers,' said Matt, raising his glass to her.

She raised hers and took a sip, eyes snapping open when she realised how strong it was.

He chuckled. 'They are rocket fuel, these martinis,' he said. 'They'll only serve you two.'

'I'm not sure I can even drink one,' she said, blinking as she took another taste and the fresh zest from the Sicilian lemon the waiter had peeled in front of them hit her nose. 'Rather delicious, though, once you get used to having your head blown off.'

Matt smiled and took another sip from his glass.

After that, the chilled liquor had slipped down rather easily and they'd chatted and laughed, talking about the ridiculous way people bought artworks for status and investment, not for the love of them.

They didn't talk about what they did, or anything else about their lives, and, for once, Juliet allowed herself just to be. Not constantly analysing the situation for dangers as she usually did.

And after they finished the second round of martinis, it seemed perfectly natural for them to take a room at the hotel upstairs and go to bed.

CHAPTER 17

Beau rang from the train. It wasn't great timing. Sophie and Tamar were in the middle of doing their first test shots for the book, trying the dishes in different pots and bowls to see what worked, and they were caught up in it. Tamar had been staying for a few days now and they'd settled into a really comfortable little groove: buying food together from all the interesting local independent shops and suppliers, cooking, going for daily swims – and now the test shots.

Sophie was happy to see how much more relaxed Tamar was. The little knot of frown had gone. She laughed a lot.

'Hello, Mama dearest,' said Beau. 'It's your great big boy.'

'Oh, hello, darling,' said Sophie, holding her phone in the crook of her neck as she tweaked a carrot two millimetres to the left and pushed two pomegranate seeds infinitesimally closer together. Nodding, her eyebrows raised, she looked up at Tamar, who pressed the shutter. Sophie immediately went over to look at the image on the camera screen.

'It's nice,' she said, 'but I think we need to bring out some more warmth, because the white of the bowl is chilling it all down and this is such a hearty dish I feel like we're losing something—'

'Mum?' said Beau.

'Oh, sorry, darling, it's just we're doing some shots here and I'm a bit distracted. Could I call you back later?'

'You won't need to do that,' said Beau. 'You can tell me to my face.'

'Tell you what?' asked Sophie, confused and a bit irritated, because doing their first shots together was a delicate phase of working with Tamar.

'You can tell me how pleased you are to see me,' said Beau, 'because I will be at St Leonards station in under an hour. Can you pick me up?'

'What?' she said, then hastened to add, 'How lovely. Text me the actual time the train gets in. Are you coming for the weekend?'

'I'm going to see how it goes. It's great weather and I feel like having a bit of a Hastings staycation. I've taken a break from the restaurant for a couple of weeks, I'm owed some time off. We can hang out and go to the beach—'

'Great,' said Sophie, trying to sound more enthusiastic than she felt, but then feeling confused about that. Normally, there was nothing she would like more than a visit from one of her boys – but why did he have to spring it on her like this? Just when she and Tamar were really beginning to gel as a creative team. It was terrible timing. He should have asked her first if it was convenient.

Then it struck her why his announcement was really niggling her – it was exactly what Matt would have done. He had never understood that the joy of a surprise was always much greater for the surpriser than the surprisee.

She glanced over at Tamar, making a 'sorry' face. Tamar beamed her lovely smile back, which made something else occur to Sophie. She had a beautiful young woman staying with her and there was nothing Beau loved more than a beautiful young woman – and they were usually pretty taken with him. There was no way she was going to let him make a move on Tamar. She had to take action and fast.

'Okay,' said Sophie, briskly. 'But it would be good if you could walk from the station. And you can meet my lovely new friend, Tamar, who is staying with me, er, us. Bye.'

As she hung up, she turned to look at Tamar and saw she now had a slightly nervous look on her face. Back to the frightened Bambi she'd been when she arrived.

'That was my older son, Beau,' said Sophie, trying to sound more positive than she felt. 'He's just told me that he'll be here in an hour. It's not ideal timing, because I am so enjoying doing this with you, but perhaps what we both need is to take the weekend off and chill out for a bit. Go swimming and hang out. You'll love Beau, he's a laugh.'

'Great,' said Tamar, not very convincingly. 'I can go back to London for the weekend, if it's too much,' she added, 'or try again to get in touch with my friend down here ...'

'Whatever's best for you,' said Sophie. 'But as I've said, you can stay here as long as you like. I want you to think of that room as your own. I love having you here and Beau really is fun. He'll get us two food obsessives out of ourselves for a bit, and if Rey's down this weekend as well, then it will be a proper party.'

But I do have to stop my lothario son hitting on you.

'Just give me a moment,' she continued. 'Play around with the lighting a bit, see if you can get some more warmth into it. Perhaps look at some other bowls?'

She nipped out of the studio and went through the front door, pulling it closed behind her before she rang Beau back.

'Hey, Mumster,' he said. 'Have you called to sound a bit more enthusiastic about my imminent arrival?'

'I am very excited to see you,' said Sophie, starting to mean it a bit more, 'but there is one thing I have to quickly say to you.' She turned her back to the door and cupped her hand round the phone, lowering her voice as much as she could. 'I have a lovely young woman staying with me—'

'Ooh …'

'Stop it!' she hissed. 'That's exactly why I'm ringing – to tell you that you are not under any circumstances to make a move on her. She's very beautiful, so I know you'll want to, but she's off limits, because she's been through a horrible trauma and I'm working with her on her first book – and it's my first book since Daddy died …' Was she wrong to throw that in? Oh, well. 'And the situation is delicate. The last thing she needs is you doing your lover boy number on her. Have you got that?'

'Absolutely,' said Beau. 'I promise one hundred per cent I will not make a move on her.'

Sophie was surprised he hadn't put up more of a fight but was relieved he'd accepted her wishes. When she got back inside, Tamar was in the kitchen.

'I'm going to start dinner, Sophie,' she said. 'If that's OK. I've done a couple more shots you can look at, but I'm ready for a break now and I'll feel less of a spare part if I'm doing something useful when your son arrives.'

'That's great, thank you.'

'Are those fantastic black and white photos of the two boys in the sitting room your sons?' asked Tamar.

'Yes. My late husband took them. He was an artist and he took really good photographs too. He had a darkroom in a shed in our garden. Did all his own printing.'

She wondered why she'd bothered relaying all that extraneous information to Tamar, but then realised it was nice talking about Matt to someone who'd never known him. She didn't have that sense of panic that she might suddenly blurt out something about the betrayal. It made him conceptual somehow.

'Can you quickly show me which one is coming?' asked Tamar. 'It will make me feel less shy.'

Sophie led the way into the sitting room, where she'd arranged Matt's portraits of the boys with the baby shots in the centre, radiating out to the most recent – the last one – at the top.

'That's Beau,' said Sophie, pointing at him. He had his finger and his thumb behind Jack's head in the classic 'loser' L shape. 'He's the older one, but you wouldn't know it from the way he behaves – as this picture shows.'

'He does look, er, fun, like you said.'

'He likes to put on a show. He's like his father and his uncles in that way – they love to make a lot of noise, live it large – but he's a sweetie underneath it. Don't be put off by the bravado.'

But don't be too attracted to it either.

Beau was relieved when Sophie relented about picking him up from the station and he strode into the kitchen, smiling broadly and flipping a stray curl away from his face as he went over to say hello to Tamar.

He kissed her warmly on both cheeks. 'Hello, Tamar,' he said, 'brilliant to meet you. I hear you're doing great book things with my mum, which is super – and keeping her company in this big house, which is also great, plus she says you're making dinner and I've never had Georgian food, so that's exciting too. It's all good.'

He was aware he was babbling. He reminded himself of his Uncle Thomas, he was so deep into the jolly bonhomie thing – had he actually said 'super'? – but he'd had to cover up the urge to go into instant Mojobo mode. He'd promised his mother.

And she hadn't been kidding. What an extraordinary-looking woman Tamar was. Tall and slender, with curly black hair, like a longer version of his, and the most amazing green eyes. And she was endearingly shy, which he also found very attractive.

He hoped that by being a blabbering twit, he could stop himself 'twinkling', which is how Jack described what he did around beautiful women. Jack said it was as powerful as a Vulcan neck grip in its effectiveness. But Beau had promised his mum – and himself – that he was going to lay off the twinkling with Tamar, although looking at her, it was going to be tough.

'The house is looking great, Ma,' he said, strolling through into the dining area, partly as a way of not looking at Tamar. 'Aah … here's Dad's old chair, but it's got a stupid blanket on it.' He snatched the shawl off and threw it onto the next chair, then ran his hands over the Mickey Mouse ears.

His mother bustled off into the studio as if she had something urgent to do in there and came back holding a plate of food, which she put on the kitchen island.

'Shame to waste this,' she said. 'Can you incorporate it into dinner, Tamar? I think you nailed that shot, the last one in the darker bowl, don't you? We can add it to the gallery when we look at them all together to see which vessels work best with your food.'

'It's starting to feel more like home here,' said Beau, walking back into the kitchen. 'But when are you going to put Dad's paintings up? It won't really be our house until then.'

'We will,' Sophie said, 'but I've had so much upheaval with the move and renovations already this year, I need a bit of breathing space. And you know how they're packed up by those art movers – just getting them out of the packaging is a major operation.'

'Joe said he'd called you about doing all that,' said Beau. 'He told me he's going to come down to unpack it all, hang them and take the debris away. You can just lie on the sofa with a glass of champagne and point. We could have a party to celebrate, this is such a great party house.' He extended both his arms in a disco move and noticed Tamar was smiling.

'Maybe down the line,' said Sophie, her voice sounding slightly strained, as it had when he'd phoned earlier – not at all enthusiastic. 'But just not right now, darling. I've already had a housewarming thrust upon me by Thomas, and I'm really enjoying getting back to work with Tamar. Her book is going to be really good and I just want to throw myself into that.'

'Of course,' Beau said, turning to Tamar and then slightly wishing he hadn't. Her mouth was a terrible distraction for someone trying not to twinkle. 'Tell me more about your book, Tamar. So it's Georgian food … what's your connection with that? And I assume it's Georgia from the former Soviet Union, not the Coca-Cola state.'

'Definitely the one in the Caucasus,' said Tamar. 'My mother was from there. She came to live in London in the nineties, with my uncle, and when I was born, my grandmother came over too and it's her recipes I'm inspired by.'

'That sounds amazing,' said Beau, getting his phone out. 'What's your Insta tag? I want to have a look. Mum says your pictures are really good.'

She told him and he scrolled through the feed.

'Wow, these are great shots,' he said. 'I can see why a publisher got in touch with you. These are really nicely lit.'

He looked at her with professional admiration, rather than the raw attraction he had felt on first seeing her, before returning his attention to her food shots. He took his own pictures for his website and Instagram feed and he knew the difference between good enough and properly done. Matt had taught him that when he was a kid.

He felt a sharp stab of sadness, like he was back in the darkroom shed with his father, watching the magic happen. He could almost smell it, but then he remembered his visit to the studio. It was like playing ping pong in his own brain.

He lifted his head to see Tamar looking at him with a concerned expression.

'Would you like some coffee, Beau?' she asked. 'Or tea? I've made a really nice cake.'

Beau smiled at her, with real gratitude. His mum had said Tamar had been through a trauma and he was pretty sure she'd recognised his distress. That was a connection he needed much more than the horizontal kind.

CHAPTER 18

Sophie woke up late after another good sleep and had a couple of beats of glorious nothingness before it all came rushing back. Knowing there were two lovely young people in the house speeded her recovery from the morning memory tsunami.

Dressing quickly, she went downstairs to find Beau and Tamar sitting side by side on the stools at the kitchen island. She was briefly furious with herself for not setting the alarm, so she would have been on hand to stop anything cosy like this happening, but then she noticed how Beau was sitting, slightly skewed away from Tamar, like he had deliberately moved the stool over a few inches.

It looked like he really was making an effort.

'Morning all,' she said, putting the coffee machine into action. 'What are you two up to?'

Her son looked sheepish. 'Tamar was very kindly showing me the shots you've done and I just wanted to compare them with her Instagram feed, because ...'

Sophie batted away a twinge of irritation that he was intruding in their work. 'Because they aren't quite as good?' she said, knowing it was the truth.

'Well,' said Beau, 'it's not a quality issue ...'

'I know, you don't need to tell me. That's what we've been struggling with, isn't it, Tamar?'

She nodded.

'We've got the same wonderful food,' continued Sophie, 'and the same brilliant photographer – and by the way, Tamar, I'm going to tell the publisher I want you to do the pictures for the book. It's your aesthetic and no one could do it better than you.'

Tamar gaped at her. 'Oh, wow,' she said, her eyes open wide, 'that would be amazing.'

'And you'll get more money,' said Beau, holding up his hand to high five her.

Sophie was distracted now, standing between them, comparing the pictures. She knew why the ones they'd taken didn't have the same atmosphere as Tamar's originals, but she didn't want to be the one to say it. She was wondering how to frame the words when Beau spoke.

'You need those lovely bowls from the Insta shots,' he said. 'That's what's missing.'

'Unfortunately, I don't have access to them anymore,' said Tamar.

Sophie reached across and squeezed Tamar's hand.

'Could you get some more sent over from Georgia?' asked Beau.

'I did look into that,' said Tamar, 'but you'd really need to go there to find some old ones, because they need to have the patina – new ones just aren't the same – and then you'd have to ship them back here and I don't have the resources for that.'

'I did ask my agent to see if we could get a trip out there,' said Sophie, 'but the publisher didn't go for it.'

Beau was studying the Instagram shot that was on the phone's screen. It featured an old-looking pot with a lustrous black glaze. 'So perhaps what you need instead,' he said, 'is an art potter to make them for you with the effect of this patina already on them.'

Sophie stared at him. It was so obvious.

'Do you know anyone?'

Sophie laughed. 'Funnily enough, I do. Come with me.'

'Olive?' called Sophie from the hall in the house next door and then up the stairs, but there was no reply. She walked into the kitchen, calling Olive's name as she went, but there was still no answer, so she went through the kitchen and out the back door, where she saw Olive on her knees in her vegetable patch – naked.

'Oh!' said Sophie. 'Sorry!'

Olive roared with laughter. 'Sorry, Sophes, didn't mean to frighten you. Just getting some vitamin D. I'll run up and get some dacks on.'

'Hold on a second, Olive,' said Sophie, starting to giggle, 'I've brought some people with me and they're in your hallway.'

'No worries,' said Olive, coming into the kitchen and grabbing her kitchen apron and a tea towel, then waltzing up the stairs past Tamar and Beau.

She was down again in no time, clad in her customary Breton top and dungarees.

'Right,' she said, striding into the room. 'Who have we got here?'

'This is my friend Tamar, we're doing a book together, and this is my older son, Beau.'

'Good to meet you,' said Olive, shaking their hands firmly, then her attention turned to the lidded pot that Tamar had brought with her.

'That's a nice little thing you've got there, darling,' she said. 'Can I have a look?'

Tamar handed it over and Olive examined it, taking off the lid to look inside before turning it upside down.

'This is beautiful. Where did you get it?'

'It was my grandmother's,' said Tamar.

'Eastern European?'

'From Georgia, in the Caucasus. She brought a lot of her old pots over with her when she moved here because that's what she felt comfortable cooking with.'

'Have you got any more?' Olive asked. 'I'd love to see them. I'm a potter myself.' She gestured to the row of vessels of different heights lined up along the mantlepiece and shelves on either side.

'These are beautiful,' said Beau, going over to examine them.

'That's why we've come to see you, Olive,' said Sophie. 'You see, the book we're doing is food inspired by Tamar's grandmother's cooking and we would love to use traditional Georgian-style pots in it, but unfortunately we can't access any at the, er, moment.'

'So do you want me to make some?'

'Well, yes,' said Sophie. 'That's pretty much it. We can show you lots of examples of the pots on Tamar's Instagram thread. So we were hoping perhaps you could have a look and see if you could make something similar.'

'I'm sure I can. I spent a couple of months with a potter in Tbilisi thirty years ago.'

'Really?' said Tamar, amazed. 'You've been to Georgia?'

'Sure,' said Olive. 'I travelled all over when I was younger, working with different potters, picking up ideas for my own work. They do interesting stuff there with smoke firing … it's all very ancient. I've done a bit of that and I'd like to try it again. So you're on, kids. When do you want to start?'

'We'd love you to come for dinner tonight,' said Sophie. 'We're going to ask Agata too. Charlie's coming and my friend Rey – so perhaps you could nip over a bit earlier and Tamar could show you her pictures to give you the feel we're hoping to recreate with your pots.'

'Sounds good. I'll come at six.' Then she turned to Beau, reaching for his hand. 'Nice rings you've got there, mate,' she said.

'I make them,' he said, holding out both hands so she could see them all.

Olive looked at each one carefully and then up at him, smiling. 'It's good work. Where did you learn to do that?'

'Well, I studied jewellery making at the Royal College of Art, but then I kind of re-taught myself.'

'Best way,' said Olive, smiling. 'See you guys later.'

CHAPTER 19

Beau was suffering. Tamar was so easy to be with, he was finding the situation very confusing. He kept thinking he wanted to twinkle, because that would be his normal response to spending time with such a beautiful woman, but then he found he couldn't, because it was more like being with a friend.

This dynamic was so different. He didn't have that permanent cliff-edge feeling he normally had with desirable women. The will-we-won't-we? – or more like when-will-we? – tension just wasn't there and he didn't know if that was because he was keeping his promise to his mother or because he just felt so strangely at ease with Tamar.

It was even fun doing food shopping together. Buying groceries with her made doing something he normally found excruciating and old person-ish into a bit of a lark. He could see that she was as discerning as his mother about what to buy. She'd been very particular in the fish shop about which bit of hot-smoked beetroot salmon she'd wanted and she'd seemed to audition each courgette personally in the greengrocers. He'd picked them up to do twirls and little routines to impress her, which had made her laugh.

'I can't believe I'm queueing for bread,' he said, as they waited in the line outside Maker and Baker in Kings Road. 'It's like being in Soviet Russia.'

'This is the sort of thing that made my mother move to London in the nineties,' said Tamar. 'Which took some doing in those days. She'd be horrified if she could see me doing this, when there's so much lovely sliced white bread for the taking in the Co-op.'

'Sorry. I didn't mean to be rude about your homeland.'

'It's fine. I'm as British as you are, but I totally understand why we would queue fifteen minutes for one loaf of proper sourdough – and once you taste this bread, you will think it was worth it.'

'Is your mum still in London?' asked Beau, just to make conversation.

'No, she died when I was fifteen.'

'I'm so sorry,' he said, realising how much more saying that meant now he knew what it was like to lose a parent. 'My dad died a few months ago.'

'I know,' she said, looking at him kindly. 'I'm so sorry. Your mum told me. It's very recent for you – is it even six months?'

'Just over seven,' he said, trying not to remember the actual date. It made it all too real. But no, he couldn't stop it – here it came, all flooding back. The phone call from Rey checking he was in the studio, where he then turned up to tell him what had happened and to take Beau home to his mum, who had been almost catatonic with shock.

Beau hadn't been sure how to take each next breath.

He felt a bit queasy just thinking about it and then something like panic started to rise in him. He really didn't want to have a meltdown in front of a beautiful woman in a bread queue in St Leonards.

Tamar was looking at him intently. 'Are you okay?' she asked, putting a hand gently on his shoulder.

He shook his head, unable to speak.

'Why don't you go into that café we passed and I'll be there in a minute? It's only a few shops back.'

'No,' he said. 'I'd rather stay here with you, if that's okay, because you know why I'm being a cringing weirdo. You understand.'

A tear rolled down his cheek, the bastard. He wiped it off roughly, mortified, but then Tamar gently folded her arms round him and held him in a firm hug, which was extremely comforting – and extraordinarily unarousing.

When they got back with the shopping, Sophie was delighted to find they'd bought everything exactly as she'd specified. Even the flowers were spot on, she said – one bunch that would be right for the dinner table and another featuring bold flowers, preferably orange.

'Perfect,' she said, picking up the rather garish lilies.

'Who are those orange ones for?' asked Beau. 'They don't seem very you.'

'They're for my other neighbour, Agata,' she said. 'The one you haven't met yet. I thought you could deliver them to her and invite her to the dinner tonight. Tell her Olive's coming and say it's the usual time.'

Beau waited so long after ringing Agata's bell, he began to wonder whether she was out or if he should press it again. Perhaps she was upstairs and hadn't heard it. But just when he was about to give up, a small figure become visible behind the frosted glass.

'Who is this?' asked a strongly accented voice.

'Hi Agata, it's Beau from next door, Sophie's other son.'

The door immediately opened. There was a tiny little woman standing there wearing a bright orange hat. It went perfectly with the flowers.

'Hello,' she said, smiling at him. 'How nice to meet the other son.'

'These are for you,' he said, handing her the flowers.

She took them and hugged them to her chest, closing her eyes. 'Thank you. Tiger lilies. How did you know they are my favourites?'

'My mum said get orange flowers.'

'I think my hat was a clue,' said Agata. 'I often wear it.'

'It's fantastic.' What a brilliant old bird. How his dad would have loved her. 'I've got something else to deliver as well, actually,' he added. 'An invitation.'

'Why don't you come in?' She stepped back to make room for him and seeing her turning awkwardly, holding the flowers, Beau stepped inside and gently took them from her.

'Shall I stick these in the kitchen sink?' he asked. 'You can do something with them later.'

'Good idea,' said Agata. 'And you know where the kitchen is, because it's like your house in a mirror. I will go into the sitting room, you come and find me there.'

Beau walked through to the kitchen and stopped in his tracks. It was an untouched seventies classic: plain teak cupboards with simple steel handles; large quarry tiles on the floor; brown, white and yellow geometric tiles on the walls.

It had been knocked through to create an adjoining dining area with a large table and Cesca chairs – bent metal with rush seats. So cool.

He ran some water into the sink for the flowers and then, seeing a filter jug on the side, he opened the cupboard above it and found some glasses. Elderly people never drank enough. He remembered that from when their granny had lived with them. He filled two glasses with water and carried them to the sitting room.

It was another perfect seventies time capsule, with Agata sitting in an Eames lounge chair by the window.

'I thought you might like some water,' he said, putting the glass down on the Noguchi coffee table next to her. 'Or I could make you a cup of tea.'

'Water is perfect, thank you. Most of all I just want to talk to you. Sit, please.'

Beau sat down opposite her and raised his glass before taking a drink. He was trying not to look round the room too obviously, checking out all the classic mid-century furniture that his friends would kill for.

'I hope you don't mind my old-fashioned house.'

'I'm obsessed with your house. It's off-the-scale cool. If only my mum had done her kitchen like yours.'

Agata laughed. 'You don't like the pink, then?'

Beau pulled a face. 'I'd never say anything to Mum. It's just such a weirdly big change from our old place, but she likes it and that's all that matters. But I totally love your house, Agata. Did you do it like this?'

'Yes,' she said, nodding. 'When we moved here in 1972. I have changed nothing since and I never will.'

'I'm so glad you haven't. This is like a dream home for me and all my friends.'

'So now I am back in fashion,' said Agata, smiling. 'For a long time this house was considered a crime. The horror on people's faces in the 1980s was ... Well, for me, very funny, because I knew they were ignorant and stupid. If something is well made and works well to live with, it will always be right and all this change, change, change ... pfff.' She flapped her hands in the air, as if brushing the idea away. 'I don't want any more change in my life, Beau. I had enough change by the time I was five.'

Beau wondered what she meant by that but didn't feel he could ask.

'And you have also had a terrible change,' she continued, leaning towards him. 'Losing your father like that. Such a shock, I am so sorry.'

He smiled at her weakly. 'Thank you.'

'And don't underestimate the effect of the shock. The way he died was so brutal and you all have to get over that before you can even start on the real grieving.'

Beau looked back at her. He'd never thought of that before. Even beyond the visceral sorrow, he had been feeling decidedly peculiar.

'It's been a bit like an out-of-body experience,' he said. 'I don't quite feel I'm here.'

Partly because of the other thing that I can't talk to anybody about, he thought, but she was probably right about the shock too.

'I understand,' said Agata. 'As I said, I had experienced a lot of change and shock already when I was a child.'

It was the second time she'd mentioned it, so he now felt he could ask – that she wanted him to.

'What happened?'

'I came to England in 1940 on the last Kindertransport,' she said, looking at him steadily with her unusually pale blue eyes. 'On my own. I was five. From Holland to Harwich.'

'Just you?'

Agata nodded. 'All the rest of my family were killed by the Nazis. Parents, older siblings, grandparents, cousins, uncles, aunties, great uncles, great aunts. Everybody. And all the neighbours and friends and playmates and teachers and doctors and rabbis and chimney sweeps and shopkeepers and musicians and dressmakers. Everybody I had ever known. Maybe a few survived, but how I would know? They could be anywhere. That is enough change for one life, don't you think?'

Beau couldn't reply. He just nodded.

Agata reached over and patted his hand. 'It's okay, I've had a long time to get used to it, but anything I can control – like the décor in this house – I must control. I'm sure you can understand.'

'Absolutely,' he said. 'What country were you born in?'

'I am Czech,' said Agata. 'Well, I was Czech, but I have lived here for over eighty years, so really I'm British.' She smiled in a complicit way he found endearing and it made him think again how much Matt would have loved her. He would have had his notebook out, drawing her as she talked. But Beau really didn't want to think about his father's notebooks.

'So you may wonder why I still sound like I just got off the last EasyJet from Prague?'

'Well,' said Beau, 'I do think you're entitled to your national identity …'

'I fake it!' said Agata, clapping her hands in delight. 'I went to school in Norfolk. I lived with an English family there until I was twenty, very good people – and of course, I spoke just like them.' She had broken into perfect Received Pronunciation. 'Cut glass,' she said, in the same voice, then switched back to her Czech accent. Then I moved to London in the fifties, where it was chic to be foreign, and I wore a polo neck and capri pants and a beret and I drank espresso ... I was fabulous. Then I met my lovely English husband, with his safe job as an engineer and we moved to this house over fifty years ago. So I'm nearly as English as you are, but I keep my fake accent, because I like it.'

Beau threw his head back, laughing. He laughed more than he had for a long time. It felt great.

'Oh, I'm sorry,' he said. 'I shouldn't be laughing when you've just told me such a terrible thing about losing your family – I'm so sorry, but your accent, it's just so ...' *So exactly the kind of thing my dad loved.*

Agata smiled broadly, clearly delighted she'd amused him. 'Well, that's our secret now, Beau. You can tell everybody the tragic story about my family – it's better they know, I would be grateful – but my accent is between us? Okay?'

Beau nodded, grinning. 'I promise, scout's honour, not that I ever was a scout, but I get the idea. Now, I'd better get back to Mum, who asked me to tell you that dinner is at our place tonight. Olive's coming and it's the usual time. Does that make sense?'

'Every sense,' said Agata, beaming with delight. 'Lovely! And you will be there?'

Beau nodded. 'I will be, plus Mum's friend Rey, who I think you've met, and his friend Tippy, who is really fun, and someone called Charlie, who I think is my uncle's friend, and another new friend of mum's, who she's working with at the moment.'

'Ah, yes. The very beautiful girl, I have seen them walking past together. You might fall in love, Beau.'

He laughed. 'Unlikely. It's the absolutely last thing I'm looking for, plus Mum has given me strict instructions to leave her well alone in that regard.'

'Instructions about love?' said Agata. 'Oh, I wish her luck with that.'

CHAPTER 20

Rey and Sophie were having brunch at the beach hut he'd bought on a wilder stretch of shingle to the west of St Leonards.

'I wanted you to be the very first person to enjoy it with me,' he said, putting rashers of bacon into a frying pan on a camp stove. 'They only finished painting it on Friday and I dressed it yesterday. Do you like it?'

'Like it?' asked Sophie, leaning back in the canvas chair, her face turned towards the morning sun. 'It's a little bit of paradise.'

'An old shed on a pebbly beach, but it weirdly works, doesn't it?'

'It's so peaceful,' she said, leaning back, her arms behind her head. 'I know I've got the beach just down the cliff path from the house, but this somehow takes it to another level. I feel like my blood pressure dropped the moment I sat down in this chair and even more so when you handed me this excellent mug of tea.' She took a sip.

'And how is your blood pressure these days, darling?' asked Rey, poking the bacon with a spatula.

'It's pretty good,' she said. 'It's great having Tamar and Beau staying.' She watched him managing to squeeze the rest of the bacon from the packet into the small frying pan. Then he took some rolls out of a bag at his feet and buttered them lavishly before tucking the cooked bacon rashers inside, four in each roll, and passed one to her.

'Ready for more tea, ma'am?' he asked. He had a second camp stove set up next to the frying pan, a bright red kettle sitting on it.

'I'll hold off until after I've had a dip. The tide is nice and high now. Will you join me?'

'Is this the Maldives?'

Sophie shook her head.

'Then, no,' he said. 'And even there, I only paddle. I've survived this long without ever swimming in the sea and I'm happy to continue that way.'

'You're missing out on a wonderful thing,' said Sophie. 'And it's weird.'

'Not if your parents grew up in the Punjab,' he said, filling another roll with bacon. 'It's a day's drive from Amritsar to the nearest coast, longer on a train, and even in this country, I didn't grow up with buckets and spades like you did. Lots of lovely picnics, though.' He patted his tummy, smiling broadly.

When Sophie got back from her swim, Rey wasn't there. He'd left the *Sunday Times* on her chair with a note scrawled across the top saying: *Please hold the fort. Gone for emergency donuts.*

She shook her head. She'd brought a cake, but there was never enough food for Rey.

She thought about stretching out on his sun lounger for a while, the sun was hot enough, but doing nothing was never a good option. It left too much space for thoughts to come in.

Opening the paper, she flicked through the magazine to the food, then picked up the *Style* section. On the contents page she noticed a striking jewelled ring in the form of an eye, with a diamond drop as a tear falling from the corner. She made a mental note to show it to Beau when she got in. She had her own copy of the paper at home.

She glanced at the newsy sections at the front and then leafed through the pages until she came to a picture that made her pause. It was of a woman standing in a chic kitchen, holding up her hands to show some rings. Nothing outlandish, but there was just something about the woman's face.

She was familiar, in a way that gave Sophie a deep sinking feeling. Could it really be that woman who had shown up at Matt's funeral? The one Sophie was fairly sure had been the Juliet he'd talked about – it had been her name, when Rey asked her.

Swallowing hard, she read the title and introduction to the piece.

RARE GEM
Self-trained jewellery designer Juliet Mylan, who broke all the rules with her dazzling Giuliette brand mixing energy crystals with precious gems, shares the story of her path to global success.

Sophie felt sick. No longer just a horrible concept, here she was in full technicolour.

Sophie's eyes went back to the picture. The woman looked much more beautiful than she had at the funeral. Of course, she would have had full hair and make up for a shoot like this, but she really was stunning – yet Sophie could still see that she looked a little bit like her. The colouring – dark blonde hair, blue eyes, darker skin than a classic English rose – and something about the bones of the face. Sophie's heart was beating so fast, she felt quite faint. She turned her head and vomited onto the shingle, just as she heard Rey's voice calling out to her. He was nearly back at the beach hut.

Thinking as quickly as she could manage, Sophie stuffed the magazine into her beach bag under the wet towel and looked up just as he came through the gap between the huts. She couldn't let him see that article. He would immediately recognise Juliet as the woman Sophie had asked him to remove from the wake. He would want to talk about it.

Not needing to put on an act, she sat back in her chair with her eyes closed, hoping she looked as bad as she felt.

'I got chocolate, jam and custard,' said Rey, dropping a shopping bag onto the beach. Then he saw the state of Sophie, who had started retching again.

'Oh, no!' he said. 'Are you sick? I hope it wasn't that bacon.'

'I'm so sorry, Rey. I think it was something I had last night. I think I need to go home.' She had to get back there as soon as possible to hide the copy of the magazine that was in the house. Beau must never see it either. Even though he was unlikely to make any connection with a random woman who'd been at his father's wake, she knew that as soon as he saw that ring he'd want to know more about the woman who designed it.

She also wanted a safe place to study the article in depth.

Sophie got into the house and glanced into the sitting room. Beau and Tamar were sprawled on the sofas reading the papers – and Beau was holding the *Style* section. She thought she might vomit again.

'You're back soon,' said Beau. 'I thought you were going to be there until sundown. We were thinking to come and join you with some chilled beverages.'

Sophie tried to think. She had to distract them.

'I got sick,' she said. 'I think I must have eaten something off. I'd better lie down.'

'Mumpty,' said Beau, jumping to his feet. 'What can we get you?'

'I think I'd like to lie on the sofa, if you don't mind me turfing you off, and I'd love some water and some fresh ginger tea, if you don't mind making it, Tamar. And, Beau, darling, could you pop up to my room and get my cashmere blanket?'

The minute they were out of the room, she grabbed the magazine and stuffed it in her beach bag with Rey's copy, before lying down again and closing her eyes.

When they came back with her requests, she told them she'd changed her mind and would go to bed after all and headed up there.

Beau sat down to carry on reading the *Style* section, but couldn't find it. Weird. He'd definitely left it on the sofa when his mum had come back.

'Have you seen *Style*, Tamar?' he asked. 'Is it mixed up in that pile there?'

Tamar had a look through all the papers heaped on the ottoman and couldn't find it. Beau was puzzled – and irritated. He'd been reading a really interesting piece about the jeweller who had started that brand Giuliette. He loved that stuff, it was bold, like his work, and it mixed up real gems with woo-woo crystals in a totally original way. He was also interested to read how she'd built up such an amazing business, all on her own, from scratch. He thought he might get some ideas from it for Mojobo.

He'd have to look her up online later, although it was tricky with that weird spelling. He wondered how you pronounced it. Gwillett?

CHAPTER 21

Juliet and Cassady were on their way to visit Granny. Cassady was carrying a bunch of paper flowers she'd made for her. Juliet had the real thing. And chocolates and shortbread from Fortnum & Mason and nice soap. She liked to spoil her mum.

'Ganny, Ganny, Ganny, Ganny,' Cassady was singing while swinging on her mother's hand.

Juliet smiled down at her head of black curls and felt her heart turn over with pure love, as it often did when she looked at her daughter. It always made her particularly emotional when she took Cassady to visit her grandmother, the three generations of them being together. The deep mutual love. The bond of their womanhood.

And for Juliet, at least, the satisfaction of knowing that she was protecting her little girl from experiences her mother had been unable to save her, or herself, from. Juliet didn't know how much her mother understood how that had influenced her decisions in adulthood. It was parked with all the other things they didn't talk about, but silently acknowledged between themselves.

Juliet called in at the warden's office so he could let her through the security door to go up to her mother's apartment.

It was a unit of sheltered accommodation for older people who could still live independently but needed someone on site to keep an eye on them. Her mother had her own kitchen and did her own shopping, but cleaning was provided and she could ask for help if she needed it to change a light bulb or whatever. There was always a warden there, who monitored each resident as they left the building and came back.

The moment Donato opened the security door, Cassady ran ahead, knowing exactly where to go. She got to the flat's front door first and knocked on it, chanting: 'Ganny! Cassady! Ganny! Cassady!' until it opened. Then she threw herself at the woman who opened it, hugging her legs.

'Hello, my little darling,' said Pauline, reaching down to ruffle her hair and then looking up at Juliet. 'And hello, my big darling.'

'Hello, Mummy,' said Juliet, hugging her mum and kissing her cheek. 'I brought these for you –' she held out the large bunch of flowers '– but Cassady has something much better, don't you? Give them to Ganny.'

Cassady held out her bunch of flowers, all carefully coloured in with felt tips. She particularly loved drawing and painting at nursery, which probably wasn't surprising, thought Juliet with a pang.

She left Pauline admiring Cassady's work and went to put her flowers in water, but when she went through the door to the sitting room, she stopped. It was so messy. The cleaners came in once a week and Pauline normally kept the place up reasonably in between but there were newspapers strewn all around – her mother had worked for the BBC and was still keenly interested in current affairs – along with dirty cups and plates with food still on them. Juliet started piling the crockery up to take into the kitchen.

'Oh, you don't have to do that,' said Pauline, coming in, Cassady holding tightly to her hand. 'I can do it later, when you've gone.'

'No, it's fine, Mum,' said Juliet, keeping her voice level. 'I thought I'd make us some tea to go with the nice shortbread I've brought, so I might as well wash these up while I wait for the kettle to boil. It's no bother.'

As she turned to go into the small kitchen, she saw her mother sweep all the newspapers that were on the sofa onto the floor so she and Cassady could sit down, seeming not to see them now littering the floor. But she had a pile of books ready to read to her granddaughter, who was excitedly looking through them to find her favourite, so that showed she had known they were coming. The mess was just a bit odd.

Juliet made the tea and took it through with the tin of biscuits, which her mother showed great delight about in her usual charming way, and then Juliet sat back to watch as her mother read one book after another to Cassady, who listened with rapt attention. It was lovely to observe them together, so happy in each other's company.

When all the books were read, Pauline handed Cassady a carrier bag which she said had a present in it. The little girl tipped it out to find a new drawing pad and a packet of crayons.

'Thank you, Ganny,' she said, hugging her. 'I'm going to draw you the best picture ever, right now. What do you want it to be of?'

'Two zebras and a hippopotamus having a party.'

Cassady jumped off the sofa onto the floor and set to, lying on her tummy, the edge of her tongue sticking out of her mouth.

'So how are you?' Juliet asked her mother.

'I am very well, thank you, Juliet,' said Pauline, smiling serenely. It was what she always said and had always said, with that same smile, even when things had been anything but well. Even when she'd been in prison, she'd smiled like that. She'd done it right through the murder trial that put her in there.

Her ability to keep up that front was one of the reasons Juliet's father had got away with his abuse for so long. No one outside the family had any idea of what he did to Pauline.

Juliet physically shook her head to stop that line of thought. It was never helpful and particularly not when she was actually with her mother. That was all over. Thanks to a human rights law project specialising in women's cases, her mother's charge had been reduced to manslaughter and she'd been released on compassionate grounds.

But the damage of several years in prison and twenty-five plus before that living with a vicious abuser – mental and sexual abuse, he was much too clever ever to put a physical mark on her – was visibly there, even beneath that automatic smile. Pauline's face was far more lined than normal for her seventy-four years, with deep grooves between her eyebrows and next to her mouth, and her eyes were quite sunken. In rare moments when she relaxed her permanent smile, her whole face seemed to sink.

'And how are you, my love?' Pauline asked Juliet, always much more comfortable talking about the other person.

'Well, the baby is coming along, as you can see ...' She stood up and pulled the dress she was wearing tight across her stomach.

'Oh, that's good,' said Pauline. 'Building Cassady's little brother or sister—'

'Sister!' said Cassady. 'I don't want a horrible brother.'

'Whoever it is, you are going to love them,' said Pauline.

'Fingers crossed,' said Juliet in a low voice. She was a bit concerned about how jealous Cassady was going to be, but she'd just have to deal with that when it happened.

'I'm a big sister,' said Cassady, standing up and running over to her mother and covering the bump in kisses.

'You certainly are,' said Pauline. 'And I'm a double granny. Aren't we lucky? When is it due?'

'Mid-September officially, but if it's anything like Miss Pickle here,' she said, hugging Cassady to her and blowing a raspberry on her cheek, 'it will take its time.'

'And is this lovely little person Cassady's complete brother or sister?' said Pauline with an expressively raised eyebrow.

Juliet nodded. Clever of her mother to ask that question subtly. Some people were very thoughtless, even in front of the little girl.

'Well, isn't that lovely?' said Pauline.

'We've got other news, as well,' said Juliet. 'We're moving house.'

'I'm going to proper school,' said Cassady, sitting back down on the floor and getting back to her drawing. 'I'm a big girl. I need more friends.'

Juliet laughed. That pretty much summed it up. For both of them.

'Where are you moving to? Far from your current place?' asked Pauline.

'Queen's Park,' said Juliet. 'You know, a bit further out, beyond Maida Vale. I've bought a house with a big garden for the kids and I know lots of very nice people up there with children the same age as Cass, so it will be much better for her.'

She knew those people thanks to Rachel Rathbone and it was making a huge difference to her life, as well as Cassady's. The house she was buying was on a street between where Rachel and Dottie lived.

'Are there good schools there?' asked Pauline.

'Yes,' said Juliet. 'And Cassady already knows children at the one she's going to. She's starting at the nursery on Thursday.'

'My friend Cricket goes to my new school,' said Cassady. 'She's my best friend and Mimi. We don't like Quiller—'

'You must like everybody, Cassady,' said Pauline.

'Whatever,' said Cassady, and Juliet had to hide her chuckle.

'I've finished,' continued the little girl, jumping up and thrusting her drawing at her grandmother.

Juliet went and looked over her mother's shoulder to see it. There were two four-legged creatures with bold pink and turquoise stripes and a bright yellow round one, all sitting round something that looked like a birthday cake.

'I changed the colours,' said Cassady. 'I think black and white and grey is boring for animals. It's the hippo's birthday party. She's called Peter.'

'Oh, this is a marvellous drawing,' said Pauline, pulling her granddaughter towards her and kissing the top of her head. 'You are clever. I'm going to put it in a frame, so I can look at it every day. Particularly Peter. She is my favourite.'

Juliet looked at the picture and tears prickled her eyes. How Matt would have loved to see it.

CHAPTER 22

Beau was sneaking around. He was in his mother's office, going through her things. It was making him feel dirty, but he had to find his father's phone. He knew she had it, but where would she put something like that? Somewhere she could find it easily – or somewhere she wouldn't come across it too often and get upset?

It wasn't in her desk drawers or in any of the cardboard file boxes she used to store stuff. She hadn't hidden it among her stationery or in the row of ring binders.

He patted his fingers against his jaw, pursing his lips and trying to think. Then Tamar made a noise in the kitchen, getting something out of a cupboard, and he jumped, looking over his shoulder. He knew Sophie was safely up in London, but he couldn't help feeling on edge.

He sat in her chair and turned all the way round in it, scanning the room. He'd looked everywhere. It wasn't in here. He'd have to go deeper.

Feeling weirdly self-conscious, he walked – casual like – into the kitchen.

'Something smells good,' he said, over brightly.

'Just testing a recipe that will also be our dinner,' said Tamar, as she stirred a pot on the stove.

'I'll keenly look forward to it,' said Scout Leader Beau, continuing on to the dining room – the opposite direction from where he was actually going. Why was he trying to put Tamar off the scent? She'd have no idea what he was up to.

He rolled his eyes at himself as he walked round into the sitting room and then back out to the hall. Then he ran up the stairs two at a time and forced himself to go into his mother's bedroom.

He stopped just over the threshold and looked at the bed. It wasn't his parents' bed, the one where he'd snuggled in for so many stories and cuddles and Christmas mornings. It was a weird new bed, with a pink velvet headboard. What was it with his mother and all this pink cringe these days? And why had she got rid of the lovely bed he'd known all his life?

She must have her reasons – perhaps the association was just too sad? – and she didn't need to feel judged. He added it to his mental list of things not to mention to her and looked round the room, wondering where to start.

It was no good. He had to face it – he was going to have to go through her underwear. Feeling more creepy than ever, he quietly closed the door in case Tamar psychically knew what he was doing and came up the stairs.

Half-closing his eyes and feeling for the phone rather than looking, he opened the first drawer. There was nothing in either of the top drawers except what felt like knickers, bras and socks. The lower drawers were jumpers and t-shirts but still no phone.

He went through the wardrobe and bedside cabinet,

finding nothing, and was just about to shift his attention to the bathroom when he noticed the hatbox on top of the cupboard. Reaching on tiptoes, he was able to knock it off and as he caught it, he heard a distinct clunk as something small and hard hit the side of the cardboard box. It sounded a lot like a phone and when he lifted the lid off, there it was, his father's mobile in its custom case, with one of Matt's most famous paintings reproduced on it. Beau's stomach lurched as he sat down on the bed, holding it in his hand.

He plugged the phone into the charger next to the bed and watched as it came to life. If only he could do the same with his father. He stared down at it for a moment, feeling slightly queasy, then got it to open on the first try. The old man had always used his own birthday, claiming it was the only number he would never forget.

Then he hesitated, wondering where to look at first. He started scrolling through the contacts, but what did he expect to find? An entry under B for 'bit on the side'? There were hundreds of names in there and it could have been anyone female.

Then he tapped open the photographs, which were meticulously filed into folders, just like the filing drawers in his father's studio. Beau couldn't help himself looking and, yes, there was a folder for him.

He scrolled through a few of the pictures, but soon had to stop. He could remember when all of them were taken and the flood of memories was too much. He flopped back on to the mattress, still holding the phone with one hand, the other over his eyes. He didn't want to do this. But he had to. In case it came out in some other way and blindsided them all.

He sat up smartly and kept scrolling through the folders, but there was nothing that looked incriminating. He wasn't sure whether to feel disappointed or relieved.

There was nothing unexpected in the emails and the WhatsApps and texts were completely predictable too. Exchanges with his mum about what to have for dinner, Uncle Seb, him, Jack, Joe at Goldsmiths and a load of other people Beau knew. The messages to people he didn't know were all perfectly innocent. Dull, really. He even checked Facebook Messenger and Instagram messages. Nothing out of the ordinary.

Then he went to the call history and right at the top of it were about ten missed calls from a number with no contact name attached. He picked up his own phone and – his heart beating fast – dialled the number. It didn't connect. He tried again and it was the same.

That was odd, especially as they were the last calls made to his dad on this phone – and they were all in the days after he died. Like someone who didn't know Matt was dead was trying to call him. Repeatedly.

Wondering where else he could look, he tapped open the diary section and scrolled back through the months. Again, there was nothing surprising, but as he got a bit further in, he noticed a pattern. There were quite a few entries that were just one letter: G. A time and 'G'. Mostly evenings, some weekends. The further back he went, the more there were, until suddenly, about five years back, there were none.

Beau felt slightly nauseous as the possibility sank in. Her name must begin with G and that was when it had started. He flipped back to the contacts but there weren't many women's names under G. There was a Gail and a Gemma, but he knew who they both were. One was in her seventies and the other one had a wife.

Even if he had found a woman starting with G he didn't know – Gillian Jones, or Gigi Faffy-Doo-Dah – how would Beau know it was her, the mystery woman at the funeral? It could be a dentist. If only he'd heard a name when he was eavesdropping on Rey and that woman, it would be so much easier.

Going back to the photograph albums, there were no women's names apart from one: Sophie.

He looked down at his father's painting on the back of the phone. He felt dirty for what he'd done. Violating the privacy of both his parents and all he had for it were the diary entries for G. Perhaps he'd be able to put that together with something he'd find in Joe's boxes. When he went back to London, he'd get onto it. Ugh. For now he was going to see if Tamar needed help in the kitchen. That would cheer him up.

But then, idly flicking over the screens on the phone he noticed something surprising on the very last one. The Snapchat icon. That was weird. As a teenager Beau had been obsessed with keeping up his 'streaks', but he didn't use it anymore and he didn't know anyone who did. What on earth had his dad been doing with it?

He tapped on the icon and as it opened, message after message arrived, all from the same contact, with no name or jolly avatar, just a circle – and all saying versions of the same thing, getting increasingly urgent with capitals and exclamation marks as they went on: 'Call me.'

They had all been sent after his father's death – the same

days those phone calls had been made. So it definitely seemed as though the person trying to contact his father hadn't known he was dead.

He stared down at the phone, feeling as though his brain was throbbing, when something else occurred to him. Snapchat messages disappear after they've been read, making it the perfect platform for exchanges you want to keep private. So that must have been how his father had stayed in touch with his bit on the side.

Smart thinking, Pops, but it didn't help his quest much. Was this mysterious G the woman in the drawing in his father's studio? And, if so, where did that leave the one at the funeral? Because clearly she'd known he was dead.

He felt more confused than ever.

CHAPTER 23

Sophie could hear the girls laughing all through the house. Tamar had shyly asked if it would be okay for her to invite a couple of her friends down from London for Rey's beach party, to thank them for allowing her to sleep on their sofas when she'd been desperate. Two young women had arrived that morning and as far as Sophie could tell, the three of them hadn't stopped giggling since. It was making her smile as she stood in the kitchen, packing up the food she'd prepared for the barbecue.

Beau was at the beach already, helping Rey set up, and Sophie was going to head over shortly. She texted Tamar – with three floors, it was easier than shouting. *Will you and the girls be ready to go shortly?*

The answer was a loud shriek, then the sound of feet pounding down the stairs. Tamar arrived first, followed by her friends, Yewande and Niamh.

'How do we look?' asked Tamar and the three of them struck poses, she and Yewande were wearing long dresses in boldly printed fabrics.

'You all look fabulous!' said Sophie. 'I love those dresses. Where are they from?'

'I make them,' said Yewande. 'It's my label.'

'Mine is a skirt and a top,' said Tamar, throwing her arms in the air to reveal an expanse of flat stomach.

'They're so great, I wouldn't mind something like that myself,' said Sophie.

'I will measure you before I go home,' said Yewande.

'What about me?' asked Niamh, doing a twirl. She had an extraordinary thing on her head, like the hair from several different-coloured troll dolls – pink, turquoise, yellow, lime green. The rest of her outfit was a pair of tartan pyjama bottoms, an old band tour t-shirt and fluffy slippers on her feet.

'You look amazing too,' said Sophie. 'Did you make that, er, headpiece?'

'Yes,' said Niamh. 'I found the wigs stuffed into a bag in a charity shop and I sewed them onto a beanie.' She pulled it off to reveal a shock of bleached blonde hair.

'You might find it a bit hot on a beach in August,' said Sophie, 'but I can guarantee that Rey will love it.'

When they got to the beach Rey was catering on a grand scale, as Sophie had known he would. He had three barbecues set up, with stacks of cool boxes full of food in the shade to the side of the beach hut and a row of plastic tubs full of ice and bottles.

'If anyone wants to drink red wine today, they can bring their own,' he said, mixing a large tub of Pimm's for good measure.

'No one is going to go thirsty – or hungry – that's for sure,' said Sophie.

'Or fungry,' said Tippy, who was wearing a full-length

psychedelic print halter-neck dress. 'That's when you're starving for funnnnn ...'

As soon as they'd arrived, Beau took the car straight back to West Hill Road to pick up Olive and Agata without really saying hello to the girls. Sophie wondered if he was regretting shaving all his hair off. Olive had done it when they'd smoke-fired the pots for Tamar's book in an old dustbin in her back garden. He'd said it was a declaration to mark a new phase in his life – which was so like something Matt would have said and done, it had given Sophie a wobble.

But she wasn't thinking about any of that today. She paused to take in the setting. A perfect August afternoon, the sky a dense blue, as though you could cut it with a knife and it would be that colour all the way through, the beach hut looking lovely with its doors open wide to reveal the bright-orange painted interior, strings of polyester marigolds festooned all around. There were various rugs and mats spread out on the shingle in front of the hut, dotted with cushions and groups of folding chairs and stools.

'How many are we expecting?' she asked Rey.

'I'm not sure. Tippy and I have invited our new friends from the Fountain, and Beau and Tamar have both asked people they know down here, so I don't know ... thirty? Forty?'

'Gosh,' said Sophie, noticing an alarmingly large speaker set up at the side of the hut. 'Have you told the neighbours?'

'A card under every door. I think quite a few of them are going to join us.'

People started to arrive and a merry hum of chat and laughter built up around the hut. Sophie didn't know any of the guests and when they asked what had made her decide to move from London to Hastings, she just said the kids were grown up and it was time for the next stage – which was the original reason. She didn't have to elaborate.

Next to arrive were Olive and Agata, who was wearing a bright blue hat with a huge brim, large dark glasses and even more costume jewellery than usual. She looked like a tiny film star. Rey sprang into action, installing her in a comfortable chair with a stool beside it for her drink and Tamar introduced her friends, who were immediately enchanted.

Sophie smiled at the happy little crew and looked round for Beau. She couldn't see him, although he had to be there because he'd just dropped the neighbours off.

When there was still no sign of him fifteen minutes later, she went over to Olive.

'What did Beau do after he brought you over?'

'Ah,' said Olive, looking a bit uncomfortable. 'He's gone back to the house. He said he just wasn't "feeling it" and if you asked, I was to tell you sorry. So – sorry.'

'That's weird. Beau loves a party. Everyone can fall in love with him and he can show off. Do you think it's the hair? Lack of.'

Olive laughed. 'I asked him that, and he said – I quote – that his virgin scalp made him feel pure and free and he wanted to be alone to commune with it.'

Sophie rolled her eyes. More Matt-osity.

She looked back towards the beach hut. The crowd seemed to have doubled in size. The young ones were already dancing, Tippy leading them in a routine to whatever song was blaring out. It was an adorable sight, but Sophie couldn't help feeling disappointed. She'd been really looking forward to having a swim and a dance with Beau and generally sharing the joy together.

She was wondering what to do when Olive grasped her shoulder.

'Come on, Soph,' she said. 'Let's go and have a boogie.'

Sophie was just taking a rest between numbers, when she noticed that Charlie had arrived. He was down the side of the hut, stashing cans of his fizz into Rey's ice buckets, and she was surprised to see he had a woman with him. Rather beautiful, with natural grey hair cut quite short, a little younger than him. Sophie didn't know he had a partner, but then she'd never thought to ask. He'd always been on his own when she'd seen him and he'd said he lived alone, so maybe this lady was more of a girlfriend. Now she felt bad she hadn't asked him if he'd wanted to bring someone when he'd come for supper. Oh, well, she knew now. And they did look right together, these two.

She went over to talk to them.

'Sophie,' said Charlie, smiling warmly and opening his arms wide.

She kissed him lightly on the cheek – sensitive to the other woman's feelings – and put out her hand to her. 'Hello, I'm Sophie,' she said to the woman. 'My brother-in-law introduced me to Charlie and he very kindly supplied his wonderful fizz for my housewarming party.' *I'm not hitting on him.*

'Cicely,' she said, kissing Sophie on the cheek. 'Charlie has told me about you. It's lovely to meet you.'

Perhaps it was quite a casual relationship or early days, Sophie thought. She'd be sure to give them plenty of space.

Heading back out to the party throng, she still couldn't help wishing Beau was there. She'd texted and called, but he hadn't answered and it was turning into one of those niggling mother worries.

She'd just got out her phone to try again when she saw him walking along the path that led to the beach huts. There was another man with him and even at a distance, something about him was familiar, but it wasn't until they got closer that she suddenly realised it was Sebastian. What on earth was he doing there?

Sophie rushed over to greet them.

'Seb!' she said. 'What a lovely surprise. I had no idea you were coming.'

'No one knew I was coming,' said Sebastian. 'Except Rey. He rang and invited me and we decided to keep it secret for laughs. I dropped by your house on my way to leave my car – and found this one there. We got a taxi over together.'

Beau looked sheepish. Sophie chucked his cheeks and kissed him. She wasn't going to lay on a guilt trip, she was just happy he was there.

'Sorry, Mumpty,' he said, whispering in her ear. 'I was having a wobble, didn't feel up to it, but I'm here now and I'm sure I'm going to love it.'

'Go and have fun,' Sophie said to him. 'There are loads of lovely people your age. Get stuck in. We all need this.'

She turned back to Sebastian. 'Welcome to Paradise-on-Sea,' she said. 'Have you got your trunks on?'

He patted his hip. 'Beau lent me his. I hadn't really thought we'd be going in, but it does look pretty appealing now I'm here. He's going to wear his underpants, of course, which I'm sure he will enjoy, knowing our Beausie.'

Sophie laughed. It was so great having someone else there who really knew them, not just Rey. It was odd when everyone around you had only known you since you were middle-aged. She'd been nineteen when she met Sebastian.

'No Freya?' she asked.

'She's in Washington. She's doing a hands-across-the-ocean exchange thing with her equivalent from the *Washington Post*. She's there for a month.'

'Gosh, that sounds impressive. Will you go out and spend some time with her? You could do some guest cartooning for them, be a Washington power couple.'

'No way. I think it's the most boring place in the world. I did suggest meeting in New York, but she doesn't want to miss a minute of Capitol Hill fun times. She loves it there.'

'Well, I think you're going to love it here,' said Sophie, taking his arm and leading him to the Pimm's bucket.

Relieved his mother didn't seem upset with him, Beau went to find a beer, but after fishing one out of a tub of melting ice, he still didn't feel like breaking into the party proper.

He was sitting on an upturned bucket at the back of the hut when Rey came round the corner.

'There you are,' he said. 'Princess Party Pooper. Where on earth have you been? Does your mum know you're here?'

Beau nodded, but couldn't bring himself to say anything. He didn't want to start blubbing.

'Hey,' said Rey, sinking to his knees in front of him. 'Your hair doesn't look that bad.' He chuckled, clearly hoping Beau would laugh too.

But Beau still couldn't speak.

Rey took his hands in his. 'I know, big boy. It's crap. You're much too young to lose your dad and it's not just that either. I can so clearly remember the stage of life you're in. Everyone thinks it's wonderful because you're young and beautiful and carefree – well, you are. I was a fat boy who couldn't come out to his Indian parents – but it's actually tough, because you're still finding your way and everything is so uncertain. You have adult responsibilities, but you don't quite know who you are yet. I was training to be an accountant when I really wanted to be RuPaul, or at the very least Alan Carr.'

That got a small smile out of Beau.

'And I know about the poster thing, Beausie …'

Beau's head shot up to look at him.

'I saw it in the *Standard*,' said Rey. 'It was horrible. I haven't mentioned it to anyone and I didn't tell you I'd seen it, because I thought if you wanted to talk about it, you would.'

'Thanks,' said Beau, quietly. Rey had always had his back.

'Do you want to talk about it?'

Yes – no, thought Beau.

'It was just so humiliating,' he said. 'The whole idea of the ring thing was not to be a disrespectful bastard, but it seems I was. I thought it was nice.'

'But it's not one size fits all, is it? What is a casual hook-up to one person is a big deal to another. You meant well, but that young woman was offended by your "ring thing", as you call it. Quite an unfortunate turn of phrase actually, in the context.' He burst out laughing and this time Beau joined in. 'So, she was hurt by you leaving the ring and disappearing, for reasons of her own that you couldn't possibly have known about, because you didn't know her as a person. She was just someone you had sex with.'

Beau took in what Rey was saying and the laughter left him as quickly as it had arrived. It confirmed everything that was making him feel so bad.

I am a sleaze, he thought. *There I was thinking I was cool and modern and a feminist, ha bloody ha, but actually I'm just a heinous sleaze. Like my dad. Everyone has always told me I'm just like him and it turns out I am. Right down to the way I treat women.*

'I've met someone.' It was like he could hear his father's voice saying it. He shuddered.

'Are you cold?' said Rey. 'We need to get you out of this shade and onto the bloody beach – it's going off down there. You'll love it. Just try and put all that crap to the back of your mind and enjoy the party. Your mum really needs this – we all do. Okay?'

Beau nodded. He would do his best. And if it all went pear-shaped, no one could say he hadn't tried to avert it.

When he emerged from the side of the beach hut, he saw Tamar waving at him. As she stood up and ran over to greet him, he felt a smile spread across his face, even while the dread deepened in his belly with every step he got closer to the happy crowd on the beach.

'Beausie!' she said. 'Where have you been, you freak? I've rung you a million times. So rude.'

'Sorry,' he said. 'I wasn't feeling well. Anyway, I'm here now and we're going to have a good time.'

'We already are, but it will be even better now you're here. I want you to meet my friends, you were helping Rey when they arrived. You're going to love them.' She grabbed his hand, but he gently pulled away.

'Let me just get a drink,' he said, hiding the unopened bottle he already had behind his back, 'and then I'll come and find you. Okay?'

'Well, don't be long,' said Tamar.

Pretending to take a fresh beer from one of the many icy tubs, he scanned the crowd to locate the person he was worried about seeing. There she was, sitting in the group Tamar had gone back to, with some people they'd met together at the Printworks bar and some others he didn't know. The challenge was how to get her on her own.

Just then Olive appeared, actually looking for a beer.

'Hey, baldie,' she said. 'You okay, mate?'

'Yeah, sorry about that. I was having a bit of a weird one.'

'No worries. It's a good party, it would have been a shame to miss it.'

'Ols, could you do me a small favour?'

'I'm not shaving your arse,' said Olive, laughing.

'Oh, you're no fun. Actually, it's about a girl.'

'I thought the whole point of your egg head was to keep you off that for a while.'

'It is,' he said, 'and I am still committed to the temporary celibacy thing, but there's a girl here I need to sort something out with about that, retrospectively.'

'Okay. Retrospective pork fork business?'

'Well, if you will put it so delicately. It's that one talking to Tamar now. Cool blonde hair. Very pretty.'

'Niamh?'

Was that her name? 'Um, yeah. Can you ask her – nicely – if she would come and speak to me, here, in the beach hut? I'll wait.'

'So is that one of your pillow rings she's wearing?'

Beau stared at her. 'How do you know about that?'

'It was in the paper,' said Olive. 'I went up to London, happened to see that issue of the *Standard*.'

'Why didn't you say anything?'

'Because your dad died and you'd already told me you were jacking in the one-night-stands gig when we did the head shave.'

'Wow,' said Beau. 'Thank you. Did you tell my mum?'

'Of course I bloody didn't,' said Olive. 'Right, I'm going to get Niamh for you. Get your speech ready.'

So Olive had known and Rey had known and they'd said nothing, which was great, but it did also make it more likely that other people knew. People like Tamar. As a former East End dweller who was totally across social media, he didn't see how she could not have heard about it – and now here was her friend, wearing a Mojobo ring. One of the 'victims'. Tamar hadn't said anything or been weird with him, but still, he was the new Beau now. He had to do the right thing.

He'd just sat down on a chair at the back of the hut when she walked in. He sprang up again. She really was very pretty.

'Hi, Niamh,' he said. 'Sorry, this is all a bit peculiar, but we've met before.'

She was looking at him with a puzzled expression, but when Beau put both his hands on his head, trying to think what to say next, her face broke into a smile.

'Oh, it's you!' she said, holding up her hand to show the ring with its big yellow stone. 'I didn't recognise you without your hair. You left me this fabulous ring.'

'I'm Beau,' he said, tentatively. 'I'm not sure we swapped names that night ...'

'No, we didn't,' said Niamh. 'No names, no numbers. I prefer it like that. Thanks for the ring, it was a lovely surprise.'

'Really?' said Beau. 'You weren't offended?'

'No. We had a good night and you weren't there when I woke up, which was a top result as far as I was concerned, and you left me this. I love it. I wear it all the time.'

'So did Tamar tell you I was here?'

Niamh looked puzzled. 'She told me the lady she was working with had a really hot son and there are lots of other smokin' guys down here, so Yewande and I broke the land speed record getting to the station and here I am.'

'She didn't say I was the "ring guy"?'

'No. Why would she? She doesn't know who I got this ring from.'

'I'm so relieved you're not upset with me. Somebody was recently and it's been rather difficult.'

'Oh, yeah,' said Niamh. 'I saw those stupid posters. What a bunny boiler. Anyway, there's a great party happening out there – and don't worry, I won't say anything to anyone. If someone recognises the ring as one of yours, I'll just say I bought it. Where could I have done that?'

'There's a shop on Borough Market that sells them,' he said.

'There you are, we have our story. Come on then, let's party down.'

Beau threw back his head and howled like a wolf, then ran out of the hut.

*

Now Beau was there – and looking like he was having a good time – Sophie really started to enjoy herself. And it was so lovely having Sebastian there too, the perfect alternative wing man to Rey, who was, quite rightly, having his own seriously good time. Sebastian remembered Charlie from the housewarming and they'd formed a little group, sitting on one of the blankets with him and Cicely.

'Sophie has discovered the joys of saltmarsh hogget,' said Cicely, when Charlie re-joined them with fresh tins of his chilled fizz.

'Ah, yes, salty coastal living, you've got to love it,' said Charlie.

'There are so many good local producers around here,' said Sophie. 'I'm having a great time discovering them all – and I still haven't seen your setup, Charlie.'

'Oh, that's a treat,' said Cicely. 'It's so great to see the land being used so well. Before Charlie decided to make the big move, we had a tenant farmer and we weren't happy with the way it was going with him, so it's a great thing all round.'

There was a lot of 'we' in that statement, Sophie noted, for people who weren't living together. Perhaps she could ask Thomas what the scenario was. Not that it mattered, but it would be good to know.

'It must have been a big deal to start something like that from scratch,' Sebastian was saying.

'It was,' said Charlie. 'But I needed a challenge at that point in my life and it gave me an excuse to go and do a course in Champagne, so that was a bonus.'

'I wouldn't mind that homework,' said Sebastian, raising his can, and they all laughed.

'We're going to start picking soon,' said Charlie. 'You can both come and help if you like. It's great fun.'

Sophie was about to ask Charlie about his production methods when a great cheer went up and they turned round to see a group of young men in swimming trunks – Beau in his undies – holding something aloft and heading towards the shoreline.

It took Sophie a moment to realise their cargo was a person. Rey. 'Put me down, you horrible little bullies!' he was shrieking.

'I'll swap places with you,' shouted Tippy, bringing up the rear as they passed Sophie and co at some speed.

'I've got to see this,' said Sophie, jumping to her feet. 'Rey has never swum in the sea before.'

'I think we should all go in,' said Charlie, taking off his shirt and pulling down his trousers to reveal board shorts with a bright sunflower print.

Sebastian did the same, and after a shared girly giggle, Sophie and Cicely shrugged off their dresses and they chased after the group, along with what seemed like most of the party.

Charlie ran ahead – clearly pretty fit for his age – and into the sea, so he was in before anyone else, with Sebastian following close behind, in what Sophie suspected was the usual spirit of Crommelin competitiveness. She arrived at the water's edge just as the boys slowed down and started to wade in, still holding Rey high. She was really hoping they weren't planning to dump him from a great height.

'Just a bit further, Rey,' said Beau. 'It's not cold at all, nothing worse than your average gin and tonic, three ice cubes. Maybe four. We're going to submerge you gently, like a baptism. Not of fire, of lovely sea water.'

'Get me out of here this minute!' screamed Rey.

'Okay, team,' said Beau – it would be him, thought Sophie, clearly fully recovered from his wobble. 'On three. One ... two ... three.'

And then they lowered Rey, fully clothed apart from his shoes, into the water.

Sophie watched in horror as his body seemed to go rigid as it hit the water, rather than bending into it to stand up again or to start swimming or floating – and his head went right under.

That was when she realised: Rey couldn't swim. That's why he didn't go in the sea. He just pottered about in the shallow end of swimming pools and got out again.

Understanding the gravity of the situation, she ran into the water towards her friend, but before she could get to him, she saw somebody was already there, holding Rey in a gentle but reassuring grip with his head above the water.

It was Charlie.

'There,' he was saying. 'We're all good. Do you want to get out?'

Rey spluttered and wiped the hair out of his eyes.

'You little fucker,' he said, pointing at Beau, who was looking a little abashed. 'You nearly drowned me. All these years I've been your devoted uncle and that's the thanks I get. Murdered!'

But he didn't look as though he minded as much as he was saying. In fact, Sophie could see he was thoroughly enjoying the attention. He turned back to look at Charlie, who was still holding on to him loosely.

'And hello to you, Silver Fox Baywatch Charlie. The last time we met you were fully clothed. I think I like you better like this.'

'Do you want to get out of the water now?' said Charlie.

'Not if you stay in to look after me,' said Rey.

'Okay,' said Charlie. 'Want a swimming lesson?'

'Does that mean you'll let go of me?'

'No. I'll just hold you in different places.'

'Ooh!' said Rey. 'Hold me anywhere, Charlie. I'm liking this party more all the time.'

Sophie looked round for Cicely and swam over to her.

'Do you think Charlie minds?' she asked her. 'Rey is flirting outrageously with him. I can practically feel the breeze from his eyelash batting over here.'

'Of course not,' said Cicely. 'I'm sure he's loving it. Charlie's secretly quite vain about his physique.'

'Do you mind?'

'Why on earth would I mind?'

'Well, some women don't like gay men hitting on their partners, even in jest.'

Cicely threw back her head and hooted with laughter. 'Did you think Charlie was my husband?'

'Well, I didn't know ...' That's why she had carefully said 'partner'. Boyfriend?

'He's my brother!'

'Oh,' said Sophie, her hands flying up to her mouth, feeling like a prize idiot. 'I'm so sorry. I just thought, actually I don't know what I thought.'

'Well, we didn't tell you, so how could you have known?' said Cicely, laughing. 'It was very rude of us, sorry, then we were talking about "our" land, so I can see why you thought that, but it's the family property, not ours as a couple.'

'I see,' said Sophie. 'That is a relief. I've been feeling really bad that I didn't invite you when Charlie came for supper.'

Cicely laughed. 'Well, I was at home in Hampshire with my actual husband. But I did hear about the dinner. He had a great time.' She paused. 'I think he's really enjoying getting to know some different people down here,' she continued, sounding as though she were picking her words carefully.

'Charlie was very vulnerable when he made the big decision to came back to the house. He'd had a tough time and was pretty chewed up. It's been great for him, working on the land, creating something amazing, but most of the people he knows here are from our parents' social world or old work contacts – so the same old, same old. He really needs a fresh milieu for the new man he is and these –' she gestured around them, lots of guests fooling about in the water, the distinctive sound of reggae beats drifting down from the beach hut, laughter filling the air '– look like exactly the people he needs.'

Charlie suddenly appeared, popping up like a seal after swimming over to them underwater. 'That was fun,' he said, shaking his head to get the water off and then slicking his hair back with his hands.

Sophie blinked. It suited him. Showed off his tanned face and blue eyes. He looked like a man who worked outside, in a good way.

'Thank God, you were there, Charlie,' she said. 'I only realised as he hit the water like a plank that he couldn't swim. In thirty years of friendship and many joint holidays, he's never confessed that to me.'

'Well,' said Charlie. 'That is why I raced to get in the water first. They've all had a few relaxing beverages and the most well-intentioned pranks can go horribly wrong in those circs.'

Sophie thought she saw something in his expression change as he said it, but just for a fleeting moment and then his smile returned.

'Now I can see the family likeness,' she said, looking from one to the other.

'Sophie thought we were married,' said Cicely.

Charlie laughed. 'Oh, that's a good one,' he said, 'but I should have introduced you properly, I do apologise. Cicely is happily married to my dear brother-in-law.'

'Did someone say brother-in-law?' said Sebastian, swimming up. 'Sophie has four of us, which I hope is a blessing rather than a curse, but she's had plenty of time to get used to our funny little ways.'

Then he disappeared under the water, popping up again suddenly between her legs and standing up so she was sitting on his shoulders. She shrieked and grabbed his head for balance while Charlie did the same thing with Cicely. The two men ran through the water, the women squealing happily above them.

All around, people did the same thing – Beau scooped up Tippy – play fighting and jumping up and down, until the sea was a white foam of splashing as the shoulder-riders fell off, only to be scooped up again by someone else.

Sophie was breathless from laughing as she climbed back onto Sebastian's shoulders to do further battle with Beau and Tippy, thinking nothing, just being in the joyous moment, surrounded by people she loved.

She wanted it to last forever.

CHAPTER 24

Beau was going round the big trade show at London Fashion Week. Every season, he found a way to get in to check out the competition and schmooze contacts among designers exhibiting their collections and the buyers and stylists looking at them. He was always photographed by influencers, which was good for getting the brand name out there, but this time, he felt a little less confident than usual about his appearance, since he'd so rashly shaved his head.

There was one good thing about that, though. When he'd got back to Hackney after his two-week break in Hastings, he'd seen Flora sitting in of one of his favourite cafés and she hadn't spotted him as he'd walked past. He was sure she would have if he'd still had his old hair.

He'd pared down the rest of his look to balance out the new barnet, swapping his wafty white silk shirts and trailing scarves for tight, plain black t-shirts. He didn't think he looked too much like the waiter he actually was again. He had one of his rings hanging round his neck on a fine gold chain, his fingers were generously furnished with them as usual and he was hoping being less extravagantly dressed and coiffed would make his jewellery the focus of attention.

This time, he was particularly looking out for buyers, because he wanted more retail outlets; he only had the one. He got some online sales from his Instagram feed and he was doing well to already have a loyal base of clients who were repeat purchasers, but he wanted the visibility and kudos of being in some premium West End shops. Liberty was his dream goal.

'Hey, Beau!' he heard someone call out.

He turned and there was Yewande, walking towards him down the aisle between stands, holding a coffee.

'Hey, Yewande,' he said, going over and kissing her on the cheek. 'I was just coming to find you. Thanks so much for getting me the entry pass. It will be so nice to have a base I can retreat back to when it gets too much. I always find doing this show a uniquely stressful experience.'

'Have you ever had a stand at it?'

'No, I just cruise around like a desperate loser, hoping to get noticed.'

Yewande laughed. 'So, status normal for you then,' she said. 'But if you want to know real stress, you should try having a stand. You still feel like a desperate loser – and you've paid several thousand pounds for the privilege. I'm just round the corner, in the cheap seats. Come with me now, I need to get back. I was gasping for a coffee, but if I don't hurry I might miss the buyer from Selfridges wanting to buy the entire collection.'

Her stand looked great. She'd covered the walls with dark brown hessian and placed bamboo furniture and big plants round the edge of the stand to break up the view from outside and make it look intriguing.

'It's very impactful,' said Beau. 'There's no question about your look.'

'Thank you,' said Yewande. 'It was also very cheap. I had to get a loan from my uncle to have this stand. The furniture is from my flat – originally from Facebook Marketplace.' She burst out laughing and Beau joined in. 'Can you stay a while? You're a good accessory. Buyers will think you're from a chic boutique in Paris and they'll be terrified to miss out on my amazing clothes.'

'Get out your order book,' said Beau. 'Let's make it look serious.'

He flicked through the rails, pulling things out and holding them up as though he was appraising them, then putting different pieces together in groups.

'So what is the percentage if I buy ten of each style?' he asked loudly in a fake French accent as some women walked past, glancing at the stand. They did a double take and stopped, then came onto the stand. Beau caught Yewande's eye and waggled his eyebrows.

She went over to the women, who seemed to be looking at the clothes with genuine interest. 'Do let me know if you have any questions,' she said.

Beau pretended to be studying a collar in great detail. 'I'll say I'm going to find my business partner,' he whispered when Yewande came over, 'and I'll come back in hour with more coffee.'

'That's great, Jean-François,' said Yewande in a slightly raised tone. 'I will see you and Renée in a little while.'

'A bientôt, ma cherie,' said Beau. 'I will be back shortly to close the deal.'

The fun with Yewande made him feel better – and gave his confidence a welcome boost. Maybe he hadn't lost all his mojo with his hair after all, which gave him the courage to do one of the things he'd specifically come to the exhibition for – to find the Giuliette stand.

Since having a glimpse of her work in the *Style* section, he'd looked at the website and been even more impressed. Her name was Juliet Mylan and she'd started off pretty much like him: making stuff and selling it, getting her break in Fenwick and then being used in shoots by *Vogue* and the other glossies. He loved the bold style of her jewellery – and he thought she might like his stuff too. It had the same sense of unrestrained glamour.

At first he'd thought of visiting the shop in Walton Street, but going to her stand at this trade fair seemed more professional and casual – he was there because he was also in the industry and he'd just happened to stumble upon her wares ...

The exhibition guide showed that her stand – a big one, by the look of it – was in the special invitation-only area of the show, where all the biggest London fashion names were located. And when he got there, he couldn't miss it: the Giuliette stand was mobbed. There was no way he would be able to get a proper look at the jewellery with so many bodies there, let alone meet her. Feeling deflated, he walked round for a bit, bumping into a couple of stylists he knew, then he picked up some coffees and headed back to Yewande.

'Hey, Bobo,' she said when she saw him. 'Get up here, my beautiful good luck charm.'

He stepped up onto the stand and handed her the drink. 'Well, hello to you. What have I done to deserve this welcome?'

'Those women who came up when you were giving your Oscar-worthy performance placed an order – and when another buyer saw me writing it up, they came to look and ordered too – and then another one.'

'Wow, Yewande. That's fantastic.'

'Those three orders have paid for having this stand and more. So thank you.'

'Well, thank you for getting me in here.'

'What have you seen on your travels?' she asked as they sat down.

'There's a jewellery brand I really wanted to look at. But it was so mobbed, it was hopeless. It's called Giuliette.' *Gwillet.*

'I don't know it.'

'It's fantastic gear. I want to meet the designer and ask her advice. I think she'd like my stuff, but I don't know how to get near.'

Yewande looked thoughtful, taking a sip from her coffee. 'There are two things you could try,' she said. 'You could come back first thing tomorrow and catch her before the crowds build up – but people can be very focussed then, getting ready for their day, so what might be better is to go back just before closing tonight. After a day of this you start to get a bit of demob fever just before home time, so you might just catch her in a good mood. And if it's a leading brand, she won't leave before the end. None of the really successful people do. Last year, I got my biggest order five minutes before the end on the last day.'

'You are a genius, Yewande,' said Beau. 'I'm going to try that. Meanwhile I'll do a bit more method acting on your stand.'

*

Sure enough, when Beau got back to the Giuliette area two hours later, it was deserted, with just one woman sitting off to the side, absorbed with something on a laptop.

He took his time examining the display. The pieces were even better in real life than in the pictures. The close work – the settings of the stones, the earring hooks, clasps, closures and chains – was all really finely done. That made such a difference and was one of the things he made a big effort with himself.

He was so absorbed in the jewellery, he didn't realise someone had come over to where he was standing.

'Do you like it?'

Beau looked up to see Juliet Mylan smiling down at him from the slightly higher level on the other side of the counter. She was very beautiful in real life. He hadn't been expecting that.

'I love it,' said Beau. 'I can't tell you how much.' He lifted up his hands to show her his rings. 'I'm a jeweller too and I aspire with all my heart to do work as fine as this.'

She smiled at him, then looked at his rings. 'Will you take them off? I'd like to see them properly.'

Then she pulled a black velvet pad out from under the counter for him to put his rings on, which he thought was incredibly cool – but also made him worry that his things would look shabby next to her beautiful pieces.

Juliet picked up the loupe that was hanging on a chain round her neck and put it to her eye to study Beau's rings. 'I really like them,' she said. 'Do you have a brand? Where do you sell?'

'My brand is Mojobo. I mostly sell off Instagram. I've got some loyal repeat clients from that. Mostly people in the music business.'

Juliet smiled. 'I can see your work would appeal to that demographic. So does mine. Do you have any retail outlets?'

'One shop,' he said, 'in Borough Market. My studio is round the corner from there. I would love to be in more shops. Liberty is my goal.'

'Well, your work is more than good enough for there, but I do know how hard it is to get into that first proper outlet.'

She smiled at him and Beau decided to go for it.

'Actually,' he said, 'I know it's cheeky, but I was wondering, would you consider letting me come and do some work experience with you? I'd be happy to do anything to help. I'll sweep up, make tea, collect your dry cleaning …'

'I tell you what,' she said, stepping back from the edge of the display case to show him her tummy. 'As you can see, I'm about to have a baby. Possibly while we're standing here talking …'

'There's definitely something in there.'

'So, I'm not going to be around at work for a while, but I'll give you the email of my assistant, Octavia, so you can contact her and arrange the work experience. I'll tell her you're going to be in touch. What's your name?'

Just as he answered, the tannoy in the exhibition hall came on, loudly announcing that it was five minutes until closing and all visitors should make their way to the exits – drowning him out.

'Okay, Bob,' said Juliet, handing him a business card. 'I'll tell Octavia to expect your email and I'll look forward to seeing you in the studio or the shop – or the dry cleaners – when I come back.'

'Thank you so much,' said Beau, registering that she had called him Bob, but thinking it would be rude to correct her. He was still wondering what to do when the tannoy sounded again.

'Oops,' said Juliet, 'I better go. I've got to lock all this up. See you soon, Bob!'

Beau walked out of the exhibition hall feeling as though he had grown wings. What a result! How lovely she was. How amazing that he was going to work in her studio.

He could handle being called Bob for that.

CHAPTER 25

Juliet was in a box at the O2 Arena to see Elton John. Rachel had invited her to join them with what she'd described as 'our favourite clients and journos', although it seemed to be mainly Rachel's family. Her mother was there and her two sisters – one with her good-looking husband, who Juliet recognised from his TV show, and two of their sons, the other with her wife.

Seeing how well they all got on – the box was ringing with laughter – Juliet absently stroked her bump, feeling more happy than ever that Cassady was going to have a sibling, to have this kind of connection in her life. Something Juliet had never known.

She was at the bar table getting a refill of sparkling water when she felt a hand rest on her stomach. On her baby. She flinched, water going everywhere as she pulled back.

A man she didn't know was smiling at her. 'Such a miracle,' he was saying, reaching his hand out to touch her again.

Juliet put her own hand in the way. 'Do you mind?' she said. 'Do you normally go around touching strangers' bodies uninvited?'

'But we're not strangers,' said the man, his smile more of a smirk. 'I'm Chaz Dowdent. Don't you remember? We met at darling Kiki's lunch.'

Juliet hoped her expression hadn't shown her instant distress. Kiki Wilmott was a very good client. It wasn't a good idea to have a standoff with someone who was – even allegedly – a friend of hers.

'Oh, yes,' said Juliet, who remembered the lunch, but not meeting this horrible man at it. 'How are you?'

'Marvellous, as always,' he said. 'But how are you, going again with the rug rats? You're a sucker for punishment.' He laughed loudly.

'Yes, I'm very happy to be having another child, thank you,' said Juliet, realising she was now at the end of the table, her back against the wall. This Chaz person was standing a little bit too close to her. She glanced over his shoulder, but everyone was caught up chatting and laughing.

'It must be a bit lonely,' he said. 'Doing it all on your own, but I've heard you have plenty of nannies to look after them, which is the only way to do it. Gives you a little private time for yourself. But it must get a bit empty without a man in your life, just your business and the brats … Perhaps you need someone to come over, to cheer you up a bit?'

He was getting closer. Juliet wondered if she would even be heard over all the happy chatter in the box and the music on the arena's PA system if she called out.

'Because you must know about the power of a pregnancy orgasm,' he said. 'So intense, from the increased blood flow to the groin. You wouldn't want to miss out on those …'

He was so close now he was touching her protruding belly with his own. She could smell his horrible breath.

'There you are, Juliet,' said Rachel, grabbing her arm and literally pulling her out of the corner where Chaz had her trapped. 'I've been looking everywhere. Come on, there are people I need to introduce you to, before the show starts.' She turned to Chaz, smiling with fake brightness. 'And Simon is longing to talk to you, Chaz. He's got a special cigar for you. A really big one. He's just outside the door of the box, if you want to pop out there.'

Rachel linked arms with Juliet. 'What a disgusting arse,' she whispered. 'I'm so sorry. He's a hateful old sleaze, but he's been Simon's client since he started the business and he's always refused get rid of him. Some misplaced idea of loyalty. But it's going to happen now. Simon's furious. Are you alright?'

Juliet let out a quivery breath, glad she had Rachel to lean against. 'I am a bit wobbly. You know how extra sensitive you are when you're pregnant? But I couldn't be too rude, because he's good friends with one of my clients, so we're in the same boat on that one. He kept touching my bump and talking about pregnancy orgasms.'

'Ugh,' said Rachel, pulling a disgusted face. 'The thought of it. I'm so sorry you had to endure that, but let's try and make everything lovely, so you can forget about it and enjoy the show.'

She led the way down the steps to the seats. 'Here we are. This is my mum, Joy, sit down next to her while I get you a fresh drink. Then I'll be right behind you with Simon. Creepy Chaz won't be getting anywhere near you again tonight, Juliet, you can rely on that.'

Juliet turned to see an older lady smiling at her.

'Hello, dear,' she said, laying her hand gently on Juliet's shoulder, in a gesture that felt reassuring, completely different from the intrusive way that awful Chaz had touched her. 'I'm so glad Rachel got you and your baby away from that horrible man. Just take some quiet breaths. You're safe here.'

Juliet smiled at her, already feeling better, then Rachel came back with the promised water and a plate of cheeses, with gherkins and cherry tomatoes. No bread or crackers – she knew Juliet well.

'Sleazebag has gone,' she said. 'Simon has ejected him from the box and sacked him as a client, so win-win. Now just have a good time – and look who I've got to sit on your other side.'

Juliet looked up to see Dottie grinning at her, flashing rainbows bouncing from springs on a headband. She was also wearing one of the more garish t-shirts Juliet had seen on the merchandise stands on the way in and a purple feather boa.

'What do you think?' she asked. 'Too much?'

'Never too much for Elton,' said Juliet, laughing, as Dottie sat down next to her, leaning past her to blow a kiss to Joy.

The three of them chatted excitedly about their favourite Elton tracks and as the lights went down and the first unmistakable bars of 'Bennie and the Jets' rang out, Juliet felt enclosed in warmth and friendship.

It was almost like having a family.

CHAPTER 26

Sophie was at the O2 arena, taking a video of Thomas and Bella, who were standing in front of a large poster of Elton John, in his full 1970s pomp, wearing angel wings and oversized diamante-encrusted spectacles. Thomas and Bella were also sporting feature specs, with flashing lights around the frames. Bella was dressed in a bright-pink sequinned trouser suit and rainbow platform boots.

'Has she explained to you yet,' Sebastian said into Sophie's ear, from behind her, 'that the suit is Gucci and the boots are Balenciaga? Just in case you thought she was cutting loose to have a good time.'

Sophie giggled. 'She did mention it,' she said, 'but good on Bella, getting into the swing of it, even if it is all from Bond Street.'

'She's only doing it for the business. That video you've just taken is for the company socials.'

'Stop being such a Grinchy cynic,' said Sophie, poking him in the ribs with her forefinger, as they followed Thomas and Bella towards the entrance. 'It's incredibly nice of them to include us in this, because you're right, it is really an event for their clients.'

'A tax deduction.'

'Stop it! We're getting to see Elton – SIR ELTON! – in a swishy corporate box, with a top view and no doubt lashings of fizz and tasty snacks. It's such a shame Freya couldn't come, though. Did she have a work thing?'

'She's still Stateside. As she probably calls it now. She's getting rather assimilated.'

'Is that alright for you?'

'I suppose so,' he said. 'The boys come and see their old man and I stay at work later out of choice, but I do feel a bit lost knocking around the house on my own – but you know what that's like more than I do.'

'I haven't really had to face up to it yet. Tamar is pretty much living with me while we do the book and Beau was down for a fortnight, but I'll have to get used to it sometime.'

'Having had a taste of it myself now, I'll make bloody sure you come up regularly to stay with us.'

He and Sophie held back while Thomas and Bella greeted some of the people who were joining them in the box, with the usual rounds of back-slapping between the men, while Bella greeted the wives with air kisses. Sophie noticed there seemed to be just one woman among the work connections and she saw Thomas automatically raise his hand to do the 'good man' back slap on her but then he hesitated, hand hovering in mid-air, before patting her lightly on the shoulder, looking self-conscious.

She heard a quiet snort from Sebastian.

'Thommo just swerved one there,' he said. 'Nearly back-slapped himself into an assault charge. He's such a gorilla.'

When they got to the box, Thomas and the bankers converged at the bar while the wives gathered round the food table.

Sebastian nudged her. 'While they're all gasbagging and pretending to eat, we can grab the best seats, then I'll nip back up and get us some goodies.'

From the moment the music started – 'Bennie and the Jets' – Sophie was transported. Every time Elton started a new number, she and Sebastian turned to each other in glee, standing up to dance in front of their seats during all the rocky ones – which made the people behind them get up too.

Sebastian glanced round during 'I'm Still Standing'. 'They are all standing,' he said to Sophie. 'Some of them are even dancing slightly. I think that's why Thomas wanted us here – as well as a jolly for the fam – because he knew we'd get the atmosphere going. Otherwise they'd all be sitting there like blocks of salt, thinking about bonds and yields.'

With that in mind, they laid it on thicker, starting a Mexican wave and turning round to high five the people right behind them. During 'Blue Eyes', Sebastian got everyone swaying with their arms in the air, phone torches held aloft.

Sophie was having a ball, borne away by the music and the atmosphere, able to put all the troubles of the past few months completely out of her mind for quite long stretches of time.

Then he played 'Tiny Dancer'.

From the very first note it hit her, like an Exocet missile to the chest. Sophie had done ballet to a high level while she was at school and Matt had always loved to watch her dance. He'd filmed her on a flat sand beach in Wales, with himself humming 'Tiny Dancer' over the top. The song had always been special to them, and his brothers had included the clip in the photo and video montage at his funeral.

As Elton continued to play the exquisitely tinkling notes of the introduction, Sophie felt like she was suffocating from the pain of her loss. It felt physical. She had to get away from that music.

Somehow getting to her feet, incredibly grateful she only had to get past Sebastian to reach the aisle, she ran up the steps to the door and out of the box. But even on the upper walkway of the arena, leaning back against the wall with her hands over her ears, the song – as familiar as her own heartbeat – filled the space and swamped her brain.

She heard herself let out something like a strangled cry before the violent tears came. She was just about to sink to the floor when she felt someone's hands clasp her shoulders.

'I'm here, Sophie,' said Sebastian. 'I've got you.'

She sank against him, feeling his arms go round her, as she sobbed into his shoulder.

He gently stroked her head. 'It's okay, dear girl,' he said. 'Let it out. The song will be over soon.'

But it seemed to Sophie to go on forever, with every note and every word bringing an image of Matt into her head. Not the cruel stranger of that final day, but the real Matt, the one who had loved her, who called her his Tiny Dancer. The one who drew endless pictures of her and told her every day how much he loved her. How she completed his world.

In those few minutes, it felt as though she re-lived every moment they'd ever spent together.

Finally the song finished and Sophie felt herself slump.

'I'm getting you out of here,' said Sebastian and he lifted her up and carried her all the way to the exit. Sophie buried her face in his neck, soaking his collar with her tears.

'Here we are,' he said, when they got out into the fresh evening air. 'Do you think you can stand up now?'

Sophie nodded and he lowered her gently until her feet touched the ground. She leant against him like a newborn foal with its mother.

She had no idea how long they stood there like that, vaguely aware of Sebastian fiddling with his phone, but eventually a shiny black car arrived and he helped her into it.

'We're going to Thomas's place,' he said. 'You can go to straight to bed, so you won't have to see them when they get back and I'm going to stay over there too, to make sure you're okay in the morning and to protect you from Bella's more intrusive good intentions.'

Sophie didn't say anything. She couldn't speak. She just rested her head against Sebastian's shoulder and, when he put his arm round her, pulling her close, she closed her eyes and tried just to be.

CHAPTER 27

Beau was starting his second week at Giuliette's Walton Street HQ – and now he knew how to pronounce it. Like Juliet, just with a weird Italian spelling, no doubt to look posher.

After getting buzzed in at the front door, which was always locked, he headed straight up to the workshop on the top floor. The shop and Juliet's office were on the ground floor, the workshop was at the top and in the basement there more offices and a safe inside a strong room, where the gold and platinum ingots and precious stones were kept, with all kinds of security protocols in place for moving the raw materials and finished pieces around the building.

Juliet was officially on maternity leave now, but she still popped in every day – sometimes twice – rushing from room to room, talking very fast.

Beau felt pretty energised himself, running up the stairs two at a time, excited to get started.

'Morning, young Bob,' said Larry, the senior jeweller, opening the workshop door after Beau had pressed the buzzer – he wasn't allowed to know the security code yet.

'Morning, Larry,' said Beau and then turned to the other jeweller, who was head down, hard at work in the corner. 'Morning, Somchai. Did you both have a nice weekend?'

'Very nice, thank you, young sir,' said Larry. 'But not so good I couldn't happily avail myself of one of your excellent mugs of tea this morning.'

'I can do better than that,' said Beau, opening his messenger bag and fishing around. He held up a packet of chocolate digestives. 'I got you something to go with it.'

'Smart lad. You know how the world turns. I imagine you're hoping to get your busy little fingers on some of the merchandise again today?'

'Well, that would be amazing. I am happy to carry on making tea and sweeping the floor as well, but I did love sizing that ring last week. It was so wonderful to work with something properly good, so if there's anything else I can do to help out, I'm at your service. But I do also enjoy just watching you two work, if it's not too annoying.'

It was true, they were both fine jewellers of great experience – Larry had trained in Hatton Garden and Somchai in Bangkok – and they'd worked at some of the biggest names in London. Juliet had poached Somchai from Graff, which had been a big deal. Her PA, Octavia, had told Beau all about it when he'd taken her out for coffee.

Larry was right, Beau thought, as he got busy with the tea, he did know how the world turned. A packet of biscuits here, an oatmilk latte there, compliments and friendly chats all round, that was how. Something else he'd learned from his father – be nice to people, make a little extra effort, but mean it. That was the secret.

When it came to the jewellery, Beau had learned loads already leaning over Larry's and Somchai's shoulders, watching them, and they seemed to enjoy showing off their skills to someone who truly appreciated them.

He'd just taken off his suit jacket and was running a mental check of how they each took their brews when Octavia came running up the stairs and punched the security code to open the workshop door.

'Bob,' she said, sticking her head round it, 'Juliet wants you downstairs, now. Her office.'

'Sorry, I haven't finished making your tea, guys,' said Beau, wiping his hands on his trousers and shrugging his jacket on again as he headed for the door. He knew from what he'd seen of her visits to the building that when Juliet said 'now' she meant that very moment, if not sooner.

Beau found her sitting on the bright red modernist armchair in the corner of her office. Her pregnant belly really was quite something now, protruding out of her slim frame like a Zeppelin.

'Hi, Bob,' she said. 'Apologies for the state of me. I can't fit behind my desk any more. This is probably the last time I'll be in for a few days and I just wanted to check in with you. Is everything okay?'

'I'm having a fantastic time,' he said. 'Larry and Somchai have been so kind, letting me watch their every move like the jewellery wonk I am.'

'Larry was very pleased with that ring you sized. And I did ask him to find some more stuff for you to do.'

'Thank you so much. I'd be delighted to.'

'But actually, there's something else I would love you to

help with. I'm short-handed in the shop, so I wondered if you would like to do a week's training in there with Luiza and then if works out, you can start in there as a paid job. You fit in so well here and you're dressed well enough to start work there now, if you would like to.'

'Wow,' said Beau, his brain whirring into gear. It would be working in the shop rather than being up in the hands-on action of the workshop, which was really his thing, but it would give him great insight into customers to see what people really responded to at this level. That could be invaluable for his own business And he could give up the waitering.

'I would love that,' he said.

'Great,' said Juliet. 'Octavia will introduce you to Gwen, who does payroll and all that. She'll be in this afternoon.'

With great difficulty, she started to lever herself out of the chair and Beau rushed over to help, offering his arm for her to pull herself up.

'Phew,' she said, making it to her feet. 'I just wanted to stand up to shake your hand to welcome you to the team.'

'I'm honoured to be part of your amazing business.'

She patted him on the shoulder and headed off towards the back office.

In the shop, Luiza, a beautiful but hard-faced Portuguese woman, appraised him from top to bottom, and Beau was glad he was wearing his best suit, a Helmut Lang his father had bought in the nineties. He always felt great in it.

Luiza seemed satisfied with what she saw and showed him how to work the till and then moved on to the more specific details of how to serve the customers.

'Okay, Bob,' she said, in her heavily accented but precise voice. 'Let's get serious.' She ushered him out from behind the counter. 'You are the customer and I will serve you. If any real customers come in while we are playing, look busy while watching what I do, okay?'

Beau nodded, taking his place on the customer side and looking back at her. With her shiny black bob and tight-fitting suit she really did look marvellous behind that counter of brightly coloured jewels. Softened by two huge rings and some earrings from the collection, her severe style set the pieces off perfectly.

'Good morning, sir. Is there anything I can help you with today?' she asked, smiling at him as though he were her long-lost son.

Beau pretended to browse the merchandise, which he already knew off by heart; he'd studied the display cases so many times since he'd been there. 'It's my wife's birthday tomorrow,' he said in a wide-boy accent. 'The old trouble and strife.'

Luiza smiled, clearly pleased he knew how to play along.

'I was thinking to get her a ring. Something sprauncy. What would you suggest?'

'Is it a special birthday?'

'Not particularly, but I've been a bit of a naughty boy recently, so I think I better get her something decent.'

'How naughty? No, don't answer that, I am joking.' She gave a little cough, one elegant hand resting on her chest, little finger raised, and resumed her more formal manner. 'Well, we have these new pieces, which have just come down from the studio. No one else has seen them yet.'

Beau's eyebrows went up.

'You see?' said Luiza. 'You have to make them feel special, like it's just for them. Then you show them the most expensive pieces, like this ...'

She opened the display cabinet with a key from a set hanging on a chain at her waist and placed a navy blue velvet tray inside, where the customer would be able to see it. With delicate fingers, she lifted up a large ring with a Cubist-style woman's head on it and placed it on the tray. Then, with a grace of movement worthy of a sacred rite, she placed the velvet tray on the countertop and gently pushed it towards Beau with both hands, her pinkie fingers exquisitely raised.

'The push is very important. You are offering it to them.' She gestured with her hands.

Beau wondered if she had once been a ballet dancer. He'd have to work on his hand dancing. Possibly get a manicure.

'That's not bad,' he said, picking up the ring roughly and thrusting it onto his forefinger before striking a pose. He turned to look at himself in the mirror on the opposite wall.

'At this point,' said Luiza, 'you don't take your eyes off them. He has turned away from me with the piece, but I am watching him in the mirror on the wall opposite. Now, sir, do you think your wife would like this?'

'I'm not sure,' he said. 'She's a bit fat, so maybe something a bit smaller, so she feels dainty.'

Smiling sweetly, Luiza presented the tray to him, making it clear he was to put the ring back on it.

'And so we take that piece back into safety, before we offer another. It is essential to keep track of the pieces. If you have a few out, they can do a simple sleight of hand in an instant and be out the door before you realise.'

'But the door is always locked, isn't it?'

'Yes, but the experienced thieves are so clever. They thank you politely, you open the door for them and you don't realise something is missing until they're in a car on Brompton Road on their way to the M25.'

'Has that ever happened to you?'

'No,' said Luiza. 'But I've seen other people get done over when I worked in Bond Street. The secret is never take your eye off the jewellery and as you can't have your eyes in more than one place, you only ever have one piece in play.'

'What if they say they want to compare two pieces, side by side, to choose?'

'Good question. You let them hold one piece and you hold the other. You do it in a way that – unless they actually are a thief and are watching the hands as closely as you are – they won't even notice, and then you swap, with you taking the piece from them, before you give them the one you are holding. You do have to pay close attention at the swap, but you'll be fine. You have fine hands. Some people have hands like spades.' She presented hers with a speedy flourish of fingers. 'They can't do this job.'

They continued with the role play, Beau enjoying himself as the tacky husband who said he wanted to buy something nice, but then tried to be cheap about how much he spent.

Luiza continued to show him rings, then earrings and a necklace – all carefully one at a time – until he made his choice.

'Very good,' she said. 'Now is there anything you noticed there?'

'Beyond how eagle-eyed and tricky-fingered I have to be?' he asked. 'I think you could do close-up magic.'

'Remember the price you just paid for the earrings for your fat wife?'

'Three thousand, seven hundred and ninety-five pounds?'

'And can you remember how much the other things I showed you were?'

Beau thought for a moment. 'That first ring was ten grand, wasn't it?'

'Yes. The first two things I showed you were the most expensive, then I showed you something quite a lot cheaper, that just wasn't quite so special – then I showed you three things in the middle and you bought the third most expensive piece I showed you.'

'Is that good?' asked Beau, beginning to feel daunted by what he'd taken on. He normally priced his stuff at triple cost, then twenty per cent above that and did a deal down to the original price.

'Yes,' said Luiza. 'Sometimes you will see that they can spend more, but for most people, it's like a wine list. You buy the third cheapest – not the cheapest. It's all psychology.'

'Do you ever sell the cheaper stuff and the most expensive stuff?'

'Yes, but we make our money in that sweet spot in the middle – and when I saw "we", I mean Juliet and us. We work on commission, Bob. You sell more, you make more. You will soon learn to judge what level customers are ready to spend at and make sure you get them to the very top of it.'

'So do you look to see if they've got a flash watch on or are carrying an Hermès handbag?'

'That can be a clue, but people dress up to come to shops like this and they will bring a carrier bag from another expensive store that is clearly not new. It's more instinctive to spot the high rollers, it's in their manner, their mood. People who are going to spend a lot might be scruffily dressed, but they have a casual confidence.'

'Do they ever ask for deals?'

Luiza laughed. 'Oh, yes, all the time – and the richest ones are the worst. Everyone thinks they are supposed to bargain. We smile and say, no, I'm so sorry, and we think, fuck off, you filthy cheapskate, try Primark. But some customers, special ones, who buy often – they get a discount. I will show you who they are as they come in. If I wink at you, it means I will take that customer and you will know it's one on my list. Memorise the face, so you don't forget if I'm not here. Even if it's a little spend, when it's often, we love them.'

Beau scratched his head and sighed. 'There's quite a lot to it, isn't there?'

Luiza shrugged. 'If it was easy it would be boring. This is a high stakes game and you will love it, I can tell. You've got the hunger – and you've got the looks, which is helpful. Right, now come behind here with me and I will show you the security system.'

He had just got behind the counter when Octavia poked her head through from the door to the back of the building.

'Hi, Bob,' she said. 'Gwen is available now. Come and tell her all your stuff so she can get put you on the payroll – as long as Luiza thinks you're up to the job.' She smiled.

'He's a natural,' said Luiza. 'And he's young and handsome. Sign him up.'

'Great,' said Octavia, 'but we will need to do a criminal-records check and all that before you start in the shop.'

Luiza mimed two fingers to her eyes and then one finger pointing at him and laughed. 'We don't take any risks, darling.' Then the buzzer for the shop door rang and the welcoming smile jumped back on to her face as she turned to see who was standing there before reaching down to buzz them in.

Beau followed Octavia down the stairs, where she introduced him to Gwen. If Luiza was like a Siamese cat, thought Beau, all sinuous limbs and cold calculation, Gwen was the little brown mouse she would chase and torture.

Gwen passed him a pile of forms and a pen. 'Can you fill these out please? And sign where I've marked it.'

Beau sat down, picked up the pen and looked at the top form. The first box he had to fill in stopped him: *Name*.

They all thought he was called Bob and to tell them now, when he'd been there a week already and had now been offered a full-time job, that he was actually called something else would make him sound like a total idiot. Or a jewel thief plant.

He cursed himself for not putting it right with Juliet the first time she'd called him 'Bob'. It would be even worse to do it now – but if he didn't put his real name on these forms, none of his data would match up and he wouldn't get the paid job. He rubbed his jaw, then filled in all the questions with his real name.

He picked up the finished forms and gave them back to Gwen. 'There's just one thing I have to explain,' he said, trying to sound shy and humble. 'You see, Gwen, everyone calls me Bob, but my official first name for National Insurance and

banking and criminal records and all that is really Beau. I just
don't ever use it because it's such an embarrassing name. I was
bullied about it badly at school. They used to call me Little
Bo Peep –' which was actually true, but he'd punched one of
them and they'd stopped '– so ever since then I've just gone by
good old simple Bob. Everybody calls me that.'

Everybody in here.

'I see,' said Gwen. 'So I will submit your details as Beau –'
she looked down at the form '– Crommelin, but you wish to
be known within the workplace as Bob?'

'That would be amazing, Gwen,' he said, quietly and
sincerely. He wasn't acting now. He really meant it. 'And I
would be so grateful if we could keep this between us. I would
hate people here to think I'd been dishonest, but that name has
been like a curse for me, I can hardly bear to say it.' *Steady on,
better not overdo it.*

'That's fine. It can be our little secret.' She smiled at him
and Beau saw that in her sweet, mousey way, she was actually
very pretty.

'Thank you,' he said, smiling back and as he headed back
to the shop to join Luiza, he made a mental note to buy Gwen
a special cupcake on his lunch break.

CHAPTER 28

Sophie pulled up in the yard next to Charlie's house, relieved to be stationary. Her sat nav had brought her straight there but the tiny winding lanes between tall hedgerows had been more stressful than driving on the M25 at peak hour; locals seemed to drive along them at crazy speeds.

She got out of the car, but there didn't seem to be any sign of life. Walking under a stone arch, she found the back door with a note pinned onto it.

Had to pop down to the vines. Back ASAP. Make yourself some tea. C

The door opened into the kitchen, which was all flagstones and beams, with an old white Aga, two butler's sinks and cupboards that looked as though they had been there since the 1920s. The space had such a lovely sense of having been used by generations of hands, it made Sophie feel queasy again about her brand new kitchen. Awfully new and awfully pink. Oh well, it would develop patina over time. A hundred years should do it.

She'd just sat down at the table with tea – after putting the cake she'd brought with her on a plate – feeling rather self-conscious to be making herself at home in a house where she'd never been before, when the door was thrown open and Charlie strode in.

'Sophie!' he said, coming over and kissing her cheek. 'I'm so sorry I wasn't here when you arrived. It's a bit hectic with the picking not far off.' He flopped down in a chair, arching his back and stretching out his legs. He was wearing the faded pink cords with braces he'd had on at her housewarming. And the pink boots.

Sophie immediately felt better. She had the Barbie pink kitchen, he had the wellies and trousers ... 'If it's a bad time, I can come another day,' she said.

'Not at all,' said Charlie, sitting up. 'It's the perfect time to see it in full grape before it all goes bonkers. Ooh, cake. Can I have a big bit? And some tea, please.'

He stood up and grabbed a mug from a hook. It was the size of a pint tankard and once Sophie had filled it, emptying the tea pot in the process, he drained it, then polished off the slice of cake in just a few bites. It reminded Sophie of the boys when they'd been permanently ravenous teenagers.

'Yum,' he said. 'Good cake. Can you leave me another bit for later?'

'I made it for you. It's all yours.'

'Excellent,' he said, jumping to his feet. 'Shall we go?'

Sophie followed him out to the yard, jogging slightly to keep up with his long strides. He seemed quite different here on his own territory. No less warm and friendly, but brisker, with a strong sense of purpose. A man with things to do.

'Here's the Batmobile,' he said, stopping next to a tiny vehicle like a squashed two-seater Jeep with a flat tray behind the seats. 'Let me grab you some head gear.' He headed into an adjacent outbuilding, then came back with a bright red helmet, which he threw to her. 'Forgive me for not wearing one, but it's better if you do. There are no seat belts on this roller skate, but I'm used to it and know when to brace.'

Feeling like a bit of a twit, Sophie put the helmet on, clipping it under her chin and trying not to let the associations with Matt form fully in her head – but in they came anyway. She let the memories run in through like an annoying commercial and then snapped herself back into the moment: sitting in what seemed rather a fun style of vehicle, with a very nice man who was a family friend, outside his beautiful house in the gorgeous countryside. It was all good. That was the thing to concentrate on.

'All set?' asked Charlie, putting on a pair of old Ray-Bans and starting the engine. 'Off we go, then.'

He headed out of the yard at an alarming pace and Sophie held on to the sides of the seat when they seemed to take off after hitting a bump. He turned a hard right along a narrow lane with trees on either side that met over the top, so it was like being in a green tunnel.

'What amazing old trees,' she said, gazing up into the canopy, the sunlight dappling between the leaves.

'It's ancient woodland. We have quite a lot of it, including one unbroken area of a couple of hundred acres where you can get properly lost in a good way. That's fun. I'll show you one day.'

The trees opened out as they came to a group of farm buildings. Not glorious old brick like the ones next to the house, but two modern barns with corrugated metal sides and a brutalist breeze-block structure arranged around a large yard. They seemed to be unused.

'This ugly lot are left over from that rogue tenant farmer we had. It was when Cicely visited and discovered he'd been ripping out hedgerows that he was given his marching orders and I decided it was time to come home.'

'Are you going to leave these buildings here?'

'I'd love to pull them down. But it seems like rather a negative way to use resources. I'm wondering if we couldn't convert them into studios for arty people to work in or something. It's quite remote, but this younger generation seem quite connected with nature, so maybe they wouldn't mind that. I've parked the problem at the back of my head for now. I'm too busy with the wine thing. The right idea will turn up.'

He continued to a gap between the buildings on the far side and when they came through it, Sophie gasped. The view was astonishing. Charlie stopped the motor and they sat there, just looking at it.

'Not bad, is it?' he said, quietly.

Sophie gazed out over a wide prospect of land that fell away into a gentle valley, rising again round the sides in banks of woodland. The flatter terrain in the bottom was all laid to vines, which, even from a distance, she could see were heavy with grapes.

'It looks like a quintessentially English version of Tuscany,' she said. 'So, those buildings would have views over this,' she said, glancing back at them. 'Or they would, if they had windows.'

Charlie nodded. 'I always think that,' he said. 'It couldn't be residential, we wouldn't get planning permission – and I wouldn't want people living so close to the vines – but that's why I thought of artists and creative people. I think this would be pretty inspiring to look out at.'

'And it must be beautiful in all the seasons.'

'It is. Every year I think, "Ah, yes, I definitely like autumn best … No, I like winter best … No, I like spring best," and so on.'

'I'm already starting to think like that about my sea view,' said Sophie. 'The light has changed so distinctly in the past week. At the height of summer, I started to feel a bit anxious about what winter would be like in an empty seaside resort, but now I'm looking forward to it. A new experience.'

'That's the idea,' said Charlie, nodding. 'Always look forward, there are no regrets there.'

Sophie felt he was referring to her loss in a sensitive, subtle way, which she appreciated, but she also had the distinct impression, once again, that he was also talking from personal experience. Since she had joined the ranks of the bereaved herself, Sophie recognised the signs in others. When the right moment presented itself, she would ask him.

She gazed out at the view again. 'Can I take some pictures?' she asked, getting her phone out of her pocket. She wanted to send them to Sebastian. He'd love it.

CHAPTER 29

Beau was doing the last thing he felt like on a Sunday morning: he was down at Goldsmiths to go through the boxes of stuff Joe had packed up from Matt's studio there. It was very good of his dad's pal to come in specially to open up and now he'd repaired to the Red Lion, telling Beau to text him when he'd finished. 'And then you can buy me a pint,' he'd said, playfully punching Beau on the bicep. Beau was still rubbing the spot, wondering how bad the bruise would be.

The ever-practical Joe – no wonder Matt had been so fond of him – had left him a Stanley knife and Beau now weighed it in his hand, sighing, as he tried to work up the courage to open one of the boxes, which had been arranged in an easily accessible circle. Beyond anything connected with the letter G, he didn't know what he was looking for, but he was terrified of finding it. The memory of that drawing of the pregnant woman in Matt's other studio was still too raw. *My girl*. Whatever that meant.

Taking a deep breath, he sliced open the first box and lifted out as much as he could in one armful. He recognised it immediately as Matt's working materials for his last show, which had been themed around the area of South East London where they'd lived and how it had changed over twenty years with gentrification.

The next box was full of catalogues from auction houses – Sotheby's, Christie's, Phillips, Bonhams, as Joe had said – and he noticed that all of them were for sales of contemporary and twenty-first century art. No Old Masters, furniture, silver, ceramics, wine or any of the other stuff they flog, the range was very specific.

He opened another and found it was full of portfolios of loose drawings, each folder marked with a label in Matt's distinctive writing, with the names of specific sales with the auction house and the dates – all part of the same project. Beau opened them up and leafed through. There were sketches of the exterior of each auction house building and of the sale rooms inside, the exhibition spaces, the cafés, restaurants and coffee counters. There was even one of a men's loo. That made Beau smile. So Dad.

In the next folder he found drawings of sales in process, with auctioneers in full flow, arms in the air, gavel raised, the men in aprons putting painting on stands and lots of bidders. Even the security guards who manned the entrances. A plug socket with a phone charging.

Despite the reason he was there, Beau found himself getting drawn in and imagined what a treasure trove this would be in the future for anyone studying his father's work.

Another crate had smaller boxes within it and inside those were cardboard maquettes of some kind of structures, put together with masking tape. Beau picked one up and looked at it from every angle, trying to understand what it was. Then he remembered what Joe had said about installations and realised this was Matt's way of starting to realise those.

But even after looking at all of them, Beau couldn't understand what that vision had been; it was still too rough. His hands dropped into his lap, still holding one of the small cardboard objects, feeling flattened by a sense of utter desolation that he would never know.

Resisting the temptation to throw the maquettes on the floor and jump on them, Beau made himself put each of the delicate little structures carefully back in its container. He hoped some academic might work it out for him someday.

Sighing deeply, about to put the folders back in the storage box, he noticed there was another portfolio at the bottom of it. He reached in to pull it out and when he saw the label on the front, he froze. It was just one letter: G.

He sank to the ground, still staring down at the folder. That letter.

For a moment Beau didn't think he had the courage to look inside, but he forced himself to open it and pull out the sheaf of paper, realising his hands were shaking as he did it.

They were all drawings of what appeared to be one woman and always in the context of the sale rooms, with details he recognised from the other pictures. He could tell it was the same woman in every sketch from her build and the hair, which came to just past her shoulders. Was it the one from the wake? Possibly. Her hair had been longer – but women change hairstyles all the time, you couldn't really go on that. She had been slim, like this one, from what he could remember. But this woman looked quite smartly dressed and the one at the wake had been very casual. In his father's old leather jacket.

Beau blew his breath out of pursed lips. He supposed they'd never see that again. Unless he found her. Was that a reason to keep going?

He picked up one drawing and studied it closely. He hadn't seen the face of that woman at the wake – Jacket Stealer – but even if he had, he couldn't have recognised her from this drawing. In all of them, Matt seemed to have sketched the face vaguely, which had clearly been intentional, because his father had been able to capture someone so you would instantly recognise them with just a few strokes of a pen or pencil. It had fascinated Beau from childhood.

Was it his mother? The hair was similar, but this woman seemed a bit taller and definitely slimmer than darling Mumpty. And Sophie didn't dress like that. She was always in jeans, or dresses for special occasions. She never wore the kind of tailoring this woman seemed to have on.

And her handbags were featured in all the drawings too. One of them appeared to be a Birkin bag. Beau knew what they looked like. So definitely not Mum. She always had practical crossbody bags.

He carried on leafing through the sheets and all the drawings appeared to be of this one woman. He could see the seasons changing in what she was wearing. It was making him feel very uncomfortable. Each sheet had the letter G written on it so presumably all these sketches had been made on the dates of the G entries in his father's phone calendar. But did that mean there was anything more to it than just someone Matt had known? She might have somehow been bound up with his obsession with the auction houses, no more than that. Or she could have been one of his regular models, who he'd posed in the auction houses as part of the project.

Simultaneously wanting to know and wanting to run away, Beau carried on sifting through the drawings until, near the bottom of the pile, he came to one that made him take a sharp breath. It was clearly the same woman – the hair and loosely sketched face were exactly the same – but she was lying down. Naked.

Starting to tremble, he carried on looking and the drawings became more and more intimate. If she was one of Matt's models, their professional relationship had clearly slipped over into something else.

There were multiple drawings of her breasts and nipples in great detail. Ugh. Dad was a tit man. Horrible. And then others, which were even more explicit.

When he came to one that was like a close-up between her legs, Beau dropped the sheets of paper on the floor, feeling oddly shocked and conflicted. It was the kind of thing he thoroughly approved of in his own life but seeing it in the context of his father's art was horrendous. Like catching your dad watching porn, which had happened to a friend of his.

Matt clearly hadn't needed that. He had his own live stream. The sleazy old bastard.

Beau closed his eyes and put his head back, trying to process it all. It was a lot. Or was he being naïve? He'd heard enough stories over the years to know that all sorts went on at Goldsmiths, just as it had at the two art colleges he'd gone to. Put a load of creative nutters in a confined space and weird stuff was going to happen. Maybe it was just on for young and old in there; free love had never died in Deptford.

He could probe Joe on that a bit when he bought him his thank-you pint at the Red Armpit.

Beau stretched his arms and moved his head from side to side, cracking his neck. He was starting to feel claustrophobic and he wasn't sure how much more of this stuff he could stand to look at.

He picked up the last few drawings, almost getting used to seeing this woman naked and from every angle, and started going through them until one made him stop suddenly. It was the same woman – she was unmistakable to him now, in Matt's consistent minimalist rendering of her face – but in this one there was a clear swelling in her abdomen. There was no doubt in his mind: it was the same pregnant woman he'd seen in the drawing in Matt's other studio.

So that hadn't been a chance sketch of a professional artists' model who happened to be pregnant, as Beau had so earnestly hoped. It was this mystery woman – and the person who had made her pregnant was all too clearly his father.

Beau forced himself to look at the last of the pile. They were all of the same woman, showing the baby bump getting bigger and bigger until finally there was a picture of her cradling a baby with her large erect nipple next to its mouth.

'Could you not have put the bloody nipple in its mouth?' Beau said out loud.

He stared at the drawing, studying the baby's face, the fat curve of a cheek with eyelashes lying against it. It was just a few strokes of pencil but it might as well have been a nuclear bomb to Beau, because it meant the words on the drawing he'd found at the other studio – *My girl, cooking* – were exactly what he had feared most: the woman Matt referred to as 'my girl' had been 'cooking' a baby. His father had a child with her. Beau had another sibling.

His father had another family.

Beau sat there, scrunched into a ball, hands clamped to the sides of his head, trying to physically contain the thoughts that were racing through it.

There was so much to take in. He might have a half-brother – or, he realised with a sudden shock which made him sit up straight – it might be a sister. A female Crommelin! That would be astonishing and even for that reason alone, he had to find them. While what his father had done was terrible, this child was his kin, his blood, and also a precious link back to his lost father. Hideously messed up although it all was, he wanted them in his life.

But what would that do to his mother?

CHAPTER 30

Sophie was sitting on the flat bed at the back of Charlie's Batmobile, holding tightly to the sides. Agata was in the front seat. Olive, Tamar and Rey had gone ahead to the vines with Cicely in her Land Rover, but Charlie had particularly wanted to take Agata himself. They'd gone out there in the afternoon so they could do the vineyard tour before dinner and were all staying the night. That had been Charlie's idea, because he wanted Sophie to be able to taste the wines and not have to hold back as the designated driver.

Agata was silent as Charlie zipped along the avenue of trees, some of the leaves starting to turn golden. Sophie noticed that he kept glancing at the old lady, presumably to make sure she was alright, but Agata seemed lost in her thoughts, a happy expression on her face, her favourite orange hat on her head, the red crash helmet on her lap.

'Are you comfortable, Agata?' he asked, in the end.

'I am in a state of bliss,' said Agata, turning to smile at him.

'Oh, that's good,' said Charlie. 'I was worried you were bored for a moment there.'

Agata laughed. 'I'm sorry not to be more chatty but I am very moved by the trees. I don't get to see many trees these days and I love them so.'

'Why don't you see many?'

'Because I live by the sea and trees don't like the southwesterly winds constantly beating them. I would have preferred to live inland like this and be surrounded by trees, but my husband loved the sea, so I live by the sea. I have an apple tree in my garden –' she shrugged and did her signature hand flick '– but that is a tree like a dachshund is a wolf. These are real trees.'

They arrived at the group of farm buildings and Charlie steered the buggy across the yard towards the view. Sophie expected Agata to make a remark about the ugly barns, but she said nothing. Even when Charlie stopped with the valley laid out before them, lined with snaking vines, the far hills slightly misty in the distance, she was silent.

Charlie looked round at Sophie for reassurance. She shrugged.

'I am quiet, Charlie,' said Agata, gently touching his arm, 'because I have spent so much time on my own that sometimes I almost forget how to speak. It is all so beautiful here. I feel privileged you have shared it with me.'

Charlie smiled at her. 'You are so welcome, Agata. It means a lot to me that you appreciate it. I lived in London for thirty years and I didn't realise how unhappy I was being away from here until I came back.'

'What happened to your wife?'

Sophie was momentarily horrified and then grateful. Agata had asked the big question she'd never found the right time to bring up.

'We got divorced,' said Charlie. 'A nasty divorce. Vicious.'

'Who's fault was that?'

Sophie tried to breathe quietly. She didn't want to intrude on this exchange. She had a feeling it might be helpful for Charlie.

Looking out at the view with his head on one side, he paused before replying. 'Our son died,' he said, turning back to Agata. 'He was seventeen. A hot day, beers, swimming in a deep quarry with signs all around it saying "Don't swim here". Such a stupid way to die.'

Ah, thought Sophie. So that was it. She'd been right about a terrible loss. It left an indelible mark that you could spot, once you knew.

'I am really very sorry,' said Agata, in that way she had of conveying deep meaning in a few words.

'It nearly destroyed me,' said Charlie. 'Well, it did really, but I am gradually coming back to life.'

'Do you have other children?'

'A daughter, but she sided with her mother in the divorce and won't talk to me. Losing Hec – his name was Hector – broke her as well and perhaps it's normal for a young woman to be blindly loyal to her mother, but then it went on too long and she was too proud to back down. But I still hold on to the hope that we'll be reunited one day.'

'How long ago did your son die?'

'Eight years. Eight years this past July.'

'For a loss like that, eight years is not long. I think there is still time for your daughter to come back to you.'

'I hope you're right. 'I'll never give up on her. She is my precious daughter and also for her brother's memory. He would be heartbroken to see his family shattered and I can't help feeling that it can't be good for him. He needs to rest in peace. I know that's silly, but you have all these daft thoughts, don't you? When you're struggling to make sense of things.'

'All my life,' said Agata.

Sophie reached out and squeezed Charlie's shoulder. He turned and smiled at her with tight lips, tears in his eyes.

'And you know too, eh, Sophie?' he said, briefly resting his hand on hers.

'We are all the walking wounded,' she said. Beau had told her Agata's story.

'But life must live,' said Agata with a sudden burst of energy, clapping her hands together. 'Not all misery. Now, show me grapes.'

Charlie laughed and beeped his horn in agreement as he set off down to the vines.

Sophie was upstairs, supposedly changing for dinner but actually standing in the middle of the room, staring into space. It was a very pretty bedroom, with flowery chintz curtains and a matching headboard, all a bit nicely faded, which made her suspect it had been decorated by Cicely and Charlie's mother many decades earlier and not touched since. The last golden rays of autumn sun were pouring in through the leaded window panes and the view looked out over the garden to a stretch of parkland dotted with ancient oak trees. Yet Sophie felt strangely flat.

She shook out the dress she'd brought to wear for dinner, but instead of changing into it, she threw it onto the armchair in the corner and climbed onto the bed. All she really wanted to do was crawl under the covers and stay there. She'd been looking forward to this dinner hugely, but now it seemed like a massive effort.

Maybe she'd been socialising too much. Was it all a bit forced and desperate, spending so much time with people she hardly knew? Sooner or later, she was going to have to face up to her new reality, as a middle-aged single woman, living alone. Jack was in Brisbane. Beau was back in London. Tamar wasn't going to be there forever.

Sophie checked the time. Charlie had said to come for drinks in the drawing room at seven. It was ten to, but she just couldn't make herself start to get ready.

And then she suddenly understood what was lowering her mood. It was the first time she'd stayed at someone else's house – apart from immediate family – since Matt had died. Her first outing as a widowed overnight guest. Another landmark.

They would have been in this room together, commenting on the delightfully out-of-date décor and admiring the view. And Matt would have been driving her nuts, sprawling his stuff everywhere and making them late.

She closed her eyes tight and squeezed them shut, tears threatening. Then something else occurred to her. Even if Matt was still alive, he wouldn't have been there. He'd have been off somewhere with Juliet, driving *her* mad with his mess and making *her* late.

Sophie would have been alone anyway.

She was still trying to decide whether that made it better or worse when there was a knock on the door.

'Come in,' she called, thinking it was probably Tamar seeking reassurance, but it was Charlie's head that came round the door – and his right hand, holding out a glass of sparkling wine.

'Are you decent?' he asked.

Sophie laughed. 'Decent enough.'

'I thought you might like to have a little heart starter up here,' he said. 'No rush to come down, everything's simmering away in the kitchen, no MasterChef timing involved. Just come down when you're ready.'

Sophie walked over to take the glass from him. 'Thank you so much,' she said, taking a sip. 'Mmm, this is delicious, Charlie. Is it your lovely brew again? It tastes a bit different.'

He nodded, smiling and looking endearingly shy. 'This is from a special stash of premium bottles from last year, better than the stuff I put in tins.'

'It's really good.'

'You better have some more then,' he said, producing the bottle he was holding in his other hand and topping up her glass.

'Cheers!' said Sophie, raising the flute.

'Chin-chin!' He put his hand on hers and pulled her glass towards him to take a slurp, grinning.

Sophie laughed.

Then he looked serious. 'I'm glad you know about my son, Sophie,' he said. 'And my divorce and my daughter. I've wanted to tell you, but I didn't want to sound like I was trying to tragedy match you or something.'

'I've been wanting to ask you,' said Sophie. 'I could tell there was something, but it never seemed like the right time to ask.'

'Fellow soldiers in suffering. But now all that's out, let's get on with living, eh? Like Agata said.'

'I'll drink to that,' said Sophie, raising her glass again. And then it seemed the most natural thing to give him a comradely squeeze.

As she wrapped her arms around him, she was surprised how good he smelled where her nose rested against his shoulder and how comforting she found the press of firm flesh from a warm and muscular male body beneath a clean cotton shirt.

Did she imagine it, or did the hug last a little longer than she might have expected?

CHAPTER 31

Juliet was in the big kitchen of her new house in Queen's Park, entertaining Rachel and Dottie and three of their respective children for a quick after-work catch-up. The four little girls were off to one side in Cassady's playroom – just close enough to hear if there was any serious distress, but not intrusive. That's what the architect had said, but she'd asked the nanny to stay in there with them anyway.

Newborn Hettie was asleep in a Moses basket on the sofa.

'So you move to our 'hood,' Rachel was saying, 'with a four-week-old baby and straight into the best house. If I wasn't so happy you were here, I'd say it was rude.'

'Do you like it?' asked Juliet, looking round the big white space, with a wall of glass opening onto the garden.

'It will be better when it's a bit dirtier,' said Dottie. 'Did you mean to buy a white sofa with two children under four, or was it an accident? It's certainly an accident waiting to happen.'

'It's got stain proofing on it,' said Juliet. 'And Cassady's not allowed to eat or drink while she's sitting on it.'

Rachel and Dottie laughed.

'Have you told her not to use felt tips, or crayons, or plasticine, or cover her entire face in your lipstick, and not to sneeze or vomit when she's sitting on it?' said Rachel.

'I had a sofa ruined by a ball of slime,' said Dottie. 'It left a bright green circle right at the front of the middle cushion.'

'Bubble mix isn't great, either,' said Rachel. 'Or wee. But you enjoy it now, Juliet. You can get lovely beige polyester loose covers made for it when it's wrecked, or a nice busy chintz. Right, Dottie, where's the magazine?'

The next issue of *Her*, with the article about Juliet in it, had just come back from the printer ready to go out with the paper that Sunday, and Dottie had brought it over to give them an advance peek.

'Here you are, Juliet,' she said, fishing around in her bag and putting the magazine on the table. Juliet was on the cover, holding up her hand with one of her famous eye rings on it.

She studied it, feeling queasy.

'Aren't you going to look inside?' said Dottie.

'Can one of you read it to me first?' said Juliet. 'This one is so personal with the pictures of Cassady ...'

'It wasn't even photographed in your own house,' said Dottie, laughing. 'We've never agreed to shoot in a location house for anyone before.'

'Well,' said Juliet, 'it worked for Harry and Meghan, didn't it?'

They laughed and Rachel picked up the magazine and leafed through to find the page. Then she held it up for Juliet to see.

'Not yet!' said Juliet, covering her eyes. 'Let me hear the words first.'

'Bloody hell,' said Rachel. 'My other clients would throw in a couple of limbs as well as our fees for this coverage. Alright, sit down for story time. This is the headline: *The Woman Who Has It All – Except a Man.*'

Juliet was quiet for a moment.

'You could have mentioned the jewellery,' she said to Dottie, who rolled her eyes exaggeratedly.

'The whole point is to make them intrigued so they read the damn article,' she said. '"This Woman Makes Nice Rings" is not going to pull them in, get it?'

'I suppose so,' said Juliet.

'Are you two going to shut up so I can read it?' said Rachel. 'Here goes. *Juliet Mylan has it all* – not a word of lie there – *Her game-changing jewellery brand, Giuliette, is worn by Hollywood stars and edgy Grime artists alike. Her unique style – invented by the self-taught designer – combines precious gems with natural crystals creating a new genre of fine jewellery, which offers her clients the energetic qualities of the crystals along with the glamour of elite stones. The company's stratospheric success is rumoured to be attracting interest from Bernard Arnault, as the possible next addition to the LVMH stable.* Bring it,' said Rachel, putting her hands in the prayer position. 'Where was I? *We visited Juliet – and three-year-old daughter Cassady – in her enviable house in Queen's Park—*'

'Or something similar in another part of London entirely,' said Dottie, laughing. 'The house in those pictures is in Wandsworth. You've made me lie to my readers, Juliet. It's shocking.'

'But it does look quite like this house,' said Juliet.

'Yeah,' said Rachel. 'It has the generic dream social kitchen. Simon's cliché nightmare that I made him have, ha ha. Hang on, let me finish.

'"Belgravia is beautiful," says Juliet, "but it's not great for kids and we have a lot of friends in Queen's Park—"'

'That's us,' said Dottie.

'"So Cassady now has a garden and plenty of pals within walking distance,"' Rachel continued. 'And children are particularly on Juliet's mind at the moment as – at the time of writing – she was nearly nine months pregnant with her second baby. So, she has business success, creative cred, a beautiful house, glamorous friends and a family – but the one thing that is missing from Juliet Mylan's apparently perfect life defines the reason she believes she has managed to "have it all" on her own terms. There is no man in her life.*

'"It is very much my choice," says Juliet. "I never wanted a husband or an involved father for my children. I knew from a young age that I wanted to be financially independent and that has been my driving force for the business. Once that side of things was stable, I was able to pursue my other ambition, which was to have a family on my own terms."'

'So, how do you have children when you categorically do not want a husband or partner, or another parent involved in the young ones' lives in any way? Juliet replies as if it's the obvious solution: a sperm donor. The same one for each of her children. "So they are true siblings, even if they don't know their father," she says. "That was important to me."'

The article went on with more about the business and her plans for the future and by the time Rachel had finished reading, Juliet was smiling broadly. She got up and gave Dottie a squeeze from behind.

'You really are a friend,' she said. 'Your journalist has written exactly what I said. She hasn't twisted it to make some controversial point. I'm so grateful.'

'What about me?' said Rachel. 'I fought Godzilla here, on your behalf, to keep Cassady off the cover.'

Juliet hugged her too. 'Thank you both, so much. You are such good friends and you're both consummate professionals as well, so I respect you as much as I like you.'

'That's lovely, Jules,' said Dottie. 'And it really means a lot, coming from someone as emotionally constipated as you.'

Rachel shouted with laughter, tea spurting out of her mouth all over the table.

'Oops, sorry,' she said. 'Lucky we weren't on the white sofa. Let me grab a cloth.'

Juliet was already on her feet. 'Don't worry, I'll get it.'

She wiped the table then sat down and looked at the pages of the magazine. 'It really is a great piece,' she said. 'Thank you again.' And then she threw the dishcloth across the kitchen in the rough direction of the sink. It landed on the floor and she left it there.

Rachel and Dottie burst out laughing.

'Yay!' said Rachel, holding up her hand to give Juliet a high five. 'You did something out of control. I bloody love it.'

'You know what,' Juliet said, sitting down again. 'I've already learned so much from you two – where to live, where to send your child to school, how to have friends. So, I'm going to do something else that's right outside my normal comfort zone – which is a very small area, as you know.'

'A jewel box,' said Dottie.

'Touché,' said Juliet. 'I know it's a school night, but if you two are game, can you call your lovely husbands and ask them to come and get your kids? And then we will drink wine – just one for me because I'm breastfeeding – and eat bad delivered food and I will tell you something I don't tell anybody, which explains why I'm such a weirdo.'

Without saying a word, Rachel and Dottie reached for their phones and started texting.

Juliet went to her study and pulled out the fat file of press clippings about her mother killing her father and all the abuse that had pushed her to do it.

It seemed a good place to start.

CHAPTER 32

Sophie was at Agata's house with the group of people she realised she had just thought of in her head as 'the Gang'. It made her smile, but that's what the quite eccentric combination of herself and Tamar, with Agata, Olive and Charlie – and Rey and Cicely when they were around – were to her now, and it meant a lot.

They met up regularly for dinners at each other's houses, which were always a hoot. So far there had been several at Sophie's and Olive's and a couple at Charlie's and Rey's, but this was the first at Agata's house – and it was the caviar and vodka setup of legend.

On this occasion Yewande had joined them too and they were gathered in Agata's sitting room, drinking Charlie's sparkling wine while Olive and Beau were busy making blinis in the kitchen. Everyone was wearing seventies clothing.

It had been Tamar's idea for them to dress in keeping with the décor of the house, after Agata had let her loose in her wardrobe one afternoon and she'd found it filled with vintage treasures. Tamar was wearing an Empire-line orange satin dress with three layers of fluttery sleeves and a silky crocheted hat pulled down low, her mass of curly hair springing out from underneath. Both hat and dress were original Biba.

'Doesn't she look beautiful?' said Agata. 'I used to look beautiful in that dress too. I wore it with high platform shoes, which is why it is long enough for Tamar with those terrible boots.'

Tamar laughed and lifted her leg to waggle a Doc Marten in Agata's direction.

The old lady was wearing another Biba outfit, grey and white print palazzo pants and a matching fitted blouse, her hat a floppy grey felt with a turned-back brim, trimmed with a silk rose.

Cicely had on an antique Afghan dress with mirror embroidery and Charlie was sporting a blue velvet suit with a satin shirt – the collar pulled out over the revers of the jacket. It was all quite convincing until his feet, where he was sporting brown brogues.

Agata was looking at him thoughtfully as he went round refreshing everyone's glasses.

'Where did you get that terrible suit?' she asked him.

'It was knocking around at home.'

'Come closer,' said Agata and she inspected the top-stitching around the cuffs and bottom of the jacket. 'It looks like real 1970s,' she said. 'They haven't made trousers that tight since then – thank God.'

'It probably is from then,' said Cicely. 'There are loads of old clothes hanging around the house. Where did you find it, Charlie?'

'Oh, it was in a random wardrobe, along with this shirt, which I think is actually a blouse. It's got darts.'

Sophie was wearing a short silver lamé dress – not too mini, she hoped – that she'd found in a vintage shop in Norman

Road, with a pair of high-heeled platform sandals she already had. The one hundred per cent manmade fabric was scratchy against her skin and she was feeling rather self-conscious. Her legs were still brown from days at the beach hut, which was something, but it was so long since she'd got properly dressed up, she felt rather exposed. She pulled the skirt down as far over her knees as it would go.

Beau popped in to tell them the food wouldn't be long. Despite his lack of hair, he was quite successfully channelling a rock god vibe, with heavy, black, Keith Richards eyeliner, a deliberately too small t-shirt and flared black-satin trousers that he'd found in the same shop where Sophie had got her dress. True to the style of the era, he clearly wasn't wearing any underwear with them. Sophie had had to bite her lip not to laugh when she saw Tamar and Yewande creasing up about it, obviously thinking no one would know why they were laughing.

Agata didn't hold back.

'So you are not circumcised, I see, Beau,' she said and everybody roared.

Charlie headed out of the room to get another bottle of fizz and Sophie noticed Tamar, Yewande and Beau having a confab, then they all got up and left the room together, giggling. She looked at Cicely and Agata.

'What do you think they're up to?'

'Who knows?' said Cicely. 'But isn't this fun? There's nothing like wearing silly clothes to get a party going.'

'Wait until we start on the vodka,' said Agata.

*

Sophie went upstairs to use the loo and as she passed Agata's bedroom she could hear young giggly voices within. She stopped to listen at the door. Not to snoop, just for the joy of it.

'The thing is, Charlie,' Yewande was saying, 'we think you ace that suit and you'd look really good with rock star eyeliner like Beau's got on.'

'You little shits,' Charlie said, starting to laugh. 'I have seen *Pirates of the Caribbean*, you know ...'

'Oh, go on,' said Tamar. 'It would look so great on you. You're such a dude. And with that groovy suit, it would be seriously cool.'

'Alright, then,' said Charlie. 'I submit to youth's ritual humiliation of maturity – it is a tradition, after all.'

They were quiet for a few moments and then there was a collective 'Yay!' so Sophie assumed the deed was done.

'That's annoying,' said Beau. 'You look better than me.'

'As Johnny said to Keef?' said Charlie. 'No? OK. Google it.'

Sophie scooted off before she could be caught eavesdropping and as she was going down the stairs again, she saw that Agata and Cicely were on their way to the kitchen, summoned by Olive, so called back to the others.

'Olive wants us at the table,' she said, just as Charlie appeared at the top of the stairs.

Sophie's eyebrows shot up when she saw him. He had heavy black eyeliner round his eyes – and it really did suit him.

He arrived at her side and put out his arm. 'May I escort you into dinner?'

Sophie put her arm through his and felt an unfamiliar sensation roll over her cheeks. She was blushing.

There was no seating plan, beyond Olive claiming the chair closest to the working part of the kitchen and Sophie sat down next to her place, so she'd be able to help easily.

Charlie appeared at her side, putting eight chilled shot glasses on the table. 'Save this spot for me, would you?' he said, patting the back of the chair next to hers. 'I need to be in pole position for the drinks service. Olive has given me my orders.'

He was soon back, holding up a frosted bottle of vodka. 'Who's for a shot of bonkers juice?' he said. He opened the bottle and reached over to fill Agata's glass first, then went round the table.

Beau arrived with the plate of blinis, followed by Olive holding a round blue tin with a small spoon sticking out of it.

'Eggs for dinner, kids,' she said, leaning over to pass it to Agata. 'You go first, Ags – show everyone how to do it.'

'But you are my guests,' said Agata.

'Stop trying not to eat and get it down you,' said Olive, taking her seat.

'So,' said Agata, 'take one blini, one spoon of sour cream, like so … and then, the heaven.' She scooped out a spoonful of the shiny black eggs, put it on the top and then placed the whole thing delicately on her plate. 'But I won't eat it yet – thank you, Olive – not until everyone is served and then we will have a toast. See this spoon?' she said, holding it up. 'It is mother of pearl, never metal with caviar.'

She handed the spoon and tin to Cicely. 'And now you.'

The tin went round the table, with everyone excitedly constructing their blinis.

Sophie turned to Charlie as he passed the tin to her and was surprised all over again by his eyeliner.

'It really suits you,' she said. 'That eyeliner. You look like Adam Ant – the later years. In a hot way.'

Charlie's hands flew up to his face. 'Bloody hell,' he said. 'I'd forgotten all about it. I hope I remember to take it off in the morning and don't go out to the farm with it on. The kids did it to me.'

'Of course they did,' said Sophie. 'Well, I like it and think you should always wear it.'

She realised she was still gazing at him when Agata spoke.

'Charlie,' she said. 'If I'm not interrupting …'

Sophie turned towards Agata. What was she doing? She hadn't even had any vodka yet.

'I am old and I am old-fashioned,' Agata continued. 'So as the senior man here, Charlie, I would like you to propose the first toast.'

'It would be an honour,' he said, standing up. 'Now everyone has their blinis and, more importantly, their caviar, I propose a toast to our wonderful friend and hostess, Agata, for her generosity in spoiling us with this very special treat and for being such a wonderful human being. Right, down in one, all. Cheers!'

'Cha cha!' said Tamar.

'Mma manu!' said Yewande.

'Na zdravi!' said Agata.

'Chin-chin!' said Cicely.

'Up yer bum!' said Olive.

And they all sank their shots.

After three more rounds of blinis with the accompanying vodka, the caviar was finished and Olive got up – a bit unsteadily – to see to the rest of the dinner, while Beau and Yewande cleared the plates.

Charlie got up to get more drinks and when he arrived back at the table, he leaned in close to Sophie.

'I hope Agata isn't one of those hostesses who makes people change place between courses,' he said. 'Because I'm very happy just here.'

'I'm happy you're happy and I'm happy too,' Sophie heard herself say, then jumped up to help Olive serve the next course, grateful for a moment to collect her thoughts. She and Charlie were blatantly flirting with each other. And she liked it.

Was a Gridow allowed to do that? There must be a rule of at least a year, surely. But for a Wronged Woman, all bets were off. In fact, she was entitled to it.

It was all so confusing. Especially after the vodka.

When she sat down again, the conversation had gone back to what they were wearing, and Agata was regaling them with a story of buying her first dress from Mary Quant in 1961.

'You were asking earlier, Agata, where I got this suit?' said Charlie.

Agata nodded. 'Maybe it's not too late for refund?'

'I think it is,' he said. 'My very cool older cousin, who I totally hero worshipped, had it for his eighteenth birthday party in 1973 and I thought it was the bee's bollocks. A few years later, he very kindly gave it to me and I couldn't ever bring myself to chuck it out. He always said it was his best pulling suit.'

And he turned to Sophie and downed his vodka in one, his eyes never leaving hers.

CHAPTER 33

Sophie woke up with the full hangover horrors. The raging thirst, the banging headache, the hungry nausea – or was it nauseous hunger? – and the shame memories of her own behaviour. She had flirted with Charlie, shamelessly. In front of them all. She put her hands over her face, wanting it to go away.

And she knew the truth. If the opportunity had arisen, she would have kissed him. She'd thought he was an attractive man from the first time she'd met him, then that mad eyeliner had just flicked some kind of crazy throwback switch in her. He and Cicely were staying at Agata's and there had been a moment when she'd seriously considered asking him to sneak away and stay with her.

She hadn't, but after even thinking it, how was she going to act normally when she next saw him? It was so embarrassing.

She sat up – aaaarggggh, too quick – and reached for her phone. There was only one thing to do. She had to see him again, as soon as possible. They were adults, they needed to meet with other people around, behave normally, possibly acknowledge the flirtation as a great joke and move on.

She texted Cicely: *Morning! Come for breakfast. I've got a full English ready to go in the fridge. Please invite Agata too.*

Cicely texted back almost immediately saying they'd love to.

Fifteen minutes later, Sophie, Tamar and Yewande were hard at it in the kitchen. Tamar was frying eggs in one pan, bacon in another and black pudding in a third while keeping an eye on the mushrooms, which were under the grill. Sophie was cutting bread, getting plates, cutlery and sauces out, and giving the sausages in the oven an occasional shake. Yewande was self-appointed barista and tea maker.

'Do you think we should fry the bread?' said Sophie.

'Definitely,' said Tamar. 'I want fried bread, don't you?'

'Absolutely,' said Sophie, necking the espresso Yewande had just put in front of her. 'My fried brain needs fried bread.' She gave the sausages another shake and, still steadying herself after standing up too quickly from looking in the oven, jumped when she heard a knock on the door.

'I'll get it,' she said, abandoning the metal spatula she was holding into the sink with a clatter. She needed to see Charlie for the first time after last night's shenanigans on her terms and in an active role. Not standing passively in the kitchen like a dope when he walked in.

'Hi,' she said, way too brightly, opening the door to see only Cicely standing there. Going on with her overly jolly tone, she gave her a hug, saying, 'Come in, come in, we're in the kitchen. How do you feel? I feel terrible. Haven't had a hangover like this for years. Did I smoke? That's how bad it feels.'

Cicely laughed. 'I don't remember you smoking, but from a certain point last night, everything is a blur.'

That's good, thought Sophie, leading Cicely into the kitchen and hoping that point had occurred sometime before the goulash course.

'Agata thanks you for the invitation, but says she doesn't eat in the morning. And Charlie will be here in a minute. He was having a bit of trouble knowing how to walk, put trousers on, that kind of thing.'

'That bad, huh?' said Sophie, laughing and trying to determine if Cicely was looking at her a bit beadily. It was hard to tell, the hangover seemed to be affecting every aspect of her mental capacities.

Yewande was asking Cicely what she wanted to drink, when there was another knock on the door. Sophie ran out of the kitchen to answer it again. Too fast, way too fast.

Charlie was standing there, which she knew he would be, but somehow the sight of him still took her by surprise. He was wearing the blue velvet trousers but with a moth-eaten sweater. Most of the eyeliner was still round his eyes.

Sophie felt her face break into a grin. The combination was adorable.

'Morning, Sophie,' he said, smiling and squinting at the same time.

She felt a bit weak and wasn't sure if it was all the hangover.

'Morning, Adam Ant, the older,' she said and went to give him the same welcome-friend hug she'd given Cicely, but it didn't go quite like that.

Charlie put his arms round her – and they were big, strong, male arms. The sort of arms that drive tractors, chop firewood and save lambs from burning buildings. He wrapped them round her and held her, close.

And then instead of the breezy social peck she was expecting, he planted his lips firmly on her right cheek and left them there for a lingering moment, before pulling slowly away.

Sophie swallowed. 'Come in,' she said, croakily. 'We're eating in the kitchen.'

'I forgot to pack any other trousers,' Charlie said, as they walked through the hall. 'Sorry about that.'

'Don't apologise. I love your pulling pants —' it just seemed right to get it all out in the open now, as he kind of had with that embrace '— and I'm glad you're still working the eye makeup look too.'

'Can't get the bastard stuff off,' he said, smiling. 'And I don't really want to. Morning, Tamar, Yewande,' he called out, as they walked into the kitchen. 'Are you two as hungover as this very old person?'

'I've felt better,' said Tamar, sliding eight fried eggs onto a warmed plate and putting it on the countertop.

'Oh, sweet holy heaven,' said Charlie, gazing down at it all. 'Fried bread. Black pudding. Mushrooms. Am I dreaming?'

'Hold on,' said Tamar, 'we haven't done any tomatoes. I'll just pop some on. I like a fried tomato with my full English.'

'Help yourself,' said Sophie, passing plates to Cicely and Charlie.

'What hot beverages would you like?' asked Yewande.

They chatted easily as they ate, remembering funny moments from the night before and recalling great hangovers of their lives. Charlie had just gone back to what he was calling 'the break-fast-boo-fay' for a third go when Beau came into the dining room.

'Hi, everyone. Morning, Mumsk,' he said, kissing her on the cheek. 'Now this is what I call breakfast.'

Charlie agreed and there was easy chat while he and Cicely finished their second coffees and the meal drew to a natural close.

Sophie saw them off at the door and turned back into the hall, feeling relieved by how easy it had all been in the end. The flirting had just been some jokey banter after a lot of strong booze in silly clothes and she didn't need to fret about it. Their friendship would be stronger for it, not spoiled.

Then there was a gentle knock at the door. She opened it to see Charlie standing there again. He reached for her hand to indicate she should come outside, then pulled the door to, behind her.

'I don't want that lot earwigging the old people,' he said, nodding his head in the direction of the kitchen.

Sophie looked at him. The eyeliner. It still got her.

'Will you have lunch with me?' he asked, quietly. 'Just us. It's great when we all get together like this, but I'd love to see you alone.'

Sophie nodded. 'I'd love that,' she said. And she meant it.

'Just one thing,' he said, looking at the ground. 'I hope I didn't come on too strong last night. The pulling suit and the eye makeup … I got a bit carried away.'

'Not at all,' said Sophie. 'I liked it. It was all part of the fun.'

'I look forward to lunch then,' said Charlie, and as he kissed her on the cheek, he squeezed her upper arm.

Sophie stood at the door watching him go, and he turned back to wave at her. Winking.

*

The kids said they'd clear up the kitchen, so Sophie made herself a pot of tea and took it back to bed. Autumn sun was streaming in through the window and she just wanted some quiet time, happy knowing the young ones were in the house.

She'd brought the Sunday papers up with her and was flicking through them rather carelessly. Her thoughts kept returning to Charlie in his eyeliner and the way he had squeezed her arm. That sexy wink.

She realised she was feeling stirrings that she hadn't had for a long time. Not since Matt died – and when she thought about it, for quite a while even before. Their sex life, once so great, had really tailed off in the years before his accident. She'd just assumed it was their age and the stage of their relationship – thirty years was a long time – but now she forced herself to accept why that had happened. Matt had been servicing his needs elsewhere.

Thinking about that broke her contented mood and she decided it was time to get up and get on with things. She'd throw herself into some boring admin she'd been neglecting while she and Tamar had worked on the book.

As she got up off the bed, the papers slid onto the floor and one of the colour supplements fell out. Sophie froze.

There on the cover was that face again – Gillette. Looking out with a mysterious half smile, a hand bearing a huge ring in the shape of an eye resting on one shoulder, the coverline bold across the bottom: *Jeweller to the stars, Juliet Mylan, on why she chooses to be a single mother.*

Sophie stared at it. She had kids?

Sitting down heavily on the bed, Sophie flicked through the pages. When she found the article, her hand went up to her mouth as she let out a kind of strangled cry.

Juliet was standing in a glamorous kitchen with a little girl on her hip. The child had a mess of black curly hair and she was laughing, her whole face creased up with joyful mirth.

She was the image of Matt.

For a few heartbeats, Sophie just stared at the picture, not believing her eyes, then she forced herself to read the beginning of the article.

The little girl's name was Cassady. One of Matt's precious Beat heroes was Neal Cassady. He'd considered the name for Jack but had then gone for Jack Kerouac Crommelin. Sophie had insisted on Beau for their first born. One time she'd got her way.

She didn't read any further. With the way the child looked and that name, she didn't need any more proof. Before they'd even run away and set up home together, her husband had had a child with this woman – and it was a girl.

What a commotion that would cause in the Crommelin clan! Finally a girl, but how they would ever know? Sophie certainly wasn't going to tell them.

Then her hands flew up to her face again as the full impact of the situation hit her. Her sons had a half-sister. Did she have some kind of ghastly moral imperative to tell them? She was pretty certain she did.

This little girl was the boys' next closest relative after her and each other – and when she grew up, she would most likely come looking for them. It was so easy now with those DNA tests.

Sophie closed her eyes. Just when she was starting to feel like she was making a new life for herself – this. It was too much.

She forced herself to pick up the magazine again. She had to read that bloody article, to find out what other horrors might be lurking in it. Right away, there it was: 'at the time of writing', Gillette had been nine months pregnant with her second baby.

Sophie didn't even need to do the maths to work out the timing, she knew exactly how long it was since Matt had died. It couldn't have happened long before the accident, but it was definitely possible.

She was still letting that knowledge sink in when she reached the part about using a sperm donor – the same one for both babies.

Sophie looked at the page in disbelief. Was that all Matt had been to this ghastly woman? A turkey baster? Sophie felt pure outrage, for Matt as much as herself, but then it occurred to her that it might have been his idea. An art project. She wouldn't have put it past him.

But that couldn't be right, because he'd told her he was going to leave her to start a new life with someone called Juliet. And this was definitely the woman from the funeral who had said she was called Juliet – and here she was holding a little girl who was the image of Matt. She'd said it was the same 'sperm donor'. They were both his children.

Then Sophie remembered that thing Juliet had said to Rey at the wake. That she wanted Sophie to know 'it's not what it seems'. What wasn't?

Sophie felt as though her head was going to explode, because she knew there was no getting out of it. One day she was going to have to face up to this, to find out the truth, so she could tell the boys.

Now she knew this awful truth, for the sake of her boys she was going to have to go and see this woman in her stupid shop. Just … not yet. It would happen, but she needed to feel much stronger first.

She picked up the magazine again, stared at Juliet's face before tearing off the cover, pulling out all the pages of the article and ripping them into tiny shreds.

CHAPTER 34

Beau was sitting in the back office at Giuliette's with Cassady on his knee. She was designing a ring. He'd already drawn about five hundred princesses and unicorns for her and had insisted it was her turn to draw a picture, so he could have a breather.

'It's going to be a very big ring,' said Cassady, pressing hard on the paper with the felt tip. 'The biggest ring in the world. This big.' She arced her dear little arms around as far as they would go.

'Will it fit on your finger if it's that big?' said Beau. 'You've only got titchy witchy fingers.'

'The finger bit will be small, you silly, but the bit on top will be big like a mountain. A rainbow mountain.'

She was spending time at the shop every day after school, because of some logistics with the nanny and the new baby. Beau usually ended up entertaining her. Gwen and Octavia were so grateful not to get landed, they waited on him with cups of tea and biscuits. Gwen had also made one of her lemon drizzle cakes.

Babysitting was no stretch for Beau. He loved kids. He was happy to lie on the floor with Cassady, making up stories involving her extensive collection of rainbow Pegasus unicorns. Jack always said Beau's affinity with children was because he had never really grown up himself. Beau was fine with that. He'd rather interact at Cassady's brutally honest level than with the bullshit thrown at him by some adults.

Which was why he was secretly glad to spend time in the back office and out of the shop. He was doing okay in there. He'd sold quite a bit of stuff, and Luiza seemed pleased with him – and he was happy with the commission – but he found some of the people who shopped there so awful it took all his self-discipline to be polite to them. Having to toady up to them to clinch the sale, as Luiza did, was just too much.

Cassady finished her ring design and jumped off Beau's lap to get some essential extra unicorns out of her bag, just as Luiza came through from the shop.

'That *puta*,' she said about a customer who had just left. 'Thinks she's a pop star, she's a poop star. Says it's for her video, wants a discount. I put the price up, then gave her "discount". She bought it. Full price. *Rego do cu*.'

Beau smiled as enthusiastically as he could. He was getting to know some interesting Portuguese insults – that one was 'ass crack', as far as he remembered – so working with Luiza did have an educational element.

'What did she buy?' he asked.

'The pendant with the big eye and the lips.'

'The one that converts to a belt?'

Luiza nodded, examining her nails.

'Isn't that twenty thousand pounds?'

She shrugged. 'Wasted on that *idiota*.'

'Nice commission for you.'

'I earn it,' she said, looking at him coolly. 'While you are working as a nanny, again. No commission for you and I'm alone in the shop. Are you happy with that? Looking after the brat?'

'Yes,' said Beau, as Cassady came running in and vaulted onto his lap, dropping two handfuls of small plastic creatures onto the desk. He gave her a little squeeze and tickled her round the waist. She shrieked with delight.

'I love hanging out with Cassady,' said Beau. *Much more than with you.*

'Well, if that's your level, you are welcome to it,' said Luiza. 'But if this carries on much longer, I will be asking our big puta to get someone else to work with me. You need to make your mind up.'

She treated him to one of the smiles she used on the customers she most despised – Beau had learned to read them – and walked out. As she got to the door into the shop, she turned round to look at him again with what seemed to be an expression of relatively sincere concern.

'Don't disappoint me, Bob,' she said. 'You're too good for that shit.' She gestured at Cassady with her head.

Beau looked down at the little girl on his knee, her head of dark curls bent over the desk as she arranged her unicorns in a neat row by size, and thought he couldn't imagine anything better than her.

He looked back at Luiza and gave her a smile as fake as one of hers. 'I hear you,' he said. *I hear you and I don't like you.*

She let the door close with a loud thump.

'Bob,' said Cassady, looking up at him expectantly. 'Let's do the one where the unicorns jump in your tea and go swimming.'

'Okay,' said Beau, 'but we better do it in the kitchen. We made rather a mess last time, didn't we?'

'Yes,' said Cassady. 'And I want to make a much bigger mess this time. The biggest mess in the whole world.'

'You're a big mess,' said Beau, lifting her off his lap onto the floor and standing up. 'You lead the way. I'll bring the tea and the magical animals.'

Cassady took off at a run towards the kitchen. Beau started to follow her then paused, picking up her drawing of a ring and studying it closely. It was really good. She'd used colours very interestingly with yellow next to orange, pink next to red and lilac next to purple, and the shapes and proportions all worked.

Cassady had definitely inherited her mother's talents.

He folded the drawing carefully and put it in his jacket's inside pocket.

CHAPTER 35

Sophie was getting dressed up for the second weekend in a row. This time it was for Thomas and Bella's joint birthday party at their place in Somerset and that was the dress code: UP.

She looked at herself in the full-length backless halter-neck dress, wondering whether she had the courage to wear something so bare, but it did seem alright. Plus, she had a long embroidered Chinese silk coat to keep out the October chill, that she could hide under until she felt more confident.

It also helped that Bella had laid on hair and makeup artists for all the people who were staying at the house, so she was feeling more glamorous than she had for a very long time.

The only thing now was to summon up the courage to go over to the marquee for the party. On her own.

Bella had put her in the guesthouse in the garden, saying it would be nice for her to have her own sitting room – although Sophie was fairly sure it was because all their important guests were staying in the main house. She didn't mind, the excuse was just classic Bella overexplain and the cabin, decorated in Nantucket beach house style, was like a luxury holiday rental, so she couldn't really complain.

It just made her feel so alone.

After one more look at herself in the dress, Sophie shrugged on the coat and headed out of the bedroom, wondering if anyone else was going to be staying in the other one. It seemed strange to leave it empty when it was such a big party and she dearly hoped someone else would be billeted there, to make her feel a little less solo.

Then she stood in the hallway, wondering whether she had the strength to go to this party at all. Perhaps she should just take the stupid dress off and sneak away. But it was a four-hour drive back to Hastings in the dark and if she just got into bed, Bella would send someone to find her. She had no choice. She had to tough it out.

Oh, why had she accepted this invitation?

Just as Sophie found the courage to approach the cabin's front door to leave, there was a loud knock and Thomas's head came round it.

'Are you ready, dear Sophie?' he said, beaming. He loved giving parties. 'I've come to escort you over to the ball, madame.'

Sophie felt bad for even thinking of bailing on the party.

'That is so kind of you, Tommo,' she said and as he pushed the door open, she saw he was wearing an entirely silver suit. He looked like a turkey ready for the oven.

'Wow,' she said. 'That's ... very silvery.'

Thomas looked momentarily uncertain. 'Do you think it's too much?'

'No,' said Sophie, slapping him on the back, in his style. 'It's your party and you've every right to shout it to the world.'

'Wait till you see the marquees,' he said, looking more himself. 'We got Nicky Haslam to design the party.'

The setup was indeed impressive even by Thomas and Bella's standards. It was actually marquees, plural. One for drinks, one for dinner, one for dancing, a Moroccan-style dark bar with low-slung seating, one just for gelatos and one full of games; all of them lavishly furnished and canopied with fabric.

Sophie was chatting to some people she'd met at previous Thomas and Bella events and was happy that none of them had mentioned her 'terrible loss' yet. Though she was still not quite able to relax for knowing it would inevitably have to come up.

The elephant in the room was just starting to turn into a woolly mammoth, with one of the women beginning to tilt her head to one side in a way that was like a flashing beacon for Sophie now – Sympathy! Incoming! – when she felt an arm go round her waist and someone kissed her cheek.

It was Sebastian.

'Guess who?' he said.

'Yay,' said Sophie. 'I've been wondering where you were.'

'I got held up at the office. A big story broke and I had to do a new drawing for tomorrow's paper, but I'm here now. How is it?'

'Better now you've waltzed in. Are we sitting together at dinner?'

'Yes,' said Sebastian. 'I haven't looked at the seating plan, but we are sitting together.'

Sophie smiled at him, immediately sure she was going to have a good time.

'Is Freya getting changed?'

'Freya's in Washington.'

'Still? It's been months now.'

'Yep. Like I told you, she loves it there. Right, let's tour this joint. Suss out the best spots for party action.'

By the time they'd finished dinner, Sophie had taken off the Chinese coat and was really enjoying herself. She'd had a lot of genuine-sounding compliments, from men and women. She felt good. It was a fun gang at their table and they'd made a team pact to get the dancing started the minute dinner was over.

No one had mentioned Matt.

'Okay,' said Sebastian, standing up and addressing the table. 'Come on, people, let's go and shake our things.'

All twelve of them hit the disco tent, launching into it and soon the whole marquee was crammed with people letting go to the music.

Sophie was loving it. Their little team from the table were all dancing together, no pairing up, just a lovely, loose, shared freak out and she felt the sense of release that only dancing can bring. She'd always had a good time with Sebastian and Freya at parties – the four of them had been one of those social combos that just really worked – and this still felt reassuringly normal. As though Matt and Freya had just gone off together to get drinks.

'It's such a shame Freya isn't here,' she said to Sebastian as they headed to the Moroccan bar for a breather. 'She's the best fun at parties.'

'Yes,' he said, flopping down next to her on one of the low kilim-covered sofas. 'We were a good party gang, the four of us.' He smiled sadly at her.

'It will still work,' she said. 'Not the same as the fearless foursome, but we three know each other so well, I think it will just become the new normal for it to be the Tearaway Trio.'

Sebastian nodded but didn't answer, suddenly seeming more interested in looking round the space. 'I'll get us some drinks,' he said.

Sophie watched him go. He'd been such a great support over the past months, she didn't know how she would have got through it without him – and somehow when she was with him, the truth about Matt didn't weigh so heavily on her. She didn't quite know why. Maybe it was because if it did ever slip out with Sebastian, she thought he would be able to take it on and understand it from every angle, in a way no one else would.

Perhaps he was the person she should tell, she pondered, not for the first time.

It was certainly something to consider, but as he came back with the drinks, she put the idea out of her mind. She was just going to enjoy this party.

A couple of hours later, Sophie was too exhausted and exhilarated to think about anything. She'd been dancing non-stop ever since a live band had started. Sebastian was a great dancer and when he took her hand and started whirling her into turns, she surrendered to it. They were grinning at each other as he pushed her out and reeled her in, dropping her into dips.

So when the music slowed and she found herself dancing close to Sebastian, her head against his shoulder and his arms wrapped tightly round her, it all seemed perfectly natural. And when she looked up at him and saw he was gazing down at

her, that seemed natural too and without realising it until after
it had happened, she pressed her body closer to his.

Then Sophie came to her senses and pulled away. Sebastian
seemed to snap back to reality at the same time. The wild
dancing and a lot of Champagne had addled their brains.

'Let's take a breather,' he said. 'I'll get us some water.'

'I'll grab my coat from the table,' said Sophie, 'and we can
go out for some air.'

Knowing the garden well, they came out of the marquee
and went down to a bench that looked out over an ornamental
lake. With lights strung along the trees from the house to the
marquees, there was just enough illumination to see, but they
weren't floodlit.

'That was so fun,' said Sophie. 'I really needed a dance.'

'So did I,' said Sebastian. 'It's such a great way to forget
everything.' He looked out over the lake, unusually subdued.

Sophie was beginning to worry he was upset with her for
what had just happened on the dance floor, when he turned
to her.

'Soph,' he said, looking serious. 'There's something I've
got to tell you ...'

She immediately wondered if he was going to tell her about
Matt's betrayal. Did he already know?

'What?' she said, quietly.

'It's about Freya.'

Thank God, thought Sophie, then immediately hoped it
wasn't anything bad. She loved Freya.

'She's not coming back from Washington,' said Sebastian.
'She's got a gig on the *Washington Post* and she's going to write
a US-based column for the *Clarion* as well.'

'So are you going to move there?' said Sophie, her heart sinking.

He shook his head. 'No,' he said, softly. 'She's left me. She's been having an affair with someone out there for some time, it turns out. That's why she wangled the placement, so she could shack up with him and she's decided to stay. We're getting a divorce.'

'Oh, Seb,' said Sophie, genuinely shocked. There'd never been a divorce in the Crommelin clan before. A death and now a divorce. It was hard to take in. 'Do your boys know?'

'Not yet. I've told her she has to come back and tell them herself. I'm not doing it for her.'

'I'm so sorry.'

'You know what,' said Sebastian. 'I'm actually not. I'm hurt and humiliated – everyone on the paper knows ...' He shook his head with a mortified look that reminded her to be hugely grateful that at least nobody else seemed to know about Matt and Gillette.

She squeezed his hand and made a sympathetic face. He squeezed back and looked at her, very sadly.

'It will be horrible for the boys at first,' he said, 'but they're both grown up now with their own lives going on and they'll get used to it and I will one hundred per cent make sure the divorce is amicable, so they won't have to choose between us.'

He paused, looking out over the lake, his face stony. 'In a funny way, I'm not really surprised. While I still love Freya, there is a little chip of ice in her heart and I've always known it. We had a great marriage, we were a good family unit, but now the boys are grown up, that toughness in her has come to the fore again and I'm quite glad to be freed from it.'

Sophie looked at him steadily, taking it all in.

'Plus it means I can do this.' He leaned forward and kissed her on the lips.

For a moment, she was too surprised to react. Then he moved along the bench and wrapped his arms around her and kissed her again, properly. Slowly and deeply.

Sophie felt as though she was melting into bliss and as his kiss became more urgent, she felt something like a jet engine fire up inside her. Then, just as she felt herself start to lift off the bench so she could sit astride him, an alarm went off in her head.

What the hell were they doing?

She immediately pulled away, realising she was panting. With lust. She looked away, taking some deep breaths to try to slow her heartbeat.

'I shouldn't have done that,' said Sebastian, quietly, touching her shoulder gently.

'Probably not,' said Sophie, 'but I'm glad you did. I wanted it, Seb. I was entirely complicit.'

'We were dirty dancing a bit, weren't we?'

Sophie nodded and then she couldn't help it – she grinned at him.

'I'm sorry, Sophie,' he said. 'But I have to confess: I've wanted to do that for thirty years.'

She shook her head at him, still smiling. 'Is this another Crommelin competition thing? Fancying your brother's wife?'

'It's not on the official list, as far as I know, but we have always flirted a bit, haven't we?'

'Yes. But it was fine, because it was all contained by the safety net of our marriages and family connections. And Matt and Freya did it too, didn't they?'

Sebastian nodded. 'It was all part of the magic between us all.' He breathed out loudly, stretching his arms over his head and putting his head back. 'I suppose the high emotion of losing Matt and now Freya ditching me, combined with the drink and dancing and how you look in that dress ... I just forgot the parameters for a moment there.'

'It really is okay,' said Sophie, putting her hand on his thigh, not too high up, but high enough. 'I enjoyed it, I'm not going to deny that. It was a release we probably both needed.'

Sebastian looked at her, his head on one side. 'Where are you staying?'

'In the luxury five-star shed thing.'

'So am I,' said Sebastian, putting his hand over hers on his leg and holding it firmly. 'Let's head back there and not kiss anymore, but just enjoy being shipwrecked together. Deal?'

Sophie nodded. 'Double deal.'

CHAPTER 36

Sophie woke up suddenly, realising she was desperate for the loo. Then her eyes snapped wide open – she wasn't alone. There was a warm body in the bed next to her.

She knew it was Sebastian, but still turned her head to check and there he was, flat on his back, the duvet down by his waist, his naked chest in full view. Sophie glanced down at herself and was relieved to see she was still wearing her dress. And her knickers.

Getting carefully out of the bed, she padded as quietly as she could to the bathroom off the other bedroom. She wasn't ready to see him until she'd gone over it all in her head.

They hadn't had sex. She was sure of that. They'd come back to the cabin and talked long into the night, drinking half the bottle of brandy laid on by their generous hosts. About 4am, they'd collapsed into bed together and Sophie had gone to sleep with Sebastian's arm round her. At the time, it had seemed the natural thing to do. It would have felt odd to go off to separate cold beds.

As she left the bathroom, she wondered if she should get into her own bed now, but her feet already seemed to be walking back to Sebastian's room. The comfort of having somebody else in the bed was impossible to resist – and they'd controlled themselves while properly pie-eyed the night before, so in the light of morning, surely it was perfectly innocent for two old friends to bunk up together?

He'd turned on his side while she was away and after she climbed back in she looked down at his shoulder. She'd forgotten about the tattoo on his bicep. It said, 'Matt'. Matt had had 'Seb' on his. They'd done it to each other with a needle and ink when they were teenagers. It was lucky that, even at that age, they could both make beautiful lettering.

Sophie put her head against the headboard and closed her eyes, too many thoughts rushing through her mind at once. Sober, in the harsh light of day, was that one – heavenly – kiss going to make things weird between her and Sebastian? She dearly hoped not.

Then she heard laughter.

It was Sebastian. She looked at him and she found she was laughing too.

'Morning, dear,' he said, smacking her thigh.

'Morning, yourself,' said Sophie, feeling shy and pulling the covers up to her neck.

'We didn't shag, did we? Please tell me I haven't had a momentary lapse and forgotten any little details like that … It would be such a waste.'

'You're fine,' said Sophie. 'We just curled up like a pair of drunk little puppies and pretty much blacked out.'

'That's what I thought. Phew. Probably a good thing. Although it was nice, though, wasn't it? That naughty kiss.'

Sophie smiled at him and nodded, glad he'd mentioned it. 'Yes,' she said, 'it was nice.' Too nice, but in such a weird situation, she couldn't see the point of being anything other than completely honest.

'It's lucky I have breath that could strip paint,' he said, 'otherwise I might try to do it again.'

'That's enough of that,' said Sophie, sitting up and prodding him on the upper arm.

She immediately wished she hadn't. It was hard and muscular and it triggered the same feeling set off by that surprising kiss. Time to get up.

After a shower – not quite cold, but much cooler than she would normally have it – Sophie got dressed and went back to stand in the bedroom door. Sebastian was sitting up, his entire upper body on display, staring out of the window, hands behind his head.

'I'm going to head over to the morning-after breakfast in the marquee,' she said, briskly. 'See you there?'

'Okay. You mosey on down. Better if we don't arrive together – Bella is like a bloodhound for any hint of illicit goings on.'

'Exactly,' said Sophie, happy she didn't have to explain. 'She told me once it was a key skill for any woman married to a wealthy man.'

'You might want to mess up the bed in the other room, before you go,' said Sebastian. 'Bit of a giveaway, in case she does a quick recce.'

After the breakfast, which Sophie felt they pulled off very naturally – mostly achieved by her avoiding Sebastian the entire time – they walked back to the cabin together. As they went, Sophie felt hyper-aware of his hand swinging right next to hers, and had to fight an urge to grab it and squeeze it. She crossed her arms as if chilly, to stop herself.

'Are you cold?' said Sebastian, putting an arm round her.

Not helpful. Sophie stepped out of his reach. 'Just walking,' she said.

'Gotcha,' said Sebastian. 'Don't worry, Soph. We'll have a little chat when we get back to the privacy of our dacha – I have heard Bella call it that, by the way – to work out how we're going to deal with this slight peculiarity. We need a game plan, to keep things normal. We've both got enough weird going on.'

'Good,' said Sophie, relieved he understood.

Back at the cabin, she made some espressos and took one over to Sebastian, who was sitting on a sofa, looking out at the garden. When she then carried on towards an armchair opposite, he put out his hand and took hold of hers.

'We don't need to avoid each other, Soph,' he said. 'Sit with me. You have been the greatest possible comfort to me since my brother died – and I hope I can continue to support you in your grief. I really don't want to let a momentary lapse of – what? decorum? convention? – come between us. As well as my widowed sister-in-law, you are probably my best friend, so I still want to be able to hug you when I think you need a hug. Is that okay?'

'You're right,' said Sophie. 'We'll just add one cheeky kiss to our list of high jinks over the years. Matt would think it was hilarious.'

'So would Freya,' said Sebastian, 'but I promise I won't tell her. She'd probably get a column out of it.'

They laughed and Sophie felt more confident they could keep their relationship – their *friendship* – on its old footing. It was way too precious to lose.

'So come up and stay soon,' said Sebastian. 'You've got the keys. I still want you to think of our house – my house – as your London base. Come next weekend, there's a great exhibition on at the Hayward and there's a new restaurant in Highgate village I want to try.'

It was an appealing invitation and normally she would have jumped at it, but after what had just happened, she didn't think she would feel comfortable alone in that house with him. A place with so many memories of Matt and them all being together when the kids were young. It would feel awkward.

But she didn't want to allow any distance to come between them either – and she could hear a new undercurrent of distress in Sebastian's voice. With what he had going on with Freya, he didn't want to spend another weekend there alone.

Then she remembered that Tamar was going away for a few days at the end of that week, so she would be all alone too. It was pointless for them both to be lonely in big houses.

'Why don't you come down to me instead?' she said.

'Great,' said Sebastian. 'I'd love to. I'll get the train on Thursday afternoon if that suits. If I need to update anything for the paper on Friday, I can scan it in and send it from your place.'

It wasn't until she got home and went to put the date in her diary that she realised that it was the Friday she had arranged to have lunch with Charlie. He'd invited her for a walk and 'huddled picnic' in the woods at his place. She had been really

looking forward to it, but Sebastian was family and he clearly
needed her support now, just as she had relied on his.

She sent Charlie a message: *Really sorry, have to postpone
lunch on Friday – a work thing has come up. Can you suggest another
day? S xxx*

CHAPTER 37

Juliet put the bottle of breast milk she had just expressed into the fridge. She'd decided to start coming in to work for a couple of hours a day to get back on top of things, which was easy to do while Hettie was still at the stage where you could safely put her down somewhere in her basket.

So far, Hettie had been a wonderful baby. Much easier than Cassady had been. Juliet glanced down at her new daughter's beautiful little face, right next to her by the desk, and felt the love that had enveloped her from the moment she had held Hettie in her arms squeeze her heart. She was such an adorable little thing.

With Hettie by her side, it felt great to be back behind her familiar desk, checking the sales figures and sussing out the prices on some special yellow diamonds she was interested in. She would probably use an agent to buy them for her – now her brand was getting such a high profile, prices of raw materials automatically started higher.

Shop sales had been good in her two-week absence and Bob had been doing well, she was pleased to see. Her instincts about him had been right. At the trade show, he'd reminded her of her own early days, trying to get appointments with buyers. She remembered all too well the knock-backs and rudeness she'd experienced from people who now begged to stock her stuff. And it made her want to help him.

Having such a personable young man in the shop also softened Luiza's ultra-professional but verging-on-scary vibe. They were a great combination. She would send Gwen an email to give Bob a bonus in recognition of his excellent start.

She started to write it, but when she got to the point where she needed to put in the amount of the bonus, she paused. She needed an appropriate figure as a sweetener but since she'd hired him in such a rush on her last day in the office before Hettie's birth, she couldn't remember how much they were paying him. She flicked over to the personnel file to check.

Realising she didn't know his surname, she looked down the first-name column of the wages spreadsheet for 'Bob'. But there wasn't one. That was odd. There was no Bob, but there was a 'Beau'. She didn't employ anyone called Beau and if she did, she would certainly have remembered that name. It was unusual, and one of Matt's sons was called Beau. She wouldn't have forgotten it.

She looked across to see the surname and her mouth dropped open. Crommelin. Beau Crommelin. She felt sick with shock. Crommelin was Matt's name. Beau Crommelin was his son's name. Was there any chance there was another young man called Beau Crommelin in London?

But even as she grasped at that scrap of hope, the reality was unfolding in her head. She pictured Bob – just through the security door in the shop – with his full lips, his swagger, his suits …

Then, sitting back in her chair, her heart pounding, a framed picture of Cassady caught her eye.

Bob looked like Cassady. Cassady looked like him.

She glanced down at her darling baby. Was there a family resemblance there too? With a small surge of relief, she thought not. Hettie was fairer, more like her. That was a blessing.

But then the full horror of the situation hit her again and she found it hard to breathe.

The young man who her little girl never stopped talking about was actually her daughter's half-brother. She had to get Bob – Beau – out of Cassady's life immediately.

And he must never find out who his little friend's father was. His poor mother had to be protected.

She stood up and took sleeping Hettie out of her basket, gently rocking her to and fro for her own comfort, and then found some relief in realising that it was actually a good thing that she had found out Bob's true identity now, before he became any more embedded in her life – or her children's lives.

Feeling a little more collected, Juliet carefully put Hettie down again, took a sip from the glass of water on her desk and then rang Gwen.

'Oh, hi, Gwennie,' she said, turning her chair so her back was to the door into the shop. 'I was just checking the payroll and I see there is someone called "Beau" on it. Who is that?'

Gwen laughed nervously. 'I was going to tell you about that when we have our meeting this afternoon. That's Bob's real name. He hates being called Beau – he says he was bullied for it at school, so everyone calls him Bob and he asked politely if I could keep his real name to myself in here and I said yes – although, obviously, I was always going to tell you.'

'Ah, that all makes sense,' said Juliet, although it didn't really. Why did he not want her to know his real name? 'Right, well, I'm afraid I'm not going to be able to stay in the office long enough to have our meeting today, after all. Something's come up and I've got to leave now. So I'll call you later this afternoon and we can go over everything on the phone, is that alright? I was looking forward to our catch-up and we will have a proper one soon, just not today, okay?'

She was fond of Gwen, who had been with her from the start, and they had a little tradition of a weekly meeting with tea. Gwen was very good at her job and Juliet wanted to hold on to her, which was why she always took that bit of time to make her feel special, but this was an emergency. She had to get out of the building right away.

She texted Ligaya, who was waiting up in the staff room, asking her to come down, ready to leave immediately, and started packing up.

Then she called her parking garage, asking them to bring the car to the front of the building and when the text alert that it was there pinged, she picked up her coat, her phone in the other hand. As she walked through the shop, with the nanny bringing up the rear carrying Hettie, she pretended to be having a tense conversation with someone on the phone, sweeping past Luiza and Bob – Beau – with just an upwards nod of her head in acknowledgement.

But as she went out of the door, she realised her eyes had fully registered Beau's face. How had she never realised how like his father he was?

*

When they got back to the house, Hettie was awake and fretful, so Juliet left Ligaya to change and feed her and went into her study, closing the door. She rang Gwen's direct line.

'Hi Gwennie,' she said. 'I'm afraid I don't have time to go over all the figures now, I'm in the middle of negotiations for some rather special stones, so I thought we could catch up with all that on Friday instead, with our tea, but there is one thing I urgently need you to sort out today.' She paused to take a breath. 'It's about that young chap Bob … or rather Beau. I've decided not to extend his contract. His trial period is up this week and I would like him to leave today.'

Gwen said nothing and Juliet found herself filling the gap.

'I know he's doing alright in the shop, but I've got some big plans on the go that will mean digging in deep for a little bit, so I don't feel we can afford an extra staff member at the moment. Luiza can manage on her own for a bit longer.' She knew it wasn't convincing as she said it.

'So, I would like you to tell him, Gwen, that today is his last day – and because it will be a bit of a shock for him, I'm prepared to give him a month's extra money as a goodwill gesture. And I will give him a good reference too. Tell him we are very grateful for the way he covered during my maternity leave, but we don't need him now.'

'What about the unpaid work experience he was doing up in the workshop?' said Gwen. 'He might ask if he can carry on doing that, even if he's not working in the shop.'

Juliet hadn't thought of that. Larry had been very impressed with the way Bob – Beau, aargh – had finished the tasks he'd set him. And she had genuinely liked the pieces he'd shown her at the trade show, they'd been well made with some interesting ideas in them. She did actually need someone else in the studio, but not him. No way.

'I'm afraid you'll have to tell him the same thing applies up there,' she said. 'Do please tell him that Larry is impressed with his work, but with the big overheads I'm about to take on, I've got to keep costs pared down and another person in the building is always a cost. Please tell him I'll give him a separate glowing reference for each job. That should soften the blow for him.'

She put down the phone and allowed her head to sink into her hands. Of course, she remembered now, Matt had told her one of his sons made jewellery. She also remembered one of them reading a poem at the funeral, but he'd had a mass of black hair like Matt's. Although now she realised that as Bob/Beau's closely cropped hair was beginning to grow back, it was exactly that jet-black Irish hair that Matt had.

That Cassady had.

Juliet shook her head, almost dizzy with relief that she'd found out before Beau's hair had grown just a little bit more and someone realised how oddly alike he and her daughter were. It had been such a close thing, but if it had happened once, could something like it happen again?

And with pictures of her and Cassady now circulating in *Her* magazine, what if Matt's wife saw them, remembered Juliet from the funeral, saw how like her late husband Cassady was and made the connection?

Yet again, she wondered if it might be better to do what she'd tried to do that day at the funeral? To go and see Sophie

and tell her the truth? That she'd an affair with her husband –
and deliberately got pregnant without telling him – but there
had categorically never been any plan for them to be together,
or for him to any active part in the children's lives. Child, as it
had been while he was still alive.

And just like every other time Juliet had gone over it in
her head, she couldn't decide which was the better thing to
do. To speak out or just keep hoping that the secret had died
with Matt.

CHAPTER 38

Beau was loading cardboard boxes and stuffed bin liners into a rented van. He'd spent the previous evening packing up everything in his flat and now that he'd done the studio, he was ready to drive it all down to Hastings. He hadn't even needed to give notice. There was such a long waiting list for spaces in the building, his had been taken the moment he'd told Sam he was leaving. It was the same with the room in the flat he'd shared for four years.

He felt like the Beau-shaped hole in the fabric of London had grown over before he'd even driven off.

That business with Flora and the posters had stripped the joy from his East London life and now that he'd been sacked from Giuliette, there wasn't anything to keep him up in town, paying extortionate rent and working all hours to cover his bills. He could make his rings anywhere. Olive had already said he could work in a corner of her studio any time.

He loaded in the last bags, slammed the van door and set off, tuning the radio to a cheesy golden oldies station with the volume turned up high and all the windows open. Waiting at a red light, he saw a woman in the next car smiling at him and doing the sexy eyes thing. Then she rolled down her passenger-side window. Beau smiled back at her. She was hot. Older, but still hot.

Still looking at her, his elbow out of the window, t-shirt sleeve rolled up, bicep on display, he sang along to the track that was playing, gazing straight into her eyes, and watched her turn quite pink.

The lights changed and he turned left, honking his horn as he went, waving his right arm out of the window. One last big stranger flirt for old time's sake. Was that sleazy?

He just wanted to make her day, to let her know she was still a sexually attractive woman to a young guy. He should have tossed a ring through her window and filmed it for Flora.

But although he was still confused about all that, he was committed to leaving that fast-love lifestyle behind in London. This move was a new start in every way. The shock of losing the Giuliette gig on top of everything else made it seem like time for a fundamental reset.

He still couldn't understand why he'd been ditched so abruptly from that job. 'Cost savings' had been the reason Gwen had given him, after plying him with tea and a slice of one of her homemade cakes. There were some big new things happening and Juliet could no longer afford an additional member of staff, she'd said. That was plausible in such a fast-growing business, but when he'd asked if he could still help out in the workshop – as unpaid work experience – Gwen had said that was over too. So it seemed like Juliet just didn't want him there.

What had he done? Was it something to do with Cassady? Had he accidentally said something inappropriate when he'd been looking after her? Used a rude word that she'd repeated at home? He really hoped not. He loved that kid. One of the worst parts of being thrown out of Giuliette was that he'd never see her again.

The unhappy ending to that all-too-brief interlude made him super glad he hadn't told his mum or Tamar – or anyone – about working there. That had been one of those Matt things Beau had found useful over the years. Never tell anyone about a project until it's absolutely in the bag had been his father's rule and it was a good one. It was just a shame he hadn't been so wise about other things.

Beau felt his mood slump, but then he saw he was coming up to the M25 exit signposted HASTINGS and immediately perked up. He was genuinely excited to be going back. He liked the quirky vibe of the place – and it had to be a good thing for him to spend more time with his mum. Didn't it?

Sam had given him heaps about being a 'loser kid, running back to mummy', asking if she had his Arsenal duvet set ready on the bed for him and his net of teddies. Perhaps he was going to find it annoying to live with a parent again, but apart from his pressing need to leave town, it seemed like the right thing to do, considering what she was going through. What they both were.

It was all good, he told himself as he merged onto the A21, heading south towards the coast. And then, of course, there was Tamar—

'No!' he said out loud. He wasn't going there. He'd made a promise to his mother and he was going to keep it.

Which made him think of something else. He hadn't actually told Sophie he was moving down to live with her. He'd planned to surprise her and now he remembered how she hadn't been thrilled the last time he'd pulled that trick – and that had only been for a visit.

He really did need to float the idea to her first, pretend they were discussing it. Although it was entirely settled in his head. He was moving to Hastings.

He pulled over at the next layby to ring an old college friend who lived in nearby Rye to ask if he could stay for a few days. With that secured, he sent a text to Sophie, saying he was 'thinking of moving down' and how did she feel about it?

Not that it made any difference. If he got any kind of vibe she didn't want him there full time, he'd just shack up with Olive. He had a jewellery project to get on with that he didn't want to have to explain to anyone and her studio was the perfect place to do it.

CHAPTER 39

Sophie was in the station car park waiting for Sebastian, who was due to arrive at any moment. She opened the car door to go on to the platform to meet him, then pulled her legs back in and closed it again. Then she flipped down the sunshade and looked in the mirror, wiping off the lipstick she'd just put on. What was wrong with her?

Her brother-in-law was coming for the weekend. It wasn't like she hadn't spent time with him before. He was probably the person she'd been on the most holidays with, apart from Matt. But of course, Matt and Freya had also been on those holidays. And she and Sebastian hadn't recently had a delicious big snog.

She put her face in her hands and groaned. Had they wrecked a great friendship with a moment's indiscretion? She couldn't bear not to have him in her life. She loved his company and he was the one person she felt really understood all the facets of her grief – apart from the one she wasn't telling him about – but now there was this other thing.

Pure lust.

How had that suddenly ambushed her? It was nothing new that Sebastian was a good-looking man who kept in shape; she could have recognised him in swimming trunks with a bag over his head. And while they had always flirted, as they'd acknowledged to each other, it had been in a platonic, mutual-appreciation way – but now, with them both suddenly weirdly single and after that one blissful kiss, had her feelings for him mutated into something completely different?

She really hoped not, but she couldn't kid herself. Just the night before, she'd had a vivid erotic dream about him. Still, she was praying that when she saw his dear familiar face, her response would be 'Hello, funny brother-in-law, dear old friend.' Not 'Rip your clothes off and get over here, Big Boy.'

She put her head on the steering wheel and groaned. Is this what it felt like to be Beau? Sex monstered?

She must have been mad to invite Sebastian to stay, but at the time, it had seemed like the best way to handle it. To meet the strangeness head on and deal with it, so their precious relationship – friendship! – within the wider family wouldn't be damaged.

Or, alone together in the house, was she secretly hoping something else would happen?

She had her head back, eyes closed, trying to eliminate that idea from her consciousness when the car door opened and she felt a fat kiss land on her cheek. Her eyes snapped open.

'Boo,' said Sebastian quietly, his face close to hers.

Sophie scrabbled to sit upright. 'Hi!' she squeaked, but he was already opening the back door to throw his bag in and then getting in beside her.

'Hello,' he said, putting his seatbelt on and smiling at her, all that mischief in his eyes.

Sophie's stomach lurched. She couldn't think of anything to say. She just looked back at him.

'So, are we going to have a picnic in the car park, in the great British tradition? Have you got the thermos?'

'Right,' she said, starting the engine. 'Sorry. I'm a bit dazed. I was having a little nap. I got here early, by mistake.'

Once they got back to the house, Sophie felt more normal. She busied herself in the kitchen while he sat on a stool on the other side of the island, chatting and topping up her wine. She was glad there was a large immovable wooden structure between them, but as they talked about work and kids, it did all fall back into place. They felt like family again.

Mostly.

The next morning, they were walking down West Hill Road, taking the scenic route over to Hastings Old Town. It seemed safer to be out of the house.

'That was so nice, last night,' Sebastian said. 'Just to watch Netflix and eat a curry together. No one needs much more than that in life to be happy, do they?'

'No,' said Sophie. 'It's nirvana.'

'That was something Freya has never appreciated, the joy of staying in. She wanted to be out every night and I had to go to so many gruesome parties with her. She often didn't even enjoy them herself – the right person hadn't spoken to her, or had been seen speaking to a rival for longer than to her. It was so exhausting, I refused to go in the end. So I suppose the cracks between us were already there and I just haven't acknowledged them.'

'I never saw that side of her,' said Sophie. 'We always had such a great time together, in our little gang.'

'Yes, the Fun Four brought out the best in her. The FOMO has got much worse recently. I think she's worried some young thing is going to come up and scoop her gig from under her.'

'That's so weird for someone as brilliant as her. To be so insecure.'

'The last time we talked was on Zoom,' said Sebastian. 'It was the first time I'd seen her face since she left. She's had loads of Botox and I think some lip plumping.'

'You're kidding me.'

'She looks like Kellyanne Conway. But less fresh-faced. Would you do that stuff?'

'No flipping way,' said Sophie. 'I am what I am. A middle-aged woman, mooching towards later life and I'm proud for my face to show it.'

Sebastian stopped and looked at her seriously then took both her hands in his. 'That's why you're so amazing,' he said, sighing. 'I know it's wrong, but I want to kiss you again.'

Sophie froze, not sure whether she was feeling thrilled or horrified, and then pulled her hands away. 'I'm sorry, Seb, I can't deny it, I feel it too, but we have to resist. It would make everything hideously complicated and we've both got enough going on. And we're out in public.'

Sebastian looked round the park. 'There's no one here. Are the trees going to see us?'

'Someone I know could walk into this park from any of the gates. It's small-town life. I don't ever leave my house without bumping into people I know. It's actually nice once you get used to it. Come on, let's keep walking.'

Sophie stopped briefly at the top of Norman Road to say hi to her hairdresser, Ken. Then, further down, Olga was standing outside the Kino, and Holly and Helen from Shop were unloading boxes of stock on the opposite corner. Sophie said hi to them all, introducing Sebastian with particular emphasis on the words 'brother-in-law'. Just to remind them both.

'Okay,' he said, as they crossed the road at Warrior Square, having greeted a couple more people on the way over, 'I get it. It's like being at school and seeing the same people constantly in the corridors.'

'That's it,' said Sophie.

They stopped for a while on a seafront bench, just gazing at the water, breathing in the cool clear air. Sophie's phone buzzed in her pocket and she pulled it out to find a message from Beau. Her eyes open wide, she turned to look at Sebastian.

'Something wrong?' he asked.

'Just surprising. It's from Beau. He's left London. Properly left it. For good. He's staying with friends in Rye until next week, but then he wants to come and live with me, permanently.'

'Ah … So no more little private interludes like this, then?'

'As many interludes as you like, but not private, which is probably for the best.'

He looked back out to sea. Sophie couldn't read what he was thinking and thought it better not to ask. She genuinely didn't know what answer she wanted to hear.

'And I have to be honest, Seb. I have been worried about how I'll be when Tamar goes, which won't be long now, the book is nearly finished. I don't know if I can cope with being completely on my own.'

'But that's the thing,' he said, sitting up and turning to face her. 'You don't need to be on your own. You've got me. If you want me that way.'

Sophie looked out at the sea now, too many thoughts chasing through her brain. She was so tired of it. Every time she got relief from the overthinking, something else happened to make her mind race and thoughts tumble. It was like Cirque du Soleil in there.

She loved spending time with Sebastian and the temptation to make it into something more serious was strong, but really, how could they? How could they tell their respective kids – two in the throes of devastating grief, the other two about to be hit by the shock of a divorce – that a weird auntie-and-uncle scene was now happening? And what would the rest of the family say?

Sophie couldn't help smiling, though, picturing Bella's face when she heard that news.

She stood up. 'Come on, brother-in-law,' she said. 'Enough of that talk. Let's keep powering on to the Old Town. There are some great pubs there and it will be nice to sit in the warmth for a bit.'

Twenty minutes later they arrived at the Crown, where Tessa found them a nice table tucked away in a corner of the snug, the cosy little room at the back with an open fire.

On her second pewter tankard of the house black velvet, Sophie was feeling deliciously relaxed, her head resting against the banquette. She turned to look at Sebastian as he told her a funny story about something that had happened at the paper the week before, trying not to think about his thigh pressed against hers.

A familiar voice snapped her out of her reverie.

'Sophie.'

She looked up to see Charlie standing there.

'And Seb,' he added, reaching out to shake Sebastian's hand. 'Good to see you again.'

'Oh, hi, Charlie,' said Sophie, too eagerly, sitting up straight and inching away from Sebastian in a way she hoped wasn't too obvious. 'Seb is down for a visit. My brother-in-law, which you know, of course, ha ha … from the housewarming and the beach party.'

Oh, God. She wasn't even speaking English.

'Yes,' said Charlie, smiling broadly as he always did, but Sophie could see something in his eyes, something that made her uncomfortable. A knowing look?

'Well, good to see you both,' he said. 'I'm on the hunt for a friend I'm meeting. I thought she might be in the back here.'

She? Sophie immediately wondered why she'd noticed that and why it was any of her business who he was meeting.

'Enjoy your drink,' he said and turned to go.

'I'll ring you about that lunch,' Sophie called after him.

'Great,' he said, half looking over his shoulder and raising a hand as he went.

Sophie felt very conscious of his back. Turned to her.

'What lunch?' said Sebastian.

'Oh,' she replied. 'I was supposed to have lunch with him today and I cancelled him – for you.'

'Good. Keep cancelling him.'

Sophie slapped the top of his arm with the back of her hand. 'I'll have lunch with whomsoever I choose, Mr Crommelin. Charlie has been a good friend to me ever since I moved here.'

'I bet he has. Just make sure he doesn't get into his sunflower swimming trunks again at any of these cosy lunches. He's way too fit for an old bloke.'

'He's only a couple of years older than you, mister,' said Sophie. *And you should see him in eyeliner.*

CHAPTER 40

Juliet had taken Hettie to see her grandmother. As they were leaving, the warden came out of his office and asked Juliet if she could pop in for a minute.

'How is Hettie?' he asked bending over the carrier to look at her. 'She's certainly growing. Please sit. Would you like tea?'

'I'm fine, thank you, I just had some with my mother.'

'Good, well, I won't take much of your time,' said Donato. 'But we need to have a little talk about Pauline. How did you find her today?'

'Well, she was very excited to see Hettie, so that was nice.'

'Did anything unusual strike you?' asked Donato, a kind but concerned expression on his face.

'The flat was in a bit of a mess. I assumed the cleaner is due today?'

'The cleaner was there yesterday. This is why we need to talk. Your mother is a very intelligent woman and she's in good physical shape, but she's not managing so well on her own in the flat these days.'

'Ah,' said Juliet. The flat hadn't just been a mess, it was dirty. Quite gross in places. 'I was going to ask you about getting the cleaner to go in more often.'

'We've already done that. With your mother's permission, the cleaner goes in every other day now. We had to do it for sanitation reasons, but even that is not enough.'

Juliet understood. He didn't have to spell it out. There had been something really unpleasant she'd had to clean up in the bathroom. She'd thought it had been one unlucky accident.

'Can they go in every day?' she asked. 'The cleaners? I'll pay for it, of course. Twice a day if necessary.'

'I don't think that's what your mother needs. I think she needs to be somewhere where all the day-to-day things are looked after for her.'

Juliet looked at him, trying to take it in. What was he saying?

'Don't worry,' he said, 'she doesn't have dementia.'

'Are you sure? I was actually shocked by the state of the flat.'

'I think it's more because of her specific experiences … I don't think it's good for Pauline to be on her own so much. She needs stimulation – and distraction. You've seen how many newspapers she reads. I think she would benefit greatly from eating her meals with other people and spending her days occupied, doing things in groups. To have activities arranged – art classes, exercise, talks, that kind of thing.'

Donato was being very kind as always, but Juliet was finding the conversation quite hard to process. She thought her mother was really well set up in this flat, where she had her independence but help on hand when she needed it – and it wasn't too far for Juliet to visit often and for Pauline to come to their house too.

'There are some new specialist places opening,' he continued. 'With a more social form of care. They do things like have a kindergarten on the site, so the residents see young children. Some of them have rooms that students live in at a very reduced rent, in return for spending time with the older people. There might be chickens in the garden and those who want it have areas to plant things. Residents can help in the kitchen, or run the library, so they are all an active part of the community, as much as they are able.

'She would have her own bedroom and bathroom, but the sitting room and dining room would be communal. I have a brochure for one which I know is very good. It's the benchmark in this country.'

He handed her a glossy-looking brochure. Juliet read the front. It said *The Elms – empathetic social care* over a picture of a large Victorian house. She turned the page and there were pictures of older people reading books to toddlers, feeding chickens, digging gardens, painting pictures, doing yoga, eating together. They all looked happy. Maybe that was what Pauline needed. Sitting alone in the flat with all those memories crowding in couldn't be good for her. Juliet felt stupid for not figuring it out sooner herself.

There were also photographs of some of the bedrooms, which looked okay, and she read that they could take their own furniture with them, which would be good. She also noticed that some of the rooms had sea views – which was nice, but meant it wasn't in London.

She turned it over to see where it was situated. St Leonards-on-Sea, wherever that was. She'd have to go and have a look.

CHAPTER 41

Sophie and Beau were in the kitchen when there was a knock at the door. Beau went to answer it and came back holding a large brown package. Looking at the address label, he beamed at Sophie before putting it on the kitchen island and bolting back out to the bottom of the stairs.

'Tames!' he yelled. 'Come down, quick! Your proof pages are here!'

Tamar came clattering down and burst into the kitchen, her hair wrapped up in a bright green towel and her face pretty much the same colour.

Her hands splayed on the package, she looked up at them, the green gunge cracking as she frowned with confusion. 'I so want to open them, but I've just put all this gunge on my face.'

Beau already had his phone out. 'Stay exactly as you are,' he said. 'I think your followers will love the reveal in Kermit mode. It really adds another element. Start opening, I'll record it.'

Tamar unwrapped the package and looked at the spreads, holding them up for Beau to film, beaming with delight.

She had tears in her eyes as she looked at Sophie. 'Thank you so much,' she said. 'It's beyond my wildest dreams.'

'You did it, Tamar,' said Sophie. 'Your food, your pictures, your concept. I just provided the space for you to work in and moved a few pomegranate seeds to optimum positions. You should be very, very proud.'

Beau went round to the other side of the island and leafed through the pages, nodding his head in admiration. 'This is a seriously class piece of work, Tames. If I had cookbook fatigue, this would snap me out of it.'

Tamar looked down, suddenly shy.

'Come here, you little superstar,' he said, wrapping his arms around her – in what he felt was a brotherly way – picking her up and spinning her round. 'Get used to feeling giddy, because this is going to go off like a rocket when it comes out.'

When he put her down, he had bright green smeared all over his t-shirt.

'Thanks, Beausie,' she said. 'Sorry about your shirt. I better go and wash this stuff off, it's starting to get itchy.' She put her hand on the proofs again and squealed with excitement before running off and up the stairs.

'It really is good, isn't it?' said Beau, leafing through the pages again.

'The best book I've been involved with for a long time,' said Sophie, standing next to him. 'I think Olive's bowls actually set the food off better than the original ones. There's just a little touch of modernity to them that cuts out any of that "ethnic food" feeling that Tamar so wanted to avoid.'

Beau put an arm round her. 'And all your brilliant idea, my lovely Mumpty,' he said, kissing the top of her head. 'We should do something to celebrate. Shall we take Tamar out for a slap-up lunch?'

Sophie was silent for a moment. 'You two go. Take the car and have an expedition. It's a really nice day for November – you could go over to Dungeness or somewhere. Tamar has spent so much time here with me, head down in the studio, then hours on the screen, working on the words, she needs to get out.'

'Are you sure? It's your book too.'

'I want her to really feel the special joy of seeing the pages laid out for her first book and not have to defer to me on it. We can do that when we have to check every word and every colour tone on every page. And while you're out,' said Sophie, from the doorway heading towards her study, 'scout some locations for the next book we're talking about doing together, all about cooking food from local suppliers. Make sure Tamar takes her camera.'

'But if you're doing it together, shouldn't you be in on that?'

'I've seen a lot of it already. I want Tamar's fresh take. And I've got stuff I need to do here.'

'Okay,' said Beau, feeling a kind of tickly excitement somewhere in his chest, or was it his belly? Definitely not any lower. He wondered what it was. The prospect of spending time with someone he knew would make him laugh and want to do the same stuff as him? Was that it? Interesting.

CHAPTER 42

Juliet was sitting with Gwen in her cramped basement office, having their weekly tea and cake catch-up to go over the figures. It was the only time Juliet ate cake. It was homemade, which made it acceptable somehow.

'I think this is my happy place,' said Juliet, looking round at the Beautiful Wales calendar and the dried flowers arrangement on top of the filing cabinet. There were pictures of a ginger cat pinned up on the notice board.

'Oh, that's nice,' said Gwen. 'I like to make it homely.'

'Well, you do spend a lot of time down here. When we move to the new premises, you're going to have a lovely office next to mine.'

'About that,' said Gwen. 'The architect has sent some new plans with the costs breakdown. Would you like to look at them now?'

'Ooh, yes,' said Juliet, pulling her chair round to Gwen's side of the desk.

The plans had just loaded when someone walked into the room. It was Luiza.

'Who's in the shop?' asked Juliet.

'Octavia,' said Luiza, her head to one side.

314

'Well, I would like you to go back up there now, please, Luiza, and whatever it is you want to talk about, we can do it another time.'

'Now is good.'

Juliet looked back at her, wondering what on earth it was about. 'Alright then. Let's get on with it, but I'm busy here with Gwen, and I need you back in the shop as soon as possible. What's going on?'

'The thing is,' said Luiza, looking down at her nails and then back up at Juliet, 'now that Bob has gone and you are not planning to hire anyone else yet, that is a lot for me ...'

Juliet said nothing, waiting to see what was going to come next.

'So I think you will agree that my commission should be raised to reflect what I contribute to the business.' She smiled again.

It's like a cloud going across the sun that smile, Juliet thought. 'Your review is in six months,' she said firmly. 'We'll talk about it then, okay? Because I'm making a big investment in the company this year, which will be great for all of us, but that means I have to really watch the budget at the moment. That's why I had to let, er, Bob go.'

'Are you sure that's his name?' said Luiza, looking Juliet right in the eye. 'I heard your little hesitation there ...'

Juliet glanced at Gwen. Had she told her? Gwen imperceptibly shook her head. They'd worked together so long and so closely they could communicate a lot without words.

'Of course it's his name,' said Juliet.

'Really?' said Luiza. 'Because I know it is actually Beau. I read the papers and I know who his dad is. Was. So sad.'

She paused and Juliet had to stop herself swallowing hard. Where on earth was Luiza going with this?

'And, of course, you knew the father, didn't you?' said Luiza. 'So it must be extra sad for you.'

Juliet began to feel Luiza was enjoying this little performance, but she was determined to keep her cool. 'What are you talking about?' she asked in a measured tone.

'One of my best friends works at Sotheby's. He's on the jewellery sales, that's how I know him, but he likes to go to all the big auctions … you know, to see what's going on, to see who's there, who they are with and where they go afterwards. It's a little sideline for him.'

Now Juliet did swallow.

'So, because of what he tells me, I think it must be very sad for you that Beau's father has died and, of course, for your poor little girls. Once you know – well, Cassady and Beau look so alike, don't they?' She laughed. A tinkly little giggle. 'And you said in that interview in *Her* magazine they have the same father, so Hettie too.'

Juliet had to restrain herself from jumping to her feet and physically pushing her out of the office. 'I don't know what you're talking about,' she said, making a huge effort to control her volume. 'You know I go to Sotheby's auctions, a lot of people do.'

Luiza looked at her straight, no smile now. 'Let's just keep this simple, shall we? I want twenty per cent more commission starting today and then this will go no further.' She paused for a moment and then added: 'My friend has photographs, so it's up to you.'

Juliet looked back at her, trying to put her racing thoughts into some kind of order. It was blackmail. But she couldn't just tell Luiza to get the hell out of her building and never come back, not with that threat hanging over her. What she needed was time. Time to think and plan a response.

'As you can see, Luiza,' she said. 'I'm having a budget meeting with Gwen, going over all the figures. How about you go back to the shop now and we'll carry on here, so I will know where I am with everything and what I can spare and then I will speak to you about your request tomorrow? Alone.'

Luiza nodded. 'You have twenty-four hours,' she said. 'Enjoy your cake.'

She left the room and Juliet got up and closed the door behind her. Quietly, although she would have liked to have slammed it.

'Shall I make a fresh pot of tea?' asked Gwen.

'I think I would rather have another slice of your delicious cake, please.'

'Are you alright?'

'Not really. She's blackmailing me.'

'Yes,' said Gwen, passing her the plate. 'There's no other word for it.'

'What do you think I should do?'

Gwen said nothing. She was fingering the little gold crucifix she wore around her neck. 'I've got to be honest,' she said, finally. 'Those things Luiza said, I have wondered about them myself. When I found out Bob's real name and I connected it with the surname, I did wonder if he might be the son of Matt Crommelin. I've read about him in the *Daily*

Mail, things he did in the name of art, like filming his own mother-in-law dying.'

Juliet said nothing. *How extreme he'd been.*

'And then the way you suddenly let Beau go when you found out his real name, that was so out of character for you and then – oh, I can't lie to you, Juliet. I looked at Beau's Instagram and there was a picture of him before he cut his hair short and he's the absolute image of Cassady, and the way those two get on …'

Gwen looked straight at her, with an expression of sincere concern. No judgement, just caring.

'Thank you, Gwen,' she said. 'Thank you for being, well, for being you. Tell me one more thing. What would you do now if you were me?'

Gwen looked thoughtful again. 'Of course, I don't know all the details and I'm not asking you to tell me – and you know I will support you whatever happens – but I always think that in difficult situations involving several people, although it's hard, it's better just to get everything out into the open, so everyone knows what's what. Then you can't be vulnerable to people like Luiza.'

Juliet rubbed her cheeks with her hands. She knew what Gwen was saying was probably right, but she just didn't think she had the courage to do it. Not yet. She'd just had a baby, for heaven's sake!

She decided she'd give Luiza the raise – for now – to buy herself more time.

CHAPTER 43

Sophie was in Charlie's car. She'd called him as soon as Beau and Tamar had left, trying to sound casual and normal, to ask if he wanted to 'catch up' some time.

It had been weighing on her heavily since he'd turned up at the Crown when she'd been there with Sebastian. She'd cancelled him for another man and lied about it. She hadn't been thinking straight.

'Now's good,' he'd said, when she rang. So he didn't seem to be holding a grudge. 'I'm already on my way into St Leonards to get something and I can pick you up right after. I'll take you on a mystery tour.'

They were on a narrow lane travelling through pretty agriculture countryside that Sophie hadn't seen before and when they came to a small group of buildings, he pulled over to the side of the road and they got out.

After grabbing a couple of blankets, Charlie led the way across the road and onto a beach. There were high cliffs to the right, and in the other direction, stretching east, miles and miles of shingle. The beach was divided at regular intervals by wooden groynes, yet it still seemed much wilder than the coast at St Leonards, and even out where Rey's beach hut was.

'This is lovely,' she said, raising her face into the breeze. 'Where are we?'

'Pett Level,' said Charlie. 'My favourite place to swim – and to decompress. I do like an autumn and even a winter sea swim, but don't worry, I'm not suggesting we go in today.'

They walked along for a while and then he turned towards the water's edge and laid one of the blankets down to the left of one of the wooden partitions, indicating for Sophie to sit. Once she was down there, she realised they were completely sheltered from the wind. She gazed out to sea and sighed deeply.

'There you are,' said Charlie. 'Let the tension out and the Pett Level calm in. Coming here always lowers my blood pressure.'

She closed her eyes and surrendered to the moment, then opened them again, looking out over the choppy waves, relishing the feeling of the sun on her face.

'This is wonderful,' she said. 'I feel spoiled. Thank you, Charlie.'

They sat for a while, silently gazing out to sea. Just being.

He spoke first. 'I wanted to spoil you, Sophie, because I think you deserve it. And to show you this lovely spot, which I knew you would appreciate, but also because I want to tell you something. I want you to know my whole story.'

'Okay …' said Sophie.

'I told you how I lost my son.'

'You did. So awful.'

'It was an appalling trauma, as you would know. A sudden, pointless, avoidable death. I went quite crazy. Which is why, as well as losing my son, I lost everything else important. I drank too much, I was angry with everybody and …'

He paused and pulled his lips together tightly. Sophie could see this was something he found hard to say. She understood that.

'I had an affair,' he said, his voice dropping almost to a whisper. 'With a young teacher at my daughter's school. I didn't even like her that much, but she flirted with me and in my insanity and my self-hate for being alive when my beautiful boy was dead, I responded. We were found out and everyone at the school knew. I looked like a disgusting sleaze – I *was* a disgusting sleaze – and my wife was so humiliated she went for everything in the divorce and got it. I didn't have the strength to fight and I didn't think I deserved anything, anyway. The stress made me useless at work and they fired me. And the worst thing of all is that, as I told you, my daughter still doesn't talk to me, so in effect, I've lost both my children.'

He turned to her, his eyes holding hers. 'There is a particular reason I'm telling you this now, Sophie. Last week, in the Crown, with your brother-in-law ...'

Sophie's mouth went dry. She looked down at her hands resting in her lap, feeling sick.

'I'm not passing judgement, Sophie,' he continued. 'It must be a great comfort to be so close to Matt's extended family, but I couldn't help picking up on a vibe between you two that day – and I'd seen a glimpse of it already at the beach party – something a bit beyond the normal in-law connection. So it's been pressing on me to tell you my story, because after the shock you've had, you could make poor decisions, as I did. I don't want that to happen to you.'

Sophie felt a tear slide down her cheek.

'I'm sorry to upset you,' he said. 'I just wanted to tell you my whole story, because if someone had given me advice then, everything could have been different for me.'

The tears came faster and Sophie couldn't help a sob escaping. She groped in her pocket to see if she had a tissue and Charlie reached into his and pulled out a large cotton handkerchief, pressing it into her hands. She wiped her cheeks.

'I kissed him, Charlie. Nothing more, but even that was too much. You see, his wife's left him and I think on top of Matt dying, it just made us both lose our hold on reality. Thank you for telling me your story. I totally understand how that happened. When everything in your life has been mangled, it can somehow seem weirdly right to do the worst possible thing.'

Charlie nodded. 'Yep, and I certainly did. But the great thing is – you didn't.'

'But I might have. Seb's as lost as I am and although it didn't go any further that weekend, he keeps messaging me, wanting me to go up to London to stay with him.'

'What are you going to do?'

'Well, I'm not going to stay with him, that's for sure. I'll have to find a way to distance myself a little bit, without damaging our friendship. I don't know quite how yet, but I'll figure it out.' Sophie took a deep breath, trying to steady herself. 'Can I ask you something?'

'Anything.'

'Do you think having all the stuff with the affair and the divorce and your daughter to deal with made it harder for you to process your son's death and deal with the grief?'

'Totally,' said Charlie. 'Just when I needed all my capacity to deal with his loss, it was bound up with all the other stuff, so I couldn't process any of it properly. Whenever I tried to address one aspect, another one would pop up. It was like emotional Whack-a-Mole.'

Sophie had to smile. That was so exactly what it was like for her. Every time she tried to deal with losing Matt, up would pop the Gillette aspect. And when she tried to work through that, she would get consumed by grief and then the anger would come again. And now she'd added confusion about Sebastian to the mix. It was exhausting and impossible.

'Well,' she said. 'There is something else I think I'm going to have to tell Sebastian, but I'm going to tell you first. In fact, you are the very first person I'm going to tell this to.'

Charlie turned to face her and took both her hands in his. 'I'm listening,' he said.

'You know my husband—'

'Matt.'

'Matt,' she said, nodding. 'My husband of thirty years who got run over by a heavy goods vehicle. Dead. Awful. But there was something else. An hour before it happened, he'd told me he was leaving me for another woman. And that was the day after we'd exchanged contracts to sell our family home and buy the one down here, so there was no going back on it. He was going to take his half of the money and go off with her and leave me to move to Hastings on my own.'

'Sheesh,' said Charlie, looking properly shocked.

It was good to see. It meant she hadn't been overdramatising this whole time. What Matt had done really was appalling.

'That's terrible,' Charlie added. 'One then the other straight after?'

Sophie nodded her head slowly. 'He destroyed me emotionally and then he got killed. So I don't know what I am, Charlie. Am I an abandoned wife or am I a poor grieving widow?'

'And you've told nobody?'

'Who could I tell? Even in the depths of the shock, I knew the most important thing was to protect the boys from it.'

'So all this time you've been the secret double-headed grief-confusion monster?'

She nodded.

'And,' he continued, 'because publicly, you're confined to the saintly widow role you don't get to enjoy the righteous revenge aspect and have to hold all that anger in. No wonder you feel confused! I'm surprised your brain hasn't exploded.'

Feeling too moved to speak, Sophie squeezed his hands. After all this time of having it buzzing round her head like a maddening bluebottle, to hear her situation summed up and understood by somebody else felt almost like a miracle.

'Ten months I've been keeping this inside. There were times when I was scared to open my mouth in case it all came out in a big scream.'

Tears filled her eyes once more and Charlie pulled her towards him. She surrendered to it, enjoying the feel of his jacket against her cheek and his lovely scent.

'You always smell so nice,' she said.

'That's because I always put on my best aftershave when I know I'm going to be seeing you,' he said, softly. 'Lucky I had it in the car today.'

Sophie glanced down for a moment, taking it in.

'You know I have feelings for you, Sophie,' he said, when she looked up again. 'I did think they might be returned, but I know you're in a very vulnerable place, so we can just leave that where it is for now, and when – if – the time is right, we can go wherever that takes us.'

'Has the thing with Seb put you off?' she asked, knowing it was pathetic, but wanting to punish herself. She was tainted. Damaged goods.

Charlie raised his forefinger and wagged it at her. 'You can stop that right away. Don't start making yourself the bad one, so there's a reason all this crap has happened to you. It hasn't affected the way I feel about you at all. Although it might take me a while to forgive him—' He chortled softly. 'I was ready to put one on him in the Crown. Could you tell?'

'Yes!' said Sophie. 'But I thought it was me you were angry with.'

'There you go again,' said Charlie. 'Stop blaming yourself, Sophie. You are in a horrible nightmare created entirely by somebody else. Don't do what I did and somehow make it your own fault.'

Sophie looked out at the sea, thinking about what he'd said. She needed to process it.

'But there is something I think you should do,' said Charlie. She turned back to him.

'Tell everyone everything. It will be difficult to tell the boys – and Matt's brothers – but it will be better in the long run. You're carrying this burden on your own. You didn't create it. Matt did, and even in death, he has to take the moral responsibility for it, not you.'

CHAPTER 44

Beau was in the Old Town, sent by Tamar on an urgent mission to the cheese shop on the High Street. He was clamping his bike to some railings and could hear a bit of a commotion going on nearby. It sounded like a child having a tantrum. Then he realised what the child was shouting: 'Bob! Bob!'

He looked round and saw Cassady across the street.

'Cassie!' he cried in delight and then saw that Juliet – with Hettie strapped to her front – was standing there, holding tightly to Cassady's hand to stop her from running across the road to him.

Beau raced over and scooped the little girl up, holding her in the air and twirling her round. She squealed with excitement and he didn't care if her mother had sacked him with no warning or apparent reason, he was still overjoyed to see his pal.

'You don't come anymore,' Cassady was saying. 'I miss you.'

'I miss you too, smelly,' said Beau. 'But I live here now.' He finally turned to Juliet, who looked extremely uncomfortable. 'Hello,' he said.

'Hi, Bob,' she said.

'How are you?' he asked. He was going to be nice. There was no point in holding a grudge; he had a fabulous new life now. Tamar was in it. Even if he didn't quite know what to do with that situation.

'I'm good. It's nice to see you.' She reached up her hand up to brush a strand of hair out of her eye and Beau saw she was wearing his ring. He'd finished it a couple of weeks before, working in secret at Olive's studio because he didn't want to explain to anyone what it was, and he'd sent it to Gwen, with Cassady's drawing, asking her to give it to Juliet.

'You're wearing my ring. Well, Cassady's ring.'

'I love it,' said Juliet. 'It was so kind of you to make it. Wasn't it, Cass?'

The little girl nodded and buried her face in Beau's neck.

'Cassady is a very talented designer,' he said. 'A chip off the old block.'

He smiled at Juliet then kissed Cassady on the head and put her down on the pavement. She grabbed his hand and held on to it tightly, swinging his arm back and forth.

'I was going to ask Gwen to contact you,' said Juliet. 'I want to start making these rings for the shop. I'll give you thirty per cent commission on each one we sell.'

'Oh, wow. That's so nice of you, but you don't have to – it's Cassady's design, not mine.'

'But you saw the potential,' said Juliet. 'Anyone else would have thrown her drawing in the bin. You kept it and made the ring. I would never have known about it.'

'Well, that's incredibly kind.'

'I'm sorry how it turned out, er, Bob,' she said. 'It was difficult, I'll explain it to you one day. I can't at the moment.'

'That's okay,' said Beau. 'I've moved down here and I'm doing my thing and it's all going really well. And I'm not distracted by this monster.' He leaned down and tickled Cassady, who giggled with delight.

'That's great. You're very talented.'

'Thanks. That means a lot coming from you. Anyway, what brings you here? Hastings doesn't seem a very Juliet kind of a place.'

'My mum has moved down here recently,' she said. 'We come down to see her a lot.'

'Get out. My mum lives here too. I've moved back in with her. Where's your mum's place?'

'She's in a specialist care home, on Frobisher Road.'

'That's practically round the corner from our house,' said Beau. 'Come and have a cup of tea later. I'll text you the address.'

'Oh, I'm not sure I'll have time today. I'm just over here to buy some treats for my mum; after we drop them off, we have to get back to town.'

'Well, why don't you go and do your shopping and I'll hang out with Cassady for a bit? You can text me when you're ready. There are lots of fun things to do here.'

'Yes!' said Cassady, jumping up and down with excitement.

To his surprise, Juliet agreed. Beau took Cassady straight down to the amusement park, where there was a carousel with a Cinderella pumpkin carriage on it.

'I can't tell you how much I've been wanting to have a go in this,' he said as they climbed in.

They both enjoyed it so much they had another go, then they went in some cups and saucers that went round and round, which made them both feel sick, and finally they went on a small rollercoaster, called the Hungry Caterpillar, which whizzed – quite slowly – through a giant fibreglass apple.

He was just wondering if it would be a very bad idea to buy her some candy floss when Juliet texted to say she was ready to go and was waiting for them at the bottom of the High Street.

'It was lovely to see you, Cassie,' Beau said to the little girl as they walked over, holding hands.

'Can we play again soon?' she asked. 'Will you take me in the Cinderella carriage again?'

'Whenever you want. Every time you come to see your granny.'

They found Juliet, and Beau gave Cassady one last hug.

'I'm going to text you our address anyway,' he said to Juliet. 'If you can't come today, come next time. There's no reason why we can't be friends, Juliet. I don't hold grudges – and I love seeing Cassady.'

Juliet smiled, but he noticed it wasn't one of her open, generous smiles. Weird, like all of it.

'Oh,' he said. 'One last thing – I should have told you at the start. Bob isn't my real name. It's Beau. You misheard me at Olympia when I first met you and it seemed rude to correct you, so I just went along with Bob. It seemed easier. Sorry.'

'It's fine. Gwen already told me. Bye, Beau.'

Beau watched them walk away, really hoping she would get in touch next time they were down, but even if she didn't, Hastings and St Leonards was so small they were bound to bump into each other again.

It was one of the things he liked about living there.

CHAPTER 45

Juliet was at Rachel's house, sitting at the kitchen table with her and Dottie. Simon was looking after the children in the TV room and the sound of happy shrieking was interspersed with deeper bellows from him.

'Stop pulling my hair, Cassady!' they heard him say. 'It's too short to plait.'

'Do you think I should go and rescue him?' said Juliet.

'No,' said Rachel, laughing. 'It's good for him. Stops him being such a puffed-up smarty pants. He loves it really. I'll just go and close the door so we can't hear his screams.'

'Cassady gets overexcited around men,' said Juliet. 'I've consulted a child psychologist about it. She's desperate for attention from them. I have to find a way to get more father figures into her life.'

'Oh, we all need that, darling,' said Dottie, refilling her own wine glass and then waving the bottle in front of Juliet's face.

She shook her head.

'Are you sure?' said Dottie, topping up Rachel's glass. 'There must be something big going down for you to call an impromptu meeting with us on a school night. What gives?'

Rachel sat down again and raised her glass to clink Dottie's.

'Yes, come on, Jules,' she said. 'What's the deal?'

'Well, it's to do with men and Cassady, actually.'

Dottie grabbed her arm, looking horrified.

'Nothing like that,' said Juliet. 'Thank God. It's something else. And I need your advice.'

'We're here and we're full of it,' said Rachel, 'and I know I can speak for both of us when I tell you that it's quite comforting to hear other people's problems. A distraction from our own.'

'Amen to that,' said Dottie. 'So what's going on?'

And then Juliet couldn't think what to say. Gwen and Luiza had both worked it out, but she'd never willingly told anyone about her relationship with Matt – and now there was all this new stuff with finding out who Beau was and the blackmail … She didn't know where to start.

She saw Rachel and Dottie exchange a glance, and wondered if she should just spin them a line about some issue to do with the Bond Street planning permission, but then Rachel reached over and squeezed her hand.

'I know we talk a lot of rubbish,' she said, 'but you can trust us, Juliet. We genuinely are your friends, aren't we, Dot?'

'With or without the press discount,' said Dot. 'You are one of the gang now and my daughter says Cassady is her absolutely best, best friend, so you're stuck with us.'

Juliet still couldn't speak.

'I know it must be hard for you to talk about personal stuff,' said Rachel, gently. 'From what you told us about your childhood, keeping everything bottled up has been your survival mechanism, but since you've moved up here and started hanging out with us you are already so much more relaxed than you used to be, so I think sharing what's on your mind now will help.'

So Juliet took a deep breath in and told them everything, from the first time she met Matt, right up to realising the true identity of the young man she had working in her shop. By the end, she felt quite exhausted.

'Wow,' said Rachel. 'That is a lot to process, let alone deal with. I don't know how you've coped, running your business with all that going on.'

'Have you got any snacks, Rachel?' asked Dottie. 'My lunch suddenly seems a very long time ago.'

Juliet was a bit surprised by the sudden change of subject, but as Rachel got up and went over to the kitchen, Dottie leaned towards her, speaking more quietly.

'Have a little break, Jules,' she said. 'It's big and real, what you're telling us.'

Juliet smiled at her. They were making this so much easier. 'So how are things with you? I'm sitting here going on about myself, how are you doing?'

'Oh, you know, work's insane and Steve has said a few things recently that make me think he might have figured out that our youngest child isn't actually his offspring and I know I drink too much … So the usual and thanks for asking, but it's fine. This is about you. We can do my problems next time.'

'And mine!' Rachel called out.

'We haven't got long enough for yours,' said Dottie and a carrot stick came sailing over from the kitchen island, landing on the table. Dottie picked it up and lobbed it back.

After what seemed like a very short time, Rachel came over with a platter of beautifully arranged cheeses, ham and rolled-up salami, with carrot and celery sticks, tomatoes, gherkins, slices of pita bread, and a big mound of hummus.

'I'll just take the other plate through to the zoo,' she said, 'and then we can get back to it.'

Juliet scooped up some of the hummus with a piece of celery, suddenly realising how hungry she was. Since she'd bumped into Beau in Hastings Old Town she hadn't been able to eat much.

'Have I missed anything?' asked Rachel, sitting down again.

'We waited for you,' said Juliet.

'Before you tell us anything else,' said Dottie, 'can I ask something? Has Matt's wife ever tried to contact you?'

Juliet shook her head. 'I've no idea what she knows or not, that's what's doing my head in.'

'I think I should tell you I've actually met Sophie Crommelin,' said Rachel. 'One of our clients supplied all the crockery for a cookery book she styled, so I did the launch party. She's really nice. Sorry.'

Juliet sighed. 'She gave an amazing eulogy at the funeral. And Beau is so lovely … of course she's nice. I feel terrible, but I can't unwish my children.'

They all went quiet for a while, eating the delicious food, lost in their own thoughts.

Rachel spoke first. 'I wonder if Sophie saw you in the *Style* piece, or in Dottie's mag? Cassady features rather prominently in that. Do you think there's any way she could have recognised you in the shots and seen Cass and put it together?'

'This is one of the things that keeps me awake at night.'

'Well, it's making my messy little situation seem like a broken nail in comparison,' said Dottie.

'Glad it's having a benefit somewhere,' said Juliet. 'But now something else has happened, which is what I really want to ask you two about, now you know all the other stuff.'

'Hit it,' said Dottie, dipping a carrot stick into her wine and chewing on it.

'So, like I told you, once I found out who Beau was, I sacked him immediately.'

Rachel laughed. 'Oh, boy,' she said. 'I hope I never get on the wrong side of you. You are ruthless.'

'I'm a survivor,' said Juliet. 'I had to get him out of the shop as soon as possible and I thought I had that all sorted, but then a woman I've had working in my shop for a while – horrible, but good at the job, she really shifted product – has worked out who the girls' father is and she's trying to blackmail me with it. She's got pictures of me and Matt together, she claims, from some sleazy friend of hers who works at Sotheby's.'

'Have you sacked her?' said Dottie.

'Not yet. I'm playing her along for now, buying some time, but now there's more …'

'Keep it coming,' said Dottie. 'I'm ready for season six.'

'Yesterday, I bumped into Beau. In Hastings, where my mother lives now and when he asked me where her care home was, he said it was just around round the corner from where he's living – with his mother.'

Rachel and Dottie looked at her with wide eyes.

'My mum is doing so well there, I really don't want to move her – but I'll have to sneak around every time I go down. Wear sunglasses and a baseball hat, put a wig on Cassady … So what would you do?'

For a moment, they both just looked at her, which Juliet found quite comforting. It wasn't just her who found it all bewildering.

Then Rachel spoke. 'It's simple,' she said. 'You go and see Sophie and you tell her everything.'

'Really?' said Juliet. Exactly what Gwen had said.

'Creeping around will do a lot more damage to everyone in the long run,' said Rachel. 'And think about your girls. They've got two big brothers. They need to know them – and vice versa. And if you don't do it now, they might do one of those DNA things in the future and find them. Imagine how angry they'd be with you.'

Rachel put her hand on Juliet's arm. 'If Sophie does know anything, it must be eating her alive too – and that's on top of losing her husband. Everyone involved needs to know everything. It's a bloody nightmare, but the only thing that will save the lot of you is being real.'

Juliet turned to Dottie. 'What do you think?'

'It might go like that,' she said. 'Or she might put out a hit on you. But actually I do agree with Mrs Rathbone. It will be unbelievably shite to knock on that door, but you have to do it. Sorry, Juliet, but it is your responsibility. And it's made me understand something too.'

She stood up, draining her wine glass and then gave each of them a hug. 'I'm going home to tell my old man the truth about our children.'

CHAPTER 46

Beau was walking along Walton Street, whistling. Now he'd bumped into Juliet and had that nice chat with her, he felt he could come back to the shop and say goodbye to everyone, which he hadn't been able to do when he left. And perhaps if he asked the guys in the studio to put in a good word for him, Juliet would relent and let him back in there to work for nothing after all. She'd said he was talented – that had been thrilling.

Most of all, though, he wanted to see Gwen. He'd made her a pendant – she wasn't really a flashy ring kind of a person – and he wanted to give it to her in person, to thank her for being so kind and lovely to him while he'd been there.

He was surprised to see a man behind the counter when the shop door buzzed open. A sleekly dressed older chap with silver hair.

'Hello,' said Beau.

'Good morning, sir,' said the man smoothly, smiling with Arctic eyes. 'What can I help you with?'

Beau saw him looking at his rings, probably thinking he was going to attempt a swap.

'Well,' said Beau, 'I actually want to see Gwen. I used to work here.'

The man raised an eyebrow slightly, clearly still suspicious. 'Is Luiza here?'

'Luiza doesn't work here anymore,' said the man, not showing any signs of warming up.

'I'll tell you what,' said Beau. 'I know you can't leave the counter – I used to work here, as I said, I know the score – so I'll just send Gwen a quick text to see if she can pop up to see me.' He turned his back on Mr Frosty and messaged Gwen.

After a couple of minutes, the door from the back opened and her head came round it.

'Bob,' she said, looking pleased to see him, but oddly nervous. 'I mean – Beau. Come on through.'

She seemed more herself when they were back in her stuffy little office and Beau was happy to be back there as she bustled around making tea and opening the cake tin. Once they were settled, a large slice of banana bread on a plate next to him, he handed her a small box.

Her face lit up when she opened it. 'Oh, it's Puddles!' she said, looking at the little ginger cat's face, which Beau had created out of tangerine quartz. 'You've caught his cross expression perfectly. How did you do that?'

'Well, you do have quite a lot of pictures of him on your Facebook feed.'

Gwen laughed. 'I can't help myself. Thank you so much, I will treasure this. You're so clever.'

'It is what I really love to do,' said Beau. 'That's what I came here for originally, to do work experience up with the boys – but I got sidetracked into the shop and then when I wasn't needed there, the other thing seemed to get forgotten.'

Gwen smiled uneasily and then leaned across the desk towards him. 'Will you help me put it on?'

He fixed the clasp and she got up to look in the mirror on the wall. 'I love it so much,' she said, turning with tears in her eyes. 'I have several friends who I think will want something similar when they see this. Would you take commissions?'

'For pet portrait jewellery? Absolutely. Give them my number. As long as there are enough photos, I don't see why it would be a problem.'

'Oh, there are photos,' said Gwen and they laughed.

Beau ate the delicious cake and looked around the cramped, windowless space with the Wales calendar, dried flowers and filing cabinets. It was so humdrum compared to the glamorous shop, but really it was the engine room of the place.

'It's good to be back,' he said. 'I wasn't here long, but I did enjoy it. How's everyone else? Where's Luiza?'

A dark look crossed Gwen's face. 'She had to leave,' she said.

'Was she lifting gear?' Nothing would surprise him about her. So tough.

Gwen pursed her lips, looking strangely uncomfortable again and fiddling with the little gold crucifix she always wore round her neck.

Beau had never seen her look so grave before. He was about to ask if she was alright when she started speaking.

'It was much worse than theft of property, Bob,' she said, sitting up straight. 'Beau. It was theft of privacy. She was blackmailing Juliet.'

His mouth fell open. 'That's horrible. But what about? Juliet hasn't got anything to hide, surely?'

'She has actually,' said Gwen, quietly but firmly. 'The parentage of her children.'

Beau frowned. It wasn't something he'd ever thought about, though he'd read about it in the *Style* section.

'Sperm donor, wasn't it?'

Gwen looked down, playing with a bit of the banana bread, crumbling it on the plate and not eating it. What was this about? Beau didn't like it.

'Cassady and Hettie did have a father,' she said, looking up. 'The same father – and it's not something Juliet ever wanted anyone to know, because he was married and already had children.'

A bit tacky, but nothing he hadn't heard before. Most of his friends had divorced parents and patchwork families with half-siblings, step-siblings, other women, other men, both. All the normal betrayals. Why was Gwen being so weird about it?

She leaned forward. 'I'm not sure how it has fallen to me,' she said, 'but I have come to the decision that I have to tell you who the father of Juliet's daughters is, Beau, before someone else does. For your sake, for those dear little girls and for Juliet, it's time for everyone to know the truth.'

Now he was feeling a bit freaked out. This was properly weird.

Gwen reached over and put her hand on his. 'It was your father, Beau,' she said.

Beau stumbled back out onto Walton Street feeling like he'd been tossed around in a tumble dryer. Water boarded. Run over by a tank. Ten tanks.

Gwen had been incredibly kind and had wanted to call a car to take him to the station, but he'd just had to get out of that building. What if Juliet came back? He'd seen his father's drawings of her nipples. And worse.

He stumbled again as the realisation hit him and he had to lean against a wall. He closed his eyes, then opened them again immediately, as those images appeared vividly in his memory. That's why Matt was suddenly obsessed with auction houses. It was where he'd met her.

He hung his head at the horror of it all, but then there was the other thing. The thing that was terrible and amazing at the same time. He really did have a mystery sibling – and it was Cassady. No wonder they had the same sense of humour – and the same bloody hair. No wonder she was so good at drawing. No wonder he loved her. They were family.

He slapped his hand onto his forehead. Cassady was a Crommelin. A girl Crommelin. And Hettie was too. There were now two girl Crommelins. The first girls for three generations, at least. It was a miracle. Tom and Bella could finally have the party. Or not.

He felt as though his brain cells were doing some kind of complicated square dance, as so many things moved around and fell into place – and out of it.

All those 'G's in his father's phone had stood for Giuliette he realised, code for Juliet.

And then, remembering all the other drawings of the mystery woman – not the grim ones he was going to have to burn – but the ones with the deliberately vague facial features, he could see now they were all Juliet. Her way of standing, her way of dressing, her hair. Her handbags. She had a bloody Birkin bag.

His father must have been absolutely mad about her. Which was horrendous, but at the same time, understandable. Juliet was an amazing woman. She was beautiful, but there was so much more to her than that, and although he hated himself for it, Beau understood why his father would have been attracted to her.

Good-looking women were everywhere and artists at Matt's level had their share of groupies, if they wanted them, but people as interesting as Juliet were much harder to find. Which made Beau reach for his phone. He needed to tell someone what had just happened, to help him process it, to help him work out what to do with this nuclear bomb of information.

But who? Who could he tell? Jack was the obvious person, but he didn't feel up to it. His own shock was hard enough to deal with – and he'd known something weird was going on even before his father had died. It would be a deadly asteroid from outer space for Jack. Rey wasn't the right person either. Too close to Mum. Uncle Seb? Too close to Dad.

The person he really wanted to tell, he realised, was Tamar. Maybe it was because she'd been through so much awful family stuff herself, he thought she might be less shocked than most people, but how could he launch all this at her? It wouldn't be fair. Especially as she was about to start another project with his mother.

His mother. Beau felt as though the blood was draining from his body. What would this do to Sophie, on top of everything she was already dealing with?

He shoved his phone back in his pocket and turned his face to the wall, groaning quietly. People walking past probably thought he was a nutjob. He didn't care.

Sighing deeply, he forced himself to leave the comfort of his wall and turn left, in the direction of Charing Cross station. He'd walk there, through Knightsbridge, across Green Park, along the Mall at the top of St James's Park, Admiralty Arch, Trafalgar Square.

Imagining the route and all the monuments and landmarks along it occupied his mind for a bit as he managed to get one foot moving in front of the other.

For the time being, it was the most he could manage.

CHAPTER 47

Beau got a reminder text from his mum when he was lying on his bed in his underpants, staring up at the ceiling. He didn't know how he was going to get through this dinner at Olive's with the people Sophie called the Gang. Since he'd got back from the visit to Gwen, he'd stayed out of the house as much as he could, working late in Olive's studio. He had a few commissions to finish, but nothing he tried to make worked out; he spent most of his time blowtorching things away. He was thinking of changing his brand name to No Mojo Beau.

Who even was he now? A pathetic loser who'd got himself an amazing work opportunity and then been sacked because his dad had been knobbing the owner and got her up the duff. Twice. The old twat had a second family.

Thank you, darling dead Daddy – you utter bastard. Beau slammed the mattress hard with his fist. Now he had to live with not mentioning it to his mother or his brother or his uncles for the rest of their lives and he could never see his own darling little sister again – sisters!

Bloody hell.

And as his sisters were going to be regularly visiting their granny just round the corner from the house he was in, he would have to creep around in disguise in his own neighbourhood in case he bumped into them and accidentally mentioned to Juliet that he'd seen her nipples. From every angle. He put his hands over his face and groaned.

There was a knock at the door.

'Yeah?' he said, not very enthusiastically.

Tamar's head appeared. That made him smile. One thing he could still enjoy – her company. The only reason he was going to the goddam dinner.

'Are you ready?' she asked. 'No. I see you're bed-y, not ready. You need to get going. It's six forty-five and you know how Olive likes people to be on time.'

'I don't know what to wear,' he said.

'Go like that,' said Tamar, laughing.

Niamh came in, wearing a bright pink eighties polyester dress, backwards. The zip was open all the way. 'What's the bants, people?' she asked, throwing herself down on the bed next to Beau.

He felt himself stiffen. Not in a good way. He wished he had more clothes on.

'Beau doesn't know what to wear,' said Tamar.

'Can you throw me my dressing gown?' he asked.

She took it off the hook on the door and tossed it over to him.

'Do you like my outfit?' asked Niamh.

'Very nice,' he said, squinting to try and block out the direct view he had of her left breast. He wished she wasn't still wearing the ring he'd given her all that time ago.

'You really need to get a move on, Beau,' said Tamar.

'Yes, you do,' said Niamh, pinching the skin on his thigh through the fabric of the robe. He tried to inch away.

Tamar opened the wardrobe and pulled out one of his silk shirts. 'Why don't you wear your classic Prince Beau look, with the floppy shirt and the long scarf and the suit?' she said. 'I like this Beau, but I miss that one.'

'I don't,' said Beau. 'But you've given me an idea.'

He jumped off the bed, happy for an excuse to get away from Niamh. Just because they'd got it on once before didn't mean he was always up for another roll around. He really liked Niamh, but he just wasn't interested in that kind of a scenario.

It was going to be a difficult night.

Tamar, Niamh and Rey were waiting with Sophie in the kitchen when Beau made his entrance.

He was wearing his favourite suit with the silk shirt unbuttoned almost to his navel, the tails hanging out, a long paisley scarf, multiple rings on each finger – and a shaggy black wig on his head. He struck a pose in the door frame.

They all looked at him, silent – then burst out laughing.

'Where did you get that syrup?' said Rey. 'Even Tippy wouldn't wear that. It's a shocker.'

'What syrup?' said Sophie, confused.

'Syrup of figs – wig,' said Beau. 'It's been in the dressing-up box forever. I'm so glad you hadn't thrown it out. The fake me is now the real me. Let's go and make this party happen.'

They arrived on the dot of seven.

'Nice work,' Olive said, as they walked into the kitchen. 'Reckon Big Ben is chiming at this very moment.'

Cicely was already there and Sophie tried not to notice that Charlie wasn't, grateful for the distraction when Olive noticed Beau's wig.

'Oh no, you've got the boufhead back!' she said. 'Where are my clippers?'

'No need,' said Rey, plucking the wig off Beau's head and throwing it to Olive, who raised one long arm and caught it. She put it in her fruit bowl, draped over a melon.

'That's better,' she said. 'Now, who wants a drink?'

While everyone was busying around, Sophie glanced over at the table, checking the number of places that were laid. Nine. Charlie had messaged her that morning to say he'd be there, so where was he? She felt weirdly nervous. She hadn't seen him since that day on Pett Level beach, a week before, because he'd been up in London having meetings with supermarkets. There'd been some WhatsApp exchanges, but she didn't know how it was going to be between them in real life now.

He'd said then that he had feelings for her, but that they should 'leave it' because she was vulnerable – or something like that, she couldn't quite remember. She'd felt much closer to him when he'd dropped her back home that afternoon, but with the subsequent gap, would that be gone?

Then she heard the front door open.

'Here are Charlie and Agata,' said Cicely. 'He went round to walk her over here.'

Of course he did, thought Sophie. That's exactly what Charlie would do. Why hadn't she thought of that?

Tamar immediately went to help Agata to a chair, and Charlie came straight over to Sophie, kissing her on the cheek, his right hand squeezing her waist, on the side no one could see.

'You look lovely,' he whispered in her ear, lingering there a little longer than strictly necessary.

'Thank you,' said Sophie, feeling her pulse immediately quicken as she breathed in that now familiar smell. 'You smell nice.'

'Got the good gear on,' he said. 'Like I told you ...'

When it was time for them to sit down, Olive asked Beau to sort out where everyone should go, which he was very happy to do because it meant he could put Niamh as far away from himself as possible – and Tamar nice and close.

'Mum,' he said, 'you go there next to Niamh, then Agata, Rey, Tamar and Charlie, you'll be here ...'

Charlie came over with the two bottles of wine he'd just opened. 'Well, that doesn't work, Beau, old man,' he said, 'because we're two to one, girls to blokes, so I can't sit next to you.' He clapped Beau on the shoulder and smiled at him. 'Niamh,' he said, in a voice that was very pleasant, but no one could argue with, 'you swap with me.'

Niamh raced over to sit next to Beau.

He couldn't believe it. How could he have made such a rookie error – putting Charlie next to himself? It was much better the way Charlie had done it, especially as Agata now had a man on either side. The only person who was in a worse position was him.

Without thinking, he turned to look at Niamh, to find her already grinning at him, her glass raised to clink. He raised his, without much enthusiasm, immediately turning away to raise it to Cicely, on his other side. He was just going to have to get to know her tonight, that was his only get out. He would be very interested in gardening. Topiary. That was the thing. He could talk about that.

After they clinked glasses, his eyes automatically flicked over Niamh's head towards Tamar, to find she was already looking at him. They held each other's gaze for a moment. Beau blinked. Had there been something in that look? Something different? He looked at her again, but she was talking to Sophie.

He glanced over at Charlie, who had just sat down again and immediately turned to talk to Agata. What a good bloke he was. Niamh was distracted, talking past him to Cicely, so he tried to tune in to listen to what Agata was saying to Charlie. That should be entertaining.

'Smooth operator, Mr Charlie,' she said. 'Here you are sitting next to Sophie again.'

'And next to you,' said Charlie. 'Don't worry, I won't ignore you.'

'Are you sure?' said Agata, smiling.

'You don't miss a thing, do you?'

Beau leaned forward a bit, under cover of reaching for the bowl of olives, hoping they wouldn't notice him earwigging.

'When you spend as much time on your own as I do,' said Agata, 'you get hypersensitive to the energies from people – and between people – when you are with them.' She paused for a moment. 'You are in love with her, aren't you?'

'Yes,' said Charlie, after a moment. 'I think it's going that way.'

'Good. Because I think she feels the same and you both deserve to be happy.'

The olive Beau had just stuffed into his gob on autopilot had nearly gone down his windpipe with the shock of this new revelation. Only a couple of days ago he'd found out his father had another family, with someone he knew, and now his mother had a fancy man. It was too much.

His coughing made Niamh turn towards him and start banging him on his back, much harder than was necessary.

'Thanks,' he croaked out. 'I'm fine, I'll just have some water.'

She stopped whacking him but left her hand on his back. Stroking it.

He stood up. Looking round for an excuse, he went over to Olive, who was still at the stove. 'Can I help?' he asked.

'Perfect timing,' she said. 'I'll put it on the plates and you can take it to the table.'

She dished out two plates of coq au vin, with a hearty portion of mashed potato and looked up at him. 'Go on then.'

'Keep going,' he said. 'I can take more than that.'

Olive looked sceptical but filled two more plates.

Beau put three of them on his left arm, picked up the fourth with his right hand and, holding the single plate above his head, rings glinting, headed for the table.

'Bravo,' said Charlie, spotting him as he came over to give the first plate to Agata. 'Proper skills. Where did you learn that?'

'I've done a lot of waiterising. Couldn't really live in London on the funds from my rings.'

'I bet you got good tips.'

'I did.'

He served Cicely next, then came back to Sophie and round to Tamar.

By the time he got back to Olive, she had the next four plates ready and he took them to the table, going straight to Charlie.

'Hey,' said Niamh. 'Ladies first.'

'Age before beauty,' said Charlie. 'Thanks, mate, I'm starving.'

Everyone tucked in and while they were all engaged with that and chatting, Sophie felt Charlie's right hand on her knee, while he ate with his left, continuing to seamlessly divide his above-table attention between her and Agata.

Sophie glanced at him nervously.

'Don't worry,' he said, in a quiet voice. 'The only person who might notice is Agata and she's already worked it out.'

Sophie frowned slightly, wondering what he meant.

'Do you remember I said on the beach that day that we should wait until the time is right,' said Charlie. 'Well, I think it's right now.'

Sophie put in another mouthful of food to cover herself, quickly checking the rest of the table to see if anyone was looking at them. Rey was engrossed with Agata, Cicely was talking to Tamar, and Niamh and Olive were both looking at Beau.

'Agata just asked me if I'm in love with you,' said Charlie, putting a forkful of chicken into his mouth. He chewed for a moment, swallowed and then added, 'I said it's going that way.'

Sophie looked down at her plate, lost for words. Then she put her hand over his on her knee and squeezed it, tightly. It seemed a more efficient way of replying than trying to speak.

*

Beau was running out of excuses to leave the table. So far he'd got extra mash, filled up the water and topped up the salt. He was praying for someone to need seconds.

Niamh was pushing her food around her plate and mainly drinking. Her speech was getting slurred and spitty. Then he felt her hand reach out and find his thigh. High up and creeping north. He picked it up and put it on her leg but back it came. Several times. He started to stand up, but Olive leaned over to him.

'Have you got ants up your arse?' she asked him. 'You're up and down constantly.'

'Yeah,' said Rey. 'What's going on with you? Have you got springs?'

Beau wondered what to do. He wished he could join Niamh's hand with Rey's under the table, that would be funny.

'Sorry,' he said. 'I'm just excited to be here with everyone and I want to help.'

'Well, start by eating your bloody food,' said Olive.

He took a big forkful, jutting his right elbow out comedically, as if portraying someone greedily tucking in – actually using it to give Niamh a bit of a shove. Then he shifted in his seat to try and get away from her, but it was no use, she just moved her whole chair over to be closer to him.

'Beausie,' she said, looking up at him through unfocussed eyes. She really was pissed. How had she got like this? They'd only had two drinks.

He glanced at Tamar just as she looked down and saw Niamh's hand moving higher up his leg. He tried to catch Tamar's eye to send an alarm message, but she just turned back to her plate. Bloody hell. She probably thought he was encouraging Niamh.

'Rey,' said Agata. She was speaking quietly, but Beau was able to hear her by putting his head on one side and pretending to be tucking in to his food. This dinner party was like being at the theatre for him, listening to other people's conversations rather than having his own.

'Yes, darling Ags,' Rey said.

'Tamar's drunk friend is driving Beau mad. I have been watching. He is not enjoying her attentions, she is like an octopus. Can you tell Tamar.'

'You're sure he's not enjoying it? I had noticed stuff going on, but I just assumed he'd be up for it. He doesn't have much form for rejecting the advances of beautiful young ladies.'

'But have you not seen how often he gets up from the table?'

'Ah ...' said Rey. 'I see what you mean. I thought he was just showing off. Leave it with me.'

Beau then saw him whisper something to Tamar, who looked surprised then immediately turned to look at Beau.

'Hey, Bobo,' she said, in a louder voice than she would normally use. 'Fancy waitering skills you've got there.'

'Years of experience,' he said and was thinking what to say next, when Niamh grabbed hold of his arm and started shaking it.

'Hey,' she was saying. 'Don't be boring. Talk to me ...'

Beau looked back at Tamar and flicked his eyes towards Niamh, then crossing them, to signal distress. Tamar nodded and held up one finger for moment to let him know: I'm on it.

Then she got up and left the kitchen. After a few moments, Beau followed her, going out to the hall and tapping on the door of the downstairs loo.

'It's open,' she whispered, and Beau went in. 'Lock the door.'

'I hope they're not going to think we're doing drugs in here.'

They looked at each other for a moment and then they both started laughing. Uncontrollable giggles.

'This is so crazy,' said Beau. 'I love Niamh, she's great – normally – but tonight she's so weird. She's all over me.'

'I don't know what's got into her. I've never seen her like this before.'

Beau looked at his feet. He had to confess. 'This is embarrassing, but I've got to tell you something.'

'What?'

'Me and Niamh ... We had a thing, a one-night stand, ages ago. I'd forgotten about it, but then at the beach hut in the summer ...' He scratched the side of his neck. 'I saw she was wearing my ring. And then I remembered.'

Tamar smiled and poked him playfully in the ribs. 'I know. You left that ring on her pillow. She told me. Said she wasn't supposed to tell me, but she did. That's what girls do, sorry.'

'You've known all this time?'

'Yes,' said Tamar, shrugging.

'And you don't hate me for it?'

'Why would I? Why shouldn't a handsome dude and a beautiful woman get it on? Big city nights. It's normal.' She put her hand on his arm. 'And I know about the posters too, Beau. I know the famous Ring Guy was you.'

His eyebrows shot up. 'You didn't judge me for that?'

She shook her head. 'No. Obviously that woman – and some others – didn't like the ring thing, but I remember when it happened to Niamh, long before I knew you. She loved it.'

'It was at least three years ago, with Niamh, and I'm not that person anymore. I've been a total monk ever since that business with the bloody posters.'

'It's fine,' she said, touching his arm gently. 'You've been through a lot this past year, Beau. Stop beating yourself up.'

'Thank you,' he said. 'But I think the problem is because of that historic event, she just assumes I'll be up for it again tonight – and I'm really not.'

'But it's more than that, isn't it?' said Tamar, frowning. 'She seems generally out of it. Something's not right.'

'Is she on drugs?'

'I really don't think so,' said Tamar. 'Not her thing. Let's go back in … I'll sit back down next to her, try and suss out what's going on. You go and hang around in the kitchen again, so she won't be distracted by you.'

From his post by the sink helping Olive, Beau could see Niamh could hardly keep her eyes open. Her head was starting to roll on her neck.

'Where's Beau?' she said, then collapsed onto Tamar.

He abandoned the dishes and rushed over to help. Everyone was suddenly paying attention.

'She's been looking crook for a while,' said Olive. 'Is she on something?'

'I've never seen her like this before,' said Tamar. 'I think something's wrong.'

'She's unconscious,' said Sophie, arriving at Niamh's side. 'Do we need to call an ambulance?'

Rey came over and raised each of Niamh's eyelids in turn and touched the skin on her cheeks. 'I don't think so. Her pupils are normal, she's not clammy. I've had quite a lot of experience of this kind of thing over the years, with my stupid friends.' He rolled his eyes. 'She just needs to sleep.'

Sophie turned to Beau. 'I think you better take her back to the house. Here are the keys. Just leave them under the plant pot for me.'

Charlie was already at Niamh's side, helping Beau lift her up.

'Just make sure she's on her side, when you get her settled there, in case she's sick,' Rey called out to them as they carried Niamh out, Tamar following close behind.

'She'll be fine,' he said to Sophie, sitting back down again. 'Looks to me like she was overexcited to be around Beau – not the first time I've seen that in action – then too much booze on an empty stomach. There's nothing of her to soak it up.'

'She certainly didn't eat anything here,' said Olive. 'I did notice.'

'Even less than me,' said Agata and they laughed.

'Well, I haven't got an empty stomach,' said Olive. 'Who wants a flaming sambuca?'

CHAPTER 48

Beau was in the sitting room, lighting the log burner, hoping Tamar would soon come down from looking after Niamh. When she finally did, she was wearing a big woolly jumper over her dress and thick socks on her feet.

He'd never seen a woman look more beautiful.

'Is she OK?' he asked.

'I think so,' said Tamar. 'I thought I'd better sit with her a while, in case she was sick, like Rey said, but she seems to be settled now. She's fast asleep. I'll go up again in ten minutes and check on her.'

'Meanwhile, let's get comfy,' said Beau. 'I've lit the fire and opened a bottle.'

With the log burner roaring, his head back against the sofa and Tamar next to him, Beau realised that for the first time in ages, he felt completely contented. All the appalling things that had happened over the past months were still floating around in his head – now with the latest weirdness of Charlie and his mum added to it – but in this scenario, with Tamar at his side, he felt he could handle it.

For a moment he let himself just enjoy that feeling. The light flickering from the flames, the squashy sofa – and her. And then he just couldn't hold it any longer. He leaned forward to put his glass down on the coffee table and turned towards her.

'There is another reason I've been celibate all this time,' he said, taking one of her hands and stroking it, looking down at their joined fingers for a moment and then up at her. 'I don't want to be with anyone else. I only want to be with you, Tamar. I'm so in love with you.'

Tamar put her glass down and moved towards him, putting her arms tenderly around him and pulling him close. 'Oh, Beau,' she said, running her hand over his head – he was glad he'd lost the wig to Olive's melon. And then she put her lips on his and they kissed, for a long time, falling back onto the sofa and surrendering to it. When they pulled apart, they stayed lying where they were, their hands entwined, gazing into each other's eyes.

'My mum's going to kill me,' said Beau.

'Why?'

'She made me promise I wouldn't make a move on you, right at the start, when I first met you.'

'She did? Why?'

'She said you'd been through a lot, and you didn't need to be harassed by a love bandit like me. And she was right, because I was a total arsehole then – but it's been very good for me, because the more I got to know you as a person, as a friend, the more I understood I wanted to be with you – and I do mean be with you, not just … you know …'

Tamar laughed. 'What you did with Niamh?'

'Touché,' said Beau. 'That was the old me. I'm over that. What I really need is to properly be with someone. You.'

And she kissed him again.

*

Despite Rey's best efforts – he tried to get a Demolition Disco going, with everyone taking a turn to choose a track to dance to – the energy was a bit flat after Charlie got back. And it didn't help that Olive didn't have a smart speaker and he had to play the music on his phone.

'I really don't mind if you all want to piss off,' said Olive, after they'd had pudding. 'It's been a bit of a weird one.'

'Let me quickly text Beau for an update,' said Sophie and her phone soon pinged with his reply. 'He says: *Niamh is fine, asleep in bed – on her side, thank you Rey.* Tamar is keeping an eye on her and we're not to worry.' She smiled at the group. 'He adds: *Keep on raving, party people.*'

'I tried,' said Rey. 'And we still haven't played "Get Lucky" ...'

'I love you all,' said Agata. 'But I think I would like to go home now. Charlie, would you kindly take me?'

'I'll help you clear up, Olive,' said Cicely, as they left.

'I'll help too,' said Sophie, 'but listen, as this has been a bit truncated, and you and Charlie are staying here, Cicely, why don't you all come for brunch at our place tomorrow? I've got enough bacon and sausages in my freezer for an army. I'll text you all in the morning, just to confirm everything's cool with Niamh.'

Working as a team, it didn't take long do the clearing up and Sophie was soon putting on her wrap, ready for the short walk home.

'It's funny Charlie's not back yet,' said Cicely, kissing her goodbye. 'But I'm going to head up to bed.'

'He's probably having a brandy with Ags,' said Olive. 'She doesn't sleep much. Spends most nights on the chair in her sitting room, dozing, as far as I can tell.'

'See you all in the morning,' said Sophie and headed out.

Beau had left the kitchen lights on, so she went in to turn them off – and got a shock. Charlie was sitting on one of the stools at the island.

'Oh!' said Sophie. 'Hi …'

'I hope I didn't frighten you,' he said, standing up. 'A strange man lurking in your kitchen, but if you will leave your front door key under a plant pot …'

He came over to her, putting his arms round her, pulling her close. 'I dropped Ags off and came here to wait for you.'

And then he kissed her. Sophie felt herself melt away. Nothing mattered except her and Charlie and the moment. When she opened her eyes again, it took her a beat to register where she was.

In the pink kitchen. Which finally felt like hers.

CHAPTER 49

Sophie was already in the kitchen, cooking, when Beau came down.

'Morning, darling,' she said, giving him a warm kiss. 'Did you sleep well?'

'Blissfully, thank you,' he said, although he'd hardly closed his eyes. He and Tamar had stayed awake all night, talking. He'd come very close to telling her everything about his father, but had held back in case it tainted the beauty of finally being with her.

Talking, holding each other, kissing and sharing secrets was all they'd done. Well, some quite seriously heavy petting, but not the full Happy Meal. Beau wanted to wait a bit longer. To relish the anticipation, to let his feelings for this amazing woman continue to grow, before they moved things on to the next stage. And possibly not with his mother in the same building.

The weirdest thing about it was that it hadn't felt weird. He really didn't know himself anymore, but he liked this new person.

'How about you, dearest Ma?' he said, snapping his attention back. 'Did you sleep the sleep of the just Mumsk?'

'Absolutely,' she said, not looking up from the mushrooms she was slicing. 'Any sign of life from the girls? I'd like to know how Niamh is this morning.'

'Er, I think I heard something stirring up there. Shall I go and see?' He was happy to do that, because he thought if he didn't see Tamar's face again in the next couple of seconds, he might drop down dead.

He bounded up to the top floor two at a time, feeling as though he had springs in his knees. The only thing worrying him was telling his mother about him and Tamar. Would she be furious? He'd made a promise. Was keeping it for four months long enough? He hoped so.

He tapped on Tamar's bedroom door then put his head round it. She was kneeling by the bed, giving Niamh a glass of water. When she turned and smiled at him, his heart did such a flip he thought he might fall over.

'How are you, Niamh?' he asked.

'Not too bad,' she said. 'I'm sorry, Beau, I was really crass with you last night.'

'It's fine,' he said, coming over to sit on the end of the bed and tickling her toes through the duvet. 'But are you alright?'

'I am now. I'm not even that hung over. I only had about three glasses of wine – but I'm taking these new anxiety pills and I didn't know you aren't supposed to drink alcohol with them.'

'It didn't seem like you, but that explains everything.'

'Was I really awful?'

'No!' said Beau and Tamar at the same time. *Yes, but we'll never tell you.*

As he smiled at Niamh, he noticed she wasn't wearing his ring anymore. Trying to be discreet, he looked round the room and spotted it lying on the floor by the bed.

'Mum's making breakfast,' he said, getting to his feet and, in one deft move, kicking the ring out of sight. 'There's the full greasy if you want that, or clean and healthy if that floats your thing. I know what I'm having and it won't be pretty. Everyone from last night is coming.'

Niamh looked horrified. 'They must all hate me.'

'Not at all,' said Tamar firmly. 'Everyone was just really concerned. They'll be glad to see you looking …'

'Normal?' said Niamh. She got out of bed, stark naked, and put the pink dress back on. 'That's never going to happen,' she said, sticking her tongue out at them and disappearing from the room.

Beau immediately took Tamar in his arms and nuzzled into her neck. 'Hello, beautiful,' he said.

She put her hands on his cheeks. 'Hello, handsome.'

'I'm so happy. I'll try not to be too embarrassing, at least until I've confessed to my mother, but I'm so happy I've finally told you how I feel.'

'Right back at you, sunshine.'

Sophie thought she was getting through the breakfast quite well. There was only one near slip, when everyone was sitting at the dining table and Charlie followed her into the kitchen under the pretence of getting more toast and started nibbling her ear, not realising that Tamar was behind the fridge door until she shut it and looked straight at them. But he moved away quickly enough, heading back out to the table, so Sophie thought she probably hadn't noticed.

Tamar also went back to the dining room and for a moment Sophie just stood by the stove allowing herself to relish the novelty of being happy and remembering how it had felt waking up that morning in Charlie's arms in the bedroom at Agata's house.

'How old am I?' Charlie had said.

'About twenty-three, I think,' she'd replied.

'Oh, good. In that case, we can carry on where we left off.'

And they'd made love again, then lay back, holding hands and smiling at each other.

She'd stroked his cheek. He'd pretended to bite her fingers and she'd giggled like a teenage girl. Was she going insane? Possibly. But she liked it. It was a lot better than the way she'd thought she was going insane not so long ago.

When Sophie went back into the dining room, with more bacon and a fresh pot of tea, they were talking about Charlie's vineyard.

'So I'm the only one here who's never had the famous tour,' Beau was saying.

'Well, we'll have to remedy that as soon as possible,' said Charlie. 'Name your day.'

'You've got a treat in store, mate,' said Olive. 'Wait until you see the view over the vines from the top of the hill. It's the Hunter Valley combined with Tuscany, but in England.'

'It's just a shame about those ugly buildings up there, though, isn't it?' said Charlie. 'Right in the prime spot. I've really got to decide what to do about them.'

'I like your idea to make them into artists' studios,' said Olive. 'We don't need any suburban shit around to survive, us makers. We can take our own lunch in. We don't need a branch of Subway.'

'Make it into a restaurant,' said Agata.

Everyone turned to look at her.

'Have artists in one barn,' she continued, 'a gallery for them to show their work and food in the one looking over the view. People now are always wanting food – and horrible milky coffee, like babies.' She flipped one of her hands in the air as if dismissing all milky coffee then took a sip of her espresso. 'Tamar can do the food. And Beau can be the waiter and charm everyone and the people will spend more money because they are both so beautiful.'

Tamar turned to Agata, eyes wide, then she looked at Beau. He nodded enthusiastically.

'That's an amazing idea, Agata,' he said. 'I'd be really into seriously talking about that, Tamar, if you would?'

'It is literally my life's dream,' she said. 'And I can't think of a more beautiful spot for a restaurant. But what about you, Charlie? It's your property we're talking about.'

'I think it's inspired,' he said. 'A great use of the building and we've already got the dream team to do it, although you would have to serve my wine, of course.'

'No other,' said Tamar.

Laughter filled the room.

'Well, come over soon and we'll have a look and really talk about it,' said Charlie. 'Brilliant thinking, Ags.' He kissed her on the cheek.

'You are welcome,' said Agata, turning to Beau and Tamar. 'And you two can be together all the time. Which is what you both want.'

Everyone laughed again and Beau stood up and took Tamar by the hand, pulling her towards him and planting a big fat kiss on her lips.

'It's official, people,' he said. 'We're an item. Best you all know.'

Everyone cheered and Sophie blew a two-handed kiss to Beau, who she could see was looking to her for approval. In the hubbub, she felt Charlie's hand find hers. She turned to him and smiled, feeling happier than she had for years – even quite a long time before Matt died, she now realised.

Thinking of him reminded her there was still the awful looming presence of his secrets to deal with, but even though she dreaded making those revelations, she now understood how it would release her from the burden of carrying of it all.

But beyond that – and growing bigger all the time – was the chance of proper happiness, for all of them. So she didn't let go of Charlie's hand. Let them see. She was done with hiding things.

CHAPTER 50

Beau and Tamar were standing outside Charlie's barn looking at the view, still beautiful in the winter morning mist, with all the leaves gone from the trees. After Charlie had given them a quick tour of the vineyard, they'd gone over the barns with him and Sophie, brainstorming ideas for how it could be converted and what to do with all the space. There was so much of it.

Then Charlie and Sophie had gone back to the house, leaving Beau and Tamar to get fully familiar with the layout and soak up the atmosphere. Sophie had given Beau the car keys so he could drive home. She was staying on with Charlie.

'It's doing my head in that we can't see this view from the inside,' said Beau. 'How could anyone put a building in this position without a single window in it?'

'Well, I suppose bales of hay and tractors, or whatever that farmer kept in it, don't really appreciate scenery,' said Tamar.

'I've got an idea. If we stand out here and intently study the view so it imprints on our retinas and then close our eyes and run inside really fast, when we open our eyes we might still be able to see it from in there.'

They both stared hard then Beau grabbed her hand and they stumbled back into the dark barn, giggling, then stared towards the metal wall.

'Just for a moment there,' Beau said, 'I think I had it.'

'I didn't. I can just about make out corrugated steel through the gloom. So what did your mystic insight tell you, oh, swami one?'

'It told me that pretty much this whole wall needs to be glass.'

'I think we knew that already, didn't we?'

'It also told me it's bloody cold in here. But the great thing is we could have acres of solar panels on the roof and be completely off-grid for electricity and have those buried heat pump things, whatever they are, so it would always be perfectly cosy. Which it would be with you here anyway.'

He folded her into his arms, still getting used to the feelings he had for her. He felt so warm and protected and nurtured by these new sensations. It was like having an amazing down coat. New with tags. He felt cocooned.

'Let's start back to the car,' he said. 'If we walk briskly it will warm us up – and if you don't mind listening as we go, I have something I would really like to share with you.'

It was time for him to tell someone. And Tamar was the someone he wanted to tell.

Sophie and Charlie were in bed. He'd done a calculation that it would take the kids twenty minutes to walk back to the house from the barns, even if they'd left straight after them so it would be a shame to waste that valuable time.

Lying with her head on his warm chest, Sophie felt completely looked after in a way she hadn't for a long time.

Well before Matt died, because he'd always been distracted so work and he'd been out of the house a lot. Of course, now she knew why.

Charlie was stroking her hair. 'That was a big sigh,' he said.

'Sorry,' said Sophie, putting her elbows on his chest and looking up at him. 'It's not because I'm not happy in the here and now. I'm ultra happy.'

'But you were thinking about things, weren't you? All those things that aren't very nice to think about, but which you know you need to face up to. Get it over with, Soph. I really think now's a great time to tell Beau. He's so loved up you could drop a bomb on him and it would bounce off.'

'But that's exactly what just made me sigh. How can I send that wrecking ball in when he's so happy?'

'There's never going to be a right time. But you all need to start moving on, which just can't happen while there are these great unspoken things looming in the background. Even though your boys don't know about them yet, the way it affects you, affects them.'

Sophie thought about that. She probably was being weird in lots of little ways. Like, she knew how much Beau wanted his dad's paintings to be put up in the new house and Jack had asked her about it too last time they'd Facetimed. She was running out of excuses why she wasn't ready to do it yet.

'You're right,' she said. 'It's time.'

Juliet was sitting in a cafe on Kings Road, twenty minutes' walk from her mum's care home where she'd just dropped Cassady and Hettie. One of the many wonderful benefits of the place was that there was a nursery on site so her mother could spend proper time with her granddaughters, with a childcare professional always nearby. Pauline and Cassady were probably feeding the chickens or collecting eggs, thought Juliet. Or sitting together in the art room, making something out of clay.

That image was a brief, pleasant distraction from what she knew she had to do. She looked down at her phone, sighing. Dottie had sent her Sophie's number the day after they'd met up at Rachel's house, saying it had only taken her one text to get hold of it. That tightly interconnected creative world again.

Now she had the number, she had no excuse for not trying to make contact and she knew she had to get on with it. She didn't want Sophie to find out from a newspaper reporter ringing for a comment, if Luiza ever went through with her threat, despite the generous pay-off Juliet had given her – on condition of her signing a non-disclosure agreement.

And it was even more pressing since Gwen had filled her with cake the day before and revealed that she'd told Beau everything, so now he knew that Cassie and Hettie were his sisters.

Juliet had been astonished at first that her most trusted employee had betrayed her like that, but once Gwen had explained her decision Juliet could see it was right. It wasn't a betrayal – it was actually a massive favour and very brave of Gwen to do it. As Rachel and Dottie had also said, everyone had to be told the whole truth, so they could all start to deal with it.

Taking a deep breath for courage, she started a message to Sophie's number.

*

Beau and Tamar were in Agata's sitting room. He'd told Tamar the whole story on the walk back to Charlie's house and when he'd asked her what she thought he should do, her reply had been immediate: 'Ask Agata. She'll know.'

So here they were. Olive was here too, because as soon as Beau had asked Agata if she could give him advice about something very serious, she'd asked him to get Olive first. 'We are a good team,' she'd said. 'I am a butterfly, she is a hammer. You will get both approaches.'

Beau told them everything, with Olive responding at key points with 'Jeez, fuck', 'Bastard!' and 'What a crock', while Agata just shook her head and sighed a couple of times.

'So what do I do?' said Beau, once he'd reached the climax with Gwen's revelation. 'Do I put gaffer tape over my mouth for the rest of my life in case I accidentally ever mention Dad's gross betrayal and the small detail of his other family? Do I never see my gorgeous little sister again?'

'You've got to tell Sophie!' said Olive. 'You've got to tell your mum and Jack and your whole bloody family everything, immediately. I know he was your dad, but what a fuck knuckle. Worst kind of bastard. No one needs to keep his filthy secrets for him. Bloody fucking wanker.'

Beau couldn't help smiling. It was strangely releasing to hear his father being assessed in those terms. He'd always held Matt up as some kind of higher being and anything a bit off he'd ever done had been excused by The Work. The precious bloody work, which took priority over everything.

He *was* a bloody fuck knuckle.

Beau glanced at Agata, who hadn't said anything yet, and she looked back at him steadily with her piercing pale blue eyes.

'I think Sophie knows already,' she said. 'I knew from the start there was something else. Not just the death. The anger.' She shrugged, raising her hands in her characteristic gesture.

'Actually, now you say it, I know what you mean,' said Olive. 'That first dinner at mine, I could see she was really pissed off, not just grieving. I recognised it because it was like looking in a mirror. I was furious with my old man for dying. He'd still be alive if he hadn't felt it was his personal responsibility to keep the whisky stills of Scotland afloat.'

'You think she knows?' repeated Beau, trying to process it.

'Yes,' said Agata. 'At least some of it, maybe not all. But if, as you tell us, a woman was asked to leave the funeral, it seems like your mother knew something, no? Even if that wasn't the same woman, it is an indication that something was not right.'

Beau had his hand on his head, trying to stop his brain from exploding. Tamar put her arm round him and kissed his cheek.

'And now I'm even more glad she has that lovely Charlie,' said Agata. 'He is a good man – and very virile for his age, I think. A betrayed woman deserves a wonderful lover.' She smiled at Beau. 'I'm sorry if that makes you feel sick.'

'Well,' said Beau, 'I'm generally feeling like I have far greater insight into both my parents' sex lives than I've ever aspired to, but, hey, I really like the guy and it will be helpful to have him around to support her when I finally tell her all this crap. Which is a fuck-knucklingly horrible prospect, but I agree, it has to be done.'

He stood up and gave Agata the biggest – and the most gentle – hug he could. He didn't want to break her.

CHAPTER 51

Sophie was sitting at her dining table, feeling like she'd just had a lobotomy.

Juliet was sitting across the table from her. Gillette herself.

Less than an hour before, Juliet had sent Sophie a text, asking if she could make a date to come and see her. With her conversation with Charlie still so fresh, and fully committed to telling the boys the truth, Sophie had replied immediately, saying yes.

And when Juliet had come back saying she was actually in St Leonards, Sophie gave her the West Hill Road address and said she'd be home in thirty minutes.

And here they were. Sophie was sitting on Matt's Mickey Mouse chair, which hadn't been deliberate, she'd just grabbed the nearest one. Matt's old leather jacket was hanging over the back of another chair.

'So that was why I said that thing to your friend at the wake – Ray?' said Gillette. Juliet.

Sophie nodded.

'That's why I asked him to tell you, "It's not what it seems", because if Matt had told you he was leaving you for me, I just desperately wanted you to know that wasn't ever going to happen—'

'Although you had been sleeping with him for a long time,' said Sophie.

'Yes. I'm sorry. Genuinely sorry. That's all I can say. I don't expect you to forgive me. It was wrong to have an affair with another woman's husband, but for reasons I won't go into – you don't need to hear my sob story – I'm able to keep emotional things quite separate in my head and, in that way, I was able to put your husband in a kind of box, on his own, with no one else around him, because that was the context I met him in.'

Sophie looked at the woman across the table. She appeared genuinely distressed, and quite haggard compared to the one who had come to the funeral and the ultraglamorous business star she'd seen in the magazines. She almost did feel sorry for her.

'I won't deny it, Juliet,' Sophie said, 'when Matt told me about you, it nearly destroyed me. We'd just exchanged contracts to sell our family home and buy this one, which meant he had deliberately arranged it so I was going to lose my home and my marriage simultaneously. He told me he was going to start a new life with someone called Juliet. It was brutal.'

'That's exactly what I dreaded,' said Juliet. 'That he'd told you that, because I'd made it ultra clear to him that I was never going to live with him, or have any kind of formal connection with him going forward.' She closed her eyes for a moment and then opened them again. 'It's really difficult for me to prove that to you, though,' she said. 'Because we only ever communicated on Snapchat, so messages were read, then disappeared. The last time I heard from him, he'd sent me a letter, which I now understand he wrote just before he died, saying that he was going to tell you about us.

'I sent him so many Snapchats asking him to ring me, so I could tell him not to do that and of course he never rang – but I didn't know why for nearly two weeks … If you look on his phone, those messages might still be there, unread.'

Snapchat, thought Sophie. The boys had been mad about that when they were still at school, but she didn't know any adults who used it and she didn't remember seeing it when she'd opened Matt's phone that time, but then, she hadn't been looking for that.

So maybe there was proof there, if she wanted to go and look but she wasn't sure she needed it. This woman had been decent enough to come to see her. Would she lie about that? More urgently, Sophie knew she had to ask a question she dreaded hearing the answer to.

'I saw your daughter Cassady in that piece in *Her* magazine,' she said. 'And I did notice her striking resemblance to my late husband. Is she his child? I mean, that is very much a name he would have chosen, with the Kerouac reference and everything.'

Juliet nodded, unable to speak immediately. 'They are both his,' she said haltingly.

Sophie let that sink in. It was a lot.

'Ah, yes,' she said. 'I remember you were in late pregnancy in that article. I worked out it could be Matt's. Just. Did you have a boy or a girl?'

'Another girl,' said Juliet. 'Hettie. That was one of the other names Matt had suggested for Cassady and I used it to honour his memory. Hettie Matilda. I'm so sorry. I know this must be terrible for you to find out, but once again, it all goes back to my stuff, which I don't expect you to care about, but that's why it's always been my plan to have a family without a man involved beyond the biological …' She trailed off.

Sophie was laughing. Really laughing. Her arms were down on the table with her head on them, guffawing.

'Oh, you must think I'm mad,' she said, lifting her head up, still laughing, 'and I'm not going to explain, but Matt fathering two daughters and no one knowing is hilarious.'

That set her off again. The thought of Bella's reaction – it was just too good. Would they have the party? Coldplay? For the two illegitimate Crommelin girls? Maybe Matt's infidelity was what it had taken to shift the family jinx.

'I know about the family thing with only sons,' said Juliet, quietly.

Sophie stopped laughing.

'Matt said in his letter that was why he had to be part of Cassady's life,' Juliet continued, 'because she was his miracle girl. He said fate had sent her to him and he couldn't spend another day not raising her. He was very insistent about it.'

'That makes sense,' said Sophie. 'The no-girl thing really is a big deal in that family and it is typical of Matt – was typical – for him to see it as some kind of sign. Is his name on their birth certificates?' It had been really nagging at her. On the birth certificate and the public record.

'Yes – and no. They both have it as a middle name, no hyphen. Cassady Pauline – after my mother – Crommelin Mylan and Hettie Matilda Crommelin Mylan. He's not listed as their father. That space is empty. He wanted to be on there, but I refused. It is up to the mother, fortunately.'

'Well, as long as the name Crommelin is on there somewhere, I'm sure that will count,' said Sophie. 'Oh, I can't wait to tell Sebastian. That's one of Matt's brothers. He had four brothers. Did he ever tell you that? They're a very close family.'

Juliet shook her head. 'He didn't tell me anything about his life. Apart from that he was married and had two grown-up sons – and the all-boys thing. And I didn't want to know any more. I did my best to block it all out of my mind.'

'It's okay,' said Sophie, aware she'd got a bit needly then, talking about the family like that, wanting to make Juliet feel like the outsider she was. It was all so confusing. She should hate this woman, but it had been very brave of her to make the approach to come and talk to her, and Sophie was doing her best to respect that. She didn't want to be horrible to her. What would that achieve?

Still, it was a lot to take in – especially as she hadn't had the chance to tell the boys anything yet. But perhaps it was better to know everything before she did that. 'Can I ask you something else?'

'Of course. Anything. That's why I'm here.'

'Where did you first meet Matt?'

'At Phillips. The auction house. I was looking at the works in a forthcoming sale. I collect late twentieth-century British art.'

Sophie nodded. Matt had started going on endlessly about auction houses and how he was thinking of doing a series of works around them from the point of view of people who really loved the art, contrasted with investors looking for 'hard currency capital gains'. That was how he'd put it.

'Who approached who first?'

'I was looking at a painting and he happened to be standing next to me. He made a comment and I moved on, because I don't talk to men in those situations.'

'And did he follow you?'

'No,' said Juliet. 'But I bumped into him again a few paintings on and he said something interesting that caught my attention. And then I saw him again by chance at another auction.'

Sophie nodded slowly. She could picture the whole thing. Juliet becoming part of the work he was doing, enmeshed in the structure he would obsessively build through preparatory works to eventually create the shown pieces.

And she now also understood how that all tied in with his refusal to accept that Juliet wouldn't move things on to the next stage with him, because that had clearly become part of The Work in his head – and when he was at that stage of developing a show, he could become quite mad. Like when he'd filmed her dying mother, against all her sobbing pleas and even the doctor's admonishments. He'd just filmed them too. He could be a cruel bastard in that state. Making The Work trumped everything.

'Look,' said Sophie, 'we can't pretend this isn't difficult. I've been living with the knowledge that my husband was having a serious affair before he died for the last, well, nearly eleven months now, isn't it?'

Juliet nodded.

'And then I saw that article and realised you'd probably had a child together, possibly two, and I had to keep all that locked up inside me, while also grieving him, to protect my sons – and Matt's family.' She paused, just to check she really was sure about what she was going to say next and decided she was. 'It's only very recently, since I finally did tell someone the whole thing, that I've understood that it would be better for everyone to know everything. And I have to say, now we've talked, I think that will be much easier for me to do that. So, just so you know what's going to happen next, I'm going to tell Beau and Jack about you and about the children. They are their half-sisters, after all. They may want to meet them. They probably should meet them.'

The front door opened and closed.

'Cooee. Anyone in?'

Beau walked into the dining room and stopped dead, looking from one woman to the other, then sat down on the chair at the end of the table and put his head in his hands.

Sophie was bewildered. 'Beau?' she said. 'Are you alright?'

He looked up again. 'Hi, Juliet.'

'Hi, Beau,' she said, quietly.

Sophie was momentarily lost for words. 'You two know each other?' she said when she recovered.

'Yes, we do,' said Beau.

Sophie looked from one to the other with a sense of creeping horror. Had Beau had an affair with Juliet too? That she would not be able to stand.

Beau stood up and walked round to sit next to Sophie, putting his arm around her shoulder. 'I think we all need to find out who knows what,' he said. 'Who wants to go first?' Then he turned to Juliet, a deep frown forming between his eyes, as something occurred to him. 'You didn't just tell her about you and you know … did you?' he asked, sitting up, clearly horrified at the idea.

Juliet looked nervously from one to the other.

'It's okay, Beau,' said Sophie, holding up one hand. 'I already knew that your father had an affair with Juliet.'

'Agata was right,' he said. 'She guessed that you knew.'

'Agata knows?'

'Yes. Tamar and I just told Agata and Olive, and they'll probably tell Charlie, who's just turned up there.'

'Hang on,' said Sophie, starting to feel overwhelmed. 'I've already told Charlie – but who the hell told you?'

Beau pursed his lips, looking uncomfortable. 'That's a bit of a long story,' he said. 'Dad gave me a hint – it was the last time I saw him actually – and then after he died, I kind of worked some things out and had others thrust upon me.'

He looked rather pointedly at Juliet as he said the last thing and Sophie wondered what that was about. It was all so much.

'So you've been carrying all this since Dad died, as well?' she said softly, feeling it was best to go back to the start of it.

'You knew before he died?' he asked, looking shocked.

Sophie nodded. 'Matt told me the day he died, just an hour before, but I didn't find it all out then. The full story has come out in bits over the months since and I've learned a lot of new things today from Juliet. One day we'll talk it all over, but for now I think we just need to sit with knowing that the time for secrets is over. What about Jack? Does he know?'

'No. But he's coming home soon for Christmas, isn't he? So we can tell him then. I don't think it's something for a WhatsApp message, or even a Zoom.'

'I'll see if he can come sooner,' said Sophie. 'He needs to be part of this, but right now can you please tell me how you

two know each other? Did Matt introduce you?' That seemed
almost as bad as them having an affair.

'No,' said Beau, looking as horrified as Sophie felt at the
idea. 'I met Juliet because we're both fashion jewellers and I
love her work, so I asked her if I could do work experience
and she didn't know who I was and very kindly said yes. Until
she found out I was Dad's son and sacked me.' He laughed, too
loudly.

'I'm sorry,' said Juliet.

'It's okay,' he said. 'I do understand why you did it since
I've had that little conversation with Gwen ... Did she tell you
about that?'

'Yes, she did. I hope it wasn't too much of a shock. I'm glad
you know – she did me a big favour.'

'Who's Gwen?' asked Sophie, starting to feel a bit irritated.

'I'll explain all that in a minute, Mum. But before we talk
about anything else, I need to ask you both something.' He
looked at each of them. 'Do you absolutely hate each other?'

'No,' said Sophie, firmly. 'We don't hate each other, do
we, Juliet? Because how is that going to help any of us? We've
just got to get to know each other – and most importantly, we
need to introduce our families to each other. All of them.'

Juliet smiled back at her shyly, her eyes filling with tears.
And then, reaching across the table at the same time, the two
women grasped each other's hands. Beau put his own hands
on the top of theirs.

'Who made the rings?' Sophie said, noticing that the
multicoloured crystal design Beau was wearing was the same
as the one Juliet had on, but bigger. 'I've seen your work in
magazines, Juliet. It could have been either of you.'

Beau laughed. 'Now that's a bit of a story,' he said, turning to Juliet. 'Does she know?'

Juliet nodded.

'Well, that's good,' said Beau. 'Because in that case I can tell you that I made this ring and the one Juliet is wearing – but they were designed by Cassady. Dad's daughter. My sister. I made them even before I knew Cassady was my sister, because I already loved her. She's the most amazing little girl, Mum.'

'I can't wait to meet her,' said Sophie, realising as she said it that she actually meant it.

'How would now be?' said Juliet.

Sophie and Beau looked at her.

'She's just round the corner, at the nursing home where my mother lives. I can go and get her. Hettie's there too.'

Beau was already on his feet. 'Tell me the name of the place and I'll get her. Can you call them and say their big brother is coming to pick up Cassady and Hettie?'

'I'd better come with you,' said Juliet. 'To explain to my mother.'

'Bring her here as well,' said Sophie, reaching for her phone to message Charlie to come round and bring all the others with him from Agata's house. 'I've got cake. Lots of cake.'

They were all going to be part of the same family. Might as well get on with it.

ACKNOWLEDGEMENTS

To have one good editor is fortunate – to have three is a miracle, but that is what I had on this book. I don't know how to convey the depth of my thanks to Anna Valdinger, Madeleine James and Kylie Mason for the enormous contributions they each made, in their own particular ways, to refining the end product. I have been known to describe the editing process as being as enjoyable as re-eating your own sick, but working with this trio, it was actually a pleasure. Fun even.

I must offer a particular word of thanks to Madeleine (Maddie), who began to feel more like a co-author than an editor. Her brilliant suggestions – some of them just tiny little tweaks, others quite big changes – were so spot on, I felt that she really understood what I was trying to do with this book. And that she cared about it as much as I did. Thank you so much, Maddie. You have been such a pleasure to work with.

And thank you once again, Anna, for your support and patience over the entire (rather extended) project, for your insights on the big picture – and another brilliant title. You really are amazing.

I would like to thank my friend Julie Tucker-Williams for allowing me into her workshop to see how a skilled jeweller works. Beau and I are very grateful.

Big cheers to Alison Brunjes who, via Mark Connolly, very generously gave me a ticket to see Elton John at the O2 (with a great seat). It was an amazing night.

A very special mention to my best friend Victoria Killay who read the book at a crucial stage and gave me invaluable insights and encouragement – and for her particular knowledge of the City of London and the man beasts who roam in it. Warburg's indeed …

I am also indebted to my friend Catherine Mayer and her mother, Ann Mayer Bird, for their book *Good Grief.* This deeply personal and universally helpful study of the experience of grieving a beloved spouse was so helpful for understanding my main character. It was from Catherine, in their book, that I got the toe-curling specifics of sympathy simpering. Aaaaaaaaandy.

I also need to thank someone whose name I have moronically mislaid. I think I deleted the key emails when I did a sweeping clear-out of my inbox a couple of years ago. This very kind person made a big donation to a charity (also lost in the email deforestation) for the naming rights to a character in my next novel. That name was Tippy Molong. I've had a lot of fun with that adorable moniker, so thank you for that and your generous donation. If you see this, please contact me via Substack or Instagram @maggiealderson.

Thanks, as always, to my wonderful agent, Fiona Inglis, and her team at Curtis Brown Australia.

A special shout out to all the lovely readers on my Substack, Style Notes. All your comments and support are hugely appreciated and I love the shared experience of the Substack flume ride.

To my daughter, Peggy, for making me laugh however stressed I am and for invaluable Generation Z explanations of the mysteries of Snapchat.

And to darling Pop, my rock, always ready to mend something with a hammer and a piece of twig. In a good suit.